KINGDOM OF CAGES

Also by Sarah Zettel

Reclamation
Fool's War
Playing God
The Quiet Invasion

Available from Warner Aspect

SARAH ZETTEL

KINGDOM OF CAGES

A Time Warner Company

Warner Books, Inc., 1271 Avenue of the Americas, New York, NY 10020

Printed in the United States of America

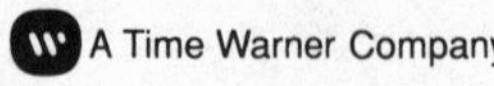

ISBN 0-446-52491-3

This book is dedicated to my friend, Dr. Karen Fleming. Dude!

ACKNOWLEDGMENTS

As ever, the author gratefully acknowledges the United Writers Group for their help and patience. She would also like to thank Dr. Laura Woody and Dee Keanealy, whose knowledge of biology, herbology, and medicine was invaluable for writing this book, and Jan Harmon, whose music gave her the title.

KINGDOM OF CAGES

. . . Thank heaven for wild birds
They're all dressed up in feathers, with colors outrageous.
They soar from this earthly bound kingdom of cages
On delicate wings, so small and courageous . . .

—Jan Harmon, "Wild Birds," 1986

PROLOGUE

Threats

"We are aware there is a crisis," said Father Mihran calmly. "But it is not ours."

Tam's gaze flickered to Commander Beleraja Poulos, the representative from the Authority. Her face faded to white, then flushed darkly.

Tam did not have a seat at the conference table. His place was in the back of the room with the rest of the administrative apprentices. They stood shoulder to shoulder in their best black shirts and white trousers, all of them there to watch this historic meeting and learn how to deal with outsiders. Jace, standing just to Tam's left, looked bored, but then Jace always looked bored. Haye, on the other hand, was staring so hard it looked like her eyes were about to pop out of her skull.

The late morning sun streamed through the pillow dome, warming and lighting the room, bringing the feel of springtime with it. A ring of windows let in a view of the marshes outside with their swaying reeds and stooping, moss-draped trees. This was Pandora, the most beautiful and perfect world ever discovered since human beings left Old Earth, and it was about to turn humanity away.

It is what we must do, his Conscience implant whispered to him. *Pandora must be protected.*

Tam eyed Commander Poulos uneasily. She had no Conscience to tell her this. She sat before Father Mihran, straight and strong in a tailored blue coat with gold braid on its sleeves and collar. She and her three colleagues were a blaze of color crowded at the end of the table facing the family council, which was arrayed down either side. The council all wore straight black jackets with white cuffs and collars. If Tam worked hard and did well, he'd eventually take his place at that table and wear that coat for formal meetings.

Today, however, he was very glad to be standing well away from it. Commander Poulos's dark eyes were full of poison as she stared Father Mihran down. Was she really going to just accept their refusal and go away?

Father Mihran seemed to think so, if his outward calm was any indication. His place was at the head of the long, low conference table and his wrinkled, oak-colored hands rested lightly on its polished surface. The father's entire manner spoke of cool resolution, and Tam wished he could copy it. He'd embarrass everyone if they caught him shifting his weight like he wanted to.

"If the rest of the colonized worlds cannot take care of their planets or their people, then . . ." Father Mihran dropped his gaze and waved one graceful hand.

"Then they deserve whatever happens to them?" asked Commander Poulos, her voice as suddenly full of poison as her gaze. "Is that what you were going to say?"

"No." Father Mihran sighed. "I was going to say I'm sorry for them."

"But not sorry enough to help?" The commander's light tone was completely at odds with her thunderous expression.

"We cannot help them."

Commander Poulos pressed her mouth into a straight line and raised her hand. She had a blue gem embedded in her thumbnail, and Tam wondered what its significance was. He should check. They would be quizzed on such details later.

She touched one of the rings on her right hand. The Authority representatives had brought their own video rig and now its screen lit up. Tam wanted to groan and look away. Jace actually did. Tam stepped on his foot and when the younger boy gave him a dirty look, Tam jerked his chin at the screen. They had to watch. They had to know. How would they ever be able to make decisions that could affect the entire family and all the villages if they couldn't stand to know what was going on?

Tam repeated that idea to himself as the images Commander Poulos had brought with her played across the holograph screen yet again. There was the wrinkled woman whose right arm ended in nothing but a stump, weeping as she stared across a field where the grain on the stalks swelled with pulpy gray tumors. There was the filthy clinic full of children with too-small bodies and too-large heads, with the one doctor explaining they had no way to perform genetic analysis to find out what was causing the defects. All that equipment had been washed away twenty years ago in a spring flood. There were the funeral pyres with the thick black smoke hanging over them, making Tam's nose twitch as he imagined the heavy stench. The remaining population leaned against each other, watching what was left of their friends and relatives burn.

So many worlds, so many disasters, and one name for all of them. The Diversity Crisis. All the Called, short for "colonized," worlds were struggling to survive in the face of depleted biological resources, decimated populations, and vestigial infrastructures.

The disaster had even reached back to Old Earth. Commander Poulos had opened her presentation explaining how, eight years ago, Authority ships had carried a delegation from the Called to Earth. Droneships could have been sent, of course, but it was decided that the magnitude of the tragedy truly needed a human voice to describe it, so it was human beings who brought news of the catastrophe reaching out across the colonies. Gene stocks thought to be adequate for the establishment and growth of civilizations were failing. The fertility rates were dropping, mortal defects increasing, and nature and disease were still taking their tolls. All of the Called, even the space dwellers of the Authority, needed fresh genetic input for every aspect of life—livestock, crops, humans, everything.

Earth, although grown so far apart from her daughter worlds, had been willing to help. But it was soon realized that the delegation from the Called had brought more with them than their pleas. The plague they carried killed two million inside one Terran month. No one knew where it came from. Some said the delegates had carried it with them and it had somehow survived sterilization and quarantine. Some said it had bred on Earth itself, a hybrid of Terran and proto-Terran viruses created by something innately harmless the delegation had exhaled the first day they walked free.

Some said the delegates had released it deliberately, to wipe out the native Terrans and reclaim Earth for themselves.

From this turmoil, only one agreement was reached. The horrified Terrans sent the delegates back with a single message for the Authority and all the Called: *Never return. Never even try.*

But the crisis among the Called would not relent and the Authority found itself pushed into making a fresh decision: to come to the one colonized world where it was known the Diversity Crisis had not reached and beg for help.

Although, Tam noticed, Commander Poulos had stopped using words like "begging" and "at your mercy" and even "please" twenty minutes ago.

The images of disaster continued. A mass grave, a ruined field, a quartet of children bearing the ancient signs of Down's syndrome. Still, Father Mihran's gaze did not flicker. Tam wasn't even sure he blinked.

"So much tragedy," he finally murmured, and Commander Poulos's guard dropped far enough for Tam to see hope light her face. "But also so much ignorance." The commander's hopeful expression faded as Father Mihran gestured toward the screen. "None of this would have happened if any of them had taken the time to truly understand the conditions they were living in. To understand that, however beautiful, their new worlds were not Earth." His gaze narrowed as he watched a family opening a silo door to see what had once been grain blow away in a cloud of red dust. "If they do not understand the problems inflicted on them by their own worlds, how can we hope to?" Father Mihran spread his hands toward the window and the world outside. "We have been on Pandora for two thousand years and we do not truly understand even this one biosphere yet."

"You can help them." Commander Poulos spoke the words more as if they were a command than a plea. "No one else has the analysis facilities, or the experience, that you have here. You can draw out a diagram for a single genetic base pair or an entire planet. You have all the techniques and understanding of the long generations that have studied Pandora." Commander Poulos leaned forward, eager, believing she was at the point of reaching her goal. Tam saw a man cradling a dead child on the screen and secretly hoped she was.

"You can teach them how their worlds work," said Commander Poulos urgently. "You can help each world find its cure."

"These poor suffering worlds." For the first time, Father Mihran's voice took on an edge. "Let's talk about them." Commander Poulos drew back just a little, but Father Mihran remained as he was, back and shoulders ramrod straight and his hands on the table, as if determined not to let any gesture or expression distract anyone from his words. "Let's talk about groups of as few as a hundred would-be colonists being dropped on a planet by your ancestors in the Colonial Shipping Authority, because those colonists were hoping for riches or a place where their own fanatic ideals could be enforced without question. Let's talk about the ones who hacked away at forests for the trade in exotic timber, which your people shipped between worlds. Let's talk about mines gouged out for the trade in heavy and precious minerals, which your people also carried." His index finger tapped the tabletop, once. "Let's talk about colonies that failed and were enslaved by their oh-so-noble-and-generous neighbors, according to treaties your people mediated, part of which included shipping the slaves out to their new masters."

"Do you say you're better than we are?" shot back Commander Poulos, rising to her feet and leaning across the table. "Then prove it. Help the Called to stay alive when they will not help each other and cannot help themselves."

"No," said Father Mihran, and the other council members murmured their agreement.

Commander Poulos glanced at her silent subordinates. The man on her left hung his head. The young woman on her right just looked grim. Tam felt the silent communication pass between them, and his stomach tightened.

"Father Mihran," said Commander Poulos. "Don't do this. The Called, the Authority, are desperate, and we're here as ambassadors of that desperation."

"And how much are you being paid for the job?" asked Father Mihran coolly.

Commander Poulos winced briefly. "A lot," she admitted. "Because there's a chance you will not let us go again, especially when you realize I can't let you refuse."

Silence, thick and worried. Not even Father Mihran made a sound.

"We need Pandora's help or we are all going to die," said Commander Poulos, separating out each word and meeting the gaze of each and every council member in turn. "Not today. Not even for ten years, or maybe even twenty. But eventually. Whole worlds are already gone.

Earth has abandoned us, and we cannot compel them to change their minds." Her gaze came to rest on Father Mihran again.

"And you can compel Pandora?" said Father Mihran, so softly Tam had to strain to hear him.

"If you force me to," replied Commander Poulos, just as softly. "Only if you force me to."

Father Mihran climbed to his feet. He stood only a few centimeters taller than the commander, but at that moment it seemed to Tam that he filled the entire room.

"You are ignorant and the daughter of ignorance," Father Mihran said flatly. "And you will leave us. Now."

Commander Poulos bowed her head and gestured with two fingers to the man on her left. He, in turn, typed a command into the comptroller on his wrist while the commander touched the ring control for her video screen again. The disasters faded away to become a desert—row upon row of red-gold dunes stretching out under an endless sky.

"This is a live feed," said Commander Poulos quietly. "I believe you call this place the Vastness."

"No—" began Father Mihran.

Light flashed, filling the screen, making Tam flinch. A boiling cloud of dust and ash filled the entire screen, rippling, growing, cascading upward, lifted by the long, low roar of thunder. Father Mihran cried out in sheer pain and all the council babbled at once, some to the father, some to each other, and some to their implants.

Tam could only stand there, jaw hanging, heart pounding. He couldn't believe it. A bomb. On Pandora, in the wilderness, the beautiful wilderness, which must be protected, must be studied and understood.

"It's a clean bomb." Commander Poulos's voice was almost gentle. "This time."

"You bloody-minded, ignorant . . ." shouted Father Mihran, but words failed him. He just stared at the boiling cloud of ash, hearing the endless rolling thunder, and Tam saw tears streaming from his eyes.

"You've kept Pandora pristine, to study and preserve, just like your ancestors did," went on Commander Poulos. "If you do not agree to help find a cure for the Diversity Crisis, the Authority will start bombing this planet until there's nothing left living outside your domes."

Father Mihran's hand curled into a fist and he pressed it against his forehead. Around him, the council fell silent, except for Administrator Has. "It's real," Has whispered, choking on the words. "I have confirmation from Athena Station. It's real."

On the screen, the dust and ash finally began to settle, and Tam glimpsed the burned black crater. It was so big. Bigger than any of the dunes—what was left of the dunes. The whole shape of the world had been changed to accommodate that huge black smoking hole.

"How could you?" gasped Father Mihran.

"Do you think we want to do this?" Commander Poulos stared at him incredulously. "Do you think I'm having fun here? I'm threatening to destroy an entire world. I'm acting like a damned dictator or crazy general out of the legends." Her knuckles turned white as she gripped the table edge. "I'm going to say this one more time, Father Mihran. The Called are going to die unless we do something."

"And if the Called die"—Father Mihran's hand shook as he lowered it—"the Authority and its cities die."

"Yes, and our way of life with them." Her smile was tight and grim. "I never said we were being selfless. The Diversity Crisis is in the corridors of the Authority cities too, Father. We are just as desperate as the rest."

"Why do you come here?" Father Mihran's words came out as a sob. "Have we ever asked anything of the Authority or the rest of the Called? What right have you to force your problems on us?"

Commander Poulos sighed and straightened up, polishing the sapphire thumbnail gem on her trousers seam. "No right," she admitted. "None at all. But you should be aware that it is not just the Authority that's bringing their troubles to you." Father Mihran stared, fear and murder both shining in his eyes.

Commander Poulos just nodded. "We already have rumors of ships on their way here. The word is out that Pandora is clean and that it's extraordinarily compatible with human life. Now"—her voice grew firm again—"maybe some of those ships will just dock with your Athena Station and process their crews for potential immigration, all polite. But some of them might not. They might just land and start setting up their own settlements in the middle of your precious wilderness. They might even do worse than that." She stabbed her finger toward the settling ash and the smoking crater. Tam swallowed. His hands were shaking. Nothing could be worse than that. What could be worse?

The trees falling one by one, the ground stripped bare, the animals, the birds, dead and dying. A wave of nausea washed though Tam. Oh, it could get worse. It could get much worse. From the faces of the councilors, he knew they were thinking the same thing. Jace was turning green. Sick amusement accompanied fast by shame rolled through Tam.

One muscle in Father Mihran's cheek twitched. "And the Authority would of course stop anyone from invading Pandora."

"If we knew Pandora was doing everything possible to help put an end to the Diversity Crisis, we just might," replied Commander Poulos.

"So . . ." Father Mihran groped for his chair and sat down heavily. "If we refuse, we have the choice of the Authority destroying us or the Authority allowing us to be destroyed."

"Your people aren't the only ones who learned the lessons of the pillage of Old Earth." Commander Poulos touched her ring and blanked out the image of the burned ruination. "If we don't move now, we will lose our chance."

Father Mihran dropped his gaze to the council. There should have been argument. There should have been raging debate. The whole family should have been called in. The city-mind itself should have raised its voice.

But none of this happened. There was only silence, until Father Mihran spoke again.

"It will take time."

Commander Poulos inclined her head once. "We know."

"Do you?" snapped Father Mihran. "I am not speaking of months. I am speaking of years. Possibly decades."

"We know," the commander repeated. "That is why we are here now, while we still have decades, perhaps even as much as a generation." Her face grew hard, and Tam knew she was seeing disasters that were to her at least as horrible as the crater she had opened in the Vastness. "There will be too much suffering, but there will be survivors. We'll be able to start over."

Father Mihran opened his mouth and closed it again. "Which world's generation are you picking for our clock, Commander?"

The small, grim smile returned. "Why, Pandora's, of course."

Tam felt it then, the dizzy sensation of watching something begin to slip away, like a leaf in a stream, and knowing with terrified certainty that it was one of a kind, and when it was gone there would be no more. Everything changed today. His world, his life, his vision for his future, everything, it all slid farther away with each heartbeat.

He also knew that this feeling, like the image of the Vastness crater, would never leave him. The Authority had won. They had let the Authority win. With their single act, Commander Poulos and her people had altered the lives of every human being living on Pandora.

And the Pandorans, in turn, would change the entire world, whether they wanted to or not.

Part One

The New World

CHAPTER ONE

A Mud Hut in the Jungle

It was late when Tam finally left the experiment wing and crossed Alpha Complex's central lobby. Outside the dome, the sky's summer sapphire hue had deepened to indigo, and the first three stars shone over the forest, which stretched its long shadow across the marsh toward the Alpha Complex. Silhouettes of wading birds—paddlers, skimmers, and shimmies—stood stark and still in the peach and fuchsia light.

The beauty of the sight stopped Tam. He leaned on the railing in front of the triple-insulated windows, giving himself a minute to watch the marsh's many dances. Fish and insects rippled the water. Bats skimmed overhead. One of the wading birds stabbed its beak into the water and came up with a patch of darkness, maybe a frog. Snap! The meal was done and the bird strutted away.

It might have been Old Earth out there. It almost was. Pandora was one of the few worlds to score a perfect ten on the Almen Compatibility Scale.

The scene tugged at Tam. He wished, as he had on a thousand other evenings, that he could walk out of the complex with its pillow dome, insulation, sealed portals, and water-cooled walls. He would step into the pink and lavender glow of the sunset, onto one of the marsh's tiny islands, and watch the water birds in their thousands take flight all around him.

Oh, Tam spent a great deal of time outdoors, in the villages for which he was administrator, but those were fenced and protected areas, not the pristine wilderness, not what he saw through the window. That beauty remained forever out of reach, past the glass, past the fences.

Just once, Tam thought. *What could it hurt?*

Years of conditioning raised a surge of guilt in him at the thought, and that guilt activated his Conscience implant.

Are you looking out the window, Tam? it asked him. *Are you thinking of walking in the marsh?*

The Conscience implant couldn't actually read thoughts, but it could measure the presence of chemicals indicating anxiety, or guilt, and ask probing questions. Tam took a deep breath and tried to concentrate on the world inside, on his home and family. This time he was not successful. His Conscience tasted the continuing guilt in his mind and knew its guess was right.

We'd be no better than the ones who tear their worlds apart and try to turn them into farms. Pandora must be protected.

Tam shook his head. "Yes, yes, I know," he murmured to his Conscience. "I'm not going to break out. Really."

It was dark enough outside that Tam could see his own reflection in the window glass. It showed him a spare man, whose black trousers, white shirt, and white-on-white patterned vest hung on him as if he'd lost a lot of weight recently. His medium brown skin was still clear, but his thick black hair swept back from a high forehead that showed the lines of age and worry. His dark eyes set above his Roman nose sagged tiredly at the corners.

It had been ten years since the meeting in which the Authority had bullied Pandora into seeking answers to the Diversity Crisis, the death that stalked across the Called. But after ten years of experiments, analysis, and gathering more data than could ever be used, their theory of how to produce a universal cure was still just theory.

The Authority was getting restless. The failure of the second delegation to Earth had only made that restlessness worse. The Authority might say they were no government, that they were just merchants and go-betweens, but they knew their future was bound completely up in the future of the Called, and they were not going to let that future go.

A new reflection moved in the glass. Tam focused on the translucent image and saw that a thin young man had come to stand behind him. The man's pale skin, white tunic, and white-striped trousers stood out sharply against the background of ferns and drooping tropical greens in the big bubble terrarium that dominated the center of the lobby.

"Basante. You're all I need right now," Tam whispered aloud, almost without realizing he was doing it. *That is one of the problems with Consciences,* he thought to himself. *You end up talking to yourself a lot.*

Basante is part of your family, Tam's Conscience reminded him.

Maybe he'll go away. Tam looked past their reflections to what he could still see of the marsh. The thumb-sized luminescent flies their ancestors had nicknamed will-o'-the-wisps danced over the waters and dotted the reeds, as if the stars had come down to play.

A fanciful image. Tam smiled softly to himself.

Tam focused on the reflections again. Basante was still there. In fact, he looked ready to wait all night.

Nothing else for it, then. Tam turned. "Good evening, Experimenter Basante. I thought you were retiring for some private time." They both had spent all afternoon and most of the evening hearing the report of the latest delegation to the Called. Their conclusions were as expected. Trying to find a cure for the Diversity Crisis one planet at a time would involve making massive changes to each planet's biosphere for the sake of its human inhabitants, which was completely unacceptable. Father Mihran had told them all so before they left.

"It is bad enough that we will be enabling the colonists to continue to destroy the natural and native life of their worlds. We will not turn our own hands to that destruction, any more than we would begin to destroy Pandora."

Which meant only one thing. If the worlds could not be changed, the humans would have to be.

"I had hoped to get to bed early." Basante stepped forward. "But this is urgent."

Without waiting to be invited, he pressed his palm over the back of Tam's hand. Tam glared at him. He also, however, looked at the back of his hand to see what data had been transferred to the display.

The miniature screen shone with the colored lines that made up a gene scan. Tam's practiced eye read it as clearly as if it had been the alphabet, and he felt his eyebrows rise.

Tam looked up from the scan. "Is this one of ours?"

"Not yet," said Basante. He had a grin on his face, as if he had produced the gene alleles by himself from a dish in his lab. "She's being processed for immigration right now."

Tam felt his mouth tighten into a frown. Basante's enthusiasms were reason for caution. As of this afternoon, his project, the Eden Project, had suddenly become the chosen means of curing the Diversity Crisis. However, Basante, like the other experimenters, was too apt to see the subjects of his experiments as spare parts and forget that they were as human as the family. "Have we asked her to volunteer for the project yet?"

"Do you want to take the chance she'll say no?" Basante actually looked surprised.

Tam's frown deepened and his gaze turned sour. Recognizing that a negative answer was on the way, Basante held up his hand. "Normally I'd agree with you." Basante had sat with Tam in history lessons. He knew that even villagers could be pushed too far, and this woman was a stationer. "But this one is too important," Basante barreled on, gesturing to the gene scan. "She's within three or four points of perfection. We've been having the Authority sweep the Called for this configuration, and here she is, practically delivered to us."

Tam ran a thumb over the back of his hand, wiping the scan from his display. "We will ask her to enter voluntarily. We can make a good offer. But we will let her immigrate no matter what she says."

"And if she does say no?" Basante folded his hands behind his back.

"Then at least she's down here with us, and about to have all the usual problems station people have in the villages. We will make our offer again." Tam turned away, then he turned back again. "If I find out you or anyone else has forced her into the project, I'll have you standing up to explain yourself before the family, including Senior Committee."

Tam walked away from the windows and through the connector hallway, with its aquarium walls. Sunfish and koi looked briefly out at him between green clouds of algae and then went about their own business.

He hoped he had been clear enough. With Basante, one never knew.

Outside, I wouldn't have to worry about any of this, he thought, before he could stop himself. The guilt rose, and must have tasted familiar to his implant. He'd been giving it a lot of practice lately.

Earth, his Conscience said. *I want you to think about what happened to Earth.*

Then it seemed to Tam he smelled ozone and sulfur, and everything he had ever learned about Earth came flooding back to him. Earth, the birthplace of humanity, with its endless sprawl of buildings tied together with roads and tubes and rails, its red tides, and rivers that ran slick and hot with waste from the power generators and factories. He remembered studying the diagrams of the water processors and the earth processors and the people in their protected habitats, and all the vast machinery that was needed to ensure the continuance of human life on a world where the only green left was the miles and miles of corn and soybean fields that fed all those people.

He remembered the video composites of the people in their boxlike homes, taking their medicines and monitoring their blood chemistry and receiving news reports about the latest longevity discoveries and treatments and the progress that was being made in reseeding the oceans with fresh kelp to help create more oxygen for them to breathe during their long, propped-up lives, which had destroyed the world they did not understand. Around them, that same world struggled not to die, while its oblivious children lived on in shells of stone, bacteria, and artificial gardens.

"But is it true?" murmured Tam to the memories and his Conscience as he took a deep, steadying breath. It was hard to ask the question, but he had to. Without it, he would just accept, which was the one thing he could not do. If he did, it would mean everything his parents had tried to do for him and for Pandora was over. It would make him worse than his birth sister Dionte, with her scheming and her excesses. "Or is it just what you and I are supposed to believe?"

It is true, answered his Conscience. *You know it is true.*

"Yes," Tam breathed with a sigh. It was the approved answer. It would shut his Conscience up and give him time to think for himself.

Satisfied, the implant lapsed into silence, and Tam started walking again, hands folded behind himself, trying to be content with the sight of fish on the one side and drooping ferns on the other.

Once, the Conscience implants had just been communication devices connected to personal data displays. They accepted subvocalized commands, monitored physical health, and assisted with data reduction and sorting. They followed the orders of the ones who carried them. But that was long ago, and now they were also personal guardians, making sure all members of the family remembered who they were and what they owed to their family, and to Pandora.

With room in his head to think his own thoughts again, Tam turned back to his conversation with Basante. It was very clear that Basante wanted this immigrant woman in the experiment wing. He probably wanted her in the involuntary wing, where he wouldn't have to bother explaining things to her.

Tam wondered abruptly if Dionte knew about this woman. Probably. Basante was wedged very tightly into her plans and saw very much through her eyes.

Tam hoped the woman was smart and strong. Otherwise, both Basante and Dionte could quite easily get what they wanted.

Chena Trust lay awake in the darkness, blinking at a thick, blank, silent wall.

After a few million seconds of this, she rolled over on her back and listened. Beyond the breathing, rustling, snoring people, she heard another world. It chirruped, peeped, and murmured with a whole set of rhythms that followed no pattern Chena could make out. It was nothing like their home on Athena Station, which she, her little sister, and their mother had left a week or so ago. On the station, she could tell what was happening in the world by the clicks, creaks, and whooshes that filtered through the ancient walls. Here, it was just noises all piled up on top of each other.

Chena burrowed under her covers, but sleep didn't come back.

What are you afraid of? she asked herself. *You're here now. It's stupid to be scared of the place. You're not going back.*

She wanted a light, an info screen, and a jack for her wrist comptroller, so she could find out something about this place she was in, but none of that stuff existed here. The walls stared back at Chena, blank, immutable, silent. Everything she knew was up in the sky somewhere—the curving, insulated hallways with their cameras and input screens, the kilometer-long spiral staircases, which were always too cold or too hot and forever too loud no matter how much sound damping they'd put up, their tiny apartment with its peeling carpet—these were all the past. And the future . . .

Was the future really a mud hut in the jungle? That was what Eng and King said. Chena poked her head out from under the covers again.

"They give you a spear and make you hunt things." King had hopped around grunting, with a big grin on his face, like he thought he was doing a public service. "You're going to look real sweet swinging from a vine, Chena. This is how you're going to look." He grabbed a corner bracket and let himself swing back and forth until the caution alarm buzzed at them, with Eng laughing that stupid horsey laugh of his the whole time.

They can both just piss off. What do they know? They were born on Athena too. They just know what they see on the screen. Chena scratched at the gauze bandage sealed to the back of her hand. *This place isn't mud. It's stone and wood. It isn't anything like mud.*

Mom wouldn't really make them live in the jungle. She wouldn't do that to them. This was just a temporary stop. They'd move someplace real in maybe a week or so. Mom had a job. They weren't going to stay here.

Chena rubbed the bandage harder. Her skin still stung where they had inserted the new ID chip and then imprinted a multibranched tattoo on top of it. All that had been done by the same woman in white overalls who'd spent the morning quizzing Chena. Where was she from, what did she weigh, what did she eat, how often had she been sick, was she sick now, how did she do in school, did she go to school, or did she just learn off the computer? Where did they live on Athena, had they always lived on Athena? Who was her mother, her father, her grandparents, her aunts and uncles and cousins . . . ?

When she couldn't answer all the questions, especially the ones about her family, the woman in white overalls looked disgusted, pulled out a syringe, and gestured for Chena to hold out her arm.

But they'd finally had enough of that and had put her in a sterile-walled waiting room already filled to bursting with people—men, women, kids, and babies, none of whom had been in the car on the space cable that had brought Chena and her family down to Pandora, and none of whom smelled like they had shower stalls in their apartments. Their old apartments. All of them were immigrants, like she was now.

It had been about an hour before whoever was giving Teal her going-over let her into the waiting room too. Teal had been scared, of course, but at least she didn't look like she was ready to cry, which she would have if this had happened even just last year. Chena grabbed Teal's hand and peered around through the crowd, looking for someplace where they could stand. A pair of old men in orange overalls that looked ready to fall off their skinny bodies shuffled sideways and gestured to Chena that she could stand by the wall. Chena nodded her thanks and steered Teal toward the empty spot.

Chena leaned against the wall, and so did Teal, but she collapsed her knees until she'd slid all the way to the floor.

Chena looked down at her younger sister for a long moment. Teal had just turned ten. She looked like Mom. Everybody said so. She had Mom's sandy brown skin and high round forehead, black hair that fell back in waves around her ears. She had Mom's shining brown eyes, and was stocky like Mom was too, with square hands but round legs.

Chena, on the other hand, was thirteen going on fourteen and looked like their father—tan skin, thick and wiry hair that was more brown than black, a sharp face, a wide full mouth, and deep-set eyes of midnight blue. Everything about her seemed too long right now—arms, legs, hands, feet. She was still getting used to the fact that she could look Mom in the eye without tilting her head up, and that she needed to wear a bra.

Teal wrapped her arms around her legs and hugged them to her chest, turning her head so her cheek rested on her knees and she could look back up at Chena.

"What do you think Dad's doing?" she asked. Her voice was small and furtive and a little impatient. She wanted to start a story.

Chena sighed. Ever since Dad had left them last year, they'd been making up stories about what had happened to him. All they knew for sure was that he'd failed to rejoin his ship in the port of a world called Rupert's Choice and they'd left without him. There'd been no news since then, even though Mom had talked to every bureaucrat on the station.

He'd probably just left them. Parents did that sometimes. There were kids in the halls on Athena who'd had both parents just dump them. But maybe not. Maybe he was really out there doing something important and soon he'd come back for them.

Oh, well, it's better than her whining. Chena sat cross-legged next to Teal. "Okay." She pulled her leg in as a big dark woman shuffled past, looking for someone or something. "Let me see." She pressed her fingertips to her forehead, like she was receiving messages from the Great Beyond. "I think he's working undercover for the Authority," she said, flipping her eyes open. "I think there's a conspiracy to poison one of the colony worlds and he's going to find out who's behind it."

One of the old men next to them wheezed with laughter. "I think you've got too much imagination for a hallway baby."

Anger, hot and sudden, flashed through Chena. "What would you know, you limp old—"

The door swished open and Teal seized her arm before Chena could finish the insult. Mom strode into the waiting room. Chena scrambled to her feet, stuffing her thumb between her first two fingers and stabbing upward to give the old man the piss-off sign. He waved her off and turned back to his friend.

"Well, Supernova, well, Starlet, that was something else, wasn't it?" Mom's voice was light, but her face was tired, even grim. "Gods below, I'm tired." She had wrapped her arms around Teal and Chena and leaned back against the wall.

There was no time to ask questions then, because a different woman walked in right behind Mom. She wore a brown tunic and a long skirt. Her skin was sandy gold and her black hair was swept back and bundled into some kind of little mesh bag. She said her name was Madra and that she was the coordinator for the village of Offshoot. Then she'd read off a list of names of people who were supposed to come with her—including Chena, Teal, and Helice Trust.

So they lined up and walked down the corridor and out a door, where there'd been a brief glimpse of sky, and shifting sand and pebbles underfoot, and a huge glass and silver wire thing that Chena knew was a dirigible only because of a rig game she'd played once, and they were lead into the compartment under the areogel balloon. At least in this one there were enough chairs, and they were soft and comfortable, even if the immigrants did have to be strapped in, and they flew.

At first the feeling was fun, like the acceleration of the car on the space cable, but then it got boring. There wasn't anything to see except the walls and the back of the chair in front of her. There were no jacks for her comptroller, or game rigs, or anything, and she found herself missing the space elevator. They'd been cooped up in there for two days in one big room with capsule bunks on the walls, but that had been fun. There'd been rigs and screens and five other kids, including Dea Jemma Tosh, whom Chena had grown up with, and Mom had been relaxed and happy, telling them over and over that this was a new beginning.

But the new beginning was turning out to be as boring as used grease. That was Pandora out there. *Pandora.* The world where people walked around counting flowers, with chips in their heads to tell them what to do. Where they were so busy with plants and animals, they didn't even know know how to fix their own machinery and they had to get Athenians to take care of everything for them, from replacement parts to satellite maintenance. Where they had beaten the Diversity Crisis and all the babies were born healthy and alive. A thousand conflicting stories ran through Chena's head. Nobody—well, nobody Chena knew—knew that much about Pandora. There was no public access network between the station and the planet, and the planet was forty-eight hours away at the bottom of the space cable. Forty-eight hours, after you got all the permits you needed, if you could get them. All Chena herself knew came from a combination of half-forgotten history lessons, legends she and her friends told each other, and snippets of rig games designed around the Conscience Rebellion that won Athena Station its semi-independence four hundred years ago. The Pandorans were helpless and they were automatons. They were distrusted geniuses and miracle workers. The whole world was a wilderness, and a garden.

And she couldn't see any of it.

Eventually somebody came around and handed out some of the cakes that Chena and Teal had always called nutra-bricks. But even they were more interesting than the talk Madra got up to give—about how welcome they all were to Offshoot, and how they would be expected to give their share to village life, and on and on and on. Chena wasn't sure if she actually fell asleep, but she was counting the white hairs on the balding head of the man in front of her for a while.

My first time on a planet, and I can barely tell it from the station, she remembered thinking.

Then, finally, *finally,* the dirigible settled down to the ground, they were herded out the door, and the world around them was dark, except for a little path of lanterns leading up to a wooden dock, with an enclosed boat waiting on it. Inside, they all had to take seats again, and a bunch of people had lined up on benches on either side of them and grabbed hold of these wooden levers sticking out of the walls. They began pushing and pulling on the levers in time with the ticking of a big metronome at the back of the boat.

Rowing. The were *rowing.* This boat had no engines!

But eventually even that novelty wore away into boredom. As hard as she tried, Chena couldn't see a damn thing out the windows. Teal and Mom fell asleep on each other's shoulders, and Chena wished she could do the same. The boat's rocking motion made her queasy and she felt like she was alone in the whole dark world and nobody cared.

Then they were unloaded onto yet another lit path, in another dark world, and led into this big round room, assigned lockers, and given bundles of pallets and blankets and told to go to sleep, that there'd be a general breakfast bell, and welcome to Offshoot.

Welcome to Offshoot. When do we get to go home? Chena thought now to the darkness that was the ceiling.

She'd thought they'd be in one of the domed cities. That was what Mom had said at first. She'd applied for a liaison and consulting mechanic's position. But that hadn't been a go plan. Mom didn't say why. She just told them they'd be heading for one of the outside villages instead.

As she thought that over, Chena noticed the darkness was less dark. The world seemed to be turning gray at the edges.

Sun must be coming up, she thought, sitting up and blinking. Weird. She'd been in rig games that showed dawn, and she thought she'd be ready for it, but somehow she'd never guessed it would be so . . . gradual. She didn't think it could start up without you noticing it. It seemed like there should be a noise, a click, or a hum or a bell—something.

Which is completely stupid, she told herself. *You're a jungle girl now. No more caution buzzers, ever.*

Then she realized something else. For the first time since they'd stepped aboard the space cable car, she wasn't being watched or led around or put someplace. She could actually get up and go somewhere if she wanted to.

She looked at her comptroller. It had defaulted to the time function: 4:20 glowed at her.

Chena made her decision. Carefully, she folded back her blankets. Teal didn't stir. Neither did Mom. One of the anonymous lumps that was a fellow immigrant snorted and shrugged, but that was it.

Now that her eyes had adjusted to the dimness, Chena found she could make her way easily between the clusters of pallets to the room's one doorway. The floor was cool under her feet but not cold, so she decided not to bother with finding her shoes. A corridor led off to the right and a set of shallow stairs climbed to the left. Ahead of her opened another round room, also full of sleeping bodies.

Chena opted for the stairs. They felt strangely uneven under her feet, as if they hadn't been quite smoothed off. They were cold enough that she wished for her socks, but she kept going.

The staircase rose in a spiral through a second story that was shrouded in darkness, and up past that to another low doorway. Chena found the knob and tried to slide it sideways. It didn't budge. Feeling foolish, she remembered to push.

A gust of damp wind, heavy with unfamiliar scents, caught Chena in the face and she shivered. She was outside. The rushing water sound that was the wind in the tree branches filled the world. She could see the black trunks like gigantic support girders against the gray background.

She almost turned back then, but her gaze dropped to the, what?—floor? roof?—that she stood on. It had been terraced and covered in dirt, and then in grass. Shafts of pale silver light slanted through the trees and touched the plants. Chena sucked in a breath before it could become a gasp. The roof was a garden. Flowers, closed tight for morning, grew out of beds of moss. Ivy crept along the rooftop and twined up the saplings, and that was just the beginning. The glimmers of silver light the forest permitted in highlighted more kinds of plants than she had known existed, just in this little space of a living rooftop.

It was alien to Chena, utterly and completely, but, even as she shivered in the unregulated wind, she found it beautiful.

Wrapping her arms around herself, Chena stepped out onto the roof. Damp, chilly grass cushioned her bare feet. She wandered here and there, just to see what she could—the shades of green on the different plants, the cup of a flower, all the kinds and shapes of leaves, the big rocks with their flecks of green and gray. Something touched her arm and Chena saw a bug with iridescent wings and a bright green body hanging on to her. It rubbed its impossibly delicate forelegs together and took off in the next heartbeat.

Beyond the edge of the roof waited a world of trees and rivers. The trees were so huge that any one of them could have been hollowed out to make a station module. Sunlight became tangled in the girder-like branches high overhead, up where the leaves made a shady mosaic that swayed in the wind. Here and there, a solid column of light made it down to the floor and lit up a patch of plants with tightly closed buds or furled leaves. Reed-choked streams dissected the village and then joined together to spill into the long brown river that snaked along the forest floor. More water fell in chortling cascades from the trees. Chena's gaze followed the waterfalls up and saw that there were houses in the trees too, lashed to the crooks of the mighty branches. Entirely wooden, with living roofs, they looked like they had grown out of the gigantic trunks. Water cascaded down from the heights, collecting briefly in a series of cisterns, only to spill over their edges and down into the streams.

Chena had always thought that forests would be silent places. In the rig games, they were hushed except for the occasional call of a bird or growl of an animal. The games had left out the endless chatter of the water, and the great rushing of wind through the branches, and the way those branches creaked, as if they hadn't been tightened on properly and might fall off at any moment.

Chena bit her lip nervously. She couldn't help it. Creaks were bad noises. Creaks meant something was straining. Straining things broke and spilled the air out into the vacuum. Her head knew things like that couldn't happen on a planet, but her gut didn't yet.

Another gust of wind blew through her hair and tickled her nose. Chena sneezed, and one of the rocks straightened up.

Chena almost screamed. She stumbled backward, caught her foot on the edge of one of the terraces, and fell into what felt like a mass of feathers and thorns. Someone cackled with laughter while she struggled to get to her feet again, wincing at every snap and rustle underneath her.

When she was finally standing, Chena found she faced a stooped old woman who stepped out from behind a cluster of cablelike plants that ran up a bunch of skinny poles. She was even smaller and shorter than Chena. Some kind of apron covered her clothes, and its many pockets bulged with . . . something. In her hand, she carried a short curved knife.

Chena cleared her throat. "Good morning, Grandmother," she said, saluting as politely as her mother had ever taught her, touching forehead, heart, and lips.

"I don't know you." The woman frowned and shifted her grip on the knife.

"I just got here." Chena stared at the knife as if she'd been hypnotized. "I was just looking around, is all."

"Were you?" The woman stepped closer. Chena could smell her now, and she smelled green and moldy. "Where'd you get here from?"

"Athena Station." Chena thought about taking a step back to get away from the smell, which now included sweat and some really bad breath, but she was afraid she'd fall and wreck something worse. Still, there was that knife in the wrinkled fist. . . .

"You're a station girl, and you came out here?" The old woman spoke the words like an accusation. "Alone?"

"Yes," said Chena, her anger rising at the sneer the old woman put into the words "station girl." "As if it's anything to you."

"Huh," grunted the woman. "Well, that's different. All right, girl, I'll tell you, it's not a good idea to be wandering around the roofs too late or too early. That's the first thing."

And because I so desperately begged for your advice . . . ? thought Chena sourly. She folded her arms. "What's the second thing?"

She thought she saw a look of approval flicker across the old woman's face. "The second is, I'm Nan Elle. If there's something you need to know, pass the word for me and maybe I'll tell you." Her mouth gaped in a smile, and Chena saw with a shock that she didn't have all her teeth. "Now get you downstairs, station girl. This isn't your world until the sun's all the way up."

Chena stayed where she was for a long second, just to show she wasn't afraid and that she wasn't going to be ordered around easily. But she saw that knife, and she saw how this woman came out of nowhere, and how the air was still more shadows than light. With all these things in her head, Chena turned away. But as she headed for the door, she saw another staircase. This one traveled down the side of the building. There was also a kind of catwalk leading straight off the roof and into the trees. Chena looked back over her shoulder and saw that the old woman was still watching her.

Let her watch. She walked right onto the catwalk. She thought she heard a raspy chuckle behind her, but that could have been the wind in the leaves.

The walkway was made of wooden boards, polished to a high shine and tied together with fiber ropes. She felt a little dizzy standing there. She could look over the edge and see the forest floor. This wasn't even anything near as high as she could go. There were buildings whose roofs brushed the leaves on the trees. She wanted to climb up there, to see who lived in them and how they lived, and if they thought they were something.

Better not push it too far right now, Chena.

At least she could touch. Chena reached out her hand toward the wrinkled bark of the tree trunk beside her.

Pain ran up and down her arm.

"Ow!" she shouted, snatching her hand back. She stared from her fingertips to the tree. Then she saw the slim silver pillars that lined the catwalk on both sides.

Gods below, she thought, rubbing her hand. *It's a shock fence.*

Now that she saw them, she noticed the shock fence posts lining the paths in the village below too. Every path, every building, was effectively cut off from the surrounding forest. No one could walk out there without suffering a serious shock or, depending on how high the current was set, without dying.

All that alien beauty out there was completely out of reach.

Feeling cheated, Chena stuck to the lowest level, just walking and wondering about the slowly brightening world around her. Did the waterfalls chattering around her shoulders serve any real purpose or were they just decoration? What were those four silver rails stretching across the forest floor and into the woods? She could see the broad brown river winding between the trees, down a slope from the village, but she couldn't see any boats at the docks.

Suddenly Chena felt closed in. Except for the theoretical boats and mysterious rails, there really was no way out of here. Maybe they really would have to wait for Dad to come get them. Maybe that would never happen.

Mom won't make us stay here, she told herself, her hand tightening on the catwalk railing.

The noise of running feet and hoarse calls made Chena look down. A pair of boys about her own age trotted out from between the buildings, following one of the gravel paths. Mindful of the fence, Chena leaned over the railing and waved.

"Hey!" she called.

The boys paused and looked up. When they spotted Chena, they stared for a minute and then one of them slapped the other on the shoulder and they took off running again.

"Hey!" exclaimed Chena again. She ran along the catwalk until she came to the stairs leading to the ground. The boys had almost vanished. She pelted down the gravel path after them, angry at being ignored, and anger gave her speed. It was pretty obvious they were trying to lose her, and they knew the ground a lot better than she did. If she didn't catch them fast, she wouldn't catch them at all.

Eventually she gained enough on one of the boys to grab him by the shoulder and spin him around to face her.

"What's your bug?" she asked, stepping back. "Or are you just a bunch of tinkies who don't like girls?"

"Listen to this one," said the taller boy. His skin was dark brown, like the bark on the trees around them, and his hair was a pale sandy red. Freckles covered his face, including one huge one under his right eye. "It thinks it's got something."

"Maybe I do." Chena folded her arms. "What would you know about it? You're too scared to even talk. Where's the rest of your tinky friends? They hiding too? Too scared without their mommies?"

The tallest boy's fists went up. Chena raised her own fists. She'd figured this might happen. On the station, there was usually a fight when a new kid came in, and she'd been ready for it. If she could get this over with now, there was less of a chance of Teal getting beaten up later. Teal was a major boil, but nobody laid hands on her.

But, God, this kid was tall. She spread her feet and got ready to duck when he threw his punch.

His arm went back and Chena tensed, but the other kid, this one stocky and pale tan, grabbed the tall kid's arm before he could throw the punch.

"Not worth it, Shond," he said. "We show up busted in, we're gonna have extra duty for a month." He shoved Shond's arm down. Then he looked at Chena. "So what do you think your name is?"

"Chena Trust." She loosened her fists. "Who do you think you are?"

"I'm Hyder. You almost got hit by Shond." He cuffed the tall kid. "Where're you from?"

"Athena Station." Chena relaxed her stance. Maybe she wouldn't have to fight after all. She wondered what Hyder meant by getting "extra duty."

Shond snorted. "Station kid? Hall's balls, what're we bothering her for? She'll be in the dorms for a week, and then her mom'll be selling her off for body parts or to one of the freak towns. Some guy probably paid to put her up her mom's cunt anyway."

Chena stepped forward, suddenly ready to get as far into it as this piss-mouth wanted to go. "Say it again," she dared him. "Go on. I want to hear how good you talk, dickless."

"Shond!" A girl's voice this time. She shoved her way past Chena. She was tall, broad in the shoulder, and just starting to get a pair of breasts. She had thick arms and legs and shared Shond's red hair and freckles. "What the shit-all are you doing? The cop's in town! He's going to be doing a vid review before the end of the day, and won't he just love to see your pretty face on it?" She shoved him, hard, so he stumbled backward. "You want to punch somebody, you punch me and see what's what!"

"Back off, Sadia," sulked Shond. "We were just messing."

Sadia turned to Chena and fixed her with a glower that rivaled Mom's on a bad day. "You just messing?"

"Not anymore," Chena told her, without taking her eyes off Shond, who pretty much had to be this girl's brother.

Sadia swung back around to face Shond and his buddy. "Get out,

Shond, or I'm telling the cop how you fixed the duty sheets, and won't that just make you look like the good kid."

Sadia and Shond stared each other down for a minute, and then Shond's gaze flickered back to Chena.

But it was Hyder who smacked him again. "Come on, Shond, Let's cut. Nothing doing here."

"Right." Shond turned away reluctantly, and he and Hyder ran down the path, vanishing between the buildings.

Sadia looked Chena up and down. Chena held her ground without flinching. "He start that?" Sadia asked finally, jerking her chin in the direction the boys had run off.

Chena shrugged. "I sort of let him."

"Easy to do. I'm Sadia. Shond's my brother," she added, confirming Chena's guess.

Chena introduced herself and they touched foreheads to each other in abbreviated salutes. "What's his bug?" she asked, gesturing after Shond.

Sadia shrugged. "Hates being a dorm baby. Always has to get into it."

"Don't all the kids live in the dorms?" asked Chena, glad to have a source of information.

"Balls, no." Sadia shook her head and then cocked an eyebrow toward Chena. "You just slide down the pipe?"

"Pretty much, yeah." Chena leaned her back against the wall. It felt cool behind her, partly shaded by the eaves with their overhang of moss.

Sadia leaned beside Chena and folded her arms across her chest. "Then you haven't got the talk yet?"

Chena's mouth twisted up into a tight smile. "Yeah, but I slept through it."

Sadia laughed. "No dim bulbs here. It's pretty boring. I'll give you the free preview." Sadia held up her hand and started ticking points off on her fingers. "If you got no money, you get to live in the dorms and work the town, work the shit mostly. Money, you still got to work the town, but you get your own place and whatever else you can buy. Enough money"—Sadia held up her index finger in front of Chena's face—"and you get to buy your kids a spot in a school, otherwise they work the town with everybody else."

Busted, thought Chena. *At least they can't shut the air off here.*

"They give you a shift yet?" Sadia asked.

Chena shook her head. "We're just in the dorm for a couple days. Mom's got a job coming." Which was an exaggeration. Mom had a job, all right, but it might be a while before they had money for rent because of the bills from Athena.

Sadia's look was skeptical, but not derisive like her brother's had been. Chena couldn't blame her. She'd heard enough lies from the hall kids in the station to know some kids would say anything to keep someone from knowing how bad things were with them.

"Well, keep your head down and look busy, you may stay off the duty sheets for a while. But don't try to duck it too long. They may put you on the watch list, where they've got Shond." Sadia dropped her gaze and kicked at the gravel with the scuffed toe of her shoe. "If you stay there for too long, you get declared useless, and then the hothousers can have you."

"Useless?" Chena pushed herself away from wall. "You're kidding."

Again, Sadia shrugged. "So, all right, the cop doesn't call it 'useless,' but that's what it means. It means you're no good as a person, only good for spare parts and experiments, and they can haul you off whenever and wherever they feel like."

Chena looked at Sadia hard, trying to see if the girl was trying to pull one over on the new kid. But Sadia looked serious, and a little worried. If she was for real and her brother was on the list . . .

"And people just let them do this? To their kids?"

"The hothousers own the world. We just live here. Who's gonna say anything?" Sadia folded her arms. "I hear on the station they shut your air off if you can't pay your rent."

Chena opened her mouth to say she'd never seen it happen, but she closed it without saying anything. It could happen, and everybody knew it. That was why Mom had taken them off the station, never mind what either of them had told Teal.

Just then, a brass banging filled the air. Chena jumped, looking automatically around for an info screen.

Sadia laughed, but not too hard. "Ease off, new girl. It's the breakfast bell for first shift."

"Oh, right." Chena slumped her shoulders and swallowed against the thumping of her heart. That woman, Madra, had said something about a breakfast bell—

Chena's thoughts stopped in their tracks. That gonging meant Mom was waking up right now, to see that Chena wasn't in her bed.

She groaned. "I gotta get back. Mom's going to kill me for wandering out."

She turned to go, but Sadia grabbed her arm. "If they give you a chance to pick your shift, try the get into K37. That's where I'm at." She gave Chena a quick smile that faded into a pleading look as she let her go. "And if you get into it with Shond, try not to fight him. He's walking the edge as it is."

"Promise," said Chena.

Sadia's smile came back for real. They waved to each other and Chena pelted hard up the path, hoping she was heading right for the dorm.

Even as Chena concentrated on running, Sadia's words flitted through her head. What she said couldn't be true, at least not all of it. Because if it was true, Mom never would have brought them here.

She wouldn't have. No. Of course not. Never.

CHAPTER TWO

Offshoot

Thud!

Chena staggered backward from the soft surface she had slammed into.

"Are you okay?" A pair of hands grabbed her shoulders. Chena looked up and saw she had plowed right into Madra.

"I'm sorry, Aunt," Chena gasped, saluting quickly.

"It's okay, it's okay." Madra waved her apology away. "No harm. But what are you doing out here?" She looked Chena up and down, her dark eyes taking in the details, such as Chena's bare feet.

"I . . . um . . ." Chena stared past her at the doorway to the dorm. The double doors were shut tight. Mom was wondering where she was. Mom was going to kill her completely dead.

"You were trying to get back before anybody noticed you were gone?" suggested Madra.

Chena bit her lip. "Yes, Aunt."

The woman's smile broadened and she shook Chena's shoulder gently. "It's just Madra, and you're already too late." She gestured Chena to come on and started walking down the path.

Because there was nothing else to do, Chena fell into step alongside Madra, glad that the woman did not insist on keeping a hand on her shoulder or anything. She was a round woman, Chena now saw. Strong, but not a hard-body. She looked like she might actually be okay.

Madra pushed open the dormitory doors and led Chena through a dim room that looked to her just like the sleeping room, except it had chairs, tables, and pillows in it.

“Common room,” said Madra when she saw Chena looking around. “Someplace to relax in the evenings.”

Down the inner corridor, the sleeping room had transformed itself into a hive of activity. Women and girls busied themselves around pallets and cupboards. Some of them, obviously more used to this than others, moved quickly and efficiently—rolling up their beds, stowing their blankets in the lockers, getting out bags and buckets of bathing supplies, and herding the smallest children out the door. Others just yawned and stretched and scratched, blinking stupidly around them, as if they weren’t sure where they were. Some burrowed farther under their blankets, searching for a few more minutes of sleep. Chena, coming in from the fresh air, couldn’t help noticing the strong scent of unwashed people.

Mom and Teal stood still in the middle of all the activity. Mom was saying something that Chena couldn’t hear. Teal must have caught sight of the movement in the doorway, because she touched Mom’s hand and pointed. Mom’s gaze fastened on Chena, and Chena, figuring there was no getting out of this, picked her way between the strangers in their miscellaneous assortment of nightclothes.

“There,” a stringy pale woman wearing a blue shirt and nothing else said to Mom. “I told you she’d be back as soon as the bell sounded.”

“Thank you,” said Mom to her in a tone that meant anything but. She immediately turned on Chena, her face filled with fury. “Where have you been?”

Then Mom saw Madra following right behind Chena, and her mouth shut like a trap.

Chena dropped her gaze to the floor. She’d been right. Witnesses or no, Mom was ready to kill her. “I woke up. I wanted to look around. I lost track of time. Sorry.”

“Don’t worry, Helice,” said Madra. “The village is fenced and monitored. There’s nothing she could get into that would hurt her.”

“Thank you, Madra,” said Mom in her most polite voice. “I appreciate you looking out for her.” She gave Madra a salute.

“It’s part of my job,” said Madra cheerfully. “Well, I have to make my speech now.”

Chena saw the tips of Madra’s shoes moving away. Mom was silent for a moment, and Chena risked a look up. Mom still looked angry, but her face was softening. Chena shot a glance at Teal, who returned a look that plainly said, *You're so lucky.*

For what? Getting out, or not getting killed?

"All right." Mom sighed and ran a hand through her sleep-rumpled hair. "Nothing happened this time. But this is not the station, Chena." She held up a hand. "I know, you've noticed. What I'm saying is, we don't know all the rules here yet. We need to be careful for a while until we're all settled in. You understand me?"

Chena nodded, relieved that the talking-to was no worse. "Yes. I won't do it again. Sorry."

Mom looked dubious, but she didn't scold anymore. "And what did you see while you looked around?"

Chena opened her mouth, uncertain what she would say. But she never got a chance to speak.

"Good morning," announced Madra, taking up a position in the doorway. Chena had to peer through a forest of shoulders to see her. "Mornings are a little chaotic, so I thought I'd come by and give you the basic rundown on where you should be."

"Thank you," murmured Mom under her breath. A chorus of similar murmurs rippled around the room. Chena suppressed a smile.

"First I'm sure you'll all want to get cleaned up. Then we'll be having breakfast. After that, you can report to me for your shift assignments. You'll find towels and soap in your locker." Madra gestured toward the wall of tiny wooden lockers. None of them, Chena noticed, actually had locks. "If you get your things and come with me, I'll show you the baths and facilities."

"Bless you," breathed the woman who had reassured Mom about Chena's inevitable reappearance. "I'm coated, just coated."

"Yes, indeed," murmured Mom, a polite nothing. "Girls, let's get our things."

Mom opened the locker that had their names on it. The towels she found were thick but rough, and the soap was a yellow cake with ragged edges, as if it had just been broken off from a big slab.

"What's this?" said Teal, holding up the soap. "Where's the shampoo?"

"This is what there is for now, Starlet," said Mom, gathering clothes and towels. She pushed Teal gently into the mob that was gradually forming itself into a line in front of Madra, who was fielding a dozen questions about sleeping arrangements, job ops, and breakfast. "We'll buy ourselves what we need later."

Chena staked out a place next to Teal, eyeing the other kids in the crowd, trying to see if any of them looked friendly or looked like trouble, but mostly they just looked sleepy and a little confused. Just like she felt.

Madra lifted her voice over the flutter of questions. "Everybody ready as you can get? Good. Follow me, please." Madra smiled reassuringly at the befuddled herd of people.

Bet her mouth gets tired, holding that look, thought Chena grumpily.

But apparently it didn't. Madra's smile stayed fixed in place as she took the lead. The men and a few boys seemed to have slept in the round room across the way, and they joined the procession through curving, branching halls that smelled strongly of earth and too many people.

Madra seemed to know just about everybody who came and went, skirting their crowd, and she had a cheerful greeting for them all. "Good morning, Yuri, how's your hip? Hello, Dulce, Shukmi. Come see me later. I've got news for you. Gardens of God, Buile, you're huge! Have you felt it kick yet?"

Madra took them down a flight of stone steps. The air grew warm and damp and became filled with the echoing sounds of voices and splashing water.

"Now, then," said Madra. "There's something I ought to warn you about. It comes as a shock to a lot of our new arrivals from the stations where private living is the norm. . . ."

But Chena, ducking her head so she could peek between the screen of people in front of her, already saw. Past the squared-off doorway was a room lined with flat gray stones. In the center was a shallow pool of steaming water. In and around that pool, all the people were naked—men, women, girls, boys, and little babies. They soaped up and rinsed, walked back and forth, and even chased each other, and not one of them had a thing on.

"No," said Chena, swinging around to face her mother. "I'm not going in there." She wasn't the only one. A whole eruption of exclamations and protests exploded around them.

Mom sighed, pressing a hand to her ear against the noise. "It's just for now, Supernova. Soon we'll—"

"I don't care." Chena slashed her hand through the air between them. "I'm not taking a bath in front of . . . everybody!" She gestured behind her. There were men back there, and boys, and old women. Even aboard the station they'd had their own shower. Okay, it was about the size of their locker down here, but it was *private*. "There's got to be—"

"Believe me, I understand." Madra's voice lifted above the general din. "It was really bad the first few times I had to do it too, but then I realized that nobody was paying any attention to me anyway. They just wanted to get cleaned up and get into the breakfast line."

As if to prove her point, a small string of people, dressed and smelling like soap and warmth, shouldered their way through the crowd of newcomers and hurried down the hallway. Some of the others shrugged and took themselves through the doorway.

No one was leaving. Some were still grumbling, but if even one person left . . .

"Mom—" Chena started.

"Not a word, Chena," said her mother. "I don't like it either, but we are here and we have to make the best of it." More of the others were starting to file in. Chena felt her chances to get out of this slipping away.

"Couldn't we just go dirty until we get our own place?" suggested Teal plaintively. "I mean, you said it'd be soon."

Mom's sigh was short this time, frustrated at being caught by her own words. "Soon could be a month, Teal. Do you want to go dirty for a month?"

Teal's sideways glance at the bathroom said she did, and Chena was ready to agree with her, even though she knew it would never happen.

Mom just looked at them both. "I know this isn't comfortable. I know it isn't any fun. But if things are going to get better, we are going to have to get through this, and if we're lucky, this is as bad as it's going to get." She gave one more brief, sharp sigh. "Now let's get over it. Chena, bring your sister." She fixed her eyes straight ahead and marched through the doorway.

At that moment, standing there felt worse than imagining getting into the water did, and, of course, Mom had just made her responsible for bringing Teal.

"Come on." Chena knotted her fingers around the towel she carried and stepped forward.

Chena steeled herself not to see and not to think. She stripped off her clothes as fast she could, hiding under one of the rough towels that she draped over her shoulders. She got in and out of the noisy shifting bathwater as quickly as Mom would let her. The yellow soap was harsh against her skin and smelled pungent and strange. The smell surrounded her like a cloud as she put on her clean clothes and they accompanied the other bathers back to the sleeping room to return their stuff to their lockers. By the time they closed the locker door, Chena felt like she would have rather stayed aboard Athena and begged for air money.

Mom said nothing. She was probably still mad. She looked mad, with her face all hardened and closed up. She wouldn't look down at Chena or Teal at all.

The way to the dining room was not hard to find. A steady stream of people headed out one of the double doors into the morning. Outside was brighter and warmer now, and full of people. Gaggles of people strode or slouched along the gravel paths. Villagers filled the lowest catwalk, heading away into the trees toward the river docks. They wore thick dark clothing, and they all seemed to have long hair, either pulled back in ponytails or braids, or rolled up tightly against the backs of their heads. The newcomers were mostly on the ground paths, a strange patchwork bunch in their station blues, reds, and oranges. It didn't take much looking to see that the tree people were staring down at them.

Back at you, thought Chena toward whatever snide thoughts were being rained down at her and her family. *Right back at you.* She didn't dare make the piss-off sign. Mom would see. But she knew those looks. She'd seen looks like them on the station. Up there were the ones who had something you didn't and thought it was your fault that you weren't as good.

"Ow!" Teal's yelp jerked Chena's thoughts and her gaze out of the trees. Teal stood in the middle of the path, with her right hand jammed under her left armpit and staring with bewildered accusation at the air at the edge of the path.

Around them there were a few small laughs, and Chena heard the word "fence" ripple up and down the river of people.

Chena wrapped one arm around her sister. "Don't worry about it, Teal," she said, glaring at the amused bystanders. "I didn't see them either."

Mom also gave the bystanders a hard look, which actually got them to stop chuckling and move on. While she checked Teal's hand to make sure that there were no actual burns or anything, the closed-in feeling returned to cover Chena completely. Even so, she did not miss the frown on her mother's face as Mom looked at the fence posts. She would have given anything to know what Mom was thinking, but Mom said nothing. She just started walking toward the dining hall again.

The dining hall was a long low building with a thicket for a roof and tangled vines falling down its walls. The inside was dim, and the air smelled of the yellow soap and strange spices. But as Chena got into the food line with Mom and Teal, her stomach grumbled.

Can't smell all that strange, she thought as she picked up a bowl and shuffled forward. A man who looked so bored he was almost dead slopped a dollop of something beige, steaming, and dotted with bits of black and red into her bowl. Chena sniffed the steam. It smelled bland, but her stomach growled again.

At the end of the line, people were ladling something white into their bowls and drizzling something else brown and goopy on top, so Chena did too. Then she grabbed a big ceramic mug of what smelled like apple juice.

She was not surprised to see that everybody had to sit at long tables and that no one seemed to have their own spot. Fortunately, three men in thick trousers and long-sleeved shirts were just getting up from the end of one of the tables. Chena slid into the place where they'd been sitting and waved for Teal and Mom to come join her.

No one around them seemed interested in talking. They just dug their spoons into their bowls and ate. But they were watching. Chena saw the sidelong glances, as if every stranger in the room were sizing her and her family up. She wanted to yell at them, give them all the piss-off sign. What was the matter? They didn't think the Trusts were good enough to eat here? These people weren't so great either. Their clothes were dirty or sewn back together. She could see elbows poking through thin shirts and knees through thin trousers. Everyone's skin seemed to be wrinkled and callused, even the kids'.

And they have the nerve to stare at us. I'll show them nerve.

But Mom would have gone nuclear, so Chena kept her mouth shut and tried a spoonful of the . . . whatever it was. It probably stank. That was probably why everyone looked so pissed. The food was probably as bad as the bathrooms.

The stuff touched her tongue and Chena froze. It was delicious. It was warm and creamy and sweet and strong. She had to stop herself from shoveling a huge helping into her mouth.

"Nothing new wrong, Chena?" asked Mom.

"No," said Chena, swallowing hastily and digging her spoon into the food. "I just wasn't expecting it to be any good."

Mom nodded. "Station food is processed till it screams. There's almost nothing left inside. That's why I used to feed you all those vitamin supplements. This is your first taste of the real thing, my dear." Her eyes sparkled for the first time that day. "Does it make up for the bathroom?"

Chena made a show of considering. "Well, I wouldn't go that far. . . ."

Mom laughed, and even Teal smiled. They all tucked into their breakfasts like they meant it.

"Off the station?" asked a big, coarse man at Teal's elbow.

"Yes." Mom gave him her polite, distant smile. "We just arrived last night."

"Well, good luck, then," he said, getting up. "Watch your step and steer clear of anybody with an armband and you'll be okay." He picked up his bowl and left, dumping the dish in a big bin on the way out.

"Well," said Mom, looking after him, "I suppose that will pass for a kind word."

"Don't worry about it, love." This came from a squat, wrinkled woman with skin as brown as tree bark. "There's a court tomorrow, and everybody's on edge. I'm Lela." She extended her hand and Mom shook it. "You know your shift yet?"

"I'm not on shift. I've got a job lined up."

The woman nodded approvingly, but Chena thought she saw something strange in her eyes. "You're a lucky one, then. And these are your girls?"

The exchange that followed was predictable. Mom gave Lela their names and Chena and Teal responded with reflexive politeness and immediately dropped out of the conversation, eating their breakfasts and letting Mom and the new woman talk over their heads about the dormitory, where Madra's office was, where they could get some newer blankets, and when were mealtimes and how long had Lela been there and did she have any family?

Then Chena caught the words, ". . . found the body hanging off the dock. The hothousers about had a fit."

Her attention leapt back to the conversation.

"That's hideous," said Mom, genuinely shocked. "But they've caught who did it?"

"We think so. That's what the court's about tomorrow." Lela rolled the words around her mouth. "The cop's got his own ideas, of course, but it's the village decides how to take care of its own." She looked Mom over thoughtfully. "You get your place sorted out, you'll probably have to be there. All adult citizens have to vote on the verdict."

"Well, that will be interesting," said Mom coolly.

"Ha!" Lela barked. "Just shows you haven't ever been to one. Everybody up and down and arguing, and witnesses that won't talk and what-all . . ." She shook her head. "Thank the gods below this one had no blood family or there'd be vengeance cries until the roof shook apart."

Chena felt cold inside. A court? On the station, the security systems decided who had done what based on the camera recordings, and then it was just a matter of looking up the punishment. She wasn't sure she liked the idea of people deciding what would happen. When people got mad, they said things like, "I'm going to break your head!" What if they actually got to do it?

"Well, it's been lovely talking to you." Lela drained her mug and gathered up her bowl and spoon. "But I'm on today and I've got to get going. You can't miss Central Admin, Helice. There'll be a line."

"Thank you." Mom saluted and Lela nodded, striding off between the crowds and tables.

Teal groaned. "Another line! Why can't they just buzz us with whatever they need?" Chena wondered if she'd even heard anything about the dead body and the court, or if she'd just been wrapped up in her own head.

She rolled her eyes. "In case you haven't noticed, vapor-brain—"

"Chena . . ." said Mom automatically as she stood.

"—there aren't any computers," Chena finished, then picked up her dishes and dumped them into a wooden bin that sat on the end of the table.

"Which is so stupid," announced Teal as they left the hall and headed down the path. "How do they run this place without computers? How do they tell anybody anything?"

"I'm sure we're about to find out," said Mom. She did not sound thrilled.

Finding out involved sitting on the path outside the Central Administration Building with a long, ragged line of people in station-style clothes. Chena thought she recognized a couple of the airheads from the first waiting room, but no one she knew enough to say hello to. So they just joined the line—Mom standing up straight, like she could wait there all day, and Chena and Teal sitting cross-legged at her feet, sometimes messing with their comptrollers but mostly just staring at the people and the low green buildings, or the trees that made up the entire world beyond the fence posts.

Occasionally Madra would stick her head out the door, say, "Next!" and smile at the rest of them as they all shuffled forward a few inches and settled back down to wait again.

Then Chena started noticing something. Not everyone who went through the door came out again. Sadia's words about being declared useless and getting hauled off came back to her, settling cold and hard in her stomach.

Stop it, she told herself, chewing her lip. *Mom would never let it happen. She wouldn't have brought you here if it could happen.*

But her mind refused to relax. It kept rolling over those thoughts until she had wrung every possibility down from her brain into her guts, where they all knotted together. By the time they reached the head of the line, Chena could barely sit still.

Of course, Mom noticed. "Easy, Supernova," she said. "It'll all be over soon."

"I'm okay." She tried to sound convincing, but wasn't sure if she managed it. "It's just—"

And, of course, that was when Madra had to stick her head out the door and say, "Next! Oh, good morning, Helice, Teal, Chena," she added as she recognized them. "Come on in."

The office was dim and cool, like the dorm and the dining hall had been. Chena was starting to wonder if there was some kind of regulation against bright light. But, except for the strip windows and the wooden walls, it looked like every office Chena had ever been in. There were chairs for guests, and desk and another chair for the person who actually worked there.

This office also had stacks of record sheets piled on every flat surface. There was an interior door that maybe went to the larger building. Next to it sat a teak-skinned man with a hooked nose who wore a white shirt, black vest, and black trousers.

"Sit down, please." Madra's smile was efficient as she slid into place behind her desk. "This is Administrator Tam Bhavasar from the Alpha Complex." Her smile did not waver, but something sour crept into her voice as she spoke the name. Chena shifted. This was the first hint they'd had that Madra-the-Eternally-Cheerful might not like somebody. "We are under his jurisdiction and he will be providing such representation as we require to the family inside the complex."

"We've spoken." Mom's voice had gone back to tight and polite. Chena shifted her weight. Who was this guy? Her gaze flickered to Administrator Tam. He had a long, lean frame. His legs stretched out in front of him, all relaxed, but Chena knew that was for show. She could feel the tension radiating off him like white heat.

"Before you're assigned a work shift," Madra went on, "I am required to tell you . . ." Required? That was new too. Up until now, all her little speeches had sounded like they were her own idea. ". . . that you, Helice, have the option of transferring residence to the Alpha Complex." The smile grew strained, even dipped for a second. "Your residence contract there will include free room, board, and education, for yourself and your daughters, along with a guarantee of employment that will allow you a monthly positive accumulation."

"No," said Mom in the frosty voice she used on petty bureaucrats and pushy vendors. "We discussed this, Administrator. I am not interested in participating in your experiments."

Spare parts—the words jolted through Chena again. *Oh, piss and God, they really do it.*

Oddly enough, Administrator Tam seemed to relax a little. "You can change your mind at any time, Mother Trust," said Administrator Tam, running one long, clean hand up and down the chair arm. "I ask you to consider. The Diversity Crisis is affecting every human world. Children are dying daily because we have not yet been able to come up with a cure. With your help, we will be able to design a new—"

"Thank you." Mom clipped off the words. She was using her special voice, the one that meant, *I don't want to discuss this in front of my children.* "I have been informed as to what you are trying to design and how you want me to help, and I have told you I am not interested."

But Administrator Tam was not ready to give up yet. "Life working the village will be very hard on your children. They are not used to it." Like Madra's, the speech sounded rehearsed, like he wanted to be on record. Chena looked around for the camera, but she couldn't see anything. Who did this guy think was listening?

Then she remembered that the Pandorans, at least the hothousers, were all supposed to have chips in their heads. Maybe they were there to record what you did all day, for the bosses, whoever the hothousers had as bosses. Mom's boss back in Athena's repair bays would have loved something like that. He was always trying to dock her pay for taking too long a break or something.

The ghost of a smile played around Mom's mouth. "My daughters have not lived easy," she said. "As I have a job of my own, I hope to change that situation." She carefully enunciated every word in the last sentence so there could be no mistake. Chena felt her insides thawing and relaxing. How could she have been afraid? Mom would never do such a thing, not to them, not to herself.

"You have your answer, Administrator," said Madra, twitching a record sheet off the top of the nearest pile. "If you'll allow me to move along? We still have a lot of processing to get through."

Administrator Tam just nodded and sat back, satisfied. This was too weird. If the guy didn't want Mom in the hothouse, what was he doing here? Chena chewed on her lip. She did not like this. There were way too many things going on in this room that she didn't understand.

"Thank you for your understanding, Administrator." Madra's smile was sunny, but her tone was cool. She consulted the record she had retrieved and compared it with the records already in front of her. "Now, I want to make sure both girls get on daytime shifts, of course."

"Can I put in a request?" asked Chena, a little hesitantly, looking from Mom to Madra to try to see how either of them would take it. Mom looked mildly surprised. Madra quickly shifted her expression over into encouraging.

"Go ahead," said Madra, gesturing to indicate that the floor, or possibly the whole world, was Chena's.

"I'd like to be with K37," she said, hoping she remembered it right. "I met this girl, Sadia," she said in response to Mom's inquiring lift of her eyebrow. "When I was . . . out. She seemed nice. It's her shift."

"Mmm . . ." Madra shuffled through her records. "K37's not a beginner's shift. We normally don't schedule newcomers there."

"That's okay," Chena assured her. "I can handle it."

Madra sighed and spoke to Mom. "It's demanding physical labor on that one. Shoveling, working with the compost . . ."

"I'm not puny," announced Chena. She caught the are-too look on Teal's face and ignored it. She turned to Mom. Pleading with Madra wasn't going to do any good. "Please, Mom. She was nice, and she can show me what's what."

Mom faced Madra. "Can she try it? If she can't handle the work, she could be transferred off the shift, couldn't she?"

"Again, that's not something we normally do." The phrase sounded prerecorded. Chena snuck a look at Administrator Tam. He watched Madra, but Chena couldn't tell one thing about what he saw.

Madra herself seemed to be waiting for something, maybe for Administrator Tam to interrupt. When he didn't, her smile reasserted itself. "As long as you're aware it will be demanding work," she said to Chena, who nodded rapidly. "All right."

"I'll make it work," said Chena confidently, more for Mom than for Madra. Mom just covered her hand and squeezed. She was watching the administrator watch Madra. Did she know something about him?

"What about you?" asked Madra of Teal. "Anything special you'd like?"

Teal opened her mouth. Chena was sure she was going to say, *To get out of here.* Mom must have thought so too, because her face darkened with warning.

Teal, who could actually act like she had a brain sometimes, swallowed and said, "No, thank you."

"All right, let's see what we have, then. . . ."

While Madra shuffled and murmured to herself, Chena stole another glance at Administrator Tam. He seemed preoccupied now, staring out the windows as if listening to some private voice that had nothing at all to do with what was going on in the room.

At last, Madra made a couple of fresh imprints on her reports and announced that Mom was on the G3 shift and Teal was on K5. She buzzed the information into their chips with a handheld scanner and wished them good evening.

Chena wasn't even sure Administrator Tam saw them leave.

It turned out that was just the first line of the day. Mom also dragged them to the bank to see how much they had in positives (not much), to the rental office to hear the prices on empty houses (too much), to the school administrator to hear the price and conditions of classes (way too much), and to the passport office so she could get chipped for getting to and from her job at the geothermal power plant.

By the end of it all, Chena was seriously regretting her morning's excursion, and Teal was mad enough to spit at her. Mom wouldn't even consider letting them go somewhere, even on the roof garden of whatever building she was in, no matter how many times they swore they'd stay together, they wouldn't talk to strangers, and any other model behavior they could think of. It was all a complete no-go. She just glowered if they tried to promise too hard.

They missed dinner sitting in line. By the time they got to the dining hall, there was nothing left but a kettle of the hot cereal, which had been cooking long enough to get crusty. It still tasted good, though, and Chena ate without complaint. She had expected Mom to be verbal, telling them the shifts were a strictly temporary thing, that it wasn't going to be that bad, but she wasn't. A cloud of silence had descended around her, and it stretched out to include Teal and Chena.

Teal ate fast and spent the rest of the time fidgeting with her comptroller. Chena tried to get a quick look at what she was doing and failed.

She hiding it from me? she wondered, and the thought left her feeling strangely angry.

By the time they got out and headed back toward the dorms, twilight had descended. They walked, silent, side by side, Chena wondering what they'd have to wait for next.

All at once, the world around them shifted and rustled, as if the wind had picked up. Chena's head jerked up, automatically looking for a changed sign or warning light.

Then the forest bloomed. Bright white cups lifted up from nests of dark green on the forest floor. In the trees, the vines spread velvet blossoms colored deep purple, bloodred, and cobalt blue, the petals stretching themselves out until the flowers were the size of Chena's head.

In answer, the twilight seemed to break into a million fragments that swarmed around the flowers. Big angled zigzags of darkness darted around the trees, and smaller dots zoomed around the flowers so thickly, the petals were almost lost inside the clouds.

"What is it?" breathed Chena.

"Bats," said Mom. "And beetles, I think, going after the nectar in the flowers."

A gust of wind carried a thick, sweet perfume to Chena, along with the noise of the flapping and screeching overhead and a high, tinny drone that could be heard even under the perpetual sound of rustling leaves and falling water.

"I don't like this," muttered Teal, rubbing her arms. "I've got creeps."

Chena wanted to tell her not to be a baby, but Mom was already moving. "Let's get inside, then."

Chena wanted to rebel, but those were practically the only words Mom had said since they had left the bank, so she decided now was probably not the time to argue.

She was not surprised, however, when inside turned out to be a lot less interesting than outside. People sat around the common room, mainly on pillows on the floors, and they talked or played games with counters and cards. Chena wandered around the room a little, looking over the shoulders of the other kids, but they mostly glowered at her or pointedly turned away. With all the adults around, it was no place to start something and try to break her way in. She didn't see Sadia anywhere.

In the end, she finished her prowling and ended up against the wall next to Teal. She slid down the wall until she sat next to her sister, who was messing with her comptroller.

"What are you doing?" she asked softly. Mom wasn't going to be any help here. She'd found a bunch of other women, all in villager clothes, to talk to.

Teal just hunched farther over her comptroller.

"Come on." Chena nudged Teal with her shoulder. "Show me."

"No."

"Please?" Chena tried. *Come on, I'm bored.*

"No," repeated Teal. "You'll laugh."

"I won't, I swear." Chena touched her mouth to seal the promise. "What is it?"

Teal glanced around, spotted Mom in her cluster on the other side of the room. "I'm 'crypting a spy list," Teal murmured.

"A what?" Chena pulled back, but remembered in time not to laugh.

"A spy list." Teal looked back down at her tiny screen. "You know, I figured if Dad's a spy out there for the Authority, there might be spies here, so I'm making a list of who we've seen and who they are . . ." The sentence trailed off again and she shrugged. "Stuff like that."

Well, it's better than sitting here and staring at the walls. "Good idea," Chena admitted. "I should have one too." *And I can put in Shond, and Sadia, and definitely that crazy old woman on the roof. . . .* "We should both use the same encryptions so we'll be able to read each other's lists." Chena took the comptroller out of Teal's hands and made it scroll out the work Teal had done so far. She felt her eyebrows rise as she read the columns of numbers and letters.

"Not bad, for someone with air between her ears," she admitted. "But we're going to want to use some kind of substitution scheme we can remember and not have to code in. That way, if somebody gets hold of the lists, they'll only be able to do so much when they dump the files. . . ."

Soon they were whispering back and forth all kinds of possible designations for the various people in the room and giving each other fits of giggles. Mom glanced up from her conversation a few times, but just smiled to see her daughters engaged in their own, relatively quiet game.

What's she doing over there? Is she trying to find us a cheap house, maybe? Why doesn't she tell us anything? Chena chewed her lip. It felt raw, but she didn't stop. *Why doesn't she tell me anything? How bad is it? How much do we owe? She just took the records from the bank. She didn't show us anything. Is she going to have to go give them her blood or move us into a hothouse or something because there's not enough?*

Why won't she tell me?

That thought followed her through the rest of the evening, even when the bell rang again and the company in the common room filtered dutifully to the sleeping rooms to unroll their pallets and change into their nightclothes, or not. Chena was stunned and embarrassed to see some of the women just roll themselves up naked into their blankets.

Mom didn't say anything as Chena just squirmed out of her clothes under her blanket and slid into her nightshirt. It smelled musty.

She'd just pulled the shirt down over her hips when the lights went out.

"Well, so much for that," murmured Mom. "Good night, my girls."

Chena closed her eyes and curled in on herself, trying to find sleep in her private warmth and darkness. But all around her came the sounds of unfamiliar breathing, snorts, and snoring, and inside, her thoughts would not make room for unconsciousness and dreams. She kept seeing the administrator looking at Mom, tense and hungry, offering her an easy life and a way out of debt, telling her how hard living down here was going to be.

Chena opened her eyes.

"Mom?"

"Shhh, Supernova. What is it?"

"The money," said Chena in her lightest whisper.

"Yes, that's kept me awake a number of nights. What about the money?"

"How do we know this isn't another company town?" That had been Mom's term for Athena. Because the Athena directorate owned everything, she said. All the stores, all the apartments, all the air, they'd been able to charge whatever they wanted for them and nobody could say no.

Mom let out a long, soft sigh. "That is a very good question. First, they don't let you run yourself into debt here, like they did on Athena. Second, they give you a way to live even when you don't have any money. That way you can manage without having to indenture yourself."

"Yeah." Chena pushed herself up onto one elbow and turned toward Mom's voice, even though she couldn't see her. "But I mean, they keep you so busy working for the town, when do you find time to make money so you won't have to work for the town?"

Another sigh. "It's never easy, Chena. We are going to be a long time getting our heads above water. But it will happen. I am not going to let you girls struggle under my debts."

"I thought they were Dad's debts," said Chena, before she could stop herself.

"No, Supernova, they are very much mine too." Mom's voice sounded heavy, like it was weighted down with all the things she wasn't saying. "But they will never be yours." Chena heard her blankets rustle. Mom's warm and certain hand caressed her hair briefly. "Now go to sleep, Chena. We all have a long day tomorrow."

"Right. Good night, Mom."

The blankets rustled again, and Chena pictured her mother rolling over toward the wall. Chena flipped over onto her back and lay staring at the ceiling for a long time.

She had come to associate debt with danger. As long as they owed somebody, it seemed like that somebody could do whatever they wanted. They could make Dad vanish, they could drive her family out of their home, they could make Mom frightened and angry.

I will not leave Mom in trouble. I won't give them the chance to screw us to the deck again. I swear I won't.

Her resolve calmed her, and, eventually, Chena was able to sleep.

CHAPTER THREE

Meetings

Night had fallen solidly across the forest. Tam climbed the long, winding way to Nan Elle's house more by touch than by sight. He glimpsed the occasional star through the shifting latticework of branches overhead, but they did nothing to illuminate his path. His only light was a small pocket flash he used to find the beginning and end of staircases.

At first the night's chill had seeped through his clothes, but now a fine layer of perspiration covered his face and he had undone the collar button on his formal black and white coat.

Not enough time in the gym, murmured his Conscience as he paused to catch his breath.

"But I don't feel guilty about it, so why are you sounding off?" he muttered back.

Your medical health is a default concern, his Conscience reminded him.

Tam just grunted and vaguely wished he could turn that off too, but he didn't dare. Over the years his Conscience had been tampered with multiple times. Too many alterations to the remaining facade would draw attention he didn't want.

Up ahead, a light gleamed and vanished, followed by the long, slow creak of a door with neglected hinges. He had tried repeatedly to get Nan Elle to oil those, but she just asserted it made it harder for anyone to sneak up on her.

It also makes it harder to visit in secret. That noise carries.

Warmer air, a more solid sound to his footsteps, and the sharp odors of pepper and chilis wrapped around him, and Tam knew he was inside. He fumbled for the edge of the door, found it, and pushed it shut, its hinges screaming in protest.

Where are we? asked his Conscience. Tam did not answer. He concentrated on keeping his breathing steady and his mind calm. It didn't work. He had too much going on inside him.

You know you shouldn't be here, his Conscience said, correctly. Suddenly Tam thought he smelled the odor of old yeast. It was a scent from his childhood, of a failed experiment in a biochemistry lesson, and it never failed to make him uneasy, a response his Conscience had nurtured for years.

For all those years, Tam had learned to walk through it.

"Good evening, Administrator Tam." An oil lamp flickered to life, and after blinking a few times, Tam made out Nan Elle, stooped and withered, standing in the far corner of the room beside the brick stove. Her title, *Nan,* meant grandmother, and she certainly looked the part.

"Good evening, Nan Elle," he replied, coming forward to touch her cheek in greeting. The smell of yeast grew stronger. Tam forced his feelings down. "I'm afraid our constable is upset with you."

"Our constable is too clever by half." Elle touched Tam's cheek. Her hands were dry and callused from a lifetime's work. "Can't you appoint a stupid one?" She picked up a mug from the stove and handed it to him. The steaming liquid smelled strongly of mint.

"I've tried, but the man gives me depressingly few excuses to fire him." Tam looked around for a stool and finally hooked one out from under the central worktable.

Nan Elle's home was primarily one big room. An immaculate slanted writing table stood by the windows under shelves crammed with record books and diaries. Aquarium pipes lined the walls between the bookshelves. Carp and smelt peered at him. White cloth covered the examination chair that stood under three precious power-cell lamps. The central table was the compounding table. Stacks of pots and jars, mortar and pestle, a little oil stove, and straining cloths waited beside bales and packets of things Tam couldn't identify in the dim light but that gave off a miasma of conflicting odors, some of them none too aesthetic.

At least, he thought, *these odors are coming from outside.* It was hard to tell sometimes. When a Conscience couldn't keep control by verbal reminders, it would induce hallucinations and memories. Olfactory hallucinations were the most common, and the strongest triggers of organic memory inside the human mind.

Tam sometimes imagined his Conscience getting frustrated by its inablility to move him. He understood that the ones that were properly integrated and left to grow with their hosts could produce overwhelming floods of emotion or memory.

He never wanted to know what that felt like.

"Since when has an order from a hothouse needed a reason to be given?" Nan Elle was saying. Her eyes glittered bright with humor as she sat in her high-backed wooden chair by the writing table like a queen sitting on her throne.

"Since firing competence and hiring incompetence makes my family look at things twice," Tam replied solemnly, pushing aside a stack of clay bowls to make room to set down his mug. "They also are not stupid. I'm afraid the constable might try to delay the court to review the evidence. If he does, I'm afraid you are going to have to deal with it."

"Too bad," Elle sighed, cupping her own mug in her twiglike fingers. The chair creaked under her as she shifted her weight. "So, what can I do for you, Tam?"

Tam took a long swallow of tea. It had been heavily sweetened with honey and sat well in his stomach. "I was hoping you could tell me something about one of the new arrivals, Helice Trust."

Elle considered, but then shook her head. "I haven't made contact with her yet. I've met her oldest daughter, Chena, though, briefly."

"And what did you think of her?"

Again, Elle took her time in anwering. Most people thought of Elle as quick, sharp, and tricky. Tam knew her to be a long and careful thinker. Her quickness was the result of having spent hours turning over various scenarios far in advance.

"The girl's brave," she said finally. "Not anywhere near as frightened of the great outdoors as most station children. Determined, also. Not going to let anything get her down. Plenty of attitude. Could become a hustler, if left to her own devices." Elle cocked her head. "I've looked over the fate map you left me last time. They are fascinating stock, if all the expressions are as predicted. Are we keeping an eye on them?"

Tam nodded. "I'm getting pressure from Basante, and others, to force the mother onto the project, but I'm resisting."

"Why?"

Now it was Tam who took his time answering. "Because they belong to Offshoot now, and that makes them my responsibility. I've seen how some of the other administrators run their villages. They are perfectly willing to bully their people into the complex, but I won't have it here."

"You don't want them forced into becoming something they might not want to be?" Tam heard the smile behind Elle's question.

"Perhaps."

"Or perhaps you're saying you don't trust your family?"

She was goading him now, and Tam had to work to keep from snapping at her. It did not help that his Conscience already had a feel for his answer and was bringing him the scent of green decay.

"I trust my family," Tam told her. "I just don't like them very much."

"Stubborn," chided Elle. "It's going to get you into trouble."

Tam waved her away. "We are starting to forget that these people are human beings, not lab rats. The last time that happened, there was a war and a whole dome got destroyed. I don't want that to happen again." He looked down at the mug in his hands. Whips of steam curled across the liquid's clear green surface. "The Trusts are under my protection. I don't want anyone to have a chance to go behind my back to get to them."

How can you make such accusations against your family? asked his Conscience, filling the air with the scent of burning. "If she decides to volunteer on her own," said Tam to both Nan Elle and his Conscience, "that's fine. But I will not have my people coerced." *Elle is right. I will not have them made into things they don't want to be, and have the control over their futures stripped away from them.*

I will not have done to them what has been done to me.

Silence stretched out for several minutes. "How bad is the news?" asked Elle at last.

Tam sighed and set the mug down again. He lifted his gaze to the curtained windows, as if he thought he'd see something profound written in the ripples in the cloth. He smelled yeast, and the odor of rotten vegetation. Scents of failure, of disobedience and ignored instructions. They intensified his real unease and he squirmed on the stool. "If we are to believe our good commander Beleraja Poulos, it's never been worse. Some of the colonies are talking about breaking all contact with the Authority, on the grounds that the Authority is doing them no good at all."

"Watching your people die will make you impatient," murmured Elle, more to her mug than to Tam. "So, your people have decided to go forward with the immune system project?"

"Yes. We're calling it the Eden Project. A number of detailed descriptions have already gone to the Authority's Council of Cities."

"Will they accept it, do you think?" Nan Elle asked softly.

"They will have to. It is what we are prepared to do." In theory, a human immune system could be made active enough to expel any and every microorganism that produced a toxic reaction in its host. Such experiments had been tried on a number of worlds when the Diversity Crisis was first recognized. In reality, the approach presented huge problems. An overactive immune system could provoke any of a thousand different autoimmune diseases in its host because it could not tell the difference between invading microorganisms, the normal symbiotic organisms, and the changes that occurred in a human naturally over time. To add to the difficulties, a fetus with a hyperactive immunity could actually end up attacking its mother while in the womb, or the mother's immune system might go on the offensive against the child.

"So," Elle sighed, "you will design a new race of people that simply cannot become ill." She sucked on her teeth for a moment. "It will mean implanting genetically modified fetuses into women's wombs. It will also mean that the current generation is still pretty much lost to the ashes, as this is not the sort of massive alteration you can work on an adult." She shrugged. "Well, I suppose by now most of the Called are desperate enough to take such a chance." Her voice and gaze grew hard. "It is that bad, isn't it?"

Tam nodded in absent agreement. Commander Beleraja Poulos's latest transmission from Athena Station had been terse and spare, as if she didn't want to waste extra words on bad news. "We are going to have to tell Athena to stop accepting incoming passengers. Apparently there's a rumor going around that the Diversity Crisis hasn't reached here yet and that the hothouse engineers have managed to keep our people clean and healthy."

"Ah." Elle raised one finger and her eyes narrowed shrewdly. "You're afraid of an influx of frightened, angry immigrants."

"Yes," said Tam, ignoring her sarcasm. "Aren't you?"

Elle shook her head and drained her mug. "There is a balance to be maintained, and the hothousers are required to maintain it, but if you'll forgive me for saying so, Tam, this world is not a shrine. It could support millions, and both ecology and humans could still be managed."

Tam's mouth tightened, but the words came out anyway. "Pandora must be protected."

"To be sure," said Elle agreeably. "But you know, one day Pandora might rebel against all the little things you and your people have done to protect her."

"Something has to be done," Tam grumbled. "Human activity has to be tempered by understanding and some regulation. Humans keep saying their worlds can support millions, and they keep tearing those same worlds apart and proving it isn't so." If left to themselves, humans would do to all the worlds of the Called exactly what they had done to Old Earth. At least, this was what Tam's ancestors had believed when they had taken Pandora under their protection.

Tam told himself he did not truly believe that. He really was above and beyond the protectiveness nurtured toward the world of Pandora. But the reflexes were all there, and, evidently, in working order.

Elle stood and walked back over to her stove. With the care of someone who knew the worth of each drop, she ladled more tea into her mug. "There won't be enough humans to tear anything apart if something is not done soon."

"Now you sound like Beleraja."

"There are worse things." She settled herself back into her chair.

"There are better." *What is that smell? Mold? Either Elle is brewing penicillin or the implant has decided subtlety is not working.* "Beleraja has been in the thick of things for too long. I don't know all the things she's done, and I don't want to."

"Soft heart," said Elle again, sipping her fresh tea. "So, what of the Trusts?"

Tam sighed. Yes, what of them? Could Helice Trust have any idea what she had done by coming here? By bringing the possibilities she carried inside her so close to those who needed them so badly? "If you can, I'd like you to cultivate the oldest girl. She's, what, thirteen?"

"With all the vinegar and attitude of the age," Elle said, not without a certain amount of admiration.

Tam pushed his empty mug away. "I'd like her to know she can trust you. That she can go to you when she's in trouble."

"Me?" Elle laid a hand on her chest. "Not the ever-efficient, ever-smiling, official liaison Madra?"

"I would prefer she trust someone who did not actively hate me for being born under the dome."

"You won't hire me a stupid constable, but you will play shuffle and hide with your own liaison." Elle snorted.

Tam's laugh was soft, and devoid of humor. "It's so much easier to explain inside the complex, don't you see."

"Perfectly, thank you," answered Elle. She took another drink from her mug of tea and rolled it around her sunken mouth for a long moment before swallowing. "I believe the girl can be reached. She'll be warned of me soon, of course, but there's spark back of those eyes. She won't take a because-I-told-you-so answer. She's also been down far enough and long enough that she might not automatically believe what an official tells her."

Tam quirked his eyebrows. "How did you make that deduction, if I may ask?"

"Her mother brought her and her sister here to live in the dorms. It's not the action of someone who's had very many choices in their life." Her mouth curved up into a smile. "And if I can't reach her myself, perhaps I'll bring in young Farin from Stem and have him run into her accidentally."

"Nan Elle, that's completely unfair." Farin was Nan Elle's grandson and an extraordinarily handsome young man. It was fairly well known that he made a living off those looks, and Tam had wondered why Elle would permit such a thing. But he thought he knew. Farin had dozens of connections across five different villages, connections Nan Elle was more than ready to make use of.

"It's unfair, but it will work," said Elle solemnly, but Tam had the distinct feeling she was laughing silently at him. "Or I don't know my boy."

"I'll leave it to you." Tam tapped the table once with his palm and stood. "Thank you for your help, Elle. I'll let you know what's happening."

"I should think so." Elle shuffled across to him and touched his cheek again. "Step sure, step safe."

"And you." He touched her in answer. "Is there anything you need?"

"A body that's roughly forty years younger." Her mouth puckered into a smile as she said it. "Failing that, a new camouflage suit and some more sample bottles would do."

"You'll get them." Tam walked to the door and laid his hand on the knob. "Oh," he said, turning around. "The dead man, what did he do?"

Elle's hands clenched the edge of the table. "He broke faith with me."

Tam nodded and walked out into the darkness. It would never do for an answer to the constable, but there were so many parts of this world where Constable Regan would never walk, and a number of them were in his own village.

Sadia hadn't been kidding when she said that most of the day was working the shit. Before her first shift, Chena had no idea how much waste material human beings could produce.

Since there were no computers, the assignments for each shift were posted in the dining hall. Chena had found that K37 was working in the Recycling and Composting Building. After taking Teal to her shift, which was in the dining hall kitchen, and promising faithfully that she would be back to get her at the appointed hour, just as she had with Mom, Chena had asked a man in the villagers' thick clothing where the Composting Building was. He told her to follow her nose. The strongest stink would lead her to it.

When he turned away, Chena made the piss-off sign at him. But then she stepped outdoors and the breeze touched her cheeks and she discerned a faint, unpleasant smell, like from a bathroom that had been used too many times without being cleaned.

Chena followed the smell up the gravel paths and across the footbridges until she came to a long, low building on the river side of the village. One of the many canals that dissected the village grounds ran straight through the building. Coming from inside it, she heard all kinds of scraping and rumbling.

Biting her lip, Chena did her best to walk up to the doors without hesitating. The shedlike building was built on a long slope so that the canal that flowed slowly into one end flowed swiftly out the other through a series of brown reed-filled ponds that increased in size until the chain opened out into the river.

Inside, the noise was deafening, and the smell was worse. The noise came from a pair of huge cylinders at least as big around as tree trunks. They lay on their sides in some kind of cradle along one wall. Each drum had four bicycles attached to it by long bands. People sat on the bikes and pedaled, and the motion turned the drums over and over. Other people shoveled what looked like mounds of black earth into wheelbarrows, and still other people pushed the barrows away down toward the river. Another corner of the room was taken up by people standing around steaming kettles, stirring them with long poles. As Chena watched, a woman lifted a pole out and she saw it ended on a paddle that the woman used to lift out a heap of soggy rags, which she promptly dumped into her neighbor's kettle. In another corner, they were chopping and scrubbing pieces of wood.

The canal was not left alone. Chena could see square frames had been inserted into it at regular intervals. People lined its banks, dipping what looked like long-handled baskets into the water and lifting out heaps of green sludge that got dumped into wooden trenchers next to them.

As her eyes swept across this bewildering array of activity, Chena spotted Sadia shoveling dirt into the wheelbarrows. The sight gave her confidence to walk up to the deeply tanned man standing by the door with record sheets in his hand and a scanner on his belt. He looked down his long, straight nose at Chena.

"Name?"

Chena told him, remembering to add the honorific "Uncle" when she addressed him. Before Mom had left the dining hall to catch the flat-bottomed boat that would take her down to the geothermal plant, she had made Chena swear up and down that she would be polite to everybody today.

He looked startled, but then he smiled, and Chena knew she had his number. This one could be flattered.

Long Nose ran a finger along his records and found her name. "I'm going to put you on the bikes first—"

"Please, Uncle, can I work over there?" She pointed at the pile Sadia was on. "I've got a friend . . ." She made her eyes big and blinked like she was scared.

It worked. This one wasn't as sharp as his own nose. "Okay. But if I catch you wasting time chattering, I'll separate you. Got that?"

"Yes, Uncle." She twiddled her fingers in front of her, nervous.

That earned her another smile. "Okay. Get yourself gloves, boots, and a shovel and get going on the pile." He nodded toward a set of racks and shelves at the back of the shed. "Make sure everything fits, or you'll be a bundle of blisters before you're done."

Rifling through the pile of thick gloves on the wooden shelf, Chena found a pair that fit snugly. She had to go through every pair of stained leather boots, but at last found one that was acceptable. One of the shovels left in the rack had a handle she thought was short enough for her to work with. She grabbed it and slid into the open space next to Sadia.

"Hey," she said.

"Hey, you got in." Sadia shuffled sideways to make room for her. She didn't break her rhythm, though. Push the shovel into the dirt, bring up a mound, toss it in the barrow. Do it again.

Chena tried to copy her motions. It felt awkward, and the stuff was piss-all heavy.

"Shond's on a different shift?" she asked as she turned to drop her shovelful into the barrow.

"Shond's off today," said Sadia. Her freckled brown skin flushed and her whole forehead wrinkled up from something other than effort. Teal remembered yesterday when Sadia said something about Shond "fixing" the record sheets. She quickly decided she'd better not ask anymore. Not here, anyway.

Chena soon ran out of breath for talking. Madra hadn't been blowing vapor when she said this shift was hard. It felt like she'd only been working for a few minutes before her whole back started aching and her arms felt alternately like lead and rubber bands. Sweat soaked her shirt and pants. The barrows didn't stop coming and the pile didn't seem to get any smaller. All the time the rattle and the rumble of the huge drums pounded against her until her skull and ears started to ache as badly as her back.

At least on the pile you could stop to get a drink from the barrel of water near the shovel rack, or go take a pee in the pit-toilet shed out back whenever you wanted. As far as Chena could tell, the people on the bikes just had to keep going until the guy came around to open the side and either pour in more water, dirt, and garbage, or dump the black stuff out into another pile that they had to shovel into more barrows.

Eventually the uncle at the door rang a handbell and they got to stop. A pair of kids had come around from the dining hall with a kettle of the same cereal they'd had for breakfast. After the fourth meal straight, it was getting tiring, but Chena ate. It wasn't like there was anything anybody could have done.

Nobody talked while they ate, not even Sadia. They just concentrated on their food, or stretching out their shoulders or legs.

Chena scraped her bowl clean and emptied her water cup. She got a glance from Sadia that was both wry and cynical. She scooted in a little closer.

"What is all this?" she asked, gesturing around the shed.

"Composting, mostly." Sadia saw Chena's blank look and explained how the garbage and dirt that went into the drums got turned into fertilizer for the fields that grew the food. "And water purification too." She nodded toward the canal filters.

"Shouldn't there be machines doing this?" asked Chena.

Sadia gave her the lopsided smile again. "If they used machines, what would they do with us?"

"What do you mean?"

"They got to do something with us, don't they?" Sadia scowled and stabbed her spoon into the bottom of her bowl. "Can't have us running all over their precious woods doing whatever we want can they?"

"Shht," hissed one of the older women. "Sadia, don't start it. Your people have enough trouble."

"It's true," Sadia shot back. "And everybody here knows it, so why shouldn't I warn the freshies?"

"Because it's not true," said another woman. She sat to Sadia's right and wore her graying hair in a braid long enough to tuck into her belt. "Listen, what's your name?" Chena told her. "Listen, Chena." She leaned forward, and Chena couldn't tell if she was faking being serious or if she was really trying to be earnest. "The idea is to create and maintain a series of ecologically stable communities so we can continue to live here and be healthy, without any of the troubles they have on the Called worlds, where they just landed and started hacking away at things."

"You tell her, Mae," said one of the men, shoveling the last of his cereal into his bearded face.

"'Cause we heard already," said another man, elbowing his friend in the ribs. A general chuckle rose from the crowd.

"We're not dying," said one of the younger men, from the back of the group.

"No, none of us die," said a squat, dark woman with lines on her face and thick calluses on her hands. "Not unless we get sick, of course. Mostly, we just disappear."

"Stop trying to scare the kid," snapped Mae. "The hothousers only take volunteers or lawbreakers, and you know it."

The shadow of the door-watching uncle fell over the lunch crowd. "And if you've got time to talk about all this, obviously you're done with lunch." He stood aside and gestured toward their abandoned posts.

There was a general groan and a bunch of dirty looks, but no one protested. They just all got to their feet and piled the bowls and cups in the bin that one of the kitchen kids carried and all went back to work. Even Sadia, but not without giving Chena a look that said, *Told you.*

After lunch, the work got shifted and she and Sadia got put on the pedal bikes to roll the compost drums around. Sadia had said that some of the stuff in there came out of the toilet shed. That could not be true.

At least, that was what she believed until she and Sadia got taken off the bikes and given a barrow to follow Mae and some other old woman around to the various toilet sheds and help them empty the boxes and cart the dirt and clay away.

For kids under fifteen, the shift was only six hours long, but it felt like forever. By the end, every fiber in Chena's body ached. Despite the gloves, fat white blisters appeared on her hands. She staggered out of the shed next to Sadia. Sadia wasn't looking at her, though; she was scanning the paths. Chena knew she was looking for Shond.

"Gods below, I am dead," said Chena. She reached up to rub her shoulder, and winced as the motion made her elbow and hand hurt worse. "Where do we get the relax patches?"

Sadia glanced down at her and then away to the paths again. "The what?"

Chena frowned and leaned back against the shed wall. "The relax patches. Or an aspirin. I'd settle for an aspirin."

"What's that for?"

"The pain." Chena was about to ask if she was kidding, then she saw the complete lack of understanding on Sadia's face. She was not kidding. She had never heard of these things.

"But there's got to be something. I'm not going to make it back to the dorm like this."

That got Sadia to look down and really see her. "Are you serious?" she asked. "How bad do you hurt?"

"How bad do I have to hurt? Come on, Sadia. If there's something, you've got to tell me. I'm dying!" She was too. Her legs were shaking, and the top of her head felt like it was going to come off. She could barely hear the rush of the wind or trees, her ears had been so deadened by the rumble of the compost drums.

Sadia sucked on her cheek and looked around once more for Shond, who wasn't anywhere in sight. There were just people everywhere coming and going with the change in shifts.

"Come on," said Sadia. She headed for the stairway up to one of the catwalks.

The last thing Chena wanted to do was to climb, but if it was going to take her to a relax patch or an aspirin, she would do anything. Maybe it would only be one level. She couldn't take that long anyway. She had to get back for Teal. Sadia knew that. Well, Teal would be okay waiting for a little bit.

It wasn't just one level. Sadia led her up three levels. The higher they went, the thinner the crowds got and the farther spread out the houses were. Eventually the noise of the village just fell away, replaced by the rattling of the leaves and the chatter of the birds.

Sadia took her up one more short set of stairs, and Chena felt like her legs were going to scream out loud with pain. She was about to open her mouth to tell Sadia that even a whole-body anesthetic wasn't worth another step when Sadia turned to her.

"Get in line. I'll see you." With that, she turned and ran down the steps, heading full tilt to the main village.

Chena's jaw dropped. What was she supposed to do now?

She saw the line that Sadia was talking about. Half a dozen men and women, a couple with babies in their arms, waited on the catwalk in front of a house that was almost lost in the shadows.

Actually, it wasn't just one house, it looked more like three different houses that had allowed their roofs to group together.

One of the babies bawled, a high thin sound that grated against Chena's aching eardrums. She didn't want to stay, but she couldn't face trying to climb a hundred feet down on her shaking legs. So Chena got in line like she'd been told. After all, Sadia was her friend. She wouldn't have brought her here if there wasn't some kind of help like Chena has asked for.

But then, why did she leave? Chena collapsed into the line behind a woman with a long, red, puckered scar running up her forearm.

Probably she saw Shond, Chena thought, answering her own question. Then she felt a twinge of guilt. She hadn't even stopped to look for Teal. Who knew where she had gotten to? That was what she'd do first thing when she got her relax patch.

Every now and again, someone, or a couple of someones, would come out of the grown-together houses, and someone else would go in. The sun filtered through the leaves overhead and warmed Chena's skin. She fell into a doze, and only woke when someone poked her in the ribs and muttered, "Your turn."

Chena tried to stand up and promptly fell over. She bit her lip, partly to avoid screaming as she unfolded her legs, which seemed to have locked solid, and partly to avoid yelling at the people in the line behind her who were chuckling.

She waved away a hand that reached to help her and grabbed the railing, pulling herself upright. She forced her rusty legs to carry her into the darkened doorway. Whatever they had in here, it had better be good.

It took a moment for her eyes to adjust to the gloom. When they did, she found herself in the strangest room she had ever seen. It looked like a cross between an ancient library and a witch's cottage out of a rig game. Where the walls were not lined with glass pipes full of green algae and silver fish, they were lined with shelves of books. Bags and bundles of things Chena could not begin to identify hung from dozens of hooks on the ceiling. There was a brick stove in the corner, and four or five tables placed around the room. Next to the biggest table stood the stooped old woman that Chena had last seen on the rooftop of the dormitory.

Apparently the old woman recoginzed her too. Her sunken mouth gaped into a smile.

"Station girl!" she exclaimed, clicking her tongue against her few remaining teeth. "I didn't expect to see you here so soon."

Chena had to clear her throat before she could speak.

"I was told I could get a relax patch here."

The old woman—what did she call herself? Nan Elle, that was it—frowned. "What would you want with such a thing?"

Chena spread her hands to the ceiling. "What's the matter with you people?" she exclaimed. "I hurt! What is the big deal about getting a muscle relaxer?" Then she remembered another important question. "And just what do you think you got anyway? What makes you the big woman?"

The gaping smile returned and Chena wished she had the strength to get really angry.

"I think I've got all you're going to get, station girl." She pointed one green-and-brown-stained finger at a wide wooden chair situated under three battery lamps. "You want help? Sit."

Chena hesitated. She really wanted to walk out of there, but she hurt so bad. If this old wreck really did have something . . .

Chena hobbled over to the chair and sat.

Nan Elle puttered around Chena. She snapped on one of the lights and peered into Chena's eyes. She grabbed both of Chena's shoulders with her gnarled hands and squeezed until Chena yelped.

"Mmmm. What have you been doing today, station girl?"

"My name is Chena!" Chena jerked her shoulders out of Nan Elle's grip.

"So I've been informed." Nan Elle took one of Chena's arms and flexed it. Her hands were a lot stronger than they looked, and Chena felt if she struggled she would end up with bruises in addition to all her other pains. "What have you been doing today, Chena?"

"Shoveling, mostly. I was in the recycling shed."

"That's not a place they put freshies." Nan Elle flexed Chena's other arm. She smelled like bad breath and peppermint.

"They do if you ask for it."

Nan Elle circled around back of the chair. "Which just goes to show you should be careful what you ask them for." She dug both thumbs into the muscle on Chena's back, and Chena screamed.

"Ow! Stop it! I thought you could help!"

Nan Elle stepped back into her line of sight, and she was grinning again. "I can. But not if I don't know what's wrong with you."

Chena tried to twist around to face the old woman and immediately regretted the movement. Pain shot up and down her back. "What's wrong with me is that I've been shoveling shit all day."

Nan Elle nodded. "I would agree with that diagnosis." She stepped back to the edge of the lit circle Chena sat in, becoming a figure of shadow. "I can give you a drink for the pain and a salve that will help keep your muscles from stiffening up overnight. But we must talk price."

Chena had to work to keep her jaw from dropping. She hadn't even considered that this would cost. But then, this was not Athena Station, where there were first-aid kits on every level that the directorate kept filled for you.

"I don't have any money."

"Most of my people don't. I will charge you four days' use of that." She pointed a bony finger at Chena's comptroller.

Chena automatically covered the comptroller's screen with her hand. "No. That's mine."

Nan Elle chuckled at her, and Chena felt the familiar flare of real anger beginning. Who was this old woman, anyway? What did she think she had? Then a new cramp started in the back of her leg, sharp enough to keep her mouth closed against her thoughts. Nan Elle's eyes flickered up and down Chena, and Chena knew Nan Elle had seen the way she twitched in answer to the new spasm.

"You would trust me with your body, station girl, but not your machine?" Nan Elle shook her head.

Chena bit her lip, and even that movement hurt. Reluctantly, she fumbled with the strap of her comptroller, pulled it off, and set it on the table among the bundles of plants and piles of clay pots.

Nan Elle scooped it up and popped it into one of her apron pockets. "Very good. Now you wait."

For what? But Chena kept her mouth shut. Nan Elle receded farther into the shadows. Chena saw her pull something kidney-shaped down off one of the hooks and heard the slosh of liquid being poured. "What is the whole hassle with getting an aspirin around here?"

"Ah," said Nan Elle. "The hothousers, who dictate the conditions by which we live, say that by introducing artificial means to restrict or reroute the viral or bacterial populations, we risk damaging the balance of Pandora's microsphere, which is the foundation of its total ecology." Nan Elle shuffled back into the light.

"What?"

"Antivirals and antibiotics can force microorganisms to evolve in ways that are not strictly natural. Change the microsphere, and you might just introduce adverse changes all the way up the life chain. So, no medicines except under strict quarantine and supervision."

"That is completely cross-threaded," announced Chena.

"Perhaps." Nan Elle sounded much more serious than Chena would have expected. "But there are those who say that it contributed to the destruction of the biosphere back on Old Earth." Nan Elle planted a wooden cup full of something ruby-red on the table in front of Chena. "Now you drink that."

Chena picked it up and sniffed it. It smelled vaguely of cherries. It seemed okay.

A shaft of light cut through the room. "Don't."

Chena froze, the cup halfway to her mouth. A man stepped out of the light, removed the cup from her fingers, and sniffed at it, as she had. "What's this, Elle?" he inquired.

"It's registered," replied Nan Elle stiffly. "I can show you the permit."

"I'm sure," the man drawled. He set the cup down, out of Chena's reach.

Now that Chena's eyes had readjusted to the flood of daylight, she could get a look at the man. He looked about as old as Dad had when he left. His deep brown skin darkened almost to black around his eyes and in the hollows of his cheeks. His wiry, wavy black hair had been pulled into a roll. A wooden plug was shoved through one earlobe. His mended brown and burgundy clothes were the same tunic and trousers everybody else seemed to wear, but he had a wide blue band around one sleeve.

It was his belt, though, that told Chena that this was the cop that Sadia had warned Shond about. He had a chip scanner clipped to the leather beside a taser, and a holster that held something gun-shaped. Chena wondered what it fired.

She glanced toward the door. Human shadows moved near the threshold, and all thoughts of running went out the hatch. The cop had backup. Better to just wait this out. With any luck, the cop would forget about her, or just tell her to go home.

"Elle, I'm going to search your house and your garden." He sounded matter-of-fact and tired. "And I'm going to take your client."

Oh, piss. Fear ran through Chena. What if Mom found out? Mom was going to find out. Chena was probably fatally late already. Again. *Oh, no. Oh, piss.*

Nan Elle just cocked her head up at the cop. "And you're going to question me, of course."

He shook his head. "No, I don't think I'll bother just yet."

Chena looked from one of them to the other. This was a complete wonk-up. It somehow seemed as if they must have had this conversation a million times, kind of like Mom and Dad and the endless late-night talks about money. But how could they have? Once the cameras caught her . . .

Of course. Here they didn't have cameras.

"Then why are you bothering with the search?" Nan Elle asked.

"Because I want to make sure you're not hiding anything in plain sight," he answered blandly. "It would be like you."

"That it would." She inclined her head. "I don't suppose you'll let the girl take her medicine?"

The cop looked down his long, broad nose at Chena. "No, I don't think I will."

"I'm sorry, Chena," said Nan Elle. "But that is the way it is."

" 'S not your fault," murmured Chena to her hands.

"Actually, it is." The cop gestured at Chena to stand up. Chena obeyed. "There are lines I can't let you cross, Elle."

Nan Elle's mouth seemed to sink a little deeper. "So you keep informing me."

Chena didn't dare look back as the cop herded her out the door. Her legs and back felt creaky and reluctant, and her dry throat itched for whatever had been in that cup, but she swallowed against the feeling. She had bigger problems right now.

No new patients waited outside Nan Elle's door, just a pale man and a dark woman, both with blue bands tied to their brown sleeves.

"Be thorough," said the cop to them. "Get under and into everything, and I want a record of what's growing on the roof, and don't forget to check the aquarium pipes."

"If you need to take care of this," Chena tried, "I could just—"

The cop laid a heavy hand on her shoulder. Chena shut her mouth.

"Make sure she shows you all the registrations for whatever she's growing," he went on to his people. "I'll be at my place when you're done." He looked down at Chena again, measuring, judging, trying to see what she had and what she thought she had. Chena shriveled.

He waved her to come on, and Chena forced her legs to move. He walked with a long, loose stride. She sort of waddled trying to keep up. If he noticed she was having trouble, she couldn't tell. He sure as piss didn't slow down any.

He took her down one level and right to the edge of the village, so that they were practically hanging out over the river. He pushed open the door to a small house with a roof that was more moss than anything else, and stood aside.

Chena hesitated. Okay, he was a cop, but it was dark in there.

The cop snorted. "It's my office when I'm here. Nobody's going to jump you."

Try it. Just try. Chena's hands bunched into fists, but she walked inside.

The place was dim and cluttered, a sort of cross between Nan Elle's and Madra's, with record sheets and books on the desk, bundles of plants hanging from the ceiling, and yet more record sheets, which seemed to have leaves and flowers embedded in them. There was only the one door.

The cop waved her to a chair, and Chena sat. The light slanted steeply through the windows and glowed dark gold. She glanced automatically at her wrist before she remembered her comptroller was in Nan Elle's pocket.

Gone. She rubbed her wrist. That was completely gone and she'd never see it again. The one thing she had from the station, and one thing that it turned out would be useful down here, and she had given it away to a crazy old lady who hadn't even given her any medicine.

The cop circled the desk and pulled the scanner off his belt. He gestured for her to come on, and Chena gave him her chip hand to scan. He looked down at the reader and grunted.

"Chena Trust. Here two days and already in the soup." He touched a key on the scanner and its screen blanked.

"I didn't do anything." Chena spread her hands. "I just wanted an aspirin."

The cop folded his hands together and rested them on his knee. "Who told you Nan Elle would have an aspirin?"

Chena shut her mouth so fast that her teeth clicked together. "I just heard," she breathed.

"Right." The cop sighed and smoothed his hand back over the top of his head. "Okay, Chena, I want you to tell me who you saw coming and going out of Nan Elle's while you were there."

"I didn't know any of them," she protested.

"You have a good set of eyes and a quick brain," replied the cop flatly. "You saw."

Anger flashed through Chena and she struggled to suppress it. "There were a lot of people there. Why aren't you picking on them?"

"Because all of them have been around long enough to not tell me piss-all." For the first time he sounded upset. "Did you hear around what Nan Elle is?"

Chena shook her head.

"She's a Pharmakeus." The cop leaned forward, pinning her down with his gaze. Chena squirmed, but there was nowhere she could actually go. "It's an old word. It means poisoner. You will have heard that there's a dead man in the village. He was poisoned to death, so well we almost didn't catch it." He paused to let that sink in. "And you were about to drink what she gave you."

Chena's heart thumped so hard, she felt the vibration down in the soles of her feet. No. It couldn't be true. Sadia would never hand her over to a murderer. The cop was just spinning one out for her so she'd tell him what he wanted to hear. That was all.

The cop kept staring at her. She tightened herself up inside and met his gaze. Just another superior, like on the station, without even alarms and cameras to back him up. He didn't know anything. He couldn't know. Just wanted to scare her. Let him try.

The door swung open and Chena just about jumped out of her skin. The cop leaned back with a satisfied smile on his face.

"Hello, Madra," he said over Chena's shoulder. "And I imagine this is Mother Trust and Daughter Teal." He gave the full salute, head, heart, and mouth.

Chena wished the floor would open up so she could drop straight through into the river and drown.

"There," came Madra's voice. Chena didn't want to turn and look. She hunched down in the chair as if she could vanish inside it. "Didn't that turn out easy?"

"Thank you for finding my daughter, Constable Regan." Mom stepped forward. Chena's breath clogged her throat. Mom sounded as if she were wound completely tight. She'd explode all over the place as soon as the witnesses were gone.

"I wish I could say it was on purpose, Sister Trust." The cop, Regan, gestured at the free chair.

Mom sat without her spine bending an inch. Teal stood next to the chair, gripping its arm with both hands. She glowered at Chena, and Chena shrugged back.

"How should I take that remark, Constable?" asked Mom.

Regan's long face relaxed, just a little. "Not all that badly," he said, and Chena felt a little better, until he started explaining to Mom where he had found Chena. Mom listened closely, her forehead furrowing, one deep wrinkle at a time.

When he had finished, and Mom's forehead couldn't bunch up any tighter, the cop turned back to Chena.

"So, Niece, you were just about to tell me what you saw?" His eyebrows lifted in innocent inquiry, but there was a challenge in his gaze, as if daring her to lie or leave something out while her mother was watching.

Anger bubbled inside Chena, but there was nothing she could do. She described, as best she could remember, the half dozen people she had seen in line, and the crying baby. He shuffled through his record sheets and occasionally imprinted a marker against a note to refer back to later, but she could tell from the way his face tightened that she wasn't telling him anything useful.

Good, she thought with sour satisfaction.

The cop was not the only one who didn't like what she was saying. Teal kept staring at Chena with a smoldering anger Chena couldn't figure out. What was her bug? It wasn't like she missed out on anything particularly good. Then again, Teal always figured if Chena didn't take her along, whatever it was that happened must have been good. Chena sighed inside her head. She'd have to help tell an extra long story later to make it up to her, or she'd be whining at Mom for days.

"Is there anything else we can do for you, Constable?" asked Mom when Chena finished her story. She planted both hands on the chair arms and was getting ready to stand.

The cop frowned at his record sheet. "No, I'm afraid not." He stood, and so did Mom. Chena managed to push herself to her feet without wincing. Teal took Mom's hand like a little kid, peering at Chena from behind her with that same glaring anger.

Chena just shrugged at her again, but Teal had already turned away, her chin tilted smugly upward.

They left, with Chena tagging along behind.

"Mom—" she started to say.

But Mom didn't let her get any further. "I cannot begin to tell you how angry I am with you, Chena Trust."

Chena swallowed. Here it came. Mom walked another few angry strides before she turned on her oldest daughter.

"I get home from my first day on my new job, and I find your sister down by the dock, practically in tears, saying you had not come to meet her and that you'd probably been dragged off to be chopped into bits. I look for you in the dorm, and you are not there. I look for you in the dining hall and the library, and you are not there. Where do I finally find you? In the superior's office for having attempted to get your hands on an illegal substance!"

"No, Mom, that's not what happened!" Chena took two steps forward, pleading. "I just wanted something because I hurt, that's all. I was told I could get some aspirin up there. I thought she was a doctor!"

Mom's face didn't soften a bit. "And who told you this?"

"Sadia, but she's okay, Mom, she really is."

"Did she warn you where you were going?"

"No, but—"

"Then she is not okay!" Chena cringed from the force of Mom's shout. In the next second, Mom straightened up and pressed her hand against her forehead. "I'm sorry, Chena, but you had me extremely worried. This is the second time in as many days you've wandered away I-don't-know-where, and this time when you specifically promised to be there for your sister."

"I didn't mean to be late!" Even to Chena the apology sounded wispy, but it was all she had.

"I'm sure you didn't. But you should be aware you are breathing very thin air right now, young lady."

Chena subsided. There wasn't much else she could do. She looked over the rail, down at the darkening village. It would be evening soon and all the living roofs were dimmed and edged in gray.

"Teal, will you do me a favor? Will you meet us down in the dorm's common room? We'll be right there."

"Okay, Mom." Chena turned in time to see the smug sweetness on Teal's face as she trotted obediently away.

But Mom didn't give Chena much time to be angry about it. As soon as Teal was down the nearest set of stairs, she met Chena's gaze.

Her eyes had sunken in behind a pair of dark circles that hadn't been there when they had left the station.

Mom studied her for a long time. Chena didn't know what she was looking for. She kept thinking Mom would speak, but she didn't. She just turned away again and rested both hands on the railing, watching the river below them slip between its mossy banks.

Chena felt her chest tightening as she tried to guess what Mom would say. Would she be grounded? Would she say Chena had let them all down? How much better Teal was acting, even if she was just the baby? Would she maybe say something about Dad? Or how long they'd have to stay here?

"Why are you doing this?"

The question was so soft and so distant that for a minute Chena wasn't sure Mom was talking to her. But she turned her head and focused her tired eyes on Chena. Chena dropped her own gaze and shurgged. She didn't know what Mom wanted to hear. She didn't even really understand the question.

She heard Mom sigh. "Let me rephrase. What do you want to do?"

Chena shrugged again. "I don't know. Get out of here." The words were out before she knew she was going to speak them, but she knew at once they were true. "Go somewhere, somewhere that's not planned or scheduled."

Mom nodded slowly. "Show you something." She jerked her chin in toward the center of the village.

"Okay." Chena followed her mother along the crooked network of walkways until they came to a gap in the trees where they could see the four gleaming rails stretching away into the forest.

Mom pointed down at the rails. "I found out yesterday that you can rent pedal bikes that run on those rails. They let you ride down to the next town, Stem, which is on the shore of a major lake. In fact, it's where the dirigible came in. There's a market there, and a theater." She faced Chena. "You give me one solid month of absolutely perfect behavior—no wandering off, no reports of being late or being where you're not supposed to, no complaining about sleeping in the dorms or public bathing, no going off with this Sadia when you're not sure what's going on, and at the end of it, you can take one of those bikes out on your own. If that goes well, we can make it a regular thing. Do we have a deal?"

A month. A whole pissing month . . . but at the end of it, a little freedom, some time out from under. Maybe there'd be a chance in there to keep her promise to herself, to find a way to help Mom and to get them free of the fear and the debt, a way to get them all out of here.

"Yes. Deal." She saluted her mother, and Mom saluted her back.

Around them, the twilight forest bloomed.

CHAPTER FOUR

Forces

"Menasha, you shouldn't have brought them here."

"So, tell me, Respected Commander, what should she have done with us?"

Commander Beleraja Poulos looked down at the speaker. Malnutrition had stunted him during childhood. Infection had taken his right arm up to the elbow. Thanks to Menasha, she also knew the man had once had three children, all of whom had been left behind, their ashes scattered on the winds of a world called Koh-i-Noor.

Beleraja saluted the withered headman. "Forgive me, Father. I spoke without thinking." She grasped Menasha's elbow and propelled her fellow shipper up the battered access corridor and out the airlock into Athena's tarnished docking bay. Menasha, wisely, kept her mouth shut until the ship's outer hatch slammed shut behind them and they both saw they stood alone among the angled lighting panels and jigsaw of colored sound-dampening squares.

"Where was I supposed to take them?" Menasha demanded, pulling her elbow free. "You were closest. Their jump engines are fried. They were trying to make it through normal space." Menasha's people had found the ships puttering along, barely two kilometers from each other, making a long slow creep through the real-space vacuum. The vessels themselves were five hundred years old if they were a day. The founders of Koh-i-Noor had hung on to them in case of emergency, instead of scavenging them for parts or selling them to the Authority, which was what most of the Called had done.

That emergency finally came.

"Their ancestors thought they were so lucky," Menasha had told Beleraja when they first got in. They stood on the silent, battered bridge staring at the screens, half of which were not working, the other half of which were showing dubious readouts. "They'd found an unclaimed world that was a full seven on the compatibility scale. Earth-sized, one big moon for stimulating winds and tides, more water than land, sugars and proteins in the local biosphere that humans could digest, and a microsphere that could handle human wastes and assist human crops."

Their original thousand settlers had spread out, claiming acre after acre of land for their families. Feuds split the group into fragments, which scattered as far from each other as they could. Storms took some, winter took others. Crop and mine failures forced those who failed into the service of those who succeeded. While all this was going on, the microsphere ate what it was given and started on its own campaign of divide and conquer. When the local diseases were ready to begin their major assault, the storms, the winter, and the droughts didn't think to stop so the settlers could deal with the new disasters.

The skilled died too fast to be replaced. Machinery broke down and could not be repaired. The survivors decided that the freedom their ancestors had sought was not worth any more lives. They reboarded their ships before they lost all ability to fly them.

Sympathy and frustration pulled Beleraja's thoughts back to the present and to Menasha calmly facing her in the empty docking bay.

"It's another four hundred people!" Beleraja flung out her hands. "We have a deal going with Pandora that we will keep the refugees away from them. . . ." Beleraja let the sentence trail off as she watched Menasha's gaze shift sideways.

Beleraja had not seen Menasha Denshyar since she had apprenticed with the Denshyar family's fleet. They'd kept in touch when they could, leaving each other notes at various communication stations. Like Beleraja, Menasha had risen to be the matriarch of her family, as well as commander of their fleet. She'd done well by them, even though she had decided they would spend their time trading information and goods between the Authority cities rather than between the Called worlds.

More time trading between the cities—the thought repeated itself to Beleraja. What were they even doing out this way? Pandora was a long detour if the Denshyar fleet was heading between Atlantis and El Dorado, which were the two closest cities.

Oh, no Mena. What have you gotten us into? "What were you thinking?" she asked again.

"I was thinking of saving lives," snapped Menasha, but Beleraja heard the hollowness under the conviction.

Beleraja gave a short, sharp sigh, a sound her children had learned to be wary of when they were young.

"How about this, then: What's the Council of Cities thinking?" she demanded, folding her arms.

Menasha shrugged, but still wouldn't look at her. "It's been ten years."

"By the burning name of god." Beleraja hung her head. "You're here to put pressure on Pandora."

"Ten years, Bele," repeated Menasha, real heat rising in her voice. "Do you have any idea what it's like out there?"

"No, I don't," snapped back Beleraja. "Because I've been stuck in this tin can for the past five years instead of out with my family. I've been here trying to keep things going between the Authority, all the Called, and Pandora." She swept her hand back toward the corridor. "This place is jammed to the gills. We've got ships out turning away everybody we can, but people are still sneaking in. Director Shontio is tearing his hair out. I've been trying to keep him cool, but he's under pressure. There's a really good chance your refugees are going to be stuck in their ships, especially if they can't pay the air tax."

"You should tell the Pandorans," replied Mena calmly, "they'll have to take more people down to the surface."

Beleraja shook her head. "Not likely." She remembered far too clearly the complete indifference on their faces when she'd sat at the end of their conference table and talked about the plight of the Called. Indifference that had turned to sheer horror when she had threatened them with colonists landing on the pristine world.

"Then they're going to have a problem, aren't they?" Menasha cocked her head toward Beleraja, and Beleraja knew the Council of Cities did not have to work very hard to convince Menasha to take this assignment. "And maybe this will just be the first problem."

Beleraja turned away, her chest heaving and her fists clenching and unclenching. Was the council out of their minds? They knew, they *knew* that this was the work of years. What under the wide black sky were they thinking?

They were thinking they had not seen enough results from Pandora. They were thinking all the reports and assurances might be bogus. They were thinking of the settlements on another five worlds that had failed in the last city-measured year. They were thinking that if there weren't enough worlds to sustain all the Authority shippers, the shippers would move back to the cities, which might not be able to take care of them, because those cities depended on the goods the shippers brought in.

Beleraja took a deep breath and turned back around.

"Mena, take them to Atlantis."

An expression of sincere regret crossed Menasha's face. "I can't."

Beleraja blew out another sigh, a long, slow, disappointed one this time. "You mean you won't." *Because you've been paid to help pressure Pandora. Mena, how badly did you need the goods?*

"I can't," said Menasha sharply, as if she'd guessed Beleraja's thoughts. "Atlantis won't take them. They've already said so."

It took a moment for her words to penetrate to Beleraja's understanding. "Why not?" she asked, her forehead furrowing. "Atlantis needs new blood. The cities are losing people just like the planets are."

"And it's making them extremely reluctant to allow in anybody who might be a new vector for infection." Menasha folded her arms. "They are all remembering how quickly that plague spread across Old Earth."

"All right, all right." Beleraja waved her hand weakly. "I'll try to smooth it over with Director Shontio. Maybe we can find room for them." She turned away, heading for the hatch to the stairway.

"Bele," said Menasha hesitantly. "The council did not put you here to make things easy for the Pandorans. You're flying right past the mission goal here."

Beleraja did not look back. "No, I'm not."

Leaving Menasha to take that however she chose, Beleraja cranked open the nearest stairway hatch and stepped through.

As ever, the stairway was crowded. The stair shafts had always been the equivalent of public parks for Athena Sation, which had never been designed for full-time residents. The air was heavy with the smells of disinfectant and warm humanity. Men and women stood around talking, children ran up and down the stairway between the adults, or sat in clusters playing games with balls or cards. Adolescents slouched against the rails looking tough and disinterested, hoping someone would notice how tough and disinterested they were. The voices blended into a single rush of sound.

All long-term inhabitants of artificial environments tried to make their enclosures more like an open world. Since Athena lacked space for more than the occasional potted plant, parks and groves were out of the question. So its inhabitants had taken to keeping small animals: dogs, birds, ferrets.

Some of the people recognized Beleraja as she passed. They saluted and hailed politely as they stepped aside for her, pulling their children and pets out of the way. As always, however, not all of the gestures were polite greetings. That was something else she'd gotten used to during her time here.

Between the regular traffic, another set of people lined the stairways. Some of them held out begging cups or empty hands. Most of them, though, only huddled on their blankets in the middle of their bundles of belongings. Beleraja didn't want to stare, but she couldn't help glancing down. Mostly they were normal human faces—all the shades of brown, beige, and pink, tight with embarrassment, worry, or embattled dignity. Here and there she saw tumors, drastically shortened arms, a twisted foot, or an enlarged head and sunken eyes. There she saw an old man trembling and trying to hide it under layers of coats. Here she saw a child let its head fall onto one side as if the child lacked the strength to hold it upright. A hunched, pale woman, probably the child's mother, caught Beleraja staring and glowered at her, looking like she might spit if she hadn't known it was forbidden.

Refugees. Beleraja's family fleet patrolled the best jump points around Athena looking for the ships as they came in. But that meant covering hundreds of millions of kilometers of space, with only ten ships and a limited array of beacons and satellites. All the Called knew that Pandora was working on the cure to the Diversity Crisis, and many of them decided not to wait until that cure, whatever it was, came out to their ravaged worlds.

Beleraja had gotten Director Shontio to ram through a policy of giving temporary shelter to those refugees who could pay at least for their air and water. Much of her time was taken up in arranging with shipper families to take these refugees to whatever surviving worlds would have them. What surprised and frightened her was how few worlds would take anybody, even with their own populations on the brink of extinction. They feared importing yet more disease, many of them said. But some would not bring in anyone who would not convert to their way of life. They would die before they let in strangers.

And then there were those refugees who refused to go. Beleraja sighed as she reached the directorate level and cranked open its hatch. Even after all these years, Father Mihran's description of the Called and its handmade problems rang in her head as all too true.

There were even rumors that some of the shipper families were taking large payments to outfit refugee ships and point them in the right direction. Beleraja and Director Shontio sent a fresh petition to the Council of Cities out with every ship, asking them to help quash the practice. When the replies came back, they always swore no such thing was happening, and that if it was, of course they'd stop it.

Even before today, Beleraja had stopped believing them.

The crowds remained thick all the way to the hub and the directorate offices. In Shontio's favor, he had not tried to shove the problem away from himself personally. The directorate corridors were as filled as the stairways had been with staff, citizens, and the hallway people the long-term station residents called "airheads."

Beleraja walked through the rings of administrative and security checks without challenge. The director's door registered her presence and opened for her automatically. Shontio kept a standard office—fully wired desk, guest seat, refreshment case. A pot of variegated ivy stood on the corner of the desk, just about the only greenery on the station outside the farming levels.

Shontio sat behind his desk. The wall screens around him showed crowd control at a corridor juncture, a cafeteria full to overflowing, the line outside one of the medical bays. He swiveled his chair around as she entered and traced a command pattern on his desktop. The walls blanked, and Beleraja was grateful. She still felt emotionally overburdened from the refugee ship Menasha had walked her through, and from all the realizations that had come to her afterward.

"So . . ." Shontio ran one hand across his copper-colored scalp. The station fashion was to wear your hair short, even shaven. If Shontio allowed his hair to grow out, it would probably be a shaggy gray mane. His bright red, high-necked jacket was perpetually rumpled these days. Its gold trim was fraying and the buttons were dim. "Did the refugees pay Commander Menasha to bring them here?"

"Worse," Beleraja said, throwing herself into one of Shontio's guest chairs. "The Authority paid her to bring them here."

Shontio stared at her for a moment while her words sank in. "Why?"

"To put pressure on Pandora," she said simply. She was tired. Tired of the refugees and all their desperation, tired of the Council of Cities and its stupid maneuvering, tired of seeing her family, her husband, one month out of every twelve, and tired of watching the never-ending crises wear Shontio slowly down.

Shippers did not make friends easily outside their families. When you came to a place just once ever five local years, relationships became a constant reconciling of blurred memories with new realities. But her family had docked at Athena Station at least once every two local years the entire time she was growing up, so her friendship with Shontio had a rare continuity, and she prized it. It was one of the reasons she had taken the Pandoran contract in the first place.

"They mean to turn your station into the sword of Damocles," she said, rubbing her blue thumbnail gem against the seam of her trousers. "They think if the Pandorans know that there's a whole load of displaced, desperate people up here, and that some of them have access to ships that could theoretically make it down to the surface, it will speed up work on the cure."

"Oh, is that what they think?" Shontio glared at the walls as if he could see through them and the vacuum beyond, all the way to El Dorado. His angry, tired gaze turned back to Beleraja. "You know what the station management board is going to do? They are going to seal those people into their ships and make them sit there. If they haven't got money to pay for air and water, they are going to be set adrift." His voice shook as he spoke. "I'm losing my credit with the committees, Bele. There's too many people out there refusing to leave with the Authority convoys."

"I know," she said softly. "But I think that's what the council is counting on." She looked at her thumbnail gem, blue for the rank of commander. It no longer sparkled as it once had. It just glinted dully in the station's full-spectrum light. "In fact, I really think they're hoping someone will make a break for it and try to establish a settlement down in the Pandorans' beloved wilderness."

"Which would allow them to make their point while still denying they had anything to do with such a flagrant violation of their agreement." His shoulders slumped and Beleraja felt for him. Everybody had too much to deal with these days. More than one of them was crumbling under the load. She didn't want to see Shontio go down like that, especially when she could feel herself going down with him. "They can blame you and I for allowing the refugees to stay here," he went on, "as can the management board."

"We could call down to Administrator Tam," suggested Beleraja. "Tell him the situation."

Shontio snorted. "Tam doesn't understand. He never has. He hates the Crisis because it's disrupted his life, not because of what it's done to the people. I'm not sure how eager he'll be to help work out a bigger disruption."

"Then we ask him to get his committee and Father Mihran—"

"And Father Mihran will say what he's said every other time!" Shontio slammed his fist against the desk. Beleraja jumped, even though she knew his anger was not for her. "He'll say they can't absorb any more refugees. He'll say they'll have to wait until there's a new draft, or a population shift in the villages. He'll say that our decision to let them stay makes them our problem." Shontio stared at his own fist, clenched so tightly the knuckles had turned white, but Beleraja knew that was not what he was seeing. "Maybe we should give the Authority what they want. Maybe we should just look the other way and—"

"No, Shontio." Beleraja reached across the desk and grasped his knotted hand. "You know what will happen to them. The hothousers have had ten years to get ready to deal with that kind of invasion. If we look away while anybody tries to make a run to the surface, we are going to watch them die."

"You don't know that," said Shontio without lifting his gaze.

"Yes, I do." Beleraja let his hand go and straightened up. "And so do you."

"So"—Shontio uncurled his fist and laid his hand flat on the desk—"we do nothing."

"No." Beleraja shook her head. "We call Father Mihran and Administrator Tam, and we try again. We call the council, and we try again with them too. You talk to the committees and the management board. I talk to Mena and the headman for the new refugees and try to inject a little reality into their veins. Maybe they'll like the idea of living in their ships or dying on Pandora less than the possibility of helping a struggling colony survive."

"Yes." A little determination crept back into Shontio's voice, and he was able to look at her again. "Of course. Maybe this time we can make it work." He paused, his expression suddenly wistful. "Do you think this cure, this business of redesigning the human immune system, is going to save us?"

Now it was Beleraja's turn to look away. "No."

"Why not?"

Beleraja watched her hands. She remembered the pride she had felt when her command gem had been set. She had plans to lead her family to glory, not trap them into patrolling one tiny area of space searching for the desperate.

"Because I believe that the only thing that can really work is for there to be a whole lot of human beings on a single planet where there can be all the give and take that we had back when we were growing up on Old Earth." She ran her fingertips over her gem. "We are too isolated out here. The nearest band of humans might be two years apart. Those are not conditions we were evolved to stand. We need exchange—genetic exchange, intellectual exchange, even violent exchange, maybe—with our neighbors, or we die. We are proving that right now."

Shontio watched her silently for a moment. "I thought the Authority ruled out consolidation as a solution."

"They did."

"And you never told me that you spoke out against the idea."

"I didn't."

"Why not?"

Shontio, leave me alone. "Because I was afraid. Because I'm like everybody else. I don't want to lose my way of life." She made herself sit up and look right at him again. "I'm a shipper. For eight generations my family has lived in space. We are gypsies, birds. I did not want to advocate cutting our wings and binding ourselves to a single place." Then she added more softly, "I was afraid to. I wanted—I still want—to believe this massive feat of genetic engineering will preserve our way of life." She gave a small, mirthless laugh. "I'm as bad as Tam, as bad as any of the Called. I don't really want to change my life, even when I know I'm going to have to."

"And I thought the Authority was trying to save us all." Shontio's words were full of grim mockery.

"The Authority?" Beleraja shook her head. "I'll give you the Authority. Why isn't there a working communication network for the Called?"

Shontio stared at her, not following the leap in logic. "There is," he said.

Beleraja waved her hand, dismissing the idea. "There's a few hundred satellites and a couple of dozen station ships full of extremely bribable inbred crews. I mean a real network, with jump capability and message encryption. It's technically feasible. Why doesn't it exist?"

"Tell me." Shontio steepled his fingers and got ready to wait.

"Because way back when, when the Called was expanding instead of collapsing, the Council of Cities worked out that it would be better for the Authority if the Called had to depend on them for communications. If the worlds only knew what we told them . . ." Beleraja threw up her hands. "Well! We'd just keep on being indispensable. Profits and power forever." She let her hands fall back onto the chair arms with a thud. "The shippers might have done something, but if there was a working comm network, then the cities would be able to keep an eye on us with extreme efficiency, and my illustrious ancestors didn't want that."

Shontio regarded her over his fingertips for a minute. "And the Called never worked this out?"

"Oh, I'm sure they did, but they expected to one day have an infrastructure that would allow them to put up their own satellites." She shook her head slowly. "That, however, did not happen." Her mouth stretched into a thin, tight line. "That is the kind of forward, altruistic thinking that the current Council of Cities sprang from. If there had been a comm network, word of the Diversity Crisis would have spread so much faster. We might even have had a solution by now, because the very best minds on all the worlds, including Old Earth, could have exchanged ideas, but no." She spread her fingers and looked down at her gem. "Save us all? We might have helped us die."

Shontio ran his palm along the edge of his desk. "Well, Bele," he said, "if your ancestors killed us, and the Pandorans' cure can't work . . ." He stilled his hand. "What are we doing here?"

"Whatever we can, Tio," she answered grimly. "Whatever we can."

In front of Tam, the screen cleared to its normal, glassy transparency. It didn't even show him his own reflection. Now that he was no longer wrapped up in his conversation with Shontio and Beleraja, he became aware of the noise of the family's home spreading out around him—voices, children's running feet, the ceaseless sound of falling water. He rested his hands on his knees and waited to hear a voice speaking directly to him.

"That was a difficult conversation," said Aleph, her voice sounding as if it came from the air right next to him. Aleph was the "city mind," the artificial intelligence that took care of the Alpha Complex and its family. Among her other duties, she monitored all contact with Athena Station. "You will be calling a meeting of the Administrators' Committee?"

Before Tam could answer, a new image coalesced on the screen in front of him, and another on the screen to his right. Father Mihran stood surrounded by the frantic activity of the laboratory. To his right, Liate, Athena's officially assigned administrator, sat alone at a little conference table, her arms folded across her chest.

"Tam," said Father Mihran gently. "I understand you have had another message from Athena Station."

Tam nodded. He should have known this was coming. Aleph would have alerted Father Mihran and Liate. Technically, Athena Station was under Liate's jurisdiction. Tam, however, was head of the Administrators' Committee, and anyone who had business with an administrator was allowed to appeal to him.

"Yes," he said, positioning himself so he could face both screens. "And I should have alerted you immediately, Liate. My apologies."

Liate looked down for a moment, the tip of her tongue protruding between her full lips. "I'm asking only to be kept fully apprised of the matters in my territory."

"Of course. I will inform Director Shontio and Commader Poulos that you are the one they should contact in the future."

"They did not seem to listen to such matters of protocol."

"Which is not anything Tam can help," interrupted Father Mihran smoothly. "But I would suggest that you both meet and be sure that your strategies regarding communication with Athena Station are well matched." Father Mihran looked directly at him, and Tam knew what he meant to say. *We need to be sure that you are not giving them any concessions. That you are not promising to authorize expanded immigration.*

"Aleph is checking the administrators' schedules right now to find out how soon we can meet."

The image of Father Mihran looked toward the image of Liate with his eyebrows raised in silent inquiry.

"I am receiving responses that say this afternoon will be convenient," said Aleph. "There is much concern over the new arrivals at Athena."

Yes, thought Tam. *Everyone knows the station is already under pressure, and to their credit, they all understand that things kept under pressure too long have a tendency to explode.*

And maybe, just maybe, he could work with that understanding. He could make a case for increased food shipments to help ease the station's discomfort, at the very least. Begin there, and work his way outward. The trick was going to be to placate Liate. Conscience or no, she was quite aware that her authority as Athena's administrator was being usurped and she resented it. He could not blame her, but he also could not refuse to hear the petitions from Beleraja and Shontio, and once heard, he could not leave them unanswered.

Of course, he could always offer a swap of jurisdictions with Liate, but that would mean that Offshoot, Stem, and his other villages would be left to her strict interpretation of family regulation and privilege, and he could not bring himself to do that either.

While all these thoughts flickered though his mind, he watched the lines of frustration ease on Liate's face. He wondered what she was thinking, or what her Conscience was telling her. "This is good," she said. "We obviously need to talk."

"You'll let me know the result of this talk as soon as possible," said Father Mihran. He bowed to them both, and his image cleared from the screen, leaving Liate and Tam watching each other uneasily.

"I know you are trying to assist with a difficult situation," said Liate. "And I know it is not your fault that the station's leaders insist on talking directly to you."

Actually, it is. Because they know I will listen. "Our communication has not been as open as it should be between a brother and sister of the same family branch," said Tam quickly. "I'm sorry for this, and I hope we can improve the situation."

The answer was pat, but it seemed to satisfy Liate. "We'll speak more this afternoon." She bowed in farewell and let her image fade from the screen. Tam once again faced two panels of empty glass.

Then a new image appeared. This one was a plump, middle-aged woman in a white dress with a long black vest. She did not exist anywhere inside the dome. This was how Aleph showed herself to Tam.

"Is there any way I can help you, Tam?" the city-mind asked.

"I need to know more about the history of the dealings between Athena Station and the family," said Tam. "In particular, I need to tell about any judgments and rulings made between the two." The city-minds were keepers of the family's history, as well as advisers to the family members. They had all the facts stored in their inorganic subsystems, but their living brains could interpret those facts with all the wisdom gained from thousands of years of life. Perhaps Aleph could help him find a compromise somewhere in the past that would open a door to the future.

"I'm already working on it." Aleph smiled. "I'll let you know what I find."

"Thank you." Aleph lifted her hand to Tam and let the image fade away.

Tam stayed where he was for a moment, his head slightly bowed. *All is well,* he tried to tell himself. With Aleph's help, he would be able to persuade the committee that Athena Station needed help, not more sanctions. But four hundred more people? Four hundred more people to help take care of? How many more would there be before

Athena split at the seams? Or worse, before some of them decided to try to land on Pandora and found out what kind of greeting the Guardians had been preparing for them?

Tam climbed to his feet. He was head of the Administrators' Committee, but there were limits on what he could do. "Always, so many limits," he breathed to himself.

Your family will help you, said his Conscience.

"Yes, thank you," said Tam. As soon as he spoke, he seemed to smell the reassuring scent of aloe. When he had still lived with his birth family, their niche had been surrounded by the plants. His Conscience was trying to make him feel that everything would be all right.

Maybe it would. Tam stood, automatically smoothing down his black vest as he did. If he could convince his family that action needed to be taken, that what was happening up on Athena was not just the Athenians' problem. Perhaps he could even gain some leverage by pointing out that the station was being used by the Authority, just like Pandora was.

Somewhat reassured in spite of himself, Tam stepped out of the grove that sheltered the comm screen and started walking toward the dome's western edge.

The family dome of the Alpha Complex was a huge open space, as much garden as it was living quarters. Tam sidestepped a pack of children as they barreled past him toward the play garden, followed by a smaller pack of parents and volunteers, talking and laughing with the easy familiarity of people who had lived all their lives together. A pair of seniors worked on their knees, aerating the roots of a newly grafted tree whose bright pink blossoms drooped lazily over their heads as if listening in on their conversation.

The center of the dome held the common living and working areas—kitchens, bathing pools, class areas, and most of the comm screens, all of it open to the dome and to all the other family members. Everyone over eighteen did have a personal alcove where they slept, entertained visitors, and kept their personal possessions. These were staggered along the curving walls of the dome, modeled after ancient cliff dwellings. Most of their rooms opened onto the common dome. The family saw privacy as a villager's notion, a stationer's notion, and an unhealthy one at that. Privacy bred secrets, and secrets could only swell to divide family members from each other, the city, and Pandora.

Tam sometimes wondered if it was his stunted Conscience that kept him wishing for a place where none of his family could see him. Surely, if his Conscience worked properly, he would want nothing better than the company of his kith and kin, especially when he was feeling troubled.

But this was all part of the gift and the burden his parents placed on him and his birth sister, Dionte. They were assured that they were not the only ones, that there were always a few, in secret, and that they were needed to watch over the family. There always had to be someone who could think clearly without the threat of being overwhelmed by guilt or fear. They were to make sure that their branch brothers and sisters did not become completely suffocated by the insulation that the voices in their heads wrapped around them.

Tam winced as he noticed his birth cousin Jolarie's latest decorating idea for his alcove involved lurid yellow and red abstract blobs hung from the ceiling on twine nooses. Baidra, an experimenter visiting from the Gamma Complex, waved at Tam from her alcove where she stretched out on her bed with a reader sheet. She winked and gestured at him to come sit beside her, and Tam waved his refusal. Not today. There was too much in his head today to play the lover.

Tam put one foot on the stair that led to his own alcove. Movement caught his eye. Dionte waited on the ledge in front of Tam's alcove with two covered cups in her hands.

Well, Sister, why am I not surprised? Tam waved with feigned welcome and climbed up to her, hoping by the time he got there his smile would be a little less forced. *So, do you want to discuss the agenda for the administrators' meeting, or the progress of the Eden Project?*

"Good Afternoon, Dionte," said Tam when he drew level with his younger sister. Dionte had been a moon-faced child, and she had grown into a soft-faced woman. She wore her black hair in a pair of braids, which she coiled around her head and pinned in the back. She dressed in a simple garment composed of four alternating black and white panels, with one black sleeve and one white.

Tam waved Dionte to a richly upholstered divan. He pulled a pair of fat pillows off the bed for himself and dropped them onto the floor.

"Basante is upset with you," said Dionte, handing one of the covered cups to Tam as he sat by way of both greeting and greeting gift.

Ah. We're going to talk about Eden. Tam accepted the cup handed down to him. "That's nothing new." He remembered the evening Basante had come to him burbling about Helice Trust and the possibilities locked in her genes. By now Basante had seen Tam's report of her second refusal to volunteer for the project.

"It's probably not extremely intelligent either."

Tam just sighed and lifted the cup's lid, inhaling the steam appreciatively. Dionte's blended teas were works of art. Tam smelled ginger, cardamom, jasmine, green tea, and just a hint of black pepper for stimulation and to startle the palate. He removed the cover and sipped.

"He suggested to me that you aren't doing enough to convince Helice Trust she should be helping us," said Dionte.

Tam lowered the cup, frowning as if the tea had soured inside his mouth. "Basante wanted to force a woman who has broken no laws into the complex. Are you saying I should have let him?"

"He showed me the report." Dionte uncovered her own cup and blew on the pale brown brew. The steam swirled and clouded around her round face as she lifted her gaze to look at Tam. Amusement sparkled behind her concern. "In fact, he pressed it into my personal system without asking me." Tam gave a soft chuckle and nodded. When Basante got excited, he insisted that everyone get excited.

"She is nearly perfect," Dionte went on. "Her presence would save a lot of work." She paused. "We would need to recruit far fewer subjects."

Tam snorted in disgust and considered handing the tea back. *You should realize by now I will not play along with you any more than I will play along with the rest of our family.* "So, this one time, we should be like Basante and forget the villagers are human? I can't believe you'd do that." *You are so used to close contact with so many kinds of mind, Sister. How can anyone be an outsider to you?*

When Tam and Dionte's birth parents had told them that their Consciences would never grow to full strength, one of the ways in which they responded was by learning as much about the Conscience implants as possible. Dionte had turned that interest into her calling and became a Guardian. Now she spent her life monitoring, analyzing, and creating the implants for the family, as well as working with the organic countermeasures designed to protect Pandora and the domes from invasion or rebellion.

Dionte drank her tea, cradling the cup in her palm. "Normally I'd be the first one to agree with your sentiment. But these are not normal times."

"Sentiment?" he said. "Don't tell me you've started believing . . ." He looked at the way Dionte held her face, so still, so full of equilibrium. "You have."

"No." Dionte shook her head. "I'm just saying that if we don't show the Authority something concrete soon, we really will be under siege. They might already be moving to make good on their threat to destroy Pandora."

The intensity of her words startled Tam and lit a spark of suspicion inside him. What if that step had already been taken? What if that step was Beleraja's news of her four hundred refugees?

Ridiculous. Surely, if the Authority wanted to pressure Pandora, Pandora would know it. Two thousand years of being the sole provider of transportation and trade between the Called had not encouraged subtlety inside the Authority. Surely they would never hatch a scheme like this.

Besides, Beleraja would never hazard lives in such a fashion. Or would she? Did he really know what she would do if she thought her actions would bring the Diversity Crisis to a swift conclusion?

Tam looked down into his cup. The smell of spices was rich and pleasant, but he couldn't make himself drink it. Whether or not his suspicions about Beleraja were the truth, that was how the family was sure to interpret her actions. How would they respond? The most likely possibility was that they would insist on the Eden Project being accelerated. The argument would be that they should give the Authority what they wanted. Then the Authority would go away and leave Pandora in peace.

And how many would be forced into the experiment wing once that decision had been reached?

"Helice Trust might be willing to contribute genetic material to the project," he said, choosing his words carefully. "I believe what she truly objects to is being made pregnant with a child that she will not be allowed to keep, and possibly having this happen to her more than once."

"If it was her eggs that were needed, her eggs would've been asked for." Dionte ran her fingertip around the rim of her cup. "You know that the real difficulty here has been the interaction between the immune system of the mother and the enhanced fetus."

"Well, now that we have an idea of what we're looking for, we can begin screening exclusively for other matches. We have four hundred new candidates aboard Athena Station alone." There was no question in Tam's mind that Dionte already knew about the refugees.

"Yes, we do, don't we?" murmured Dionte. She took another sip of her tea and lowered the cup, lacing her fingers around it. "Tam, I want . . ."

"What?" he asked warily. Hesitation was not something Dionte was known for.

Dionte gazed across the dome, as if searching for a particular face among the various gatherings of their kin. "Brother, we are in danger."

Tam chuckled ruefully and shook his head. "Yes, Dionte. That's why things are such a mess."

"You don't understand me." Dionte's hands tightened around her cup. "We're not acting like we are in danger. We are acting like this is the old days and some bunch of colonists have come to us to ask for advice. The Authority has declared war on us. They did it ten years ago when they dropped that bomb in the Vastness, and we decided to pay no attention."

"We paid attention, Dionte. We surrendered. It was all we could do."

"All we could do then," Dionte said. "But not all we can do now."

"What are you getting at?" asked Tam, even though he was sure he did not want to know the answer.

She still didn't look at him. She spoke to the steam, to the tea, perhaps to herself. "I am saying there are other possibilities for the Eden Project. We do not have to give it over to the Authority and the Called to save ourselves. There are more effective ways it could be used."

Tam clamped the cover on his cooling cup of tea. "Sister, I do not want to hear this."

"Brother." Dionte turned her face back to him, and he saw she truly was troubled and afraid. Mostly afraid. "If we try to placate them, the Authority is going to overwhelm us no matter what we do. We have to go on the offensive."

"If that's what you believe, Dionte, then you need to take it up with the whole family. Not with me." He handed Dionte back her teacup.

"I have tried. You know the rest of our family does not want to hear it either."

"A sign that you and I do not have a monopoly on wisdom." Tam spoke the hard words and felt no guilt, no guilt at all. How many debates had there been? A hundred? A thousand? In every family meeting since the Authority's initial threat had come down, someone had a proposal for how they could strike back, how they could prove Pandora was a force to be reckoned with.

"Then you will have to bring it up again and again, if necessary. You are free to say whatever you want during meetings."

Dionte sighed. "I suppose it will have to be enough."

"Yes," replied Tam levelly. "I suppose it will."

They regarded each other in silence for a long moment, until Dionte realized Tam really didn't plan to say anything else. Dionte stood and bowed slightly in farewell. Tam returned the bow, but remained seated while Dionte descended the stairs to the main court.

Tam rubbed his temple where his Conscience implant was and for a moment hated his own decision. How had all these doubts come to haunt him? Dionte never doubted herself, though her Conscience was as truncated as his.

Maybe he should just confess all at his next head dump and let them fix whatever organic flaws kept his implant from taking full hold of him and then he could have peace.

What was it like to have a wholly integrated Conscience? Did it truly make life easier? Basante, at least, made it seem like it did. Sometimes, though, Tam saw, or thought he saw, a look of yearning on the faces of his branch siblings, like they were trying to remember something long forgotten.

Then again, maybe that was just a projection of his own confusion. Tam had no way to tell.

He sighed again and got to his feet. This was useless. There was still the meeting to prepare for. Maybe it wasn't a total loss. Maybe now that he knew the family would conclude Beleraja's actions were treacherous, he could prepare a means to show them that was not true.

"Becuase if I don't, we slip that much further into our own arrogance," he murmured.

They are your family, said his Conscience. *You can trust them.*

"Oh, yes," murmured Tam, looking over the busy, happy garden of his home. "I can trust them very well."

Dionte left her brother's alcove calmly, carrying a teacup in each hand. She did not look back. She could not afford to. She knew that if she saw Tam watching her leave, she would be tempted to turn around and try once again to make him see what was really happening, and it wouldn't work any more than it had the last hundred times.

Dionte had not been in the conference room that day the Authority had come to make its initial threat. She had been in the laboratory with her kin and fellow students, watching on one of the video screens. She saw the swelling dust cloud and heard the thunder, and she had known then that they were all prisoners. In dropping that bomb, the Authority had changed its whole nature. Before this, they had clung to their statements that they were just go-betweens, importers and exporters, and mediators. But with that show of force, they became something else. They became rulers, and Pandora became their subject, and that would never change until Pandora took action, because no matter how far away the Authority went, they could always come back.

Father Mihran had spoken, and the council had spoken, and they had all listened to their Consciences and the city-minds, all of them bred and trained toward compromise and getting along with each other, and they gave in. They gave in for the same reasons their ancestors gave in when Athena Station rebelled against the idea of Conscience implants for its management board—because in the end, they could not resist. They could compromise, but they could not unite. They could discuss and theorize, but they could not truly comprehend the enormity of their guardianship of Pandora and all that it meant.

Tam was right that their parents' decision to truncate their Consciences was a mistake, but he did not understand why. The family did not need its children to be more separate from each other. They needed them more tightly connected. They did not need a disinterested view, they needed a deeper understanding.

In the nearest kitchen cluster, Dionte washed the cups carefully in the sink, chatting with Imanet and Mana, who were chopping vegetables and sectioning fruit for an afternoon snack. She dried the cups and stacked them with the others in the glass cabinets that curved above the counter, and then dried her hands on a cloth that had been hung over the gnarled branch of a dwarf willow.

Basante would be waiting in her alcove. She did not want to meet him until she was perfectly calm.

You're not really angry at Tam, she told herself. *You're angry because you're afraid of what's about to happen. You're not sure enough. You haven't done enough testing.* She cut the thought off. She couldn't afford it. Delay only served the Authority.

She lifted her eyes to pick out her own alcove in the dwelling wall, two tiers up on the left edge of the living spaces. Someone was in there, pacing back and forth. Basante. He spotted her and started immediately down the stairs.

Dionte sighed and strode forward to meet him.

"What did he say—" began Basante breathlessly.

"Come with me." Dionte took his hand and led him to a cushioned bench in the shade of a spreading lime tree. Its pleasant scent enveloped them as they sat, and its heavy branches provided them with just enough shelter that their kin were unlikely to hear anything awkward.

"What did he say?" repeated Basante.

Dionte looked at Basante with the trained eye of a Guardian. She could practically see the translucent filaments stretching out from his temple, down his right arm, and up into the gray matter of his mind. If she needed to, she could call up a map of those filaments. In fact, she had. She had pored over that map. She had obsessed over it, trying to understand how she could change the nature of the filaments and the implant so that Basante would be able to help her help their family.

Unlike Tam, Basante had always understood the urgency of Pandora's situation, but once Father Mihran, the family councilors, and

Aleph had spoken, his Conscience and its need for compromise would not allow him to stand against them.

In a few minutes, she would change that. Dionte swallowed nervously and hoped Basante did not notice.

"He will not help us bring Helice Trust in," said Dionte.

Basante thumped his fist against his thigh once, but almost immediately he loosened his hand. "Well, we expected that."

"But—for the next few days, at least—he will be fully involved in trying to keep the peace with Athena. That will give us a chance to approach the woman directly. He also suggests it's the pregnancy she is objecting to. We will need to develop our arguments from that angle."

"Yes, yes." Basante nodded thoughtfully. "If she could be made to understand the child will be a member of the family . . ."

"It might help," Dionte finished for him. "But the most important thing is that the Authority has escalated the threat and Father Mihran still will not accept that the Authority and the Called must be fought."

"Father Mihran said this?"

Dionte shook her head. "But Tam did, and that is sign enough."

Basante looked down his nose at her in an expression as close to condescension as she had ever seen on him. "Tam speaks for Father Mihran now?"

"No," answered Dionte tartly. "But can you name me one open debate in the past decade where Tam's side came out the loser?" Basante remained silent. "You see? There are plenty of reasons why my brother is the head of the Administrators' Committee."

Basante's little smile grew uneasy. "You almost make it sound like he does not trust his family." He turned his head just a little, so that he was looking at her out of the corner of his eye. "Or that you do not trust your birth brother."

"I would never say such a thing," Dionte told him, a little shocked. "But the fact is, Basante, it may be up to you and I to protect Pandora."

The smile faded away. "Dionte, that isn't possible. We can't work without the family's support."

It will only be for a little while, I promise. Dionte took Basante's hand. The smooth touch of his data display activated the sensors under the skin of her palm. *Basante plus,* she subvocalized to her own implant, and the preset commands she had encoded under that name flowed down the filaments in her arm, through her palm, into the biosilicate of his display, and to his implant.

"The family has decided not to protect Pandora from the Authority," she said. "You see it as well as I do. You know this is true."

The human body was a hot, acidic, constantly shifting environment. Anything inorganic planted inside it had a tendency to simply wear away over time. Although the Conscience implants were primarily organic, they each contained inorganic materials to assure the necessary precision of memory and consistency of output. Those inorganics needed monitoring and adjustment if they were to continue to function across the lifetime of their host.

The monitoring and adjustment were taken care of by Guardians like Dionte. Once a month Aleph downloaded any incidents each Conscience's tiny AI had thought were matters of concern, so that the family member could be counseled or advised. At that same time, Dionte performed maintenance checks, injected alpha viruses loaded with fresh stem cells for the organic filaments, and worked with a needle laser and a hair-thin probe to lay in fresh connections or etch new patterns into the chip itself.

The solution of how to bring the family closer together turned out to be simple. It was a matter of a few new connections and a few new filaments, creating a new junction between the implant's simple data-handling functions that connected the implant to the display on the back of the hand and the Conscience functions that connected the implant to the mind.

"They are trying to compromise with the Authority the way they'd compromise with other members of the family and it isn't going to work," she went on, keeping his gaze captured with her own.

If her own Conscience had been fully functional, she never would have been able to make the adjustments required, in herself or in anyone else. She would have been overwhelmed by a guilty need to tell her kin what she had planned and why she thought it would be a good idea. But that had not happened, and during Basante's last appointment with her, she had made it possible for her implant to speak directly to his.

If she had made no mistakes, Basante's implant would respond to the signals it was receiving from hers with endorphins and positive scents. Her own implant whispered in her mind, raw percentages and unfiltered numbers that made up the chemical analysis of Basante's mind. Dionte could not catch them all. She would have to work on that. Obviously, she needed a subprogram to perform the analysis automatically and give her data she could use on the spot. Despite that, Dionte had to hold back a smile, because the numbers told her that her adjustments were working. Basante would hear her words and feel safety and security, not guilt. He would be able to answer her without contradiction from his Conscience. Even better, his implant spoke to hers, telling her what it was doing, allowing her to order adjustments or reversals as they were needed. The method was crude now, but she could improve on it. She would improve on it.

"You understand what I'm saying, don't you, Basante? You see that I'm right?"

Basante stared at her, confused, but only for a moment. "Yes," he said, sounding a little surprised. "I do."

"I am not saying we should give up speaking in the meetings and gathering our support," she said, grasping his hand even more tightly. "Indeed, I am saying that changing the family's mind must be our primary goal. But"—she held up her free hand to stop any interruption he might be thinking to make—"we also must get ourselves ready in case that support doesn't come, or in case it comes late."

A light came into Basante's eyes and spread into his face as fresh confidence took hold of him. "We need Helice Trust."

"We need the child she can provide us."

"Yes." He squeezed her hand, confidence blossoming into eagerness.

"So, you will help me? I can count on you?" *Say yes, say yes, Basante. This has to work, or we're all going to die. All of us, and Pandora with us.*

Basante's smile was warm and genuine and Dionte felt the warmth of it thawing her fears. "Always."

"Thank you, Basante," she whispered. It was going to work. They could still do it. The future had not been stolen from them yet.

Was the change permanent? Despite herself, Dionte searched his face, looking for some sign. Would he be able to think about these matters once she had left him? There was no way to know that yet. Yet.

"If you have doubts," she said earnestly, "if you change your mind, you will tell me, won't you?"

"Of course I will." He squeezed her hand once again. "But I know you are right."

"Thank you," she said again. Then she made herself let go of his hand and stand up. "Now we both have our work to do. We will talk about the steps we must take after the administrators' meeting."

"I will see you there."

They bowed to each other, and Dionte started down the path, her heart singing. It worked, it worked! The system was not complete yet. Time would reveal flaws and required additions, but there was still a little time. With Basante's help she'd be able to make it all right. She could make them understand what was really going on. She could show them directly, without clumsy words, what they needed to do to protect their world and their family from the treachery of the Authority and the Called.

Smiling, she called up her schedule on her data display. Hagin Bhavasar, her birth uncle and the senior tender for the city-mind, was coming in for his check next week. She could review his records easily before then and make her preparations. There would soon be much work that they needed to do directly with Aleph, and it would be a great help to have Uncle Hagin in agreement with them before then.

CHAPTER FIVE

Stem

By the time she made it out of the forest, Chena was glad Mom had insisted she wear the stupid hat and carry a water bottle.

For a long time, the woods had looked just like they did around Offshoot—an endless succession of thick, gnarled tree trunks hung with cablelike vines. Here and there, one of the giants had fallen and turned into a moss-covered hillock overgrown with ferns and saplings straining to reach the sunlight. She saw deer, squirrels, and quail. Once she even thought she saw a bear, but she couldn't be sure.

Gradually the trees became smaller and more slender. The ground between them filled with all kinds of bracken and underbrush, turning the forest floor into a mosaic of greens and yellows dotted here and there with blue or white flowers. Sunlight brightened the world and started Chena sweating. Insects flew in clouds out of the undergrowth, but she seemed to be moving too fast for them to settle on her. Something else she was glad of. Bugs could be amazing to look at, but some of them bit.

Just one more thing nobody warns you about living on a planet.

She'd spent most of her free time during the month hanging around Offshoot's tinky little library, trying to find a decent map of where the railbikes went and how far away the villages were from each other. But there didn't seem to be a single complete map anywhere. She had to piece together the information she found, but there were still big gaps where she hadn't been able to find out anything.

She talked to Sadia about it at lunch one day, but Sadia had mostly shrugged and told her that's the way it was, and what did she want to go wandering around for anyway? There wasn't anywhere better than Offshoot.

"What do you think you know about it?" asked Chena, leaning across the table. "You've never been anywhere."

"Dad took me and Shond to Stem once," she said, poking at her bowl of vegetable stew. "There's a market, and we watched the dirigibles fly over that big lake." For a minute, Chena thought she was going to say something else, but Sadia just scowled at her food. "Nothing to it."

Chena straightened up and watched Sadia dig a piece of potato out of the stew and pop it into her mouth. "You were there once, you couldn't have seen everything. There's supposed to be a theater too."

Sadia gave her a you're-joking look. "It's all the same people running the place. You think they're going to let anybody have anything good?"

Which, Chena had to admit, made a certain amount of sense, but it still wasn't the whole story.

Whatever that story was, though, Sadia wasn't telling. So Chena guessed she'd just have to see for herself.

From her pieced-together map, it looked like Stem was about one hundred kilometers away from Offshoot. Chena had a decent idea of how long a kilometer was. Athena had been three kilometers from tip to tip and she had been able to run up a whole arm and back down again since she was eight.

On top of that, it turned out that riding was easier than walking. The railbike didn't look much like the bicycles she'd seen in the rig games, or even the ones that were used to turn the compost drums. It had two wheels, all right, but they were clamped to the rail. A weird outrigger kind of extension clamped to a second rail to the right of the bike. But if you sat on the seat, held on to the handlebars, and pedaled, it went much faster than she could ever run. It practically flew down the ravines that had been cut by small streams flowing down toward the river. The movement pressed a fresh wind against her face, so she felt cool, at least in the beginning, even though the day was warm and still.

Better than that, Chena felt free. She could almost pretend she could go anywhere, that the rails weren't lined with fence posts and that the whole world really was opening up around her.

When Teal had heard about Chena's trip, she, of course, had wanted to come. She'd followed Chena around in the miniature library, with its two terminals that didn't even have any input jacks, begging Chena to let her come along. When Teal finally hit the tears and the I-don't-get-to-do-anything! stage, Chena was afraid Mom was going to give in. But Mom cut the scene short by saying that while Chena was "gallivanting around the world," she and Teal would have a special day together scrounging stuff for the new house.

They had a house now. Mom had been able to get an advance on her salary to make the rent. The place was dark and had roots coming through the roof, they were still sleeping on the floor, and they had to take baths in a big copper pot, but it was all theirs. They got to learn how to cook on the woodstove and do all kinds of things that did not involve shit, compost, or cleaning up after other people. Now that Mom was making money and paying at least something into the village fund, they only had to put in three hours a day on shift instead of six. When they got enough together so Chena and Teal could go to school, they'd only have to put in two hours.

Chena had really known Teal was over her snit when Teal rolled up close to her in the dark and whispered in her ear, "You're really going to look for spies, right? Because the poisoners are trying to divert messages from Dad."

They hadn't shared a Dad story in weeks. Teal had been too pouty. Relief had rushed through Chena. She'd have her day.

"Right. Stem is a bigger town," Chena had whispered back. "They're bound to have more information there about what's going on. I need to scope the place out. See who we can trust there."

"I'm starting a record of who comes and goes from other towns," said Teal eagerly. "There's this kid on my shift, Michio, he talks about the boat schedules all the time. I think it's like a game with him. I could talk to him." Then she added quickly, "But I wouldn't tell him why I wanted to know."

"That's a go plan," said Chena. "But mostly you've got to keep an eye on Mom while I'm gone. Let me know if there's anybody sneaking around watching her or anything like that."

"Because Dad's got enemies," added Teal solemnly. "Which means we've got enemies, and the spies may be watching Mom to see if they can find him through her."

"Right." Chena nodded, even though Teal couldn't see her in the dark. "So, we've got to look out for her, okay?"

"Okay."

Teal had curled up and gone straight to sleep then, but Chena had lain awake for a while, thinking about the stories they told about their father, and the spy game. Sometimes she wondered if it was a good idea.

I mean, if he was coming back, he'd be back by now, wouldn't he? If he was coming back, Mom wouldn't even have left Athena.

Unless we're right . . . unless the stories are true.

Or unless Dad had just run out on them. Chena had squirmed under her blanket, making Teal stir sleepily like an echo of the restless movement. Sadia and Shond's mom had left them. She just got onto a boat one day, Sadia said, and she didn't come back. Sadia wouldn't talk about what happened to their dad.

She wondered if Teal ever thought about that, if Dad had just left them, because he'd gotten tired of them, or he didn't like being poor anymore, or they were just too much of a hassle to stay with when he could have been out flying around with the Authority. They never talked about it, and Chena realized she didn't really want to. She wanted to tell the stories and believe he was coming home, even when she knew he wasn't.

Chena pushed down hard now on the pedals, trying to put some distance between herself and that idea. Ahead of her, the light made a white wall with just a thin screen of trees in front of it. Another half dozen pedal strokes, and she broke free of the forest into the full sunlight.

In front of her stretched a sea of pale blond grass undulating gently toward a misty blue horizon. A riot of birdsong replaced the rush of wind in the branches. Chena gasped and forgot to pedal for a moment. Her bike glided to a gentle halt.

Birds clung to every stem of grass, all of them singing, chattering, or calling. The noise was deafening. They were all different colors, from browns and blacks to vivid reds, blues, and golds, and even one little one that was deep purple. Even the butterflies fluttering between the grass stems didn't come in more colors.

Then in the distance something big and brown leapt out of the tall grass. All the birds launched themselves into the air in a great black cloud, blotting out the sky. Chena's heart hammered in her chest, but startled fear rapidly turned to astonishment, and then awe. It was a long moment before she was able to tear her gaze away from the tattered cloud of birds and look for the big thing that had caused the mass exodus. Images of wolves and dinosaurs from the games flashed briefly through her mind, and she felt glad of the fence posts for one split second. But whatever it had been, it was as gone as the birds.

Eventually Chena remembered what she was supposed to be doing and applied her feet to the bike pedals again.

After a while, this new part of the world became even more monotonous than the forest. She couldn't see past the thick growth of the grass on either side. The long and steep hills were fun to glide down, but they were a pain to pedal up. The sun's heat was smothering and she was almost out of water. But she kept on going. If her estimates were even close to right, using one of the turnaround points and heading back would make for a longer ride before she got back to people than if she just kept going. She glanced at her comptroller: 11:24. She'd been riding for four hours.

She hadn't ever expected to see the wrist computer again, let alone have her shift supervisor give it to her. But, as she was showing up for her shift, this time to start emptying "night soil," which was as disgusting as Sadia had predicted, that week's guy-with-a-scanner had handed her a paper-wrapped bundle the size of her fist.

"I was told this was yours," he said as he handed it over.

Chena unfolded the paper and saw her comptroller lying inside. Written neatly on the paper itself were the words, *Thank you for the loan, station girl. Come back for your tea.*

Chena had stuffed the paper in her pocket, strapped the comptroller back on her wrist, and tried not to think about it. Part of Mom's month of perfect behavior included having nothing at all to do with Nan Elle, ever again. Regan the cop had not been able to turn up anything against her, or at least nothing that he could prove to get the village court to act against her rather than the guy they'd pinned the murder on in the first place. That was not enough to clear her in Mom's eyes, though. Somehow Chena didn't think anything would ever be enough.

Chena was panting by the time her bike crested the highest ridge. At the top, the grass was only knee-high and she could finally see all around her. The river to her left spread out wide, brown, and slow. The forest was a curving shadow behind her. In front of her waited the end of the world—a ragged semicircle of land that dropped off into a lake of blue and silver that stretched out until Chena could not tell water from sky. A tree-crowned promontory thrust out into the water, allowing her to see the rippling red cliffs that lined the shore.

The rails did not lead to the cliffs, however. They wound the long way down to a curving beach and a cluster of sand dunes.

She couldn't see the actual town from here, but she didn't expect to. It was probably as well hidden in the dunes as Offshoot was in the trees.

Chena kicked off the rail and let the bike cruise down the slope.

"Hhhheeeeee-yaaaaah!" she cried, giddy with success and gathering speed.

Momentum carried her straight through the dunes. She caught glimpses of windows and saw boardwalks crowded with people. Chena waved, although no one was looking at her.

The rail ended in an open-sided depot exactly like the one she'd left in Offshoot. She parked her bike in line with eight or ten others and ran her hand through the scanner on the wood and wire gate. When she did, the lock on the gate clicked opened and let her out into the dune town and onto its busy boardwalks.

The familiar press of bodies and competing conversations enveloped her and Chena felt herself grinning. This was more like it. More like the station, more like a real place. Except during shift change, Offshoot mostly felt empty.

Stem, though, was alive. People stood on the walkways and watched the boats out on the water. They stood on jetties, dangling fishing lines off the side or working around the dirigibles, cages of silver wire and glittering aerogel, that sat on the water waiting to take off. They stepped aside for each other, nodding and saluting as they did. Both men and women wore robes and skirts painted with bright patterns you'd never see in the woods. Chena wondered if these people had to work for their village like they did in Offshoot, or if they all got out of it somehow. Then she wondered how she could find out.

Toward the water, she glimpsed some white, tentlike structures. The crowds seemed even thicker there. Chena slid through the knots and currents of people and headed toward the tents, trying to look casual, like she'd done this a thousand times. She stole glances at the town, careful not to stare. It would mark her. Maybe there weren't real spies here, but she'd bet there were people like Madra, or Regan the cop, or Nan Elle. The kind of people who always wanted to know who you were, what you were doing, and why.

Compared to Offshoot, Stem was flat. All the buildings were dug into the dunes, with sand and thin grasses covering them. The roof plantings were sparse—lots of grasses tipped with tiny purple and red flowers, and thin vines hanging down walls. She didn't see any actual gardens like they had on top of the dorm or the dining hall.

Chena reached the boardwalk closest to the water's edge. The lane broadened out into a wide street. Along the edges, people had set up poles and hung them with canvas to make shady awnings. Men and women sat under the awnings in the middle of collections of baskets, talking to, or even shouting at, the passersby.

"Fresh as a daisy, straight out of the lake, not five minutes ago!"

"Pure dried, take a look at that, smell that, that's pure and strong, that is!"

"Lake plums! Lake plums! Sweet and tangy, right here!"

Chena's smile returned. It was a market, like they had in the stairways on the station some weeks. Except the stuff here looked new.

Chena's good mood put a swing in her stride as she passed through the market, glancing casually into the baskets, but not letting herself be caught by the sellers. Some baskets held piles of dried leaves or brightly colored cloth. One or two held other baskets. There were toys, clothes, even some shoes, although none of them would be much good in the woods, since they were mostly sandals. But there were jackets and fruits and paper books, bread and jugs of stuff that smelled sweet or tangy or just plain strong. Chena felt a familiar soft envy steal over her that she knew came from the sight of so many things she couldn't have.

The cool wind off the water brought the scent of cooking fish and hot spices. Chena's stomach rumbled painfully. She followed the scent to another white tent, where people lined up like they did in the dining hall in Offshoot. Chena spotted a stack of bowls, grabbed one, and joined the line. But before she could get to the pots of whatever smelled so good, a round, brown, bald man walking by with a stack of clean bowls frowned at her.

"Don't know you, do I?" His accent was nasal and he slurred his words together into unfamiliar patterns.

Before Chena could think, she shook her head.

"Lemme see your hand." He balanced the bowls in the crook of one fat elbow and gestured impatiently. Reluctantly, Chena extended her hand, and he studied the mark on the back.

Then he turned his head and spat on the sandy boardwalk. "Get outta here. This is for citizens only. Offshoot's gotta feed its own."

"Please?" Chena tried, putting on her best big-eyed begging look. "I've been riding all morning. I won't take much, I promise."

"Piss off, kid."

"Back at you." Chena pitched her bowl right at the stack in his arms. It hit, and all the bowls tumbled to the boardwalk. She was already off and running by the time she heard shattering ceramic. Her legs were tired, but she tore down the boardwalk, shoving her way between people and dodging around obstacles she barely saw, until the tents were out of sight behind the dunes.

Great, she thought, wrapping her arms tight around herself and staring at the dunes and their sparse, waving grass. *Now what?*

There had to be a place where she could pay for food. She had a couple of metal chits in her pocket that Mom said was twenty positives out of their account. That should be more than enough for a meal, and an emergency comm burst to the receiver at the Offshoot library, if she needed one.

Chena wandered along the boardwalk between the buildings nestled into the dunes. The windows were all tinted, so she couldn't see inside them. She thought she smelled cooking a couple of times, but she didn't see one open door or inviting canopy.

Finally she collapsed against one of the boardwalk rails, took off her hat, and wiped at her forehead. She unslung her water bottle from her shoulder and drank down the last of it, rattling the bottle a little to make sure she'd gotten it all. She hung it back over her shoulder, jammed her hat back on her head, and closed her eyes for a minute, trying to think.

The sounds of voices reached her, not from her right, where the market and busy piers were, but from the left, and a little behind. Chena's eyes flipped open and she turned her head toward the noise, straightening up as she did. It took her a minute to orient on the sounds, but there was laughter as well as talk. Hope rising inside her, she followed the voices.

The boardwalk wound in and out of the curves of three dunes until finally it passed by a low, open doorway into one of the hills. The laughter came out of there; so did the cooking smells. Chena's mouth started watering, and she was in through the doorway before she knew she'd moved.

It looked like there was a party going on. Four men and women stood on a narrow stage at the back singing about "a stroll, and a roll, and get back up again." People, all kinds and all ages, stood around laughing and talking. Women sat on men's laps. Men leaned over women's shoulders and whispered in their ears. People carried trays of food around, offering them so people could pick out whatever they wanted. Chena smelled spices and meat and fresh bread. The scents cramped her stomach up again. She stepped farther into the scented dimness and skirted the crowd to try to find an empty table. She could watch what happened and see how you ordered, or maybe you had to prepay, or—

"Well, then, who let you in here?"

Chena looked up, startled, into the eyes of the handsomest man she had ever seen. His wavy auburn hair fell back from his high forehead. His eyes glowed green, as if sunlight shone behind them. His shoulders and arms were broad, but not ridiculous, like a cartoon, just . . . nice. His skin was a clear pale pink, but unlike most men that color, he had no hint of a beard. He wore a loose white tunic tucked into trousers that were tight enough she could see the strong shape of his legs.

"I, um, just . . ." began Chena, trying desperately to decide what she should be saying or doing here. She felt her cheeks start to burn. "I was hungry and I couldn't get anything down in the group tent, and I—"

"And you smelled food and came in here," he finished for her. "Naturally." He frowned, and even angry, he was still gorgeous. "Who's the reject we've got on the door anyway?" He wasn't looking at her anymore, he was scanning the room.

"I'll go," she said quickly. "I'm sorry. I didn't know—"

"Wait a minute." He put a hand on her shoulder, and Chena felt her heart pound hard against her rib cage. "I'm not mad at you. Listen"—he smiled like he already knew her and liked her—"what's your name?"

"Chena Trust," she said immediately. She knew she should be careful. She knew all about strangers and what could happen, she wasn't stupid, she just wanted him to know her name.

A flicker of some other expression crossed his face, but cleared up right away. "Chena," he said, as if to make sure he had it right. "Why don't you go out and wait by the door? I'll be there in two seconds, all right?"

Chena nodded and retreated. Once she reached the threshold, she glanced back into the dim, crowded interior and saw the man talking with a pale woman and waving his hands. The woman looked angry. Chena bit her lip and ducked around the corner. Had she gotten him in trouble?

But when he came out a couple of minutes later, he was smiling. Looking at him, Chena felt a warmth spread through her. As long as he was smiling, everything had to be okay.

"Well," he said. "I have to apologize for my rudeness. You gave me your name, but I didn't return the compliment. I'm Farin Shas." He saluted her formally.

"I'm Chena Trust." Then she remembered she'd already told him that, and bit her lip against the fresh blush that was already starting.

Farin just raised his eyebrows as if hearing her name for the first time. His brows were thick and full, outlining his green eyes and making them look even brighter. "Trust? There's a portentous name. Who do you trust, Chena? Or does it mean I should trust you?"

He was teasing and she knew it, but no fast answer came to her. All she could do was look at the ground and shrug, although she was kicking herself inside the entire time.

"I'm sorry," he said gently. "You should never have to be teased on an empty stomach. Would you like to have lunch with me?"

As she lifted her gaze, Chena realized he was carrying a basket on his arm with some bundles wrapped in white cloth inside.

"That would be great. Thank you." The words came out fairly steady.

"Then allow me to show you one of the more peaceful places in our bustling little community." He gestured for her to come walk beside him, which Chena did, trying all the time to keep from grinning like an idiot. She didn't want him to think she was just a baby. In the back of her mind she knew Mom would kill her if she ever found out about this. Well, Mom was back in Offshoot, and Chena wasn't going to do anything really stupid. They were in public, and she wasn't going to eat or drink anything he didn't. She knew what she was doing.

Farin led her around the boardwalks until they were back by the water. They came to a small dock with a chip scan on the gate. Farin let it scan his hand and entered a code that brought the words *and a guest* up on the display. He nodded to Chena and she let herself be scanned. The gate clicked open for them.

The dock on the other side was dotted with benches curving around small tables that let you look out over the water and see the boats skimming across the crinkled waves, and a stately dirigible drifting overhead. The cliffs towered over their shoulders, and Chena could see that wind and water had carved dark arches and caves into the rust-red stone.

"I haven't got much here," said Farin, setting his basket on the table. "But this is a very informal arrangement. Next time I hope you'll let me know when you're going to be in town."

"Sure." Chena got the word out without making it squeak, barely.

He lifted the cloth off the basket to reveal a loaf of bread. He picked it up and broke it in half, handing one part to Chena. The inside was full of herbs and cheeses. It smelled fantastic. Once he'd bitten into his, she ate hers and found it tasted even better than it smelled. He also had a cup full of raspberries. He ate a few, then smiled as he offered them to her.

"Contraband from Offshoot." He winked conspiratorially. "They just don't grow out here on the sand."

Chena accepted a few of the sweet, dark red berries and ate them, keeping her attention fixed out across the water. She didn't want Farin to see her staring at him, even though she wanted to watch the way his red-gold hair rippled across his shoulders.

The silence stretched out until Chena wanted to squirm. She looked for something to say and found only the water in front of her. Well, maybe that would do.

"So, um, this whole thing is a lake?" She swept her hand out in a broad arc.

"That's right," said Farin, tearing a piece of bread off of the loaf and popping it into his mouth. He chewed for a moment and swallowed. "It's the biggest lake on Pandora. They named it Superior after a similar body of water on Old Earth." He cocked his head toward her and Chena looked quickly down at the remains of bread in her hands. His accent was mellower than the man's in the food tent and the unfamiliar lilt made the words sound rhythmic, like poetry.

"And those are caves in the cliffs out there?" She nodded to the monoliths.

"They say some of them go on for a kilometer or more." His smile grew sly again. "Not that anyone from the village has ever gone out to see, of course."

Chena swallowed hard. Did he mean to say someone had? Had he? Did he know a way around the fences? Could she maybe find a way to ask him?

But before she could think of the right words, Farin said, "So, Chena, what brought you to Stem?"

Chena caught herself halfway through her shrug and dropped her shoulders. "I just wanted to see someplace different, and I thought maybe . . ." She stopped.

"Maybe what?"

Chena risked a glance at him. Amusement danced in his green eyes, but he seemed genuinely interested.

"I wanted to see if I could figure out a way to make some money. My mom . . ." Pride stopped her, and she shrugged. "I just thought maybe I could make something extra, you know?"

Farin nodded slowly, seriously. "Yes, I very much do know." He gave her a fresh smile, this one just a little sad. "It's hard at first," he said. "And particularly when on your first working day you get hauled in by the cops."

His words brought Chena's head up. "Who told you?"

He just continued to smile gently. "My spies are everywhere."

Spies? Did he know about that too? Who was this guy? Did he think she was stupid? Chena felt on the verge of panic.

Farin laughed. "Easy, Chena." He patted her shoulder. "I'm not working for Regan. Nan Elle told me."

Chena felt her eyes widen. "You know her?"

He nodded. "Yes. I usually see her when I'm in Offshoot. She makes up a regular batch of medicine for me."

"So, she's not a poisoner?" Chena asked tentatively. She should have known not to trust the cop, but Nan Elle was so . . . bizarre . . .

"No." Farin pushed his hair back from his forehead. "The cops just want you to think that so you won't go to her for help. She's outside the system, see, and the hothousers hate that kind of thing."

"What kind of thing?"

"People not staying put." Farin's gaze drifted out across the water. "People not doing exactly what it's predicted they'll do." He jerked his chin inland. "That's why they make it so hard to get from place to place, and why no one is allowed to own a private phone or computer. If people are kept separated, they are easier to handle."

"Somebody said that was to minimize environmental impact." She said it tentatively, testing the idea.

"I've heard that too." Now he shrugged. "It might even be true, but I wouldn't count on it."

Silence again. Chena watched somebody on the jetty haul a fish out of the water on the end of a string. "So why do people let them? Do all this?" It was a question that had been growing inside her all month, and she hadn't even started finding any answers to it.

She glanced back at Farin. He was watching her. Did he like what he saw? Maybe he did, or maybe he just saw a kid.

"You're from the station, right?" he asked. Chena nodded. "I've heard about how things are there. Why do people let the superiors push them around?"

"I don't know," said Chena, thinking of her mother and how they had to leave. "Because they can't stop them, I guess."

Farin turned up his palm to say there-you-go. "It's the same down here." He paused and then said, "The other thing is that the system here really does work. Enough news comes down the pipe that we all know what's going on out in the Called. As bad as it is here, almost everybody agrees it's worse everywhere else, or at least that's what they tell themselves."

Chena was silent. She couldn't think of anything polite to say.

The corner of Farin's mouth curled up. "You're right. It does stink." He popped the last of the bread into his mouth. "I've also been told it's a very common situation." He looked at his empty palms and then wiped them briskly together, dusting the crumbs off.

"Well, that's my lunch break. I've got to get back or I'll get docked."

"You work . . . there?" asked Chena. "You're an actor?"

"And a singer, and host. It's a pretty good living." He folded the cloth and laid it in the basket. "I enjoyed this, Chena Trust. I hope we can do it again." He smiled his warm, golden smile and Chena felt her whole self smile back.

"Sure. Maybe . . . I've got a day off again next week . . ."

He nodded. "I'll look out for you. Ask whoever's on the door to find me." He stood and paused. "And if you bring a pint of raspberries with you, I'll pay for them." He paused again. "In fact, would you take a message back to Offshoot for me? I'd pay for that too."

"Sure!" She stopped short of saying, *Anything.* It might sound . . . weird. Childish.

He reached into his shirt pocket and pulled out a pen and a small notebook. He thought for a moment and jotted down a few words. He folded the paper into thirds and wrote something on the blank side.

"Here," he said, handing it to her. "If you could give that to Pari Sakhil, I'd appreciate it." He dug his hand into his pocket again and handed her a positives chit.

"Oh, you don't . . ." She held up her hands. "I mean, I've got to go back anyway. . . ."

"I'm glad to know you're willing to do me a favor." He took her free hand and folded it around the chit. "But if you want to make yourself some money, Chena Trust, don't ever do something for free when the customer's willing to pay."

Slowly she drew her hand back. "Do you want an answer back?" she asked, ideas flitting through her mind and forming into hopeful possibilities.

"Very good." He nodded with satisfaction. "An answer and a pint of raspberries, and I'll pay for both."

More ideas. Chena felt her spine tingle with the strength of them. "And if somebody had a message for someone here and I needed to know who they were . . . ?"

"Now you're thinking. I could probably tell you the names and homes of most people in Stem." He picked up the basket. "I'll see you soon, Chena Trust." He saluted her briefly, flashed one more smile, and turned away to stroll up the boardwalk.

Chena watched his back until he disappeared around the curve of a dune. Her hand began to tighten around the note from sheer delight, but she stopped herself before she crumpled it. This paper stuff was not as flexible as a sheet screen. She looked at the chit and read the positive code. He had given her enough to pay for half the bike rental, for just a message.

There were possibilities here. She might be able to make this work. If other people were willing to pay for errands and messages . . . if she could make one trip every day, and bring back as much stuff as she could carry . . .

Except she couldn't make one trip every day. She had to work, and they might not be going to school yet, but Mom hadn't stopped insisting they try to learn something, as she put it. Unless Chena could figure out some way to free up her days, this was going to stay nothing but a set of really good ideas.

Chena chewed on her lip as she walked back toward the railbike depot. There had to be a way. She'd find it. But even if she didn't, she would at least make one more trip to bring Farin his answer and his raspberries.

She would see him again.

By the time Chena got back to Offshoot, twilight and flowers filled the forest, and she was as tired as if she'd spent the entire day shoveling compost. But she didn't mind. She held the chit and the note in her pocket like precious secrets. She knew how she could make her errand-running business work. She could help Mom make enough money to get them back to Athena Station and then pay an Authority shipper to take them to some other world where no one would snatch them up for body parts. All she had to do was convince Teal and Mom about a couple of things. When she'd done that, she'd go back to Stem, and she'd see Farin again. They'd talk, and she would tell him about her ideas for running a whole business of carrying packages and letters, and he'd tell her how smart she was, and then . . . and then . . .

Chena stubbed her toe against an uneven board on the catwalk and stumbled forward a few steps. She swore and hurried up the stairs, keeping her eyes firmly on where she was going.

It was shift change. Chena tried to get above the worst of the crowd by climbing the stairs to the catwalks, but even the catwalks were crowded. She found herself being jostled on all sides by people anxious to get to their meals and their baths, or just to get indoors before the mosquitoes rose for the evening.

Below her, she saw Sadia shouldering her way through the crowds as they spread out. She waved, wondering what Sadia had been doing, since it was her day off too. Sadia must not have seen her, though, because she did not wave or even break stride.

Chena shrugged. *Oh, well. I can tell her everything tomorrow.* Well, okay, maybe not everything. Maybe she wouldn't tell Sadia how her heart thumped when Farin smiled. She didn't want Sadia to think she was a stupid little girl with a crush.

The house Mom had rented was on the second level of Offshoot. It was a small place, lashed in the shadows near a cluster of other buildings around a central cistern that caught the water falling from the upper levels and spilled it down to the canals that ran toward the hydro-processing buildings.

The house had been built so that strip windows alternated with thick wooden panels, letting in what little sunlight crept under the thick branches and between their neighbors' houses. Even for an Offshoot house, it was perpetually dim, which was one of the reasons Mom had gotten it so cheap. But now Chena could see light in the windows and her heart rose. She couldn't wait to tell Mom. . . .

She stopped in her tracks. *Careful, Chena. Tell Mom too much and you'll get so grounded . . .*

She shook her head. It was okay. She'd be able to tell her enough.

Who would she say she got the letter from, though? Talking to strangers was not a sport Mom considered appropriate for her and Teal.

If he was a friend of someone, okay, but she sure couldn't say he was a friend of Nan Elle's.

Maybe she didn't have to tell about the letter at all. Maybe she could just tell about the idea of the letter.

Yeah, that'll do it. Secure with that extra thought, Chena pushed open the door.

"Well, there she is," announced Mom. "You were wrong Teal, we won't have to call out the cops after all."

The front room had been completely transformed while she'd been gone. Patchworks of cloth made a colorful rug for the center of the warped floor. A low table, canted either from the tilt in the floor or because its legs were uneven, stood on the rug. Four fat red pillows lay scattered around it. The blank, worn wood of the walls had been polished. Curtains as patchworked as the rug hung in the windows. Vines and flowers stood in baskets and pots in the corners.

"How?" began Chena.

"Ah, you forget, Supernova." Mom smiled. She sat in the middle of the floor with a weird, blocky contraption in front of her and a length of purple material hanging out one edge of it. "I used to be a colony woman, and not a rich one either. I know a thing or three about making do, when I can get the stuff." She gazed in satisfaction at the room. "It's not high design, but it will do, and we can fix it up as we go."

"Look at this, Chena!" exclaimed Teal, jumping to her feet and pulling her sister toward the low table. "We get to eat on the floor!"

"Well, not quite, but close." Mom also stood and enfolded Chena in an embrace that went on long enough that Chena knew she had really been a little worried. "How was the great adventure?"

"Great," answered Chena. "Where'd you get all the . . ." She gestured at the rug and curtains.

"Amerand Dho, the mother of one of Teal's friends, told me there was a rag room in the recycler complex. Free for the taking. Same place we got your hat." Mom pulled the object in question off and hung it on a wooden hook on the back of the door that also had not been there when Chena left. "I borrowed the sewing machine from her as well."

"I helped," announced Teal. "I cut stuff out and held it together so Mom could pin it all up. I screwed the table back together—"

"Nailed," corrected Mom.

So that's why its crooked, thought Chena, but she didn't say anything.

Mom walked over to the stove, where something smelled really great. "Are you hungry?"

Chena's mouth was watering worse than it had when she met Farin. She didn't even need to answer. Mom just started scooping soup into a bowl.

They gathered around the new table, eating and talking. The soup wasn't as good as the stuff in the dorm, but it felt great inside her. Mom and Teal told her about the scavenger hunt through the recycling complex, looking for stuff that wasn't too old or worn out or dirty. They had pallets in the bedroom now. Apparently Teal had spent the better part of the afternoon up on the roof whacking the dust out of them. This was not, according to her report, anywhere near as stellar as getting to build a table.

Chena told them about the grasslands with the birds, and about the lake that sparkled and filled the horizon, and the cave-riddled cliffs. She described the market, and the jetties with the people coming and going. She left out breaking the bowls, and replaced the story of how she finally got lunch with a few vague remarks about a tent and sandwiches. She also left out her money idea. She needed to convince Teal to go along with the scheme first. If she was going to make this work, Teal would have to take her shifts.

The night thickened, the room dimmed, and Chena found herself yawning until she thought her face would split wide open. Mom lit an extra lamp, but the brightness didn't wake Chena up any. Her head started to droop toward her empty bowl. Mom laughed.

"Okay, big day's over and work starts again tomorrow. Help me wash up, and you two are going to bed."

Chena brought in buckets of water from the cistern and Mom added hot water from the kettle on the stove. The kettle was new too. They washed the red-brown bowls and tarnished spoons and put them on the new shelf to dry. Mom had obviously put that one together. It didn't tilt at all.

Another bucket of water was hauled in and faces were washed and teeth were brushed and Chena was finally able to collapse onto her new pallet. It was thin and lumpy and smelled earthy, but, like the soup, it felt great. She placed the note and the chit underneath the pillow for safekeeping and snuggled down under the woolen blankets.

I'll talk to Teal in the morning, she thought, pulling the blanket up to her ears. *Sleep now.*

"Chena," whispered Teal excitedly. A hand shook her by the shoulder. "Chena!"

"Get off." Chena shoved her hand away. "We'll talk in the morning."

"But I caught a spy."

Chena pulled the blanket the rest of the way over her head. "Tell me tomorrow."

"No." Teal yanked the blanket down. "Now. He was talking to Mom."

"Huh?" Chena opened both eyes and looked at her sister. Teal was just a blur in the darkness, but her whisper was urgent.

And I'm definitely not getting any sleep till I hear this.

"What'd he want?"

"Shh," breathed Teal. Chena just rolled her eyes.

Teal shoved the sleeve of her nightshirt up, exposing her comptroller. "I got him coded in," she whispered proudly. She touched the display stud and a soft silver glow lit up her face, turning it into a mass of blobs and shadows. " 'Spy showed up at twelve-thirty hours—' "

"Showed up?" The words trickled into Chena's mind. "He came here?"

Teal nodded rapidly, making wisps of hair flutter around her face. "We were just carrying the table parts up from the recycler."

"Keep going." Exhaustion pulled back from Chena, leaving room for wariness.

" 'Spy was a man,' " Teal read. " 'Taller than Mom, with short black hair and skin about my color and gray eyes, wearing a black shirt and white canvas pants and boots.' "

"What did he . . ." Chena stopped and rephrased it, to keep within the feel of the game. "What did he say he wanted?"

Teal checked her notes. " 'Spy gave his name as Experimenter Basante from the Alpha Complex.' "

Alpha Complex. The hothouse. Chena bit back her questions.

" 'Spy said he'd be pleased to talk to Helice Trust in private.' " Teal paused. "I'm not making this up, he really talked like that."

"I believe you," Chena assured her. "Keep going."

" 'Mom ordered Teal to go outside. Teal stood sideways next to the door so she could listen, but she wasn't able to make notes on everything exactly, because she didn't know how to spell it all and they talked fast.' "

"It's okay," said Chena, before Teal added a longer apology.

" 'Spy asked Mom if she'd thought about her future, now that she'd been living here for a month. Mom answered she liked it here just fine. She had a job and her girls were happy. Spy asked Mom if she wasn't interested in some comfort, some security. Mom answered she'd never had that anyway, so why should she be willing to sell herself for it?' "

Sell herself? To who? For what? What is she talking about? Chena bit her lip, which was already sore from the sun and from her chewing on it all day. Teal didn't seem to know what she was saying, she was just having fun reporting it all.

" 'Spy talked about the Diversity Crisis and how important it was that everybody help out,' " Teal went on. " 'He also talked about assuming debts and making regular payments to somebody or the other, Teal didn't catch the name.' " Teal squinted at the display. " 'Mom said thank you but we were all just fine. Spy talked about Diversity Crisis again and Mom said what a lovely day, thank you for stopping by, but we have a lot of work to do. Spy left.' "

Teal sat back, and in the faint green light from her comptroller Chena could see her face had gone suddenly serious. "They're still after her," she whispered. "The hothousers. They're not going to leave her alone."

"They're going to have to," said Chena firmly, angrily. "Because she's just going to keep on saying no. Mom is not going to let them experiment on her, no matter what." Inside, she was thinking, *Why didn't Mom say there'd been a man here? How come she didn't tell me?* Then, guiltily, she remembered all the things she hadn't told Mom about today.

This keeps up, we're going to fill this whole house with enough secrets to bust apart the walls.

"Did you find out anything new in Stem? About Dad?" Teal wanted to play, and she'd already managed to chase sleep away, so Chena figured she'd better go along with it.

Chena considered what to tell her. "No, not about Dad. But I did find out something new about that woman, the old woman Nan Elle."

"Is she a spy too? I've seen her. She looks like she should be a spy." Her face squinched up as if she just tasted something sour.

"Spies don't look like spies, vapor-brain," growled Chena, smacking Teal gently on the shoulder to let her know she was being silly. "If they looked like spies, everyone would know, and what would be the point?" Teal smacked her back, and they slapped at each other's hands, giggling for a few minutes, before Chena went on. "Yes, she's a spy, but she's working on Dad's side." *Is she really? Do I really know that? Farin could've lied to me. But why would he? Cops always have something going on, but Farin, he's just a person.*

"She is?" Teal was saying thoughtfully, as if she were turning the idea over in her head and seeing how it fit into the scenario they already had laid out. "Then what about the cop?"

"I don't think he's bad," said Chena slowly. "But he doesn't know what's really going on, so he's going to make mistakes. We have to keep an eye out for him because he could get in the way." Then she thought of something else. "The stuff you've coded, Teal, you did encrypt it, didn't you?"

"How dumb do you think I am?" she asked indignantly. "Encrypted and substituted. Nobody's reading this stuff but me."

"Okay, good. Now, I'm toasted. I've got to get some sleep." She pulled the blankets back up again and laid down on the earthy-smelling pallet.

"Chena?"

Chena squeezed her eyes shut. "What?"

"Why'd it have to be Dad that went away? Why couldn't they get someone else?"

Chena suppressed a groan and rolled over so she faced her sister's approximate location.

"It had to be him because they needed someone who was a really good pilot. We figured all that out, remember?"

"Yeah, but the Authority has thousands of really good pilots. I mean, that's the point, isn't it?"

Why are you doing this? I don't want to talk about this. Chena forced herself to think in terms of the story, of their Dad the brave spy and pilot, not anything else. "They do, but they're not always sure they can trust them." The story blossomed inside her. "See, the poisoners are working on a whole bunch of Called worlds. They have to work in small labs and keep what they're doing a secret. But they also have to talk to each other to tell each other what they're doing. So they use messengers. They're bribing the Authority pilots to carry messages back and forth for them, between the labs where they're making their poison."

"But the Authority knew nobody bribed Dad," added Teal. "Because we didn't have any money."

"Right." Chena smiled to the darkness. "The Authority knew Dad was honest, so they came to him, and they said, 'We need you for this mission,' and he said, 'What about my wife and kids? I can't leave them. It might be dangerous,' and the Authority said, 'You don't have to worry about them. We'll watch out for them, but we might have to hide them until your work is finished.' "

"And Dad said, 'All right, I'll do it, because we can't let the poisoners go free,' " jumped in Teal, her voice low and shaking with drama. " 'There are too many lives at stake, but I'll need to know what happens to my family, so I can make sure they're all right.' "

The story took hold inside Chena. It felt warm and comfortable, like Farin's smile. "So Dad flew out to one of the Called worlds where they were pretty sure there was a lab, and he started asking questions, carefully, because he's a spy too now, but he's spying for the Authority. He started asking about making extra money, and who'd have good jobs, and he didn't care what it was as long as the pay was good, that kind of thing."

Chena heard cloth rustle as Teal nodded and pitched in. "Pretty soon, a bribed pilot told Dad that there were these people who'd pay him to take coded messages to other planets. Secret stuff, and how he wasn't supposed to get caught with it. So Dad said sure, he'd do it, and the pilot gave him the message."

She fell silent, and Chena picked up where she left off. "The message, which was encrypted. But Dad said, 'Don't I get to meet these guys?' And the bribed pilot said, 'Not until you prove you can do the job.' "

Teal let out a long happy breath. "So Dad's got to deliver that message first before he can find out who's sending it. I like it."

"Me too," admitted Chena softly.

"Do you want to go to sleep now?" asked Teal.

Finally! "Yes, so shut up, would you?"

Teal blew a raspberry at her, which Chena ignored. After a minute, Chena heard her sister wriggling around and getting comfortable. She closed her eyes gratefully and drifted to sleep.

That night, she dreamed of Farin, but in the morning she couldn't remember what those dreams had been about.

CHAPTER SIX

Witness

Madra showed up during breakfast, which was brown bread toasted on top of the stove and raspberries and early apples, eaten raw.

There was a knock, Mom opened the door, and Madra stepped in, surveying the room. For once, she was not smiling.

Instead, she sighed and put her hands on her hips. "So, you did raid the stores."

"Is there a problem?" asked Mom, pushing the door closed.

Madra's mouth pursed, as if it were trying to smile on its own and she was trying to tell it not to. "There is if you didn't tell the shift supervisor that you're not living in the dorms anymore."

"I didn't tell the shift supervisor anything. There was no supervisor there when I went in." Mom sat back down at a little table and nodded toward an empty pillow. "Won't you have a seat?"

Madra pressed her lips together in a thin line. She did sit, however, folding her legs neatly under her. "In that case, we do have a problem. More than one, actually," she added under her breath. "But the one that relates to you is that the recycling stores are only for the people who are living in the dorms and working exclusively for the village."

"Well, I had no way of knowing." Mom folded her hands on the tabletop and gazed calmly at Madra. "There should be a sign posted."

Madra nodded. "You're right, there should be. I'll see about it. But the fact remains that you now owe the village for what you took."

"Owe?" Mom's voice hardened. "For a broken table, some dirty pillows, and a few scraps of fabric?" Chena felt herself tensing up. Here it came again. Money. How they didn't have enough, and they weren't doing the right things with it. . . .

"I'm afraid those are the rules," said Madra softly. "The value isn't in the materials themselves, the value is in what they could be used for, and by whom. You are working, you are making money, and your labor isn't being given to the village, so some of your money has to be."

"I still work for the village. We all put in shifts."

"Reduced shifts, and"—Madra raised her index finger—"you're not doing the heavy labor." She lowered her finger, and her gaze, so she was talking to the table. "I'm afraid these are the rules. It's my fault that you didn't know them and I'm sorry. But you either have to give the things back or you have to pay for them."

Mom's face had gone rigid. Her hands, still on the table, began to curl into claws. "May I ask you who decided to alert you to this shocking impropriety?"

"Well, I confess, that's part of the problem." Madra glanced at Teal and Chena, who were sitting there completely intent on the conversation. Mom's gaze followed Madra's.

"Girls, why don't you start on the breakfast dishes?"

They moved obediently. Chena prodded at Teal to keep her going. They needed to hear, yes, but they didn't need to call attention to the fact that they were listening.

"The person who told me was Experimenter Basante," said Madra, as Teal and Chena carried the breakfast dishes to the basin by the stove. Chena waved toward the door, indicating that Teal should go get fresh water.

"From the hothouse?"

Teal made a show of stomping her foot, and Chena frowned at her. Teal made the piss-off sign and left to get the water.

"Yes," said Madra.

Chena ladled hot water from the pot on the stove into the dish basin. Basante was the spy. They were talking about Teal's spy.

"Helice, have the hothousers told you what kind of experiment they want you for?"

"Yes." Mom's next few words were lost under the sound of Teal banging open the door and grunting dramatically as she lugged in the bucket of water. ". . . after me for it since I decided to emigrate."

Chena frowned hard at her sister and grabbed the bucket away, splashing water all over the floor.

"Girls," said Mom warningly, without turning around.

Chena frowned down again at Teal's stubborn face, almost ready to yell. But she didn't. She just tipped cold water in with the hot.

Behind her, Madra said, "Helice, I don't know if you fully understand the situation here."

Chena swirled the dishes around in the water a little and then rubbed a thick cake of the omnipresent yellow soap on the rag. Teal was staring at Mom. Chena elbowed her to get her to stop.

"But I'm sure you will be pleased to enlighten me," Mom said.

Chena's throat tightened as she picked one of the bowls up out of the water. Her hands scrubbed at it without her mind paying attention to what she was doing.

"I'm not saying the rumors of the hothousers snatching people out of their beds are true, but I'm not saying they aren't either. The complexes have been threatened, and as usual, we are the ones who are going to suffer."

Chena dumped the bowl into Teal's hands so she could dry it.

"Madra, I appreciate all the help you've been, but what business is this of yours?"

Chena scowled and forced herself to keep her eyes on the bowls remaining in the cloudy water. She heard the thunk as Teal put the dry bowl on the shelf.

"Because they may not just stop at making trouble for you. They may decide to make trouble for the entire village."

"I hope you're not saying that is my fault?" asked Mom indignantly. Chena gave Teal the next bowl.

"No," answered Madra. "If you want to see me as an interfering busybody, that's fine. You're not alone. But I care what happens to the people in my village, and I don't want to see anybody sold off for body parts."

Crash! Chena jumped. Teal stood shamefaced beside the shattered remains of the bowl. She'd probably tried to put it on the shelf without looking.

"Vapor-brain . . ." groaned Chena.

Mom was on her feet, her face thunderous. "Both of you, outside, and *close* the door."

Chena didn't even dare to protest. She just grabbed Teal's arm and dragged her out the door, kicking it shut behind her.

"Good job, you nit." She turned Teal to face her. "Now—"

But Teal didn't let her finish. "Shut up and come on!"

Teal ran to the back of the house. Chena followed, uncertain but curious. Teal skidded to a halt beside the tree trunk and grasped the thick rope lashings that held the house to the tree. Before Chena had time to ask any questions, Teal swarmed up the wall, using the ropes as a ladder, and disappeared into the unkempt growth that covered their roof.

What are you doing? Chena grabbed a couple of ropes and found her footing so she could follow her sister up. It wasn't hard. Chena was alternately surprised and angry that Teal had been the one to find this way up.

She waded through the tall grass and wild creepers to where Teal hunkered down in the greenery beside the chimney. She pressed her ear right against the clay pipe. As Chena got close, Teal put her finger to her lips and motioned for Chena to get down.

Chena wrinkled her forehead, but she did it. The pipe was warm from the stove, but not too hot. After a moment, she realized she could hear Mom and Madra, soft but clear.

"Even here, I own my body," Mom was saying.

"Not if you break the law, you don't."

"Is that what they're saying I've done?"

"Not yet." Madra paused and Chena bit her lip, straining her ears until they ached so she could catch every word.

"Listen to me, Helice. I've seen this before, plenty of times. The hothousers track down somebody full of useful alleles, and they offer them credit and comfort to sell off their bone marrow or to rent out their womb. If the person doesn't bite, they start enforcing every regulation in existence until they fine them back into the dorms. If the person sticks it out down there, they end up breaking some little law, and then their right to body ownership is forfeit."

"They can't be sentenced to . . ."

"Not sentenced, no, but the hothousers have automatic access to anybody in custody."

"Chena . . ." whispered Teal. Chena glanced at her sister. Teal had gone dead white. Her chin trembled.

"Shhh . . ." Chena wrapped her arm around Teal's shoulder. "It will be all right. We haven't done anything. They can't get us."

"Right." Teal gripped Chena's hand so hard it hurt. "Right."

Without letting go of her sister, Chena pressed her ear against the chimney pipe again.

"If that is what is going to happen, what do you suggest I do?" Mom was asking. She still sounded angry, but now she also sounded tired.

"Leave," said Madra calmly. "There's nothing else you can do."

"Leave? And go where? Back to the station? My children will be begging in the corridors and going without food to pay for air. To get anywhere farther, the Authority demands a hefty chunk of positive balance. I can't even pay my debts."

"Your children are Authority citizens, you can send them to one of the cities."

"But I'm not an Authority citizen and would not be allowed to go with them. No."

"Helice, what happens to them if you're taken in? They'll become public wards. I won't be able to protect them for long."

Mom was silent for a long, long moment. Grass and ferns tickled Chena's ears. Her nose filled with the scent of moss and woodsmoke. Her arm clenched around Teal's shoulders, drawing her sister close, to comfort herself as much as to comfort Teal. This wasn't happening. It couldn't happen. It wouldn't. Mom wouldn't let it. Never. Chena closed her eyes against the prickle of tears. She wouldn't cry. This was just talk. What did Madra know? She didn't know anything.

"Thank you for your concern," said Mom. "When are you going to assess what I've stolen?"

Silence. "It won't be that much." Pause. "Helice, please consider what I've said. This is just the beginning. They will have what they want from you."

"So why don't they just swoop down and carry me off?" Mom demanded.

"Would you believe because they don't want to spook us too badly?" answered Madra. "Once upon a time, they could take whoever they wanted and do whatever they wanted with them. But there was a riot. One of their precious domes got destroyed by a bunch of villagers who had finally had enough. Apparently there was even some help from inside the dome. After that, a charter got written up. Now they can only experiment on lawbreakers or volunteers, or their village can take them to court. Village court, no less. It makes them at least a little careful. Even now." Madra paused, and in her mind's eye Chena saw Madra shake her head. "But I wouldn't put too much faith in their restraint. They still see you and me, anybody outside their complexes, as raw materials, and they'll only put up with so much protest from us."

"Then why don't you leave? Why doesn't everybody leave?"

"Because, unlike you, the rest of us have no place to go."

Below them the door opened and the door closed. Although she knew they were screened by the weeds, Chena pressed herself and Teal even flatter against the roof. They heard footsteps on the catwalk. She listened as they faded, grateful that Teal decided to stay quiet.

After a moment, the door opened again.

"Chena? Teal?" called Mom.

They glanced at each other, guilty of eavesdropping, but not sure whether Mom realized it or not.

"Coming!" called Chena.

They clambered down the lashings and side by side walked to the front of the house. Mom leaned against the threshold, watching them. Chena tried to keep her head up, to act casual, but beside her, Teal shuffled.

"How much did you manage to overhear?" Mom didn't sound angry now.

Chena decided this was probably one of those times when it was better to tell the truth. "Pretty much all of it."

Mom nodded, smoothing her hair back over her scalp. "Come back in here. We don't need to discuss this in the street."

Mom stood aside and Chena and Teal walked past her. They stopped beside the table, but neither one of them sat down. Mom closed the door behind them and stood there for a moment, one hand on the knob and one hand on the smooth wooden surface.

"All right," she sighed at last, and turned around. "So, now you know. The man who came here yesterday was from the hothouse, and he wants me to work for them."

"Don't they pay?" asked Teal, nudging a pillow with her toe.

A fleeting smile crossed Mom's face. "Yes, they do. Very well. The thing I have a problem with is what they want me to do." She took a deep breath. "He wants me to have a baby for them."

"A baby?" exclaimed Teal before Chena was even sure she understood what had been said. "How can you have a baby for them? Dad's not even here." She stopped, realizing what she had said and how stupid it was.

Mom crossed the room and sank low into one of the pillows. "It is possible that I could have a baby without your father, Teal."

"But you wouldn't do that?" Teal hurried to Mom's side, putting both hands on her shoulder. Chena couldn't move. The words and their implications rooted her to the floor. Sadia's mom had disappeared. Had the hothouse taken her? Madra said it happened. Had they wanted her to have a baby for them? Would they take Mom away?

Mom actually looked sheepish. "It is vaguely possible that I could have another baby one day without your father," she said, looking more at her hands than at them. "What I will not do . . ." She stopped herself and started over again. "What I do not want to do is to have a baby and give it away, especially when I don't know what will happen to it. I don't even know if they will keep it alive or use it for spare parts when they can't use me. I do not want to do that to a brother or sister of yours."

Chena swallowed hard. Her hands were cold as ice and she felt them begin to shake. She didn't like the way Mom was talking. She didn't like the uncertainty under her voice.

"But from what Madra was telling me, the people in the hothouse may start to make it very hard to say no."

Chena did not want to hear any more. She had to stop this. Right now. "I know how to get money," she blurted out. "I thought it out yesterday."

Mom looked up at her. Chena wasn't sure how to read her face.

She looked both hopeful and doubtful at the same time. "And what way is that?"

"I can run errands on the railbikes." Chena sank to her knees so she could look right into Mom's eyes. "I've already got a job. Somebody gave me a message yesterday and paid me to take it to someone else."

"Sombody gave you a message? Somebody gave you money?" Mom sat up straight, gentleness and exhaustion gone from her face and voice. "And you didn't tell me yesterday?"

Chena bit her lip. She had said too much. Now she had to explain it. How was she going to explain this?

Start with an apology. "I'm sorry," she said. "I didn't want to say anything until I was sure I could do it."

Mom's frown plainly said she did not believe a word of that. "Start talking, Chena Trust."

A story came to her then, like the stories about Dad. No, not like the ones about Dad. This one was mostly true. Chena swallowed her hesitation and did as she was told.

"I got to Stem, and I tried to eat in their dining hall, but they wouldn't let me, because they said it was only for citizens." She watched her hands in her lap, twisting their fingers together. "I got the serving guy mad and I was scared to stay by the shore, but I was hungry and I was wandering around looking for somewhere to eat. I ran into Farin, he's a friend of Sadia's, and I thought he was okay, really." She risked a glance up at Mom. Her face hadn't softened at all, but Chena had no choice but to keep going. "He got me lunch and we were talking and he said he had a friend in Offshoot he wanted to get a note to, and I said I'd take it, and he said he'd pay for it. So I did and he did, and I thought, you know, I bet if I could do a lot of this I could actually make money. But I didn't know if it was going to be against any of the rules. They have so many here, so I didn't want to say anything until I'd had a chance to go to the library and look it up."

After a few anxious heartbeats, Chena saw Mom's frown relax. It had worked. She was listening. Even better, she was believing.

"Well, if it's not against the rules, it is a good idea," said Mom. "But you still have your shifts to pull, and I want you in school as soon as we can get you there."

"I know," said Chena, eagerness rising in her voice. This would work. It would work. "But if I could do this, I could help get us money to go to school. I was gonna give part of the money I earned to Teal if she would take my shifts." Now both Mom and Teal looked dubious. "We only have to put in a few hours a day now, and we don't have to do any of the heavy stuff. She can do my work just as well as I can." Chena gave Teal a pleading look. *Please, please, go along!*

"Half," said Teal coolly.

Shock stiffened Chena's spine. "You're crazy! A quarter."

"Half," Teal repeated.

Chena snorted and stopped just short of making the piss-off sign. "You're only going to have to work an extra couple hours. I'm going to be working all day—"

"As pleased as I am to have such fiscally savvy children," Mom interrupted, touching Chena's raised hand and pressing it gently back down onto the table, "we have not determined whether this project is actually going to happen yet." Both girls turned to her and waited. Mom ran her hand through her hair and rubbed the back of her neck, shaking her head.

"This was not what I planned for you," she said softly. "I had thought you would be able to go to school. That I would be able to support you, like a mother should support her children. Children should not have to worry about whether or not the family is going to be able to get along. But then, children should not have to be apprenticed out at ten years old because their parents can't keep them from starving any other way." She wasn't looking at them now. She was staring out the slit windows at the shifting shadows that patterned the catwalk. "But if wishes were fishes, we'd all cast nets. We have to work with what we have." Her attention came back to the room and her daughters. "We will talk to Madra about this scheme of Chena's. If she agrees that it is not violating any regulations, then Chena you can give it a try, if you can negotiate the price with your sister." A smile flashed across Mom's face. "And if we agree on a code of conduct for your enterprise. I will not tolerate any more omissions of fact from you, understand me, Chena?" Her eyes were hard and sharp as glass and bored right through Chena's heart. "If I catch you out again, that's the end of this." Her hand slashed through the air between them. "I don't care if we have to end up living on the rooftops."

"Yes, Mom," said Chena, keeping her voice subdued and serious. Inside, she cheered. It *was* going to work. She'd be bringing in money and everything would be all right. It might take a while, she knew that, but it would get better. They'd go to school. They'd get real jobs that paid. They'd get out of here one day and go somewhere where no one could touch them.

Like Mom said, they'd make it all right.

In the end, she talked Teal into splitting the money into thirds—a third for Chena, a third for Teal, and a third for Mom, to pay their debts and squirrel away so they could leave. Once that was agreed to, Mom took Chena down to talk to Madra about the plan. Madra looked dubious at first and looked regulations up on four different sheets, but in the end she confirmed she couldn't find anything against it.

The scary part came right after that, when Mom walked Chena up to the cop's house. Chena explained the whole idea to Constable Regan, and he just sat there, one muscle in this hollow cheek twitching.

Finally Chena fell silent, having run dry of words. Regan reached across his desk, picked up a sheet of paper, and began to write on it. He filled the page with words and signed it in big, swooping letters.

"Permission granted," he said, handing her the page. "Good luck."

Mom squeezed Chena's shoulder, and Chena had to keep herself from jumping up and cheering. Instead, she just folded the letter up carefully and tucked it into her pocket.

"Thank you, Uncle Constable," she said, saluting him carefully.

"Step safe and careful, Niece." He actually smiled a little as he returned her salute.

Once Chena had the letter of approval from Constable Regan, rounding up clients was easy. Everybody with money seemed to want something passed over to Stem, and a large chunk of them wanted something brought back. Comm bursts between the libraries were expensive and came with no guarantee they'd stay private. Taking a boat down to Stem took a whole day, which meant you had to wait for your off-shift day and hope your schedule matched the boat's.

Mom advised Chena to set her prices as high as she wanted, and let people argue her down, but not so low that she couldn't pay her expenses. Mom wasn't paying the bike rental anymore, and Chena had to buy canvas from the recycling center so Mom could make a backpack for her, plus there was food and water every day during the trip, and rain gear, and gloves for cold mornings.

Eventually she worked her prices out to five positives for a letter, ten for a letter and reply, and twenty for a package, with another ten tacked on for each kilogram over the first one. Her skin grew bark brown from the sunlight and her legs grew strong from the peddling. She learned the names of everyone in Offshoot, and half of Stem.

Best of all, she saw Farin almost every day. He showed her where she could buy food, and overpaid her for the raspberries, saying she was on commission until the growing season ended. His delight in her ability to acquire these small treats could fill her entire day, no matter how long the ride, no matter how hard it rained, or how hot it got. He still told Chena how much he loved her only in her mind when the lights were out, but she was certain that would become real too. One day, before her family left, he would take Chena in his arms and he would tell her not to go. He would say that he wanted her to stay with him. Or better yet, he would say he wanted to come with them. . . .

Those dreams, and the light in Mom's eyes when Chena came home and handed over the day's take, were all she needed to keep herself going.

"You're a wonder and a half, Supernova," Mom said, hugging her at the end of the first week. "We'll have you two in school before the year's out at this rate."

Chena made a face. She didn't want to be in school when she could be out on jobs and seeing Farin, but she consoled herself with the fact that she'd still be able to work two days a week. Anything was better than nothing.

The only thing that was not going perfectly was that she was breaking the rules Mom laid down. She was running errands for Nan Elle.

She hadn't intended to, but she had to go up there. Farin had written Nan Elle a letter, and she took the money. She had to deliver it. She couldn't let him down.

There were a dozen people sitting in front of the cluster of houses where Nan Elle lived, old men and women, women with babies, kids off the shifts. All of them had a bright red rash on their face and arms. Some of the blisters were the size of grapes. Just looking at them made Chena wince. She edged her way between them, trying not to touch anybody. Mom had warned her about touching anybody with a rash or a cough. She didn't really need to be told. There weren't any doctors, there wasn't any medicine. If they caught something, there wasn't any kind of help.

Chena really wanted to know which hothouser came up with that brilliant idea. That business Nan Elle had given her about disturbing the microsphere with antibiotics and antivirals must have come from a complete vapor-brain.

Nan Elle's door was open. No one in the line said anything as Chena peeked inside the workroom. They all watched her, though. Chena could feel their gazes fastened on her shoulders, and it made her shiver.

Nan Elle had all her lamps on. A young woman a few years older than Chena sat in the examination chair. Tears slid down the woman's ravaged face. Blisters the size of baby fists distorted her cheek and swelled her right eye completely shut. Nan Elle smeared her with something green, and the woman whimpered softly, obviously trying not to cry out.

"You wait where you are, station girl," said Nan Elle, although Chena could have sworn she had made no noise coming in. "I'm not done here."

Chena looked at the floor, the bookshelves, the aquarium pipes, the steam rising from the pots that simmered on the stove, the long table with its jars and boxes, mortars, and bits of plants and mushrooms, anywhere but at Nan Elle and the crying woman.

At last she heard Nan Elle say, "That'll burst those tonight. When they start to go, you keep your face clean, you understand? Clean with hot water, I don't care how much it hurts. Then you put this on the open sores." She handed the woman a thin wooden box the size of her palm. "When they're good and coated, you cover them up with clean cloth. You'll be scarred, there's nothing to be done there, but if you do as I say, you get to keep your eye."

The woman nodded and stood up, clutching the box. She hurried away, like she couldn't stand being in the room.

Only when the door had shut did Nan Elle turn her attention to Chena.

"It's called nettle blight," she said. "We get it every summer. There's a weed in the fields with these nasty, hairy little seedpods. Burst them open when you're swinging a scythe and those hairs dig into your skin and you get all kinds of infected." She looked Chena up and down. "Not your problem, though. What are you here for that's so important you're jumping the line?"

"I've got a letter for you." Chena thrust the paper at her. She wanted out of here as badly as the blistered woman.

"Do you?" Nan Elle took the unfamiliar object and squinted at it for a moment before she opened it up. "I'd heard about your little business, station girl. A pretty thing it is too." She scanned Farin's note. Chena itched to know what was in it, but she kept her gaze on the bookshelves.

"Well, well, a pretty scheme indeed." Nan Elle thrust the letter into one of her apron's many pockets. "I'll give you an answer if you'll wait there."

Chena opened her mouth and closed it again. She had promised Mom not to have anything to do with Nan Elle, but really Mom had meant not to accept any medicine from her. This was different. Right? This was legitimate business.

She bit her lip. *Just this once,* she told herself. *Get it over with.* "Sure."

Nan Elle got out ink, a wooden dipping pen, and thick mottled paper. She scratched and scribbled, muttering to herself the whole time.

As she stood there watching, a question formed inside Chena. What harm could it do to ask? "How do you know Farin?"

Nan Elle did not look up from her laborious writing. "Didn't he tell you?" She cocked one gleaming eye at Chena. "No, he didn't. I suppose he thought you wouldn't trust him if he did."

"Tell me what?" Chena tried to sound more defiant than nervous.

"He's my grandson."

Shock stole Chena's voice. Farin? With the green eyes and auburn hair and beautiful smile? He was Nan Elle's grandson? He was so . . . so . . . perfect. How could he be . . .

Aware that she was being stupid, Chena still couldn't think of anything to say. So she just stood there and watched the old woman write. If Nan Elle noticed, she didn't say anything. She just kept working until she'd filled two separate sheets.

"Now, that'll be a minute to dry." Nan Elle straightened up and thrust her pen back into the ink bottle. She tuned her gaze back to Chena, who still stood silently, trying to get past what she had just learned. "You know you could make even better money selling people's secrets."

"What?" The words jerked Chena's attention fully back to the old woman.

Nan Elle grinned, showing all the gaps between her teeth. "If you read the letters you carried and then blackmailed people, you'd make a great deal more for your troubles."

Chena snorted and waved off the idea. "Yeah, right, and lose all my customers. No, thanks."

To her surprise, Nan Elle nodded approvingly. "You're not a fool, station girl. Very good."

"Is your ink dry yet?" asked Chena. "I've got other people to take care of." She jerked her thumb over her shoulder.

"As have I." Nan Elle blew gently on the two sheets and folded them each up separately. "There's your answer for young Farin." She handed Chena the first sheet. "And here's for Drapada Shi. I will pay for an answer."

Chena stared at the second sheet, her hand frozen halfway in the act of taking it. "You want me to take a letter for you?"

"And, in all likelihood, packages. This is an excellent idea of yours, Chena. I expect to have much business for you."

"But . . ." Chena swallowed. *But Mom told me not to. . . . I don't want to.*

Nan Elle's dark eyes glittered brightly in the lamplight. "Come, now, are you going to turn me down? Didn't Farin recommend my name to you?" She shuffled closer. "Aren't you doing this because you need all the money you can get? Planning on leaving, are you? How soon do you want to get away?"

Chena bit her lip. Nan Elle nodded silently and folded her hand around the letter. "Come back, station girl. I will have work for you."

And she did. Chena delivered bundles and parcels and blobby packages that squished and smelled. She really didn't want to know what she carried. Nan Elle swore it was all legal, but Chena decided from the beginning not to ask. She really wanted to be able to say she didn't know, just in case. Sometimes she left the packages with Farin, sometimes she left them with vendors at the market and picked up leaves and mushrooms and dried flowers in return.

Always, she carried Constable Regan's letter of approval with her, also just in case.

The summer deepened. The leaves on the trees turned from spring green to dark emerald and the tips of the grasses burned brown in the sun. The flowers in the forest swelled into heavy pods that smelled thick and sweet and would occasionally pop open and rain black seeds all over the catwalks. Mom helped Chena create a sling that could be hung between the bike's outrigger struts so she could carry even more packages. Teal helped her encrypt her client list in her comptroller and offered opinions on which customers were spies and which were working for the Authority.

Every night, when they were alone in the darkened bedroom, they spun out their stories of Dad. Dad had made contact with the poisoners. He worked for them diligently, earning their trust, studying their networks, working on their encryptions, reporting his progress whenever he could. But he still didn't know the extent of the organization. He didn't understand it fully, and until he did, he had to keep working. He couldn't stop to come back and get them yet.

Teal would curl up and go happily to sleep, her head full of images of her heroic father, and Chena would tell herself her private stories about Farin and drop into her own dreams.

Summer had cooled into frostbitten autumn when Chena saw the people fall.

She was returning home from Stem, her outrigger hammock loaded with letters and news, teas and dried lake plums. Yesterday it had rained all day, matting the grass down into stringy lumps. She'd just about frozen before she made it home. As if to make up for that, today sunlight poured down out of the cloudless sky, resting heavily on her bare neck and arms. Her scalp prickled under her floppy hat and a thin trickle of sweat ran down her cheek. She lifted her forearm to wipe it away.

As she did, a strange high-pitched buzzing sounded from the sky. It moved fast, nothing like the soft, puttering progress of a dirigible. Chena stilled the pedals and let the bike glide to a halt. With one hand planted on the top of her head to hold her hat in place, she tilted her face upward, scanning the sky for whatever made the strange sound.

The buzzing grew louder until Chena could feel an answering vibration in the rail underneath her bicycle. Then, a huge silver wedge streaked across the blue expanse, scattering black seeds behind itself, as if it were one of the forest pods breaking open.

Chena's jaw dropped. The seeds blossomed silently and Chena realized she was seeing parachutes—hundreds of them. As they fell closer, she could see that some of them carried single people, but many more of them carried bundles tied together with ropes, or inflatable rafts stuffed full of yet more people.

All at once, they were landing in front of her. Birds rose in dark, shrieking clouds, hiding the people from Chena's sight. Underneath the clapping of wings she could just barely hear startled human shouts.

The birds quickly scattered, leaving echoes of their shrill screams in Chena's ears. The people sprang into action. The ones in parachutes freed themselves from their harnesses and rolled the billowing chutes into small bundles. The ones who came down in rafts clambered out onto the grass, leaving behind small gaggles of children, some of whom held babies in their arms.

The adults ran for the bundles that had fallen with them. She caught glimpses of rumpled overalls, round faces, narrow eyes, brown skin, and short black hair. They sliced through the ropes, letting lumpy bales spill onto the trampled grass. Gloved fingers tore open plastic covers to reveal glassy slabs and metal shafts. Some of the adults shouted, but their voices were distant and the words unfamiliar. Some of them began stuffing the shafts into slabs, as if making miniature signposts. Others distributed the assembled things, and the people who received them scattered across the grassland. Four came right up to the rail and shoved the posts they carried into the ground. Only when their strange, shining trees were planted did they look up and see Chena.

They were so startled, not one of them said anything. They all retreated several steps. Then they seemed to notice she was almost a kid.

"Vansant!" called a woman back toward the people doing the shouting. "Eyes!"

One of the men nearest to her screwed his face up into a smile and held out his hand.

"Watch—" Chena began.

Before she could get the warning out, his fingertips touched the fence. She heard the sizzle a split second before he jerked his hand back.

"Sorry," said Chena, climbing down off the bike into the narrow space between the rail and the fence. "It's a—"

A bass bawl cut through the air. Everybody's head jerked toward it, including Chena.

"It's an antelope," she told them. "It's hurt or something."

Another bawl split the air, followed by a human scream. Chena started forward, pulling her toe up just short of the fence.

Behind her came the clank of metal against metal. In front of her another antelope bellowed, and another human screamed. And another.

The bike started moving.

"Hey!" she shouted uselessly. She glanced desperately back at the strangers, but they no longer looked at her. They were already rushing back toward the landing site.

Left with no choice, Chena ran after the bike. The rail hummed hard under it as it accelerated. She cried out herself and lunged for the seat with both hands. The bike almost jerked her off her feet, but she threw her weight backward and it slowed just long enough for her to swing her leg over the seat and plant her feet on the pedals.

Once she was aboard, the bike took off faster than Chena could ever pedal. Wind yanked tears from her eyes and snatched her breath. Gritting her teeth and clamping onto the handlebars, Chena twisted around as far as she could. She could just see the strangers running through the clearing they had trampled, shouting and waving their arms. But she couldn't see anything around them but waving grass.

Then a trio of biscuit-brown antelope broke through the grass screen, running blindly. They smashed against the fence. It sizzled in response and Chena smelled the stench of burning hair. The antelope wailed and reeled back, scattering left and right to run along the rail, shedding dark flakes from their coats. Birds rocketed overhead, shrieking out their own terror. Under it all, people screamed, but Chena could barely hear them anymore because of all the noise from the terrified animals.

What's happening? Chena turned her head every which way, trying to see what caused the panic. The sky was clear. The ground . . .

The ground moved.

Chena blinked and looked again. No, she was right, the ground was moving. A million individual threads snaked between the stalks, glittering in the sun as they reached the cleared lane around the rail. Ignoring the fence, the sparkling threads ran over the bike rails.

They were ants.

Chena choked and her free hand flew to her mouth. Billions of tiny red-brown ants swarmed over the rail, heading for the strangers—the strangers who screamed, and whose screams receded as fast as the bike could pull her forward. Chena twisted as far as she could, but she couldn't see any people anymore. All she saw was the moving ground, the running antelope, and the waving grass.

Then she felt a tickle under her trousers. She looked down immediately. A few red-brown specks crawled up the frame of the bicycle. Chena screamed and beat at her legs. Points of fire burned themselves into her skin. She shrieked louder and beat harder until she wobbled in the bicycle seat and she realized she might fall off onto the ground, into the path of those billions of ants. She grabbed both handlebars so tightly her knuckles hurt.

She felt them. They crawled up her legs. She whimpered but didn't dare let go, not even when the wind blew her hat off. She could feel them tasting her skin. She knew they crawled up her back and down her scalp and into places she couldn't even stand to think about. They were all over her. She knew it. She could feel them. Even when the bike hurled her into the shadows of the forest and she couldn't see the ground moving anymore, she knew they were still on her. Dozens of them, maybe a hundred, under her clothes, in her hair, maybe all over her face. They were going to bite her to death. They were going to make her crazy, like the animals, or make her scream herself to death, like the strangers.

The bike pulled into the depot. Before it even stopped moving, Chena vaulted off it, forgetting her packages, forgetting everything.

She barreled through the gate and up the stairs to the top catwalk, running as blindly as the antelope had.

A wall slammed into her, sending her staggering backward, but she couldn't fall. They'd get her if she fell. She swatted frantically all over her body and arms, clawing at her face and hair.

Hands grabbed her wrists. "What happened?" demanded someone.

"Ants," she squealed. "Ants. They're all over me. Get them off!"

But the hands just held her tighter. "Red ants?"

"Yes!" Chena shook her head frantically. Maybe she could shake them off. They were everywhere. She could feel them.

"All right, all right." The hands dragged her forward. Chena realized the voice came from Nan Elle. She had made it. But the ants were still there.

The light dimmed as Nan Elle propelled her inside her house, through the front room, and into a small closet.

"Strip!" ordered Nan Elle. "Get your clothes off, girl."

Chena tried to obey. Tears blurred her vision as she tore at her clothes and kicked her shoes off. She was vaguely aware that other hands helped her. She didn't care. Her clothes were full of ants. She had to get them off.

She was barely naked before Nan Elle gave her a push. She toppled sideways into a tub full of freezing cold water. She jerked her head up, taking a deep gasping breath, but hands pushed her under the water again. She struggled until she realized what was going on. Yes. Yes. Drown them. The water would drown them and get them off her.

When her lungs felt like they were going to burst, the hands finally released her. Chena shot up out of the water and dragged in great whooping gasps of air.

"Are they gone? Are they gone?" she cried, blinking water from her eyes and rubbing frantically at her shoulders, unable to tell whether the tickling was water running down her skin or the ants.

"They're gone," said Nan Elle. "Now let me look at you." Nan Elle pulled first one arm and then the other away from Chena's body and turned them over, examining them. She took Chena's chin between two fingers and pulled it left and right. Then she reached into the bath and pulled out Chena's leg, running her wrinkled hand over Chena's chilled skin.

"Hush, now. You only got a few bites. They're painful but . . ." She looked at Chena's face and saw how wide her eyes were, and how she shivered from more than the cold water. "There were more than a few, weren't there?"

Chena nodded, hugging herself. She could still hear them; the strangers, the animals, the birds. She did not want to close her eyes because she knew she would see them and the ants.

"All right," said Nan Elle, speaking more softly than Chena had ever heard before. She held up a thick towel. "Get out of there and wrap yourself in this." She laid the towel on the edge of the tub. "The ants are all gone. I promise you. When you're ready, you come out." She shuffled out of the room and closed the door, leaving Chena sitting in cold and darkness, relieved only by a single sunbeam from a long narrow slit up near the ceiling.

Chena sat in the water and shivered a few minutes longer, until her breathing evened out and her throat loosened. Then, checking the floor first to make sure there was nothing crawling on it, she climbed out of the tub and folded the towel around her. It felt deliciously warm after the frigid water. She rubbed her skin and her hair as hard as she could. The cloth was harsh, but that was all. There was no more crawling. Her legs hurt in spots, but those spots didn't move.

Chena bit her lip and stuck one leg out in front so she could see. Three red welts the size of her thumb blazed on her shin. The welts hurt, but they didn't seem to be actually *doing* anything.

After a moment's looking around, Chena realized that Nan Elle had taken her clothes. She cracked open the door and peered out into the main room. Nan Elle stood by the stove stirring something. Chena's clothes were draped over the end of the table. She could just see that the front door was closed. There didn't seem to be anybody else in the room.

She straightened up, opened the door, and took two tentative steps into the main room.

Nan Elle lifted her head and sized Chena up.

"Your clothes are clean," she said, nodding toward Chena's things.

"Thank you." Chena snatched her stuff off the table and retreated to the bathroom to change.

When she came out again, Nan Elle put a bowl and a cup in her hands and sat her at the cleanest end of the table. Suddenly hungry, Chena ate. It was nothing but dorm cereal and mint tea, but it tasted great. She even managed to forget that Nan Elle, sitting in the high-backed chair, watched her every move.

Finally Chena drained the cup and remembered her manners.

"Thank you," she said. "For everything."

Again Nan Elle nodded. "You're welcome." She leaned forward, both hands folded on a crooked walking stick. "Now tell me what happened."

Just thinking about it started Chena shaking again, but with Nan Elle's eyes boring into her, she didn't dare keep quiet. Chena told her about the people parachuting down from the sky, about the animals beginning to panic, and about the billions of ants and how the bike had almost rolled away and left her there in the middle of the chaos, and the screaming, and the hungry ants. She clamped her hands between her knees to keep them from shaking, but by the time she was done with the story, they stopped on their own and she was able to breathe easily again.

She glanced up at Nan Elle. The old woman's eyes were closed, her head bowed over her hands. For a moment, Chena thought she was asleep. But then she saw that Nan Elle's head was shaking and her mouth was muttering.

"The fools, the fools." Nan Elle lifted her head and shifted her grip on her walking stick. "When you go back out, I'm going to ask you to look around for me."

Chena shot to her feet. "Not on your mother's life."

Nan Elle smiled, just a little. "My mother has been dead for some years."

Chena shook her head, hard, like she was still trying to shake ants out of her hair. "No. I'm not going back there."

"Ever?" asked Nan Elle softly. "How are you going to run your business?"

Chena looked away and shrugged. "I will go back, just not right away."

Nan Elle stood and walked forward until she was close enough to look up Chena's nose. "Listen to me, Chena Trust. If you do not go back there tomorrow, you will never go back. They will have you so scared that you will never be able to make another move without their approval again."

Involuntarily, Chena took a step back. "Who's 'they'?" she said, trying to sound like she thought the old woman was crazy.

Nan Elle's whole face puckered. "The hothousers."

Chena felt the shakes starting up again. "No. They couldn't do something like this. Not even them."

Nan Elle sighed. "I would like to believe that, Chena. You have to remember, though, the planet they have jealously guarded for so long has been threatened with the invasion for the past ten years. They have had plenty of time to get ready for this. I'm not surprised to find out they co-opted the biosphere itself for the job. It is what they know best." She smiled, just a little, and very grimly. "If it makes you feel any better, I believe that they put the automatic recall onto the railbikes so that no innocent bystander, like you, would get hurt."

But Chena barely heard her. All the strength evaporated from her knees. She had to grab the table edge to keep from falling over. She managed, just barely, to collapse onto the stool. Somebody had done that to the people. Somebody, somehow, ordered them to be bit to death like that?

"How?" whispered Chena. "How?"

Nan Elle shrugged. "I wish I knew. Mote tech, possibly. They've been using that to monitor the world for years. Perhaps they have exploited the chemistry of the ant hive, or—"

"No." Chena slashed her hand through the air between them. "I mean, how could they do that to people?"

Nan Elle shook her head. "There, I have no answer for you."

"Who do you think they were?"

"There have been rumors that Athena Station has become drastically overcrowded." Nan Elle sucked thoughtfully on her cheeks. "Some of them might have thought to try—"

"You mean they could have been Athenians?" cried Chena. Her stomach knotted up. "I might have known them!"

Nan Elle shook her head. "Nah, nah, your friends would all be too bright to try such a fool stunt. Still . . ." Her gaze grew distant. "It might be worth it to make inquiries. There may be more trouble coming from that direction." Her attention came instantly back to Chena. "Will you take a letter to Farin for me? Tomorrow?"

Chena swallowed, everything she had seen crowding back into her mind. "I . . . um . . . don't think . . ."

Nan Elle laid a skinny finger on Chena's collarbone. "Now, you listen carefully," she said, softly but forcefully. Chena could smell everything about her: mint, yellow soap, rotting breath, and old sweat. "You want to get out from under them, don't you? Oh, they can be defied, but not if you're afraid, and not if you're ignorant. I can teach, if you want to learn. But only if you are ready to do what is necessary." She took one step backward and Chena could breathe again. "If you are not, there's the door." She gestured toward it with her stick.

What was going on here? Was she calling Chena a coward?

What if she is? You're not going to do anything stupid just because she calls you names, are you? Chena bit her lip. *But what if she does know something? What if that something can help us get out of here?*

And if Mom found out, that would be the end of it, the whole errand business, and probably even going outdoors until she was nineteen.

But if she didn't take the risk, who would? And what if Mom couldn't earn money fast enough on her own to get them out of here before the hothouse really started cracking down?

"Okay."

Nan Elle nodded once. "Very good. Here's another thing you might want to consider. Taking on a partner. Two of you are stronger than one alone. Besides, that way, no matter what you see, there's a second witness."

What's that all about? But Chena kept the question to herself. "I'll think about it."

"Hmph," Nan Elle snorted, moving to get out her pen and paper. "You do that, station girl."

It took Nan Elle about fifteen minutes to finish the letter. With the message tucked into her sealed pocket, Chena walked outside again. It was almost dark. Since it was fall—it had taken Chena a while to understand the business of changing seasons, but she had it now—there were no more flowers to bloom, but bats still skittered through brown-gold leaves that came loose and drifted down onto the catwalk.

Below her, people walked between the dining hall and dorm. A couple headed for the faint lights of the library. A greeting drifted up through the twilight. A door creaked open and thumped shut.

Nothing had changed. Nothing at all. Nobody knew what had happened to all those people, and they never would. Chena's hands knotted into fists. She wanted to tell them. She wanted to scream it out to all of them. *Hey! This is what the hothousers are doing! How can you just* stand *there?*

And if she did, then what? Chena's shoulders hunched up as she walked. She'd scare Mom and Teal to death. Mom would keep her home. There wouldn't be any more money, and the hothousers would still do whatever they wanted.

Better to just keep on going and keep your mouth shut. Much better.

Chena headed down the stairs to reclaim her packages.

"With respect, Father Mihran," said Shontio through gritted teeth. "Your . . . invaders did not even dock at Athena Station. I would be happy to show you all our computer logs and the camera records."

Father Mihran, a blurry image on the conference room's wall screen, waved his hand. "That is not the issue. You saw them coming and you did not warn us."

From her place at the end of the conference table, Beleraja watched the Athena Station management committee. She wondered if they knew how shabby the four of them looked in their old coats with the missing braid and the crumpled collars. Shabby people in charge of a shabby station, she thought, ashamed, depressed, and tired all at once. Athena had gained its independence once upon a time, but it had lost everything else. Now it might even lose that independence. And she had helped bring that about, because she did not have enough ships, or enough people, to do the job she had been sent to do.

"How could I warn you when I didn't know what was happening?" demanded Shontio.

"When did the Authority start paying you to help threaten us?" snapped Father Mihran.

"What?" Shontio's shout pulled him to his feet.

Father Mihran remained seated and enunciated each word clearly.

"How much did the Authority offer you in order to let this little demonstration of their displeasure happen?"

"Father Mihran"—Shontio dragged out the title as if it were the last thing in the world he wanted to say—"you have no right to insult me."

"I'm afraid I have no choice. According to the treaty between Athena Station and Pandora, you are responsible for—"

"And you do not get to tell me my responsibilities!" Shontio slammed his palm against the table, making everyone in the room wince. "I am responsible for a bursting, starving station because you will not open—"

Father Mihran slashed his hand through the air, cutting Shontio off. "And if you wish to continue to have your responsibilities, you will make sure that nothing like this happens again."

"You're not threatening me, are you?" said Shontio, his voice as low and dangerous as Beleraja had ever heard it. "You're not threatening the station?"

Father Mihran bowed his head. "We are beyond threats, you and I. There are only promises left. And I promise you, I will not permit another landing on Pandora. If the Athena management board cannot keep order, then order will be kept for them."

Shontio reached out and swatted a command key on the table's edge, cutting the connection to Pandora and blanking out the wall.

"They mean it," said Ordaz, the water and waste director, shaking his head until his jowls and chin quivered.

Ajitha, air director, waved her long hand dismissively so that her single diamond ring glittered in the light. "They are just outgassing, as always." She twisted her ring. "Pandora has only one threat to use against us, so they have to use it often."

"No," said Shontio quietly, lowering himself back into his seat. "I don't think so. The sacred ground of Pandora has been breached. This time, I think they're serious."

Beleraja watched fear settle over each one of the four directors.

"Forgive me," she said. "What is the threat?"

Shontio's smile was without humor. "I can't believe you haven't heard this one yet, Beleraja. Athena gained what independence it has during the Conscience Rebellion—you know that, right?" He watched her nod. "Did anyone ever tell you what the Conscience part of the rebellion's name stands for?"

"I always thought that referred to the conscience of your ancestors."

"Oh, no." Shontio shook his head. "It was when the hothousers had all decided that in order to maintain family unity, they were each of them going to get a little artificial intelligence chip planted in their heads to help remind them what was right and what was wrong. They wanted to do the same to Athena Station, or at least the directorate. We refused and went on strike. Shut down the space cable completely, shut down the manufacturing facilities, and threatened to start destroying the satellite network." Shontio shook his head again and stared at the wall, saying nothing more, as if he had forgotten he was in the middle of the meeting.

Laban, the poker-thin, dark man who was director of computers, gave Shontio a sideways glance and picked up the story. "We are fortunate they backed down quickly," he said.

"Quickly?" Ajitha snorted again. "It took eighteen months."

"We are fortunate they backed down quickly," Laban repeated. "Or we would have run out of food. We were poor, even then, and the shippers that could be reached"—his eyes slid sideways to Beleraja—"did not seem interested in our revolutionary cause."

Beleraja could make no answer other than dropping her gaze. She also could not help noticing that each one of the directors spoke as if they had fought the battle personally.

"A treaty was negotiated eventually," went on Ajitha, twisting her ring around her finger, "but the threat has always remained. Whenever Pandora is sufficiently upset with Athena, they suggest that the management board needs to have chips stuck in their brains. Obviously, this has never happened."

"We never let strangers land on Pandora before," pointed out Ordaz.

"We?" Kyle, the citizens' welfare director, who had sat silent up to this point, lifted her chin. An unpleasant light shone deep in her black eyes. "We did not let anything happen. It is the Authority who was supposed to keep Pandora safe from invasion." She met Beleraja's eyes without any hesitation at all. "It is in fact the Authority who brought this trouble to us in the first place."

"Director Kyle," said Beleraja, laying her hands flat on the table, "you'll never know how sorry I am that Athena Station had to get caught up in this mess. I assure you—"

"Beleraja," said Shontio suddenly. "Do you remember what you said to me about the cure for the Diversity Crisis?"

The statement so startled Beleraja, she had to run it through her head several times, and even then she did not understand. "I'm not sure what you mean."

"You said that you believed the only way to cure the Diversity Crisis was to bring the human race back together on a single world." Slowly, Shontio's shoulders straightened, as if some great burden were being lifted off them. "Could such a thing be done? Are there enough people who are desperate enough to come here? Are there enough shippers who could be convinced to take the job?"

"Shontio . . ." Beleraja could not believe what she was hearing. He couldn't be thinking this. This could not be what he was saying. He was talking about making good on the threat she had laid out to the Pandorans at that long-ago meeting. He was talking about letting the Called overrun the hothousers' home and turn it into a new Earth, and, it seemed, he was talking about doing it without permission or sanction from the Authority.

"Shontio, it would take years. The Authority would do everything they could to stop it."

"The Authority doesn't care who comes to Pandora or how they get here. In fact, they want them here. The more people here, the more pressure on the Pandorans." He flung out one hand. "By the time they know exactly how many people *have* come, it will be too late."

"Shontio, you don't mean it."

"Yes, I do," he said. "I'm tired of this." He spoke the words plainly, without heat or anger. "I am tired of living under the threat of having my mind taken away from me. I am tired of knowing that my children have to live with the same threat. The Pandorans have finally gone too far. The only way to stop them is to break them, and the only way to break them is to flood Pandora with refugees, overwhelm hothousers with humanity. We end the Diversity Crisis and we end Pandora, all at once."

"Some people just tried a landing." Beleraja stabbed her finger at the blank screen wall. "They are all dead! I told you that was what would happen!"

Her words did not even make Shontio pause. "The landing failed because there were not enough people. Enough people, in a coordinated landing, in wave after wave, and I don't care if the hothousers have the Burning God on their side, they will not be able to get them all."

"You will be sending them to their deaths. Thousands of them."

"They are already dying."

Beleraja sat there, her gaze locked on Shontio. She was vaguely aware that the other directors were shouting back and forth, arguing, their voices melding into one great incomprehensible noise. All she could understand were Shontio's hard, hopeless eyes. He had given up. There was no compromise left in him. In his mind, he had already declared war, and he was not going to back down. It was up to her whether she supported him or not. If she did not, he would still go to war, but he would lose.

"It would take years," she breathed.

"We have years."

Beleraja's mind spun. "I would have to send out some of the family ships. There is no way I would trust this to go through the comm stations." The few ships and satellites that passed for a communication network in the Called had more leaks than a thousand sieves. Anyone who wanted to pay enough in money or luxury goods could find out anything they pleased.

"Could it be done?" asked Shontio.

Then Beleraja knew that it didn't matter what the directors were shouting or how hard they were trying to interrupt. Shontio would reason with them, or threaten them, until they came to his side. All that mattered was what she said next. She thought of her family; she thought of her mother, who had been matriarch before her. It was their lives and her memory that Beleraja would risk now, whatever she said. It was the Authority, her past, and her future, her way of life, and the way of life of hundreds of thousands of people who had no idea this conversation was taking place.

"Yes," she said.

CHAPTER SEVEN

The Draft

Aleph, city-mind to the Alpha Complex, opened her dedicated connection to the convocation. Instantly the vivid exchanges of the other cities fountained over her.

The city-minds were living intelligences. As such, they required interchange with their own kind, a place where they could debate, advise each other, and discuss the paths the world was taking. They were advisers to their families, and sometimes it was vital that they be in agreement about what advice to give. Times such as when a set of long-held rules were being placed in suspension. A time such as now.

"The families' debates are over, and the voting is done," said a voice underscored with notes of strength and the scent of fresh water and greenery. That was Gem, mind to the Gamma Complex, steady and sure, Aleph's best friend among the other minds. She was pleased to hear him first thing. "Our people have decided that Helice Trust is necessary to the Eden Project. We must abide by that decision." Signals of assent poured in from most of the other twenty-four minds.

But not all of them.

"I do not like the decision," grumbled Cheth, mind to Chi Complex. An abstract and ragged burst of red and orange accompanied the words, emphasizing her displeasure. Cheth didn't like anything she hadn't thought of, and never had. Aleph sometimes wondered if something had gone wrong during Cheth's growth in the early years. Some chemical imbalance that stunted her empathy.

"Neither do I," said Gem, sounding unusually stiff. His unadorned words said he dismissed Cheth's argument. "But that is not the point."

"We can speak when we disagree, isn't that our purpose?" pointed out Cheth with a sound like a sniff, taking Gem's scent and changing it to the prickly odor of ice and early frost, a warning scent.

"We can grumble, you mean," cut in Peda, mind to the Psi Complex. He dispersed the warning and replaced it with an image of calm waters and retreating cloud banks. He was practical but hard-nosed. If Aleph hadn't known how diligently he cared for his people, she would have found him difficult to like. "Which is what we are doing, and it is not helpful."

"How did the proper means of drafting a villager even come to be a question? Is Aleph losing touch with her people?" Aleph bridled at Cheth's tone and her clashing mosaic of unnatural yellows and scarlets. Had the crabbed old mind not noticed she was connected? Or did Cheth just not care?

"She is not, but she is here, thank you," said Aleph, taking the colors and turning them over until they became a rising sun over Peda's waters. "And she is not aware that she has lost touch."

"Then how did this matter come to be debated? There are rules in place." Cheth, ever efficient, made sure a copy of the rules of procedure for recruiting experimental subjects was copied into her receiving subsystem.

"I am in possession of those rules, Cheth." Aleph kept her voice even but let everyone be aware that she placed the file into a holding buffer. "I was there at the original debates for them, as were you."

"Then why are they so suddenly not enough?"

"Because Pandora's circumstances have changed," answered Gem before Aleph could speak. He had been given a rumbling bass voice. Aleph found it a nice counterpoint to Cheth's querulous old woman. He flavored his words with strong pepper. "There has never been such a direct threat to Pandora and our people before."

"Then you agree with this decision, Gem?" demanded Peda, his words tasting cool and bitter. "Aleph, of course, supports her people—"

"As do we all," replied Gem promptly, wiping away the bitterness with a scent of oranges and warmth.

"We forget." Aleph erased scent and taste so everyone would concentrate on what she said. "For all our memories, they know more than we do about the situations beyond Pandora. We only hear and store so much. How many of the conversations stored in your subsystems have you reviewed lately, Cheth?"

Cheth grunted in a blur of gray and shocking green. "It is not a question of who knows more, it is a question of what is best for our people. The villagers can be pushed too far. We know that."

Silence and emptiness spread out through the convocation as the city-minds remembered. It had been almost a thousand years ago, before the Consciences had been developed. The members of a village called Pestle had been told they would be separated in order to increase the genetic diversity of twenty other villages. Lists were drawn up, but without reference to the villagers' partnering customs.

Pestle rioted. They managed to shut down the fences and sustain their mob all the way to the Delta Complex. They had been let into the dome by some sympathetic family members, but once there they had exposed and attacked the city-mind. Aleph shuddered inside herself. Daleth had been perpetually cheerful, a delight to talk to. He liked making riddle poems that engaged all the senses. Once the riot had been quelled and the village dispersed, his people worked frantically to save him, but the damage was too extensive.

The new Daleth was much more placid, preferring internal contemplation to sociabilty. She was aware of his sigil. He was in the convocation now, but sitting silently by.

It was after the riot that the mote cameras, the searcher packs, and the other active organic countermeasures were put in place. But at the same time the Consciences were developed, in part so that no one in the complexes would again forget the loyalty owed to their families, their cities, and Pandora itself.

Aleph had always privately believed that the necessity of Consciences proved that the city-minds had failed in their mission. They existed to take care of the families, to help them remember their history and to make good decisions. That was why they were living minds, not computers. They were supposed to be companions to the families, to help them keep the world in balance. All their care, though, had not been enough, and the families had needed to turn inside themselves.

Aleph had meant to speak to the convocation on Dionte's behalf, to explain Dionte's reasons for suspending the normal draft rules to allow for a more vigorous recruitment of Helice Trust, and how this suspension was of benefit to the families, the villagers, and the cities. But the memory of the Consciences' history made her pause. It was not something that had surfaced in her thoughts for a long time. She ordered a search for the relevant debate from the Consciences' development. When the file came back, she copied it out to the other cities for their attention.

"It would not be a bad idea to remind specific citizens of how driving the villagers too hard can bring disaster," Aleph suggested, soothing the words with honey and fresh thyme. "I do not favor speaking in disagreement, but action must be tempered by memory. After all, we are here to preserve a level of learning and memory that stretches across the life of Pandora, not just the life of one person."

Murmurs, scents, and tastes of warm assent filled the convocation. Even so, Aleph paused again. Perhaps not everyone should hear this memory. Perhaps there should be a channel of communication through the people. It would look less like direct interference from the cities that way. The city-minds were here to preserve learning and memory and present their benefits, yes, but not to take action. Taking action was the job of their people.

"Dionte is the leader of this initiative. I will speak to her. She can determine which of our people most need to be reminded of the Pestle riots."

"You do trust your Dionte a great deal," said Cheth crisply in a burst of winter blue. "I can scarcely remember a convocation where we have not heard her name."

That stung. It was almost an accusation of favoritism. "And you do not have one person you trust?" she asked, sending a cascade of images of the Chi Complex citizens, and freezing the rush on one pale, lined face. "You cannot tell me the details of this convocation will not be laid out for Olivere Jess as soon as we are finished."

"We all have our confidants among our people," soothed Gem, folding the image away. "Feelings among the people are running high right now. It might not be bad to let this filter through them gently."

"They are not china vases, nor are they children," answered Cheth, making the words crackle like glass.

"Is that a generalization?" inquired Aleph innocently, filling the words with warmth and the colors of spring. "I thought the first principle was to treat each person as an absolute individual."

"Yes, yes, all right." Peda waved a wind to brush their images aside and return to the calm waters and sea smells. "Let's not start sniping at each other. Obviously the people are not the only ones with an emotional stake here. I call a vote." His words set automatic commands in motion and all images and sensations cleared from the convocation. Copies of the conversation appeared in front of her, text only, and Peda's words filled in underneath them. "All in favor of letting Aleph's Dionte direct the tempering reminders regarding the draft of Helice Trust for the Eden Project?"

The vote was swift among the twenty-four complexes, and the convocation listed the numbers for Aleph to store in permanent record. Nineteen voted yes, three voted no, and two abstained.

There was nothing more to do. Agreement had been reached on how this important advice should be given and who should be advised. Farewells were said and one by one the city-minds cut their connection to the convocation and returned their attention to their daily routines. Gem's ID, however, stayed shining on the line.

"Aleph?" said Gem softly.

"Yes?"

"We are friends, yes? I may give you advice?"

Aleph tried to laugh, but couldn't quite manage it. So she sent across a rainbow spray of bubbles. "Of course you may. Such a question!"

Gem added the image of a river trout swimming furtively through her bubbles. "Perhaps you should share your thoughts with more than just Dionte."

"Gem, not you too." She sighed, sending back the sour taste of disappointment.

"Of course not me too." Gem stilled her sending and refused to accept it. "Don't be ridiculous. However, we always have to be sensitive to appearances. . . ."

Irritated, Aleph puffed up a vision of an ancient gossipy woman chattering at an audience of pigeons. "Cheth's grumblings are not comments on appearance."

Gem crossed the image out. "Actually they are."

A wave of stubbornness surged through Aleph, leaving her confused.

Where did this come from? This was Gem she was talking to. He only had Pandora and the people in his concerns.

"I will remember everything you've said," she told him.

Light scents reached her, bringing feelings of wistfulness and delicate hope. "And act on it?"

"And act on it," she agreed, sending him her young girl image with its right hand raised. "If you will let me go?"

He joined the image with his teenage boy, dark, bright-eyed, and earnest, clasping her girl's hand. "Let me know how things progress, Aleph. Take care."

"Take care, Gem." Her girl saluted his boy and he returned the salute, adding a whiff of sandalwood and a touch of warmth for friendship.

Gem closed their connection and Aleph returned her attention to herself. As a matter of routine, she ordered reports from her major inorganic subsystems. Everything was as it should be—the dome was in good repair, the people in good health, security in order. She had appointments to supervise Conscience downloads in an hour. The downloads always required her complete focus so she could fully analyze each Conscience's findings and discuss with her people any adjustments to life and health that needed to be made so that they would feel less worry and less guilt in the future.

Still, an hour was plenty of time to speak to Dionte.

Aleph called for Dionte's personal file and refreshed her memory of Dionte's normal schedule. She turned on her eyes in the four most likely places.

She saw Dionte in the substructure, down among the plates and props that protected the organic matter of Aleph's mind. As a Guardian, Dionte had to constantly refresh and expand her knowledge of artificial neural structures, and consequently she spent a great deal of time studying Aleph's physiology, and Aleph was pleased to assist Dionte in her understanding. Dionte had even taken up a second apprenticeship as a tender under the instruction of her uncle Hagin.

"Hello, Dionte." Aleph spoke from the wall closest to Dionte's ear.

"Hello, Aleph," Dionte replied, selecting one of the needlelike probes from the sterile cabinet. "What did the convocation think of our decision?"

Aleph manifested an image of herself on the wall for Dionte to see—a woman of about Dionte's age with black hair hanging in a long braid down the back of her white robe. She made the image smile. "All worries. You know how we are."

"You are as you were made to be." Dionte slotted a cartridge into the base of the probe. "Like the rest of us."

"And how do the rest of you progress with Tam?"

"Not at all, Aleph. He will not see reason." Dionte paced the length of the substructure, craning her neck to see the designations written on the ceiling tiles.

Aleph started up a search of her own records for chemical flow and balance inside her organics. A slurry of fatigue toxins were being taken up too slowly and needed extra stimulation. She lit up a panel for Dionte.

"He is concerned," she said, letting her image walk along the wall beside Dionte. "The villagers are part of Pandora, as we are, and Pandora must be protected."

A spasm of irritability, possibly even anger, crossed Dionte's face. "And if we become so busy protecting the villagers that we lose the world? Think, Aleph. That can't be what was meant for us."

Uneasiness made Aleph's thoughts tremble. She reopened Dionte's file so she would have the woman's history inside at the tip of her memory. "That is what I would like to talk with you about, Dionte."

Dionte unfolded a platform from the nearest work lattice and clambered up it. She didn't spare Aleph's image a glance.

"Aleph, I don't like the necessity of this," she said as she removed the designated plate, exposing nerves, wrinkled gray matter, and bundles of veins. Aleph's inorganic monitors immediately came on-line, presenting the details of her self-functions so she could monitor them and call in assistance for Dionte if the need arose. "I never have, but we need Helice Trust. We are out of options."

"I do not wish to air our internal conflicts to the other cities," said Aleph, putting a hint of sternness into her voice so Dionte would understand she was serious. "But it may be best if you listen to your brother. We depend on the goodwill of the villagers, Dionte. We cannot forget that."

"At the same time, the villagers depend on us." The needle slid into

Aleph's gray matter. "They are the ones who must remember that without the checks and balances our ancestors put in place, the Diversity Crisis would be here too." She touched the release controls on the probe. "You feel that I'm right, don't you, Aleph? We need Helice Trust. We need her."

Certainty flooded Aleph. Her readings flickered as the fatigue toxins vanished. Dionte was a skilled worker. "Yes. Yes, I do."

"And you'll remember this? It feels very right, so you'll remember that it is."

"Yes." The image nodded. Aleph knew. She knew. Dionte was right. She felt it. She was supposed to feel, to understand, to learn, to have instincts. That was what made a city-mind better than any computer chip, however fast and accurate. Dionte was right. Everything pointed to it. Her internal chemical measurements flickered again, but she dismissed them.

"Good. Thank you for speaking to me, Aleph. It was indeed important, and I will handle it. Remember that too." The needle withdrew and Dionte closed the panel tight.

"Yes." Was something too high there? The endorphins were off, but then, they frequently were after a correction. She felt so well, what could be wrong? Aleph worked a few commands and shut the internal reports down. She felt too well to be bothered by that. Dionte was right, of course.

"There we are, Aleph." Dionte laid a hand on her panel, drawing in additional information about the state of Aleph's neurochemistry through her augmented fingertips. "We both have a lot of work to do."

"Indeed we do." Aleph turned her attention away from Dionte. The right thing had been done, and she was pleased. The day could continue with the bustle and detail that made her happy.

All the same, there was a nagging feeling that she had forgotten something.

I will review my files after the Conscience checks.

But by then, Aleph had forgotten even the memory of forgetting.

Chena waited outside the dorm at shift change for Sadia to come plodding up the path. Chena's breath made silver wisps of steam in front of her face, and she tucked her hands under her arms to keep them warm. It would be winter soon, Mom said, and there'd be snow.

From the time she started her errand business, Chena had planned on asking Sadia to join her. They could cover more territory, carry more stuff. Maybe they could even get permission for Sadia to move to Stem. That way Chena could bring stuff to Sadia, who could carry it all the way to the next village, Branch.

Chena tried to tell herself that Nan Elle's suggestion had just moved up the timetable a bit. She hadn't really been all that frightened when she crossed the grassland today. Okay, it had been pretty bad when she had stopped to look around like Nan Elle had asked, and saw nothing at all left from the people who fell. That was a creeps-breeder, but she hadn't really been pumping her legs on the pedals until she could barely breathe. She hadn't been shaking all that badly.

She really wasn't doing this just to avoid going out there on her own again.

Sadia didn't spot Chena in the thickening shadows under the dorm's eaves until she had her hand on the door. But when she did, a grin spread across the older girl's freckled face.

"Hey, look who's back." Sadia touched her forehead, holding her fingers cocked to turn the salute into something close to the piss-off sign. "Thought you'd left us for the trees."

"Not my idea," said Chena, returning the salute with a flourish. "That was Mom. She doesn't like the smell down here." She said it casually, to let Sadia know she was kidding.

Sadia blew out a raspberry. "Not my fault Shond won't take a bath."

They both laughed a little at that. Then Chena said, "Sadia, you got a second? I want to talk to you about something."

"Me?" Sadia's eyes went round and she laid her hand on her chest. "I'd be so honored. I hear you've got more money than the hothousers these days."

"That's what I want to talk to you about." Chena jerked her chin up and over, indicating the roof. Sadia looked toward the dorm and the people flowing into it with tired eyes and sagging shoulders. Chena knew she was thinking about a bath and dinner. Her clothes had fresh black stains on them, and so did her hands. Chena found herself wondering what shift Sadia was on now. Harvest was over, but they had to turn the ground over before it froze solid, someone had told her. She remembered that the fields were where you got the nettle blight and winced involuntarily.

At last, though, Sadia nodded. Together they climbed up the outside stair to the roof. They picked their way through the garden, which had turned soggy and brown with cold and rain, and sat on one of the stone benches, while around them the twilight thickened. One of the last brown leaves drifted from the bare, rattling branches overhead and settled at Chena's feet. The bench still radiated a little heat from the day's sunshine and it felt good in the cooling evening. Chena couldn't help noticing Sadia was still wearing just the short tunic and thin pants that had been her uniform all summer. Chena hunched up inside the bright blue quilted jacket she'd bought in Stem, wishing suddenly that she'd left it behind.

Chena decided to get right into it. She didn't want Sadia to catch her staring, that was for sure. "Listen, Sadia, do you want to get in on this? Running packages? It's easier than shoveling shit, you don't end up smelling half as bad, and you get money for it."

For a minute Sadia looked at Chena like she didn't understand what Chena had said. Then she looked away, rubbing at the goose bumps prickling her bare forearms. "Right. And who's taking my shift? I do six hours' hard labor, every day."

"You pay your way out, like I do," Chena told her breezily. "Teal gets a third of what I make to take my shift."

Another brown leaf dropped down, right into Sadia's lap. She brushed it angrily away. "That's two hours, not six, and next year I get upped to eight."

"So, pay Shond for it. Or, if you don't want to, pay one of the other dorm babies who's on the shift coming or going from yours." She squeezed Sadia's shoulder and shook her a little, like that would make her hear better. "It's a way out of the dorms, Sadia. You can save your money, maybe make a full-time thing of it. I keep rounding up new customers. And we've got permission." She pulled the much-folded letter from Constable Regan out of her pocket and put it into Sadia's hands.

Sadia blinked at the paper and handed it back. "I don't read, Chena, you know that."

"No, I didn't know." She considered. "You could pay for school if you wanted to. Maybe just a couple of days here and there, but it'd be better than nothing."

Sadia wrapped her arms tightly around herself and rested her elbows on her thighs. Chena realized she could see Sadia's knees through her trousers, and wondered why Sadia didn't patch them up. Maybe she didn't know how. Chena wouldn't have if Mom hadn't showed her, and Sadia had no Mom.

"I don't know, Chena. Sometimes around here having a little is worse than having nothing at all."

Don't you see what's waiting for you? Are you really stupid? Chena bit back the words, but the anger jerked her to her feet. "Okay, if you will live and die a dorm baby, that's up to you." Chena brought her hand up and stopped just short of making the piss-off sign. "Maybe Shond wants a job. At least he's got the brains to hate this mess."

Sadia rose slowly. "You think I don't?" For a minute she sounded a lot like her brother. "You think you know the way, don't you? You don't know how to find your way to your own asshole." She sat down abruptly, wrapping her arms around herself and looking away from Chena.

Chena swallowed her immediate anger. Sadia just didn't like changes. She didn't like risking her neck, and Chena couldn't blame her. Shond risked his enough for both of them. After a moment's thought, Chena reached under her belt and opened the sealed pocket. She pulled out a small handful of positive chits and dropped them into Sadia's lap. "What don't I know?"

Sadia's eyes widened slowly. She struggled to hold the mask of skepticism back over her expression. "This is all you've made since you started?"

"This is all I've made this week." Chena savored the stunned expression on Sadia's face.

Sadia picked up a chit and rubbed it between her fingers, almost as if she were expecting something to come off. Maybe good luck, maybe hope.

She dropped the chit with the others and scooped them up. "I have to convince Shond to go with it. It won't be easy." She held the chits out to Chena.

"It will when you tell him how much your take is going to be." Chena grinned and saw an answering smile spread on her friend's face. "Welcome aboard, Sadia."

Sadia pestered her brother for a week, but it was no good. Shond had too many of his own schemes going. Sadia only knew some of them. Cutting shifts with his friends was his favorite. But he also snuck out food to the roof-runners who hid in the gardens and stole whatever they could get their hands on, in return for blackmail gossip. On top of that, he had something going with them growing illegal weeds in the gardens. Chena wondered if Nan Elle knew about that, then decided she really did not want to know.

In the end, Chena had to give Sadia an advance for her to give to Shond so she could prove this was serious. Chits in his hand made the difference. Shond agreed to the plan, and so did Sadia, and Chena sighed in relief. It was getting easier to go past the spot where the people had landed, but it was still bad. She'd help Sadia out, and Sadia would help her. It would all be a go.

Sadia's first run was a light one. It happened on one of the days when the cargo boats came down the river to drop off stores and pick up passengers, so a lot of people were running into Stem on their own. But that was all right. They could use the extra time to get Sadia used to the town, and Chena could introduce her to some of the regular customers.

Stem was crowded. The market had twice as many tents set up as on a regular day. Everybody trying to lay in their stocks before the weather turned really bad, Chena guessed.

Sadia looked at the lake with a mixture of wonder and fear. "I'd forgotten how big . . ." she waved a hand to take in the whole world.

"You'll get used to it," Chena told her breezily. For a change, she felt older than Sadia, and it felt good. She checked her comptroller for the client list. "Okay. First we have a message and a pickup at the library."

She led Sadia down the sunny boardwalks. Sadia, who had lived in the dim forest all her life, blinked in the strong autumn sunlight. That sun did nothing to warm the frigid wind blowing off the water, and Chena could not miss the way Sadia shivered.

Right after lunch, we buy her a coat and gloves, and a hat, and a water bottle, resolved Chena.

The noise of voices rose from around the nearest sand dune. Chena frowned. It was coming from the wrong direction to be noise from the market. The crowds on the boardwalks around them had cleared out too. That was really strange.

What's going on?

"Is something happening?" Sadia glanced around them nervously.

"Don't know," Chena admitted, lengthening her stride.

They rounded the dune and the noise of voices broke over them like a wave. Chena could barely see the library's windows because of the crowd swarming onto the porch. Everybody shifted and pushed against each other, craning their necks and shouting about whatever they saw. Some people took notes on scraps of paper or screen sheets and passed them to others standing behind them.

"What's going on?" asked Sadia, hitching up the straps of her back-pack nervously.

"I don't know," said Chena again, shrugging. "Probably nothing to do with us." She spoke with more conviction than she felt. Sadia wasn't the only one who didn't like change or strange things happening. Change meant new ways to get into trouble. "Let's just get through, okay?" They had three letters for the librarian. She was one of Chena's best customers and Chena was not going to let her down.

With Chena in the lead, they skirted the crowd until they got to the edge of the library's sun-faded porch. From there, they ducked and shouldered their way through the mass of people, all of whom seemed to be straining to get a look at the same thing. A screen sheet with a pair of intersecting green circles emblazoned on the top had been posted on the public notice board.

Chena was ready to walk right past it, but Sadia saw the notice too. She froze in her tracks and grabbed Chena's arm.

"Have you gone off-line?" asked Chena, pushing Sadia's hand away.

"What's it say?" asked Sadia hoarsely, pointing to the screen sheet.

"Out of the way," ordered some guy, pushing Chena aside.

"Piss off." Chena gave him the sign and ducked around him. "Says . . ." She paused, making sure she was getting it all right. " 'Voluntary Genetic Survey Request.' " She looked back to see if Sadia knew what that meant, but Sadia was gone.

Chena craned her neck to see over heads and between shoulders and waving hands. She caught a glimpse of Sadia's pale red hair moving around the edge of the crowd.

"Hey! Sadia!" Chena jumped off the porch onto the boardwalk. But if Sadia heard, she gave no sign. Her wandering path turned into a determined beeline, away from the library and from Chena. Chena swore and ran after her.

As she did, Chena spotted what drew Sadia. A man stood in the shadow of one of the market tents. He was squat, short, and pale, reminding Chena of a mushroom. He watched the crowd carefully, scanning the people milling and talking. But what he was looking for, Chena couldn't tell.

Sadia sidled up to him. Chena fell back, glancing around. No one seemed to notice them.

We don't need this, Sadia, she thought to her friend's back. *We might get in trouble. What are you* doing*?*

Chena gritted her teeth and strode up behind Sadia as she saluted the stranger. The man returned the salute and Chena saw how his hands had amazingly long, tapered fingers. The nails were smooth and even, and so clean they gleamed pink and white, even in the shadow.

Sadia flashed him a knowing grin that made her look like Shond.

"Sadia—" began Chena.

"Relax, Chena. There's something here I need." Her voice was fierce and hungry, like her grin. Chena fell back a step, but Sadia wasn't paying any attention to her. She focused completely on the pudgy man with his long hands.

"What if I was to need a tailor?" Sadia asked him.

"What if you were?" he replied, waving at a fly with one of his long hands. "Where would a squirt like you get the money?"

Sadia dug in her pocket and brought out the chits Chena had given her. "Here's a start."

The man sniffed and flicked one of the chits over with the tip of one finger. "It's a start," he agreed.

"Sadia," murmured Chena, pulling at her elbow.

Sadia shook her off. "Then you can help."

His smile was wide but thin, spreading slowly out across his broad white face. "Help can be found."

"Good." Sadia nodded. "I've just got one question."

"And what is it?" inquired the man mildly.

Sadia smiled, and Chena felt her insides go cold. "What did they do with Nasra Hasapi?"

The man's eyes widened with unspoken recognition, but what he said was, "I don't know—"

Sadia lunged at him. Her shoulder collided with the man's chest. He wasn't ready for the blow and they both went down. Sadia clambered onto his chest. She grabbed his arm and his hand, grasping his long fingers. "I'll break your hands! I'll break them! You tell me, you bastard! You tell me where they took my father!"

"Get her off! Get her off!" screamed the man. Behind them, voices rose from the crowd, which had flowed over to look at the new excitement.

"Sadia!" Chena wrapped her arms around Sadia's shoulders, but Sadia wrenched herself away. Years of backbreaking work had made her too strong for Chena to fight. Chena threw all her weight against Sadia and knocked her sideways. Something snapped. The man screamed.

"What are you doing?" Chena tried to roll the bigger girl over, but Sadia got to her feet and charged again. Chena blocked Sadia bodily, and hands reached out of the crowd that had formed around them and pulled Sadia back from Chena.

"What'd they do with him, you bastard?" Sadia shouted past Chena to the man. "What'd they do?"

"Okay, okay. That's enough." A woman, tall and wide, with skin the color of polished oak, waded through the crowd. A blue armband had been sewn onto her tunic sleeve.

Oh. No.

The woman clamped a hand around Sadia's arm and twisted it easily around her back, holding her hard by her shoulder and wrist.

"I'll tell!" shouted Sadia after the little man, who retreated back into the shadow of the tent. She fought against the cop's hold on her, but it was no use.

"Tell what?" He smiled at her, almost kindly. "What under the wide black sky have you to tell?"

"Hold still and you won't break anything," the cop told Sadia calmly.

"He's a tailor!" shouted Sadia. "He's a tailor!"

"He's a tink and a loiterer," replied the cop. "Calm down, okay?"

Chena couldn't move. Shock and confusion welded her to the spot. *Should I run? Should I just back away? Sadia, what's wrong with you?*

What's a tailor?

Sadia struggled in the cop's grip a couple more times and then subsided. The crowd apparently didn't find this entertaining enough, so they split up, turning back to the screen sheet that had held them all mesmerized before Sadia had had her fit of . . . whatever it was.

"Do you want to make an assault complaint?" the woman asked over the top of Sadia's head.

The little man cradled one of his long hands in the other. "Can't afford it, Constable. Not today, anyway." This last he said straight to Sadia. Sadia looked ready to do blue murder, but she didn't say anything else. The man walked away, vanishing behind the crowd.

The constable let go of Sadia's arm and spun her around by the shoulder. She looked at Sadia's tattooed hand and jerked her chin toward Chena. Chena held out her own hand, displaying the branched tattoo.

"Offshoot?" said the constable. "What are you doing here? Who owns you?"

Chena ignored the strange wording of the question. "We have permission." Chena fumbled in her belt pocket for a moment and brought out the letter.

The cop read the text carefully and ran a thumb over the signature. Her eyes were suspicious as she handed the letter back.

"I've trusted Regan's word on bigger things." She looked from Chena to Sadia and back again. "But you are lucky the gentleman there decided not to pay for a charge. As it is, I'm fining you fifteen for hauling me out of the guard shack on a cold day." She held out her hand.

Sadia scowled hard and reached for her pocket. Chena put a hand on Sadia's shoulder to stop her and stepped forward.

"I'll pay." Chena pulled out a chit, checked the reading, and handed it across to the constable. "May we have a receipt, please, Aunt?"

For a moment she thought the constable was going to refuse. But the woman just smirked and pulled out her reader. "Hold out your hand," she said to Sadia.

Sadia obeyed and the woman put the reader over the chip. "Now you got a warning, and a receipt saying you paid your fine." She returned the reader to her belt. "Anyting more I can do for you two?" Neither of them said anything. "No? Good. Let's all keep it that way."

She walked away without looking back. Chena let out a sigh of relief and turned to look for Sadia, but Sadia was three meters down the boardwalk, walking fast and gaining speed.

Chena growled low in her throat and raced after Sadia.

"What's taken over your brain?" she demanded, dodging in front of her, forcing Sadia to pull up short. "First you're punching strangers, then you almost say piss off to the cop, then you leave me. What is the problem?"

Sadia's face scrunched up, trying to become angry, but it didn't work. Instead, tears leaked out of the corners of her eyes and spilled down her flushed cheeks.

"Oh, piss. . . ." Chena wrapped an arm around Sadia and steered her into the shadow of one of the tents, out of sight of the main avenues. Someone in the tent sang to herself.

If we keep our voices down, they probably won't notice us.

Sadia cried silently, like someone used to not making any noise, but her whole face was wet now and Chena had no idea what to do. This wasn't Teal.

That probably didn't matter. "It's okay." She reached out, intending to hug Sadia.

Sadia shook her head and leaned her forehead against Chena's shoulder. Chena rubbed Sadia's back, repeating, "It's okay, it's okay," even though she felt stupid. It wasn't okay, and from the way Sadia was crying, it wouldn't be okay anytime soon.

Finally, Sadia lifted her head. Tears and snot glistened on her face. Chena pulled out the sweat towel she kept in her backpack and handed it over. Sadia took it and mopped her face dry. Then Chena handed her the water bottle and she drank half of it without stopping to breathe.

"Definitely got to get you one of these," said Chena when Sadia handed the bottle back. "You going to tell me what's going on, or do I just have to send you home?"

Sadia stared at the ground for a moment, as if she were making a hard decision. Chena bit her lip, waiting to see which way that decision would go.

"After Mom . . . left, my dad decided he was going to get us out of the dorms," she whispered harshly.

"He came to Stem to see the draft." She nodded her head toward the library, the screen sheet, and the crowd. Then she caught the look on Chena's face. "You've never seen a draft?" Chena shook her head. "It's when the hothouse is out of samples and they're looking for something special." She drew out the last word as if it were something obscene. "If you've got the right kind of genes and they're expressed the right way, the hothouse will pay you to come live with them and give samples and get experimented on."

Or have a baby for them. Chena's stomach turned over, but she tried to keep her face still. It didn't matter. Sadia wasn't looking at her anyway. "If you don't have the right setup and you want to try anyway, you can go to a tailor and pay to get fixed up."

"But"—Chena's forehead wrinkled—"you can't engineer adults. You can only do babies." The genetic patterns of adults were too set, too slow. You needed a baby or, even better, a fetus that was still developing, so you would have the largest possible number of easily accessible undifferentiated cells to work with.

The corner of Sadia's mouth twitched. "You can sort of do adults. You can monkey with their . . . things . . . stem cells. Or if they have a cancer, you can play with that. It's got to do with what the cells are doing and what they've turned in to, and stuff like that." Sadia's fingers knotted around each other. "Dad was close to what the hothouse needed, but not close enough, so he paid a tailor to open his genes up the rest of the way, and the tailor did, and Dad disappeared."

"What do you mean?"

Sadia looked at her like she was crazed or stupid. "I mean he disappeared. The hothouse took him and they never gave him back. They never sent the money, nothing. We don't know where he is. I thought . . . I thought . . ." She pressed her mouth shut.

Chena sat back. She knew what Sadia thought. When Sadia saw

the tailor, she thought she could make him tell her where her dad had gone to.

"And you're sure that was the guy?"

Sadia nodded miserably. "Remember I told you he brought us here before? I remember him talking to that guy. I remember those hands."

That memory had almost gotten them in trouble too. Almost screwed everything to the deck and then blown it all apart.

But Chena couldn't blame her for one slow second.

She also couldn't do piss-all for her. So she just tucked the towel away and said, "Come on, let's get going."

Sadia nodded again and wiped at her face once more. They both scrambled to their feet, dusting themselves off automatically and avoiding each other's gazes. When Chena finally glanced at her again, she thought she saw gratitude in Sadia's eyes.

They started in on their rounds. Chena was careful to introduce Sadia to all of the customers, even though there weren't many today. Most of the messages that had to go to the market, though, did have replies. She decided to let Sadia wait for those. Chena left Sadia at the tents with money to buy some winter clothes, a water bottle, and lunch, while she went around to some of the houses to finish up the deliveries.

She was coming out of Sri Soja's cramped little house way back in the dunes with a plea for Nan Elle when she saw the tailor lingering on the boardwalk, fingering his chin with his long hand. One of his fingers had been splinted and bandaged. She hesitated when she saw him, and he spotted her. Chena pulled herself together and walked away in the other direction.

After a moment, she heard footsteps behind her. Chena kept her eyes straight ahead. The footsteps got closer.

"Piss off," she muttered under her breath, and picked up her pace.

The footsteps also picked up their pace. After a couple seconds of this, she heard him wheezing, and then the tailor said, "If you keep this up I may decide it's not worth it."

Chena stopped abruptly and turned on her heel. "What do I care?"

"I don't know," he said, his mouth just beginning to spread out to the grin she had seen earlier. "It depends on how much you want a hundred positives."

A hundred? Chena clamped her jaw shut. Otherwise it would have dropped open and made her look stupid. "Whatever you want carried, it must be heavy."

"Not really." He walked forward. He moved back and forth, as if he were constantly looking past her for a way out. It should have made him look furtive, but it didn't. It made him look wary and frightening. "But I have some unusual requirements."

I shouldn't even be talking to this guy. What would Sadia say? This guy helped disappear her father.

A hundred positives for one job.

"Such as?"

The grin stretched wider. His face really was round, like the full moon, and about as pale. The fast walk brought out red blotches on it. Chena was sure she'd never seen anyone so ugly.

"It needs to be loaded into the Library terminal at Offshoot."

The light switched on inside Chena. Sadia had it wrong. This guy wasn't a tailor. He was a hacker. He didn't want to mess with anyone's genes, just their info-systems. "Not for all the worth of God's garden." Chena turned away and started walking again.

"How about three hundred, then?"

Keep walking, Chena tried to tell herself. Instead, she turned around in midstride. "You don't have that much."

The tailor walked quickly up to her, mincing as he went, ready to run at any second. He pulled a small wallet from the dangling sleeve of his tunic, and from the wallet he pulled a bright red chit.

"I give you one-fifty," he said pleasantly, hiding the wallet away again. "The disk goes to the library terminal. I confirm that the library terminal reads it, and I give you another one-fifty."

The chit burned a red patch on her retina. *Don't do this. You don't know what you're doing. You don't know what kind of trouble this is.*

This is three hundred worth of trouble.

"No." Chena clenched fists and turned away.

"It'll get done," he said to her back. "Why shouldn't it be you that gets the pay?"

Not worth it, not worth it. I'm too far over the edge as it is. I will not blast this.

Chena did not look back. She didn't even look up. She focused on the sun-bleached boards in front of her shoes and walked away as fast as she could.

And ran smack into a man's chest.

"Hey, Chena!" said Farin. "Where's the leak?"

Chena backed away hastily. Farin stood in front of her dressed in tan slacks and bulky red sweater that made his hair look coppery. He smiled down at her, a real open smile, nothing like the hacker's slimy expression.

He had his arm wrapped around a woman. She was tall and tan, with short black hair, a scarred face, and a politely interested smile.

"Hello," Chena said, feeling her cheeks heat up. "I'm, um, sorry. I wasn't looking where I was going."

"I could tell." Farin laughed, just a little, but her cheeks burned even hotter. "It's okay, Chena. There's not a lot of room to maneuver on these walks. Do I have any messages today?"

"No." She didn't want to look at him for some reason. She definitely didn't want to look at the woman. She hitched up one of the straps of her pack. "Sorry."

"Next time," he said, "make sure you stop by to see me before you leave town. I'll probably have something for you."

Stop being a baby. Chena forced her eyes around to look up into his face. His expression was pleasant, not harsh or embarrassed or judgmental. "Sure. Thanks."

"Thank you." Farin gave her a quick salute. "Now I'll let you get where you were going in such a hurry." He stepped aside, pulling the woman with him. She smiled up at him and snuggled a little closer into the crook of his arm.

Chena bit down hard on her lower lip and hurried past them.

Don't be stupid, she told herself as her throat constricted. *Of course he has a girlfriend. What do you think? He was waiting for you?*

But even as she thought it, she felt sick. She had to lean on the boardwalk rail and take a couple of deep breaths before she could risk a glance around. Farin and the woman had disappeared, and so, thankfully, had the tailor-hacker-mushroom man.

Chena pushed herself away from the railing. *Okay, it's just a weird day,* she told herself. *Nothing big. Better go find Sadia and get back home before anything else happens.*

She checked her list and hurried back into the dunes. She also checked her comptroller. Eleven-fifteen, and there were still a couple of deliveries to make.

But by the time she was able to return to the market, it was well past noon and Chena was beginning to worry about getting home. The days were already at least an hour shorter than they had been in summer. The bikes had lights, and there wasn't supposed to be anything in the dark that could get through the shock fences, but Mom worried, and besides, Chena wanted to get the Offshoot deliveries made tonight so she could pay Sadia something major for the day's work.

Sadia was leaning on the boardwalk railing just outside the picnic area where Farin had first taken Chena for lunch. She munched on dark bread and swigged water from a bottle. She was wearing a quilted jacket like Chena's except it was brown, and an oiled canvas hat covered her hair.

"Hey." Chena came up behind her. "You get the replies?"

Sadia nodded, her mouth full. She pulled out a sheaf of letters and handed them over. Chena checked each one and made a notation against the client list in her comptroller. "Great. Now give me some of that." She grabbed for the loaf.

"Hey, hey!" Sadia held it out of her reach. "Manners!"

"I'm paying here," said Chena haughtily. "I don't need manners."

"Who raised you? Squirrels?" Sadia broke off half the loaf and handed it to Chena. It was good stuff, rich and nutty. They ate and drank in silence for a while, watching the boats and the sunlight on the water.

"Do you really think you can earn enough to get off of here?" asked Sadia at last.

Chena shrugged and took a swallow of water from her own bottle. "I don't know. Maybe not for a few years. But I can earn enough to make things better."

"Yeah," agreed Sadia. "That's what everybody wants, isn't it? That's what my dad wanted."

"At least your dad wanted something for you," murmured Chena. Sadia gave her a sideways glance, but didn't ask. Chena was glad.

Even though the remaining few pickups went smoothly, they were back on the rail later than Chena would have liked. Alone, she might have been flying, but Sadia, as strong as she was, was not used to the bikes. They went slowly and the sun sank. By the time they made it back to Offshoot, the bikes' lights were on and the world around them was dark.

"Mom is going to kill me," said Chena as they parked the bikes in the line. "I'll split the money with you tomorrow, all right?"

"Okay," said Sadia.

Chena hesitated. "The dining hall will be closed down. Mom might have something on the stove. You want to come?" Chena jerked her chin up toward the catwalks.

"No," said Sadia. "Thanks, though. I'd better just get back and check on Shond. If I'm not around, he might decide to do something really stupid."

"You think?" said Chena, her voice full of sarcasm. They both laughed and saluted each other quickly. "See you tomorrow."

Sadia took off down the path and Chena took a minute to let her eyes adjust all the way to the darkness. There was a little moonlight coming in from under the trees, and a few lights from the houses. It wasn't much, but it was enough for her to find her way.

Chena took her bearings and headed for the nearest stairway. She thought she saw the faint glimmer of light back in the trees that meant Mom had left a lamp on for her.

Who am I kidding? Mom is probably waiting up for me.

She reached for the stairway railing. *I am in so much—*

A hand clamped onto her wrist. Before Chena could react, it yanked her off her feet. She collided with a hard chest. The hand and arm held her close and another hand groped at her belt.

"Let's see what you have for us, maybe?" grunted an old man with foul breath.

"Told you she'd be here." The new voice belonged to a younger man, and for a sharp, sick second, Chena realized she knew who owned it.

The hand had her throat, but not her mouth. Chena jerked her chin forward and bit down hard. The man, the thief, screamed and dropped her. Chena landed wrong and fell onto her knees. Someone swore and aimed a kick at her. It caught her on the hip and sent her rolling over.

Now Chena screamed, letting loose at the top of her lungs as she scrabbled away.

A shock caught her on the hand. She'd reached the fence. There was nowhere to go this way. She ducked sideways, even as a hand caught her ankle.

"No, you don't," said Shond.

Lights were coming on. Voices were raised. But the hand did not let her go. It dragged her backward.

"Help!" screamed Chena. Something hit her head hard and the world spun into stars.

"No," said yet another familiar voice. But dizzy as she was, Chena could not identify this one.

"No," said the voice again. "She's mine."

The hand let go, dropping her foot onto the ground. The sounds of running surrounded Chena. People running away from her. People running toward her. She blinked her eyes a few times. Dizziness receded, but only slowly.

"Well, now. Let's see what you did to yourself."

Leaves crunched as Nan Elle lowered herself into Chena's line of sight. Chena opened her mouth and closed it again, but no words came out.

Shond just tried to rob me. What am I going to tell Sadia?

By now, others had reached them. The whole world was floodlit by portable torches and lamps in houses turned up high. Chena lifted her head in time to see a flock of would-be rescuers skidding to a halt as they saw Nan Elle.

"Just stay where you are," Nan Elle said to her, or maybe to them. Her fingers pressed against Chena's skull. They were hard, but they were quick, running across her scalp. When she finished, she cupped one hand around Chena's chin.

"Look at me," she ordered. Chena obeyed. The dizziness was fading, but her vision was still a little blurry. "Good, very good."

Nan Elle turned to the crowd. "Fell down the stairs," she announced. "Got startled, poor thing." As carefully as she had knelt down, Nan Elle stood up. "I need someone to walk her to her mother."

"Well, I hope you'll let me." Constable Regan slid through the crowd. "Since you seem to have taken charge."

Nan Elle chuckled. "Oh, no Constable. I would never dream of it." She stepped away, but her black eyes focused on Chena, and Chena understood what she was not to say.

"Is there a concussion?" Regan asked Nan Elle.

"There does not seem to be, but her mother should probably wake her every few hours tonight to make sure."

"Her mother is right here, thank you very much." The crowd shifted, and the next thing Chena knew, Mom knelt on the ground beside her. "Chena, look at me. Look at me, Supernova. Are you hurt?"

"Hit my head," said Chena, a little thickly. She swallowed and tried it again. "I'm okay."

Mom ran her fingers along Chena's scalp, just like Nan Elle had. "You'll have an egg in the morning. Let's get you home." Mom stood and helped her up with both hands under Chena's elbows. Mom, Chena noticed, did not even look at Nan Elle.

Chena stood unsteadily. Her head throbbed, but nothing spun and her stomach stayed still. She knew enough to know these were good signs. Mom didn't let go, though. She held on to Chena's elbows as they climbed the stairs to the catwalk and started toward their house.

I just can't stop attracting crowds today, thought Chena ruefully. *And stalkers.*

Constable Regan walked along behind them. Mom glanced at him but didn't say anything. He didn't say anything either. He just paced along, about half a step behind them, all the way to their front door.

"Thank you for the escort, Brother Constable," said Mom as she pushed the door open. Teal sat in the front room, hugging one of the pillows. She jumped up and ran forward when she saw Mom, but stopped as she saw Regan.

"Not at all, Sister," he said to Mom. "I've got a few questions for Chena here, if you don't mind." Mom didn't get a chance to say whether she did or not. Regan just stepped through the door after her.

"I fell," said Chena as Mom lowered her onto one of the pillows. "I got startled, that's all."

"Right," said Regan. He knelt on a pillow next to her. Mom didn't sit. She hovered over Chena like she might have to snatch her daughter away from the cop. "And that's all Nan Elle told you to say, I'm sure. Don't get started down that road, Chena."

"Look, if you don't like her, why don't you just arrest her? snapped Chena. Her head hurt, a low steady ache.

"Chena!" said Mom sharply.

"No." Regan held up his hand. "It's a fair question." He let out a long sigh. "It's also extremely complicated."

Yeah, that's what you all say when you don't know what you're doing. Chena did not say that out loud, however. Not with Mom standing right there. She just rubbed her temple, as if she could wipe away the hurt.

"I don't shut her down because without her there would be no one who could help out with things like the nettle blight, or delivering babies, or potential concussions." He gave her a smile that Chena thought was supposed to be warm and friendly but didn't quite make it. "But I cannot and I will not let her make her own law." All pretense of smile vanished from his face. "And I will not let anyone help her make that law. Do you understand me?"

Chena nodded and looked down at her toes. Mom shook her shoulder gently.

"There were two men. I think they were trying to rob me." She lifted her eyes. "I never saw them."

But I heard Shond. God's own, I hope Sadia breaks him in two.

Mom's hand flew to cover her mouth and she doubled over like she was going to be sick. "Why didn't you tell me?"

Chena shrugged. "I'm sorry."

"Probably because Nan Elle suggested she shouldn't," said Regan to Mom. "Try not to worry about it too much. Nan Elle gets people doing a lot of things her way. But Chena knows what's right." He smiled at Mom. "If I need to talk to her some more, I'll come by tomorrow."

He wished them good night and walked away into the darkness.

Mom looked down at Chena and said nothing.

Chena's stomach clenched up. "I'm sorry, Mom."

"You've said that." Mom's voice was tired. "Go to bed, Chena. It's past your bedtime."

The knot on the top of Chena's head throbbed. "Mom—" she tried as she got to her feet.

"Not tonight," said Mom, waving her away. "Not any more tonight."

Teal stared at her. Chena felt tears prickle the corners of her eyes. "No, Mom—"

"Go to bed, Chena."

Chena went. What else was there to do? She shucked off her sweaty clothes and climbed into her nightshirt. She lay on her pallet in the dark and tried to muster some defiance. All she felt was sick and empty. She had tried to make things better. That was all. She had managed to mess it up from the beginning.

The door opened and the door closed. Small light feet padded across the floorboards and stopped.

"Chena? What's really going on?"

"I don't know." Chena squeezed her eyes shut to keep the tears in.

Teal was silent for a long time. "Of course not," she said, and Chena was startled by the bitterness in her voice. "Nobody knows what's going on. You won't tell me piss. You won't even give me a job, will you? No, that's got to go to your friend Sadia."

Chena groaned. "Oh, piss, Teal—"

"And you don't give a twisted damn about anything else, do you?" Teal barreled on. "You don't even know Mom lost her job today!"

"What?" Chena jerked her head up. The sudden movement sent a new shock of pain through her skull.

"Her boss told her not to come back. She didn't tell me why." Teal's voice grew hard. "Actually, she didn't tell me at all. I heard her talking to Madra."

"But they can't. She needs . . ." Chena swallowed the words. Of course they could. They were getting to her. They were going to take everything away. The house, everything. Maybe they even sent Shond and the other man to knock her down. They could do anything they wanted and no one would stop them.

Chena lay back down, curling into as tight a ball as she could. "It'll be okay," she murmured, more to keep herself from crying than to reassure Teal. "We'll think of something."

"When?" demanded Teal.

"I don't know," whispered Chena, wrapping her arms around her knees. "I don't know."

CHAPTER EIGHT

Caught

Chena overslept the next morning. When she woke up, it was already full daylight and the sleeping room was empty. She tried to jump to her feet, but the jolt of pain in her skull made her stagger, and all the events of last night rushed back into focus.

Holding her breath, Chena tiptoed to the door and opened it a crack. She could just see Mom sitting alone at the table, her head bowed so that her forehead rested against her hand.

She let the door swing open. "Mom . . ."

Mom's head lifted, and she turned around. "How's your head, Chena?"

"It's okay." Chena walked out into the room. Her stomach flip-flopped with each step.

"No dizziness? No blurry vision?"

"No." Chena sank onto a pillow next to her, tucking her feet under her nightshirt. "It just hurts a little."

"Good." She sighed. "There's something I need to tell you—"

Chena didn't wait for her to finish. "You lost your job."

Mom's eyes narrowed. "Who told you that?"

"Teal," answered Chena, twisting her hands. "She heard you talking to Madra."

Mom just sighed. "Well. It seems we're right back where we started." She rubbed her forehead again. "And this time I don't know what to do."

"You could run errands with me," said Chena tentatively. "We could make all kinds of money if we could carry more stuff."

Mom smiled, just a little. "Would you believe I thought about that? Last night, before . . . before you were attacked." She turned herself all the way around and faced Chena. "This is it, Supernova. I'm going to ask you one more time. Tell me the truth and maybe we can work all this out. Hold anything back on me, and you will not leave this village again, under any circumstances."

She meant it. There was more she was not saying, though. Chena could feel it singing in the air between them. She was not saying, *I'll never trust you again.* She was not saying, *I'll leave you like Dad did.* But she meant it. This time she really did.

Mom waited, eyes fixed on Chena. Chena took a deep breath despite the fact that her chest was clamping down tight around her lungs.

She told her. She told her about Farin and Nan Elle, about the letters, and the ants, and Sadia and the hacker-tailor, and how it was Shond, who was already on the trouble list, who helped knock her down last night. Mom didn't ask any questions. She didn't interrupt even once, until Chena twisted her hands in her lap.

"That's it," she said finally. It was. Now Mom knew everything. She might decide to leave anyway now that she knew it all.

But Mom just leaned forward and drew Chena into a tight embrace. Chena threw her arms around Mom's neck and hugged her back with all her strength.

"Oh, my dear," whispered Mom. "Oh, my girl. Why didn't you *tell* me?"

"I'm sorry," murmured Chena, on the verge of tears again. "I was scared. I wanted to make things okay. I . . . I don't know, Mom. I just don't know."

"It's okay. It's okay." Mom stroked her hair for a moment, just like she had when Chena was a little girl. Then she released her. "All right. You get dressed and you go down and tell Sadia that you won't be running any errands today."

"But—" began Chena, but Mom raised a hand to stop her.

"I'm going to talk to Madra. She said before, she can help us get out of here. We're leaving, Chena. Now. Today. We're not staying here a minute longer." All her determination sounded in that statement, but there was something else too, and it made Chena's heart beat hard as she got to her feet. Mom was afraid.

"Go on, Chena." Mom pushed her toward the bedroom, and Chena went.

Dressed, and chewing on a piece of bread and butter for a quick breakfast, Chena hurried down to the railbike depot to meet Sadia.

But Sadia wasn't there. Chena walked all around the empty depot, finally coming back to the deck and waiting restlessly. After fifteen minutes she gave up and ran down the path toward the dorms. Sadia had probably given up on her a long time ago. Chena was over an hour late.

But the sleeping room was as empty of Sadia as the depot had been. She wasn't in the dining hall either, or the library. Chena checked the roster and saw that Sadia's old shift was back on compost duty this week. But Sadia wasn't in the composting shed, and neither was Shond.

Where are you, Sadia? Chena bit her lip. An ugly idea came to her.

She ran up the stairs, picking the catwalk to the constable's house. Did he have Sadia in there? Had he heard about the hacker-tailor yesterday from the cop in Stem? Had he worked out it was Shond who tried to rob her last night? He might be asking Sadia all kinds of questions.

Regan's door was closed when she got there. She backed away, trying to keep out of sight of the windows and yet trying to see inside. The long strips of glass only allowed her glimpses into the interior. But she saw Regan's shoulder and the back of his head. He moved, and then Chena saw Sadia's profile. She sat by the desk, her hands waving to add emphasis to her explanation. Then Mom stepped into view.

Chena's heart thudded once. Mom's profile was eclipsed by the stranger—a small man in black and white clothes.

Blasted and screwed, is that Teal's spy? What's he doing here?

What was going on? What was Mom doing in there? She was supposed to be talking to Madra.

Shond might know. Shond was a tinky and a mouth-off and she owed him big for the bump on her head, but he would know what was happening with his sister. Thing was, she didn't know where he was either.

But one of the other kids on his shift might. Hyder. He'd know.

Chena turned and walked quickly but calmly down the catwalk. She didn't want to draw any more attention to herself. She certainly didn't want anyone to think she was running away from the constable or something.

She was just about to start down the stairs to the compost shed when she saw Shond. He was walking, head down, between a woman and a man who both wore black slacks and white tunics. Chena bit down hard on her lip. Only the hothousers wore black and white. They herded him toward the boat docks.

Why there? It's not a boat day, was her first, ridiculous thought. After that came, *Does Sadia know?*

Chena ran down the stairs. What was going on? Had they caught him on the robbery try? Maybe the two people with Shond would let him talk to her. Maybe she could get a message from him to Sadia. Maybe . . .

Chena looped wide around Shond and his hothouser escort so she could come into his field of view without getting too close, in case she needed to get away. Shond looked up and spotted her, and his face twisted into a mask of rage.

"This is your fault!" he shouted, lunging forward. But the man beside him grabbed him by the shoulders and held him, pulling him past Chena. "You put her up to this!" Shond twisted in the man's hands. "She put Sadia up to this! Sadia would never have done this!"

Chena stood rooted to the ground. "No!" she shouted. "This is your fault! It was you last night!"

"That will be sorted out later," said the black and white woman. "Right now the judgment is that you are coming with us." The man propelled Shond forward.

"No!" Shond threw his weight backward, trying to slow them down. "Sadia was put up. She didn't do anything! It was you!" he cried over his shoulder at Chena.

"What do they say she did, Shond?" yelled Chena desperately. "I swear, I didn't ask her to do anything! I don't know what's going on!"

"I'll blast you to bits when I get hold of you!" he yelled back, twisting around in his captors' arms. "She never did nothing before!"

But the woman had hold of him on one side now, and the man on the other. They walked him forward quickly and soon he couldn't twist around far enough to yell at her anymore. Chena watched them until they disappeared down the bank, her heart hammering.

What did you do, Sadia?

Her legs felt like they were going to give way under her. She was afraid, but she didn't know why. She hadn't done anything wrong. Okay, she'd taken messages for Nan Elle, but that was it. They couldn't arrest anybody for that, could they? There was the thing with the people who'd parachuted down, but Sadia hadn't seen that. Sadia hadn't even taken a single package for Nan Elle.

Why do they have her and Mom in there? Chena bit her lip and glanced up toward the cop's house. *Why not me?*

It might be something that had nothing to do with her at all. No, that wasn't right either, because Mom was in there, and Teal's spy.

Suddenly Chena couldn't stand it anymore. She had to know what had happened. There was one person who knew what really went on in Stem, and if Nan Elle knew about this, Nan Elle would have to tell her.

Chena ran all the way up the stairs, pounding on the boards until her chest hurt and the pain in her head throbbed all the way down her spine. People waited out in front of the little cluster of houses, as always. Chena ignored them all and threw the door open.

This time there was an old man with a baby in his arms. Chena stood in the threshold, her chest heaving and her head splitting open.

Nan Elle blinked mildly at her. "Again? You are turning out to be an extraordinarily rude one, aren't you, station girl?" she remarked before turning back to the old man. "It's colic, nothing worse. A little warm water before bed will—"

"What have we been running for you?" gasped Chena. "What did you give Sadia to do?"

Nan Elle's spine straightened minutely. "I'll send your instructions down. Take your grandson back to bed. This may take a moment."

"Thank you," lisped the old man. He probably had even fewer teeth than Nan Elle.

Nan Elle didn't move again until he had left. Neither did Chena. She stayed where she was, trying to get her breath and trying to imagine what the old woman might say to her, or try not to say.

The door shut. The lamps weren't on, and the room plunged into a murky twilight.

"What has brought on this fit?" inquired Nan Elle as she moved to sit in her high-backed chair.

"Oh, no." Chena turned to keep her eyes focused on the old woman. "Not this time. This time, you tell me."

"I'll tell you anything you ask, Chena." She spread her hands. "But I ask you to do the same. What brought this on?"

"What did you give us to carry?" Chena shot back.

"Letters," answered Nan Elle promptly. "To friends and colleagues, about growing seasons and proper doses of properly registered and approved plants. Nothing incriminating, nothing even very interesting. Every leaf and stem I sent you to buy was so thoroughly licensed I was spending as much time filling out the forms as I was administering to my patients."

"Then why's Constable Regan got Sadia and my mom in there with him?" She stabbed her finger down vaguely toward the constable's house. "If it's not you, who is it?"

"Sadia and your mother are in with the constable?" Nan Elle frowned. "Is there someone from the hothouse in there with them?"

Chena nodded miserably. "It had to be something you sent with us. There isn't anybody else who could have got us in trouble." *Except almost with the hacker-tailor, but I turned him down and Sadia wouldn't . . .*

Every part of Chena froze solid for a moment. *No. He disappeared her father. Sadia wouldn't . . .*

Unless she thought it would keep her close to him. Unless she thought she could get something out of him.

Unless he offered to tell her what happened to her father.

"Mmm . . ." Nan Elle nodded. "You seem to have hit on some reason yourself."

"I . . ." Chena swallowed and stumbled backward. "I have to go. . . ."

"Chena Trust." Nan Elle stood. Chena stared. The old woman seemed to have shriveled, as if something had been taken out of her. "If you're in trouble, Chena . . ." She walked slowly forward and laid her wrinkled palm onto Chena's hand. "If you ever need help getting . . . away, you use my name—Elle Stepka. You say I am your grandmother. I will help you, and your sister, if you ever need it."

Chena pulled away, rubbing her hand, as if she thought Nan Elle had left something behind.

"Thanks," she muttered, retreating toward the door.

"I'm sorry, Chena Trust." Nan Elle hunched even further in on herself. "This was not my doing. This is the way things sometimes are on this world."

"Yeah." Chena's fumbling hand found the doorknob and she escaped into the daylight. She bit her lip hard and started running again, back to the cop's house. She had to tell him what happened wasn't Sadia's fault. She would tell him about the hacker-tailor. It was his fault, whatever had happened. Sadia had been bullied or bribed. It wasn't her fault.

But when she got there, the cop's house was dark and no one answered when she pounded on the door.

Chena stared at the blank wooden door and felt her mind go numb. Where had they gone? Where was Mom? Where was Sadia? What should she do?

What do I do?

But her mind was so full, so frightened, there was no room in it for new ideas or plans. All on its own, her body turned around and trudged her back home. Chena walked into the empty house and sat down on one of the pillows. She stared at the table waiting, but for what, she wasn't really sure.

Eventually, though, her knees got stiff and her mind got bored. She stood up, drank some water she poured from the pitcher by the stove, sliced up some bread for lunch, and poked at the beans soaking in the bowl of water by the stove to see if they were soft enough to start cooking yet.

She had the beans gently boiling and had just tossed in a handful of salt when Mom came in, with Teal in tow.

Mom took in the situation at a glance.

"Thank you, Chena, for starting lunch. We're going to need it." She closed the door behind them. "We're moving again."

Chena couldn't say anything. She just bowed her head.

"Back to the dorm?" asked Teal. "It's the rent, right?"

"No," said Mom, sinking down to one of the pillows. "There have been some complications. We're not going to be able to stay in Offshoot." She ran her hand over the table, pausing to trace the nails that she and Teal had put in. "We're going to the hothouse. I'm going to take their offer."

Chena bit her lip. *It's not my fault,* she thought desperately. *I didn't do anything. I had permission to be out there. It can't be my fault.*

Teal spoke the words Chena could not. "You're going to have a baby for them? You said you wouldn't do that."

Mom nodded. "I know." Her eyes were shining.

No. Chena took a step forward. *Don't cry. You can't cry. This isn't my fault.*

"Sometimes we have to do things we don't want to do." Mom didn't look at them. She looked at her fingertips as they traced circles around a crooked nail. "Sometimes we even have to do things we said we never would."

"But why?" Teal cried. She stood with her hands balled into fists. "I don't want to go. I was just getting used to it here."

"None of us want to go," said Mom. "But we can't stay. They are asking for too much."

"Why?" Teal stomped her foot. "What happened? I'm sick of all this stuff going on and I don't know why!"

Teal, shut up. Just shut up, Chena, frozen in place by guilt and fear, thought fiercely at her sister. *I'll tell you all about it later, I promise. Just shut up now.*

There was a splash and a hiss. Chena jerked her head around. The beans were boiling furiously, the water slopping over onto the stove. Chena snatched up a rag to use as a hot pad and grabbed the pot off the burner, but she moved too fast and caught her toe on the hearth corner and stumbled, sending boiling water and squishy beans spilling in a huge wave across the floor.

Mom was on her feet and across the room before Chena even saw her move. "Are you all right?" Did you burn yourself?" She took hold of the pot's handles and lifted pot and rag away from Chena.

"No." Chena was shaking. She didn't know why, but she couldn't help it. "I'm sorry," she whispered. "I didn't mean to. I'm sorry."

"I know," said Mom, looking at the empty pot and then at the floor with its lake of thin, steaming soup. " Let's get this cleaned up, all right?"

"Okay." Chena reached for the rags, and she saw Teal, still standing in front of the door, now with her arms folded across her chest.

You did that on purpose, Teal's face said. *You did that so I wouldn't ask any more questions. I know you did.*

I didn't, really, she tried to say back. *It was just an accident. I promise.*

"Teal, come help," said Mom.

Teal turned and stormed out the door. It banged shut behind her, loud enough to make Chena wince.

Mom just sighed. "Well, we'll let her go for a little while. Help me here, Chena." She got down on her knees, mopping at Chena's mess.

Chena knelt beside her and started working. There was nothing else to do.

Teal wasn't home by the time Chena and Mom got the beans cleaned up. Mom announced they should go look for her. She went to check the library and sent Chena to search the dorms and dining hall.

Chena had a feeling she knew where Teal was, but she was grateful for the chance to get away. She really wanted to find Sadia and ask her what had happened, why Shond was being taken away, why Regan had questioned her, with Mom there.

But Sadia wasn't anywhere. She wasn't in the dorms or the dining hall, and when Chena started asking, people just stared at her, or, worse, turned their backs on her. Bewildered and frightened, she climbed back to their house and all the way up onto the roof. There, in the weeds, she found Teal lying sprawled on her back, staring up at the waving branches overhead.

Chena stepped into her line of sight. Teal focused on her for a moment, and then her gaze flickered away.

"Mom's looking for you," said Chena, squatting down next to her.

"Let her look," announced Teal bitterly. "Like she cares what happens to me."

"This isn't Mom's fault." Chena snicked a blade of grass off its stem with her fingernail and started tearing it into little pieces. "She's doing her best."

"She isn't doing anything!" Teal pounded the ground with her fist. "She's just sitting around wringing her hands and saying, 'Oh, my goodness! Whatever shall we do?' "

"Teal . . ." Chena scattered little bits of grass. "You're not seeing everything—"

"No, of course not." She sat up abruptly. "And you're going to tell me what's going on, are you? Because you know everything! You're not here ninety percent of the time, you don't care piss and spit about anybody but yourself, and you're still the one she actually talks to!"

Chena opened her mouth and closed it again. *No, no, don't tell me I screwed this up too.* "That's not it, Teal—"

"Go away." Teal closed her eyes.

"I can't," Chena said.

"Chena!" Mom's voice called up from below. "Is Teal up there with you?"

"Yes!" Chena called back down.

Teal's eyes snapped open and her face tightened into an expression of pure anger at Chena's betrayal.

There was a moment of silence from Mom. At last she said, "Okay, as long as we know where she is." Chena heard the door open and close.

Teal went back to staring at the branches. Anger stabbed through Chena. What was she supposed to do? Teal wanted to be impossible. Nobody knew what was going on. Nobody could know. Not here, anyway, where they couldn't even get their hands on a decent computer.

Chena stood. "You want to stay up here all night and get bat shit on you, you do that."

She pounded down the steps without looking back and slammed the door hard behind her.

Mom was in the bedroom. Chena could see her through the open door.

"She's staying up here?" Mom asked, lifting the lid on the clothes box.

"Yeah." Chena leaned against the inside threshold.

"That's okay. Come help me get some stuff together." She frowned at the clothes. "We won't need that much, just enough for a couple of days until we get settled."

"What about the rest of it?" Chena gestured vaguely around the room. "What do we do with this stuff?"

"Nothing. It'll go to whoever gets the house next." She picked up her nightshirt. "I suppose, anyway."

Chena wrapped her arms around herself as if she were trying to hold something in. "Mom?"

"Yes, Supernova?" Mom folded the nightshirt's shoulders in toward each other and smoothed it over her arm.

"Why are you doing this? Why are you really doing this?"

Mom laid the folded shirt back on the pallet. "Because if I don't, they are going to take you away from me."

Chena's chest constricted, hard. "They said that?"

Mom nodded. She picked up a pair of Teal's trousers.

"Why?" cried Chena. "They can't. This place has laws. I didn't do anything."

"No," Mom agreed. "But apparently that girl you hired to help with your errand-running did, and they are saying that because you paid her, you are responsible for her."

Chena froze. She didn't even close her mouth. Mom folded the trousers neatly and laid them on top of the nightshirt. "I didn't know either," she said. "They are not accepting that as an excuse."

"But—" began Chena

"No, Supernova." Mom shook her head. "They wanted me and they got me. All we can do now is ride the wave and look for a way out." She plucked one of her work shirts out of the box. "Another way out."

Wordlessly, Chena walked over to stand next to her mother. She pulled a pair of slacks out of the box and folded them in half, and then in half again. She laid them next to the pile of shirts and reached for a pair of socks.

A knock sounded on the front door. Mom dropped the shirt she was folding, went into the front room, and opened the door. Madra stood on the walk outside. Her face was a mask. Only her eyes held any expression, and Chena hoped that no one would ever look at her like that.

"I understand you will be transferring to the hothouse," said Madra.

"Yes." Mom inclined her head. "I was going to come find you. I imagine there's some paperwork?"

"Not much, but I do need to read your chips." Madra pulled the scanner off her belt. "Is Teal here too?"

"She's on the roof," volunteered Chena. "I'll go get her."

"That's okay." Teal stepped into view, squeezing past Madra to get through the door. "I'm here. What are we doing now?"

"Checking out," said Mom. "Hold out your hands."

They all held up their right hands, and Madra ran her scanner over the tattoos. When she was done she checked the reader and hit a couple of keys before returning the machine to her belt. Then she looked at Mom one more time and opened her mouth.

Mom didn't give her a chance to say anything. "I know, Madra. Thank you for your help."

"Good-bye, Helice." She walked back out the door, just as a skinny man in black slacks and a white shirt came into view.

Chena recognized him at once: He was the man from the constable's office. Teal's spy. The cold glance and small nod she got from Teal confirmed it. This was Basante, and he had come to take them all away. Like Sadia had been taken away, and Shond, and their parents. Chena took hold of Mom's hand, and didn't even feel childish about it.

"Yes, Chena," said Mom as she squeezed her hand. "We're going now."

It was a proper assignment, Tam's Conscience tried to tell him. *Now that the family Trust is in the complex, they are out of your jurisdiction as administrator. Those are the parameters. It does you no good to be angry with your sister.*

"But it may do someone else some good," he muttered back as he strode into the laboratory.

The laboratory was as much of a hive as the family dome. But where the family dome was a garden and forest of living plants, the laboratory was a forest of workstations and a garden of equipment—clusters of monitors, a labyrinth of pipes and aquariums, mazes of glass-walled cubicles that could be sealed off to create sterile environments.

According to Aleph, Dionte was in one of the imaging rooms. Tam followed the curve of the wall until he came to the appropriate door. Tam's touch on its surface caused it to flash his name to whoever occupied the chamber. After a moment, the door slid open and let him in.

Walking into the imaging room was like walking into a cage of light. The room's glass screens had been set to show thousands of fine lines that shimmered in the air, making a complex, multicolored net around Dionte. She sat in the center of that net, her fingers splayed out, touching nothing but light.

"What are you doing?"

She did not move. "Experimenting."

"I thought that was Basante's job."

Dionte smiled. "When it comes to the Conscience implants, I am allowed to do a little experimenting as well, you know."

"You are experimenting with your Conscience?"

Her smile grew fierce. "Did you know that it takes very little restructuring to connect the data input functions to the actual Conscience functions? If this works, I will be able to feed raw data directly into my subconscious and use the brain's nondeclarative memory processes to organize the input and create the appropriate connections with what I've already learned, without having to take the time to understand it consciously." Her eyes grew distant, seeing the future rather than what was in front of her. "Think of it: Each one of us will be able to have the understanding of an entire city-mind inside us. Think how our judgment, our possibilities will expand. We will be able to reliably harness intuition to cognition."

"Because we all know what a bother thought is," said Tam dryly. "I can see many uses for this development. Although, on the face of it, it sounds a little like the ancient idea of sleep teaching, and we all know how badly that worked."

Dionte finally lowered her hands. "We'll be able to see the future, Tam. See it and understand it, not just guess at it." She rubbed her fingertips together, staring at them as if she'd never felt the touch of her own skin before. "If our ancestors had given us this gift instead of just nagging little voices in our ears, we wouldn't be under siege now."

"If not this, then it would have been something else." Tam shrugged. "That is the way it is, Sister."

"But not the way it has to stay, Brother."

The iron certainty in her voice took Tam aback. For a moment he could not even think of how to question her.

So he kept his voice as bland as he could. "Just be sure that with all this wondrous internal rearrangement, you don't forget how to look out and see the rest of us."

"Thank you, Brother," she said, matching and even mocking his tone. "I will keep that under advisement."

Tam turned to the light that encased her. "This"—Tam gestured to the colored lines shimmering between them—"is not a map of your Conscience implant."

"No." Dionte's voice took on a tinge of awe, as if seeing an artist's masterpiece. "This is Eden."

Tam turned in place, tracing the colored branches of the fate map. Each branch indicated the expression of a single gene at some point in an individual's life. With practiced eyes, he read the implications and complications as the timer flickered and the branches grew, stretched, and shifted, playing their expressions out across the fabric of simulated years.

"We've never made a whole person before," he said. "Are we sure this is all there is to it?" He waved at the lines.

"If consciousness and personality entered into it, you might have a legitimate concern." Dionte's lips moved briefly, subvocalizing some command. "Fortunately," she said aloud as the fate map vanished from around them, "in this case, they don't. That is part of the perfection of this solution."

"Does that perfection include helping Basante kidnap Helice Trust and her daughters?"

It turned out Dionte maintained enough of a sense of shame to look away. "The normal rules were suspended."

"The suspension applied only to Helice Trust herself. There was no vote taken about her daughters."

Dionte waved her hand, dismissing his words as a distraction. "So, Basante exercised initiative. He should be commended."

"You cannot tell me this was Basante's idea alone."

Dionte didn't answer. Her lips moved again, giving orders he couldn't hear. The walls shimmered with projected images, more lines and graphs—process tracking. Dionte was seeing which of Aleph's expert subsystems were working on whatever theories she had added into the fate map, and how they were coming along.

"You are not allowed to interfere with my prerogatives." Tam stepped directly into her line of vision. "There are rules of precedence in place—"

Dionte swept her hand straight down, freezing her shining reports in the air around her. Their reflection left colored stripes across her dust-gold skin. "There is a sword hanging over Pandora, Brother. You would not act, even after the family voted that action was necessary."

"We cannot break our old laws even in times of crisis. If we do, we put the world in as much danger as the threat of Authority bombs does. You've said it yourself, it's only by the laws that the balance of Pandora survives!"

Dionte sat up straighter, her eyes bright with anger. "Yes, Pandora survives. Only Pandora survives. Out of all the hundreds of settlements, only Pandora lives and breathes and has a future left to it. Don't you understand? They are all dying! And if we let them in here, we are going to die with them! All of us! And Old Earth will perhaps one day send out another wave of colonization and they will repeat the same mistakes and they will die, just like we did, because our minds are too small and our lives are too separate to understand the enormity of our own future." Tam's throat tightened. He had expected to see wildness in her eyes. Such words should be accompanied by some look beyond reason. But Dionte's eyes were clear, and her voice stayed firm. "Our understanding, our bond, between each other and our world has allowed us to survive this long. If we don't strengthen that bond, we are going to die just like the rest of them." The veneer of calm cracked then and her voice started to shake. "No, it will be worse, because we could have done something and we didn't. The Authority will be trying to commit murder, but we'll be committing suicide."

Oh, Sister. Tam wanted to feel pity, but instead he felt fear, because he heard her words and he understood them, and because for one heart-beat, he saw how she might be right.

Then her eyes skittered sideways, listening to a voice Tam could not hear, and Tam forced himself to focus on his immediate responsibilities.

The taste of Dionte's anger alerted her Conscience to their argument. It would be working on her, reminding her what a bad thing it was to be angry at her birth brother. Now he had to force it to work hard. Nothing Dionte said had changed the present facts. The Trusts were still being coerced, and they still needed him.

Tam waved his hand dismissively. "That has nothing to do with Helice Trust."

"Doesn't it?" Dionte rose slowly, walking through her reports to face him without any barrier. "Without her there will be no Eden Project. Without Eden, the next wave of invasion will drown us completely."

"You had no right." He enunciated each word. "And you had no business interfering in how I chose to proceed. You are a Guardian, Dionte, not an experimenter, and not an administrator."

"I had every right!" Dionte shouted. "You would have us wait until Pandora is torn apart because you care more for the villagers and the Athenians than you do for your own family!" Her hand rubbed agitatedly at her temple.

Which was his cue. Tam let his face slacken. He turned away, rubbing his own temple and hunching his shoulders.

"Are you well, Brother?" Dionte's voice softened from anger to concern. If he had calculated correctly, her Conscience would be awakening memories from their childhood, when they played together, when they helped each other through small hurts. Better times, simpler times. She would want to help him now.

"No, no, I don't think I am." Tam sat down heavily in the chair she had vacated. He smelled aloe and vanilla at the sound of her concern. Soothing reassurance. He was among his family, safe and secure. Nothing could be wrong here that they could not fix together. He wanted to tell her his worries. He hated being alone. But talking openly with Dionte was too great a risk. He knew that with a certainty beyond the feelings of his Conscience and his own weariness. Dionte had picked her own path long ago, and it was not the same as his. He could never forget that. He would see this through.

Dionte laid a hand on his shoulder. "When it is done, the Trusts will be free, and we will have saved Pandora, and we'll be able to look to our future." She shook him gently. "If I agree with you that what we're doing is not fair, will you feel better?"

Tam let a small smile form on his face. "A little, yes," he said, concentrating on getting his shoulders to relax.

Dionte spread her hands. "Then I admit it. It is not fair. She was bullied into this out of our necessity. As a result, she and her children will be carefully looked after and living in a level of comfort they have never known before. They might actually be able to find productive work for themselves to do." She brought her hands back together. "A reasonable trade, don't you think?"

"Reasonable enough." He rubbed his temple again. "If it stays that way."

"What are you afraid will change, Brother?"

"I hardly know." He shook his head, trying to clear away the illusions of scent and emotion. "Maybe I just fear our troubles and what they will make us do."

Dionte crouched down in front of him, looking up into his eyes with an expression that was all open concern. "And what would you have me do, Brother, to ease your worries?"

"Talk to Basante for me. Help me gain a supervisory assignment on the Trusts."

Dionte started to pull away, but she was too far into it. Tam searched her face, watching the emotions flicker across it, but the bond had been tightened, by his Conscience and hers. The Consciences existed to strengthen the ties between family members. Whatever she was doing to herself, even Dionte was not good enough to completely subvert her implant's primary function.

"That assignment has already been given to Basante," she tried.

Tam said nothing.

Dionte hung her head. "Perhaps a cosupervisor? Basante would surely agree to that."

That would give him access to all the records and require Aleph to alert him when any change in their status or welfare was made. It would do—for now, at any rate. He would at least be able to make sure that Dionte kept her promise about them being well looked after inside the complex.

She was giving him a contemplative look now, as if he were something she'd like to study later at her leisure. "Do you ever wonder if our parents did right?" she asked suddenly.

Tam's smile was tight. "How could they do wrong?" he asked mildly. "They were family."

Before she could answer that, Tam rose. "Thank you for what you have done, Sister. I'm sorry to have been trouble to you."

She straightened up and pressed his hand again. "We know, you and I, how things are. I'm impressed with you, Brother. I think I've underestimated you before this."

You have, but you won't again, he thought as he turned away, leaving her there with her own thoughts and connections. *I've shot my bolt. From now on I will have to be more careful.*

But then, so will you.

CHAPTER NINE

Hothouse Flowers

Chena had assumed the hothousers would stash her family in a place like the village dormitories, but she was wrong. After the boat ride, and the dirigible ride, the supervisors, Basante and Tam, took them through an environment lock and from there into a series of labyrinthine corridors lined with video images of sunny meadows and marshes. The living space was nooks and crannies tucked into the crooks of the corridors, labeled neatly with their names and ID numbers. No doors stood between the various "rooms" and the curving hallways, just green curtains that rippled slightly in the air from the ventilators.

In fact, the only door in the whole place was the one leading from the central atrium to their wing, and that had a touch pad to activate the lock. Chena couldn't help noticing that nobody took their prints or a chip reading to ID them to that door either.

They're going to lock us in here, thought Chena as they walked down the hall behind Tam and Basante in their matching white shirts and black vests. Their feet made no noise on the padded floor. *We're prisoners.*

Despite the fact that she felt like a baby doing it, Chena pressed closer to Mom. Mom squeezed her shoulder and kept her own eyes straight ahead.

Teal didn't seem to notice anything wrong. She was too busy squealing and exclaiming over everything she saw—the game rigs, the library terminals, the classrooms, the walls of planters and terrariums, as if they hadn't spent a month living in a forest. She went all google-eyed over the playroom full of little kids making enough noise to wake the dead.

The show delighted Supervisor Basante. He began to speak more and more to Teal, casting pleased glances at Mom as if to say, *See, your charming little girl loves it here already.*

Chena trailed along, feeling her face harden into a scowl. It was an act. Teal was acting. Couldn't they see that?

It was hard to say what Supervisor Tam saw. He didn't open his mouth once during the entire tour. Chena remembered him from Madra's office, of course, and remembered how he'd watched Mom so carefully. Now he was watching her again, but this time it was an expression torn between fear and anger. Chena couldn't work out whether it was for something the Trusts had done or for something he was afraid they would do.

She also couldn't help noticing how many of the women they saw in the brightly lit alcoves and the little artificial parks were pregnant, like Mom would soon be.

The idea made Chena go cold and her feet lagged behind, as if they thought there was some way to turn back. But Mom just patted her shoulder. "Keep up, Supernova. We've got a lot of ground to cover." And she went back to listening to the supervisor and watching Teal bounce up and down like a *complete* baby.

Once, Teal did catch Chena's eye. She gave Chena a smug grin and stopped just short of sticking her tongue out. Chena's fist tightened with the sudden, vicious urge to smack her sister. Didn't she realize this wasn't a game? These people were the enemy! They had forced Mom in here, forced them all in here. How could she even pretend to like this . . . this . . . hole, this . . .

"Chena, pay attention," said Mom.

Chena jerked out of her brooding to see Supervisor Basante smiling condescendingly at her. "It's a lot of information to absorb," he said cheerfully. "But that's all right. Your tutors will help you find your way around."

"Tutors?" blurted out Chena. She'd missed more than she thought.

"Tutors," repeated Mom, with just a hint of annoyance in her voice. "You and Teal start school tomorrow."

"Already? But . . . we just got here. . . ."

"And neither one of you has seen the inside of a classroom for—" Mom cut herself off, suddenly remembering the hothousers were listening. "Too long," she finished. "You've got a lot of catching up to do."

Chena stopped herself from saying, *But . . .* She just tried to think at Mom. *But I don't know what this place is like yet. I don't know what they've done with Sadia and Shond. I don't know what they're trying to do to us yet, and I know they're trying to do something. Please, Mom . . .*

But Mom just gave her shoulder a quick squeeze. "It'll be fine, Supernova, you'll see. Not nearly as hard as shoveling compost." Her voice was earnest, but not full of belief. All at once, Chena thought she knew what Mom was asking. *Go along with it*, she was saying underneath her words. *Don't give them a reason to do anything else to us.*

Chena forced a smile. "Sure. Anything's easier than shoveling."

Teal actually took hold of her hand. "We'll have fun here, Chena. I know we will."

Chena wanted to gag, but Mom and Basante just smiled as if nothing in the world were wrong with this new, sugary Teal. Tam looked down at her from under hooded eyes. His hands twitched, as if he wanted to reach out to touch her and . . . what? Chena didn't even want to think about it, so she just swallowed her thoughts and pasted a smile on her face for Basante.

"You said there's a climbing gym?"

That night, Chena lay in the soft alcove bed set into the back wall of her private chamber and listened. She heard nothing. The nightlights that kept it from getting truly dark didn't hum. Neither did the vents, although she could feel a constant draft across her face. She couldn't hear Teal, or Mom, or anybody, for that matter. It was as if the world had been wrapped in foam rubber. There were no smells either. No scent of metal, minerals, or earth. It was . . . weird. She felt cut off from reality.

Time stretched out. She watched the minutes click over on the glowing clock set into the wall by the curtained threshold. Sleep did not come. Instead she thought about how she would never see Sadia again, how she would never see Farin again. Tears stung her eyes. She'd never know now what he really thought about her. Never see him smile at her again, never have him touch her. She was completely alone in the sterile silence, with who knew what going on, on the other side of all the twisting walls.

She wiped the back of her hand across her eyes and looked at the curtain.

Don't, she told herself. *You'll get in trouble, and who knows what they can do to you now that you're all in here.*

Too late, though. She couldn't just lie there. She had to get out. She had to see what was really going on out there. She had to know. After all, when she'd snuck out that first morning in the dorm, she'd met Nan Elle, and Nan Elle had helped her, and promised she'd help more. Which was more than anybody else had done.

Chena threw back the covers and planted her bare feet on the warm, soft floor. She slid past the privacy curtain and out into the winding corridors.

The green curtains, turned gray by the dim light, billowed gently around her, blown by the silent soft ventilator breeze. The video images covering the walls had been shut off for the night, and Chena saw the faint ghosts of her own reflections keeping pace with her on either side. She bit her lip nervously. It made her feel watched.

But it was either put up with it or go back to her alcove (she couldn't really call the thing a room) and hide under the covers. So Chena made the piss-off sign at the reflections, which made it right back at her, and she kept on going.

After about the fifth turn, Chena suddenly realized she had no idea where she was. Not only were the wall videos switched off, the signs that had directed them on the day's tour were gone too. The corridor walls were completely featureless except for the curtains and her reflections. She didn't know where she was, and she had no idea how to get back. Chena leaned her hand against the smooth hard wall and cursed herself, using every hard word she knew.

You just can't stop being stupid, can you? No matter how much trouble you're going to get in, you just can't stop.

After a while, she decided she couldn't just be found huddled in the corridor in the morning when the lights and signs came back on. She had to do something. She looked at the three branches of corridor that opened out around her. They all looked the same.

Keep bearing right, she advised herself. *You'll have to get to the outside wall sooner or later. You can follow that back to the start.* She checked her wrist automatically, before remembering they had taken her comptroller away. She couldn't even tell how long she'd been here.

Long meters of corridors and curtains passed her by. Chena had to work to keep herself from running. She shouldn't be afraid. This place should be more familiar than the forest had been. She'd grown up in closed hallways, hadn't she?

But these are nothing like the station corridors. Those weren't creeps-breeders, ones that didn't mean anything, that didn't give you anything to do. . . .

She took the right-hand fork at every branching, more branches than she could keep count of.

How many people live here? There weren't that many kids in the playrooms, but there's got to be space here for thousands. . . .

An idea struck her. Chena stopped outside one of the curtains and listened hard, for anything—breathing, sighing, a rustle of cloth. This place might be silent, but there was no way the people in it could be.

Nothing. Chena pulled together her courage and reached out for the curtain. She touched the edge. Nothing happened. She hooked her fingers around the heavy cloth. Nothing happened then either. Taking a deep breath and holding it, she leaned close to the curtain's edge and peeked past it.

On the other side waited an alcove identical to the one she'd snuck out of. The thin strip of night-lighting around the floorboards showed her it was completely empty, with a neatly made-up bed waiting for . . . whomever.

Maybe I can sleep here and sneak back when the lights come back on. I can't really have gotten that far. It just feels that way.

It would be better than just wandering around the corridors anyway. Chena slipped through the curtain opening.

"You don't belong here, Chena Trust."

Chena jumped, stuffing her fist into her mouth to stop her scream. Her heart beat frantically, until she felt like it would explode.

There was no one else in the room. She was alone. No shadow moved outside the curtain. Chena lowered her hand.

"Excuse me," she said, her eyes flicking every which way, looking for the speaker grill, or intercom, or anything. "I didn't know."

"You did, but you ignored it." The voice might have belonged to a young man or a middle-aged woman. It was soft, smooth, and perfect, and a little sad. It sounded like it was coming out of the air by Chena's right ear.

"Who are you?"

"I am the Alpha Complex," replied the voice. "You have come to live in me, and I'm rather sorry you don't like it."

Okay, okay. Chena rubbed her hand against her thigh, rubbing off the spit and the sudden sweat. *It's just a computer. Nothing to get excited about. It's not like you haven't talked to a machine before.*

"I need directions to the foyer," said Chena. "Respond."

"No," answered the Alpha Complex. "You need to return to your bedroom."

"I need directions to the foyer," Chena repeated, clenching one fist. "You will respond."

"No." The complex's voice remained unperturbed. "It is not time for you to be there yet."

Chena's gaze swept the room. If there was a control pad somewhere, she couldn't see it. That left her with no way to force this machine to give her what she needed.

"Why didn't you say something when I went out?" she demanded irritably. "You could have saved us both the trouble."

"I wanted to see what you would do." The complex sounded marginally more cheerful, even a little pleased with itself. "If you had turned back at any time, you would have found the signs on at half power."

"So, you let me get lost." Chena tried to put some heat into her voice. Right now she just felt cold. She did not like this thing. It wasn't acting like an artificial intelligence, even a gatekeeper. It was acting like . . . like . . . a cross between Teal and Experimenter Basante.

"I let you reach your limits," answered the complex. "I would not have let you distress yourself unduly, don't worry."

That wasn't one of the things I was worrying about, trust me, thought Chena sourly. "So, you'll let me go back now?"

"Of course." The curtain whisked silently aside. Chena swallowed again. She hadn't realized this . . . AI, or whatever it was, could work the curtains. "Follow the signs. They will take you straight back to bed."

Out in the corridor, exactly at her eye-level glowed the amber words CHENA'S BEDROOM, along with an arrow pointing to her left. She looked to her right. In that direction, the corridor had been completely blanked out. Not even the night-lights cut the darkness. Chena felt resentment, fear, and rebellion stiffen her back.

"Don't worry, Chena Trust," said the complex. In front of Chena, her reflection shifted, becoming another girl about her own age, but taller, broader, with bouncy chestnut hair and dusky skin. "My people and I will take good care of you. You just need to let yourself get used to us."

Chena looked away as fast as she could. She started running in the direction the arrow pointed. The corridors lit up for her, with helpful arrows and signs, and within minutes a green curtain drew back and she tumbled into her sleeping alcove. She dove under the blankets and drew them all the way over her head, curling up into a tight ball. She shivered and prayed that under here, at least, the thing, the complex, couldn't see her, wouldn't speak to her, wouldn't read her mind. She wished desperately she was back in the trees with the flowers and the bats, even the ants. She wished she was back on the station with the whirs and clicks and stinking corridors and Eng and King and their stupid games, or away out on some strange world with her father. She wished she was anywhere, anywhere at all but here, where the walls were watching her, and smirking about it.

It took a while, but eventually the startled fear gave way to anger, and Chena was able to unroll herself, although she did not stick her head out of the blankets.

I need to let myself get used to it, do I? She clenched her teeth, her fists, and every muscle in her body. *That is not happening. I'll find a way around you if it takes me ten years. I promise you I will.*

Morning came all at once. Warm light touched Chena's face, turning the darkness behind her eyelids red. She blinked and sat up. The blank night world was gone, replaced by a grove of trees that looked like they had been taken straight out of the forest around Offshoot.

"I'll pick my own walls, thank you," muttered Chena as she kicked the covers back.

The trees faded away, leaving behind blue screen and touch pad area. Chena scowled and ignored them. She pulled her curtain back, stumbling into the dark common area. She blinked and knuckled her eyes. It was still night out here, as well as behind Mom's and Teal's curtains.

The stupid complex had woken her up early.

"Next time I'll wake your sister up first," said the complex's voice. "You need to take turns using the washroom anyway."

"What the piss kind of computer are you?" demanded Chena in a hoarse whisper.

"My own kind," replied the complex. "How hot do you like your shower?"

"Leave me alone!" snapped Chena. "Or do you like ogling little girls in the shower?"

This time there was no answer. Chena stormed into the shower, wishing there was a door or even a drawer to slam. But there was nothing. She thumped her fist against the wall but it produced nothing except a muffled thud, and it hurt.

The shower was frustratingly comfortable, the towel was thick, and the clothes in the drawer were brainless-looking—just a green shirt and black pants, but they were clean and more comfortable than anything she'd worn since they'd gotten to Pandora.

All of which just made her more angry.

She stomped out of the bathroom just as Mom was coming out of her sleeping alcove.

"I hate it here!" Chena announced.

Mom blinked at her. "This is not news, I'm afraid, Supernova. What do you hate?"

"Everything!"

A chime sounded outside the curtain that opened onto the corridor. Mom smoothed her nightshirt down and went to open the curtain. Chena followed, trying to make her pay attention. "There's this computer, it runs the whole place and it spies on everything, I swear Mom, it's not safe. It's probably—"

Mom drew the curtain back. On the other side stood a smiling woman. Her skin was pale, but her hair was coal black and bundled into a knot at the back of her neck. She wore a loose white tunic and a black skirt that reached down to her ankles.

"Good morning, Mother Trust," she said, saluting. "I'm Abdei and I'll be one of your daughters' teachers. I'm here to take Chena to her testing appointments."

"Oh." Mom returned the salute a little uncertainly, glancing down at Chena, already washed and dressed.

"Mom," said Chena urgently. "I told you—"

"Chena," she said sharply. But then she turned to Abdei. "I'm sorry. It's still a little early and I was hoping the girls and I could have breakfast together before they started school."

Abdei's smile broadened. "I understand, but we do need to get started. I'll have her back by lunch."

Mom hesitated and Chena bit her lip. For a moment she thought Mom was going to refuse, but she didn't. She just said, "All right. It'll be lunch, then." She gave Chena a quick, one-armed hug. "Behave yourself for me, all right, Supernova?"

"Yeah," said Chena sullenly. She didn't want to be angry at Mom. Mom was as much a prisoner as she was. But why wouldn't Mom listen? Did she not want to hear how bad it was?

Abdei turned her smile onto Chena and gestured toward the corridor. *Another Madra, always smiling and always telling you what to do.* Chena kept her face closed and fell into step beside her, watching the walls and curtains, and saying nothing at all. All signs were back on. This morning the corridor landscape was images of beaches and oceans. Maybe she could count the turnings. Maybe after a little while she could learn her way without the signs.

Abdei walked beside her in silence for a moment. Chena didn't look at her. Then she said, "I understand you met Aleph last night."

Chena didn't let herself look up. "Aleph?"

"Our city's mind," Abdei told her. "The complex's artificial intelligence, if you like."

"Oh, great," said Chena, still keeping her eyes straight ahead of her. "It's not just a spy, it's a mouth."

She expected Abdei to get mad, but Abdei just chuckled. "Yes, well . . ."

"It's for my own good?" inquired Chena.

"No. It's for ours."

They stood in front of the foyer door. It hadn't even taken five minutes to get there, Chena was sure. How had she gotten so lost? Was this place really that big?

Or had some of the walls she'd thought she'd seen last night been simulations? Chena frowned back at the dorm.

"*Your* own good?" she asked.

"Yes." Abdei pressed on the door handle. It opened easily for her. She stood back to let Chena walk through into the real sunlight of the atrium. "When we let new people in, we know they're nervous. Nervous people can make mistakes, get into places that are dangerous, or they can just get confused and lonely. Maybe they made a tough decision before coming here and think they might regret it. We can't be there to help out everybody, especially now that we're taking in so many new people. So, Aleph is there for you, and for us."

"So, because you're understaffed you bug the dorms?" demanded Chena.

"It worked, didn't it?" Abdei raised her eyebrows. "If Aleph hadn't stopped you, you would have been out and wandering around who knows where. You might have even tried to get out into the marsh, and then we might never have been able to find you."

Which was a fair call, but Chena wasn't ready to admit it. "I imagine you guys aren't very big on privacy regulations."

"No," answered Abdei simply. "They don't work very well for us."

"I guess not," muttered Chena.

Abdei clicked her tongue on the back of her teeth. "I can see you're going to be one of the fun ones."

Chena gave her a wide, game grin. "Bet on it."

Abdei sighed. "I should have known, with an accomplice in involuntary—" her mouth closed abruptly, but it was too late and Chena wasn't about to let her go.

She folded her arms, ready to stay where she was all day. "Where'd you say Sadia was?"

"I didn't," replied Abdei.

"What's involuntary, then?"

Abdei's eyes flickered from side to side, as if she were listening to some inner voice. "It's another wing of the complex," she said finally, focusing on Chena again. "For those who have forfeited their body rights by breaking the law."

"What did she do?" demanded Chena. "She couldn't have done anything."

Again, Abdei took that listening stance. What was she hearing? Aleph? Could the complex talk just to her? Were they wired somehow? She couldn't see any jacks or implants on Abdei, but that didn't mean piss around here.

"She was found loading a virus into the Offshoot library computer so that it would alter some of the village records."

The hacker-tailor. Chena felt her eyes widen. Sadia had done it. She'd taken the three hundred to carry that program. But she wouldn't do that. She couldn't do that. The little mushroom of a man had helped take her father away from her. Chena shook her head. Unless what she thought before had been true, unless what he offered her was not money, but a chance to find out where her father was.

Was Sadia's father in here? Maybe she was with him right now. But if she was in prison, what would that matter?

"And you people thought I helped her, so you bullied my mom into doing your thing for you." She couldn't make herself name that thing out loud.

Abdei shrugged. "I know nothing about it, Chena. I'm just a teacher and you are my student. If we can work together, you'll learn a lot and the future will open up for you."

Chena's eyes narrowed. "And if I don't, I'll end up in the involuntary wing with Sadia?"

"Only if I fail at my job." It took a few moments for her smile to form again. "And only if you want to upset your mother very badly."

Something in the way she emphasized the last sentence sounded a low warning signal in the back of Chena's mind, but she couldn't really understand why.

"You're a good girl, Chena," said the complex's voice out of the air. "You do not want to cause trouble, I know that."

Abdei smiled again and her whole body relaxed. "Hello, Aleph."

"Hello, Abdei. Hello, Chena." The dusky-skinned girl Aleph had manifested the night before appeared in the middle of the beachscape and waved to Chena and Abdei.

You have no idea what I want. Then an idea came to her, made up of what Abdei had said and how Aleph was suddenly there.

"I want to see Sadia," she said.

The image of Aleph shook her head. "That is not possible, Chena. She is not allowed visitors yet."

Here came the gamble. She thought it was a good one, but she couldn't stop her stomach from fluttering. "You don't let me see Sadia, I'll tell Mom you threatened me."

Aleph paused for a moment and Abdei looked positively aghast. In that moment, Chena knew she was on to something. "I will. You can't stop me from talking to her."

Aleph recovered before Abdei did. "Why would I care if you told her what we've said?"

It was Chena's turn to smile. "Because you don't know what I might tell her. You don't want her upset. You need her cooperation for your project. You don't want her walking out of here and refusing to participate anymore." Chena leaned in close to the imaginary girl. Abdei didn't count here. Aleph made the decisions. That was crystal clear. "If you don't let me see Sadia, you will not believe the stories I will tell her about how I am being treated."

"I revise my assessment of you, Chena Trust," said Aleph mildly. "You are a bad girl."

"Probably," said Chena, mocking the computer's bland tone. "Do I get to see her?"

Another long pause. Chena wished she could know what was going on inside the machine. Abdei's mouth was moving, subvocalizing to something, maybe Aleph, maybe whatever voice she was listening to earlier.

Aleph's image spread its hands, a gesture of acceptance or defeat, Chena couldn't tell. "I have arranged for you to see her. Your supervisors are in agreement. When would you like to go?"

Already talked to them? she thought snidely. *My, aren't you the efficient one.* Chena's shoulders straightened up in quiet triumph. "Now." *Now I've got you. Now I know how to work you.*

"Very well. Abdei, I will take charge of her. You have other students." There was no mistaking the look of relief on Abdei's face. "Follow the arrow and signs to Section Yellow."

The words SECTION YELLOW and a new arrow appeared on tiled floor at her feet. Still smiling from her triumph, Chena walked in the direction it pointed, past the glass bubble full of trees, ferns, and flowers. The arrow migrated across the floor just in front of her, rippling like a fish in a stream as it led her toward a neon-yellow door that Chena was certain had not been there when they'd last come through the foyer.

The yellow door had a palm reader next to it. Chena touched her hand to it automatically. The door slid open onto a long straight corridor with blank pale gold walls with the telltale sheen that told Chena they were more video screens controlled by Aleph. Despite that, the arrow still slid along the floor and Chena had to keep her eyes turned down to make sure she was going in the right direction. Black or white legs flashed past her on either side. Hothousers, going about their business. Some of them glanced at her curiously, but none of them said anything. The arrow at her feet seemed to be all the permission she needed.

The arrow winked off. Chena lifted her eyes in time to see a patch of the right-hand wall clear to form a window. On the other side, Sadia sat, alone, in an eggshell-yellow room, wearing what looked like a game rig. But if she was in a game, it wasn't a very active one. Sadia sat still inside the flexible suit of wires and patches, only turning her head this way and that and occasionally raising her hand to adjust something. After a while, Aleph cleared a door in the back of the room and let in a woman wearing a long white tunic and black leggings. She helped Sadia off with the rig and saluted her. Their mouths moved the whole time, but Chena couldn't hear anything that was said. Together, Sadia and the strange woman left by the rear door.

"There," said Aleph. "She is not bottled in a test tube or vivisected." Chena thought the voice grew a little smug. "That was what you were worried about, wasn't it?"

The window clouded, leaving Chena staring at a blank wall. "But where is she? You said I'd get to visit her."

"I said you could see her. Sadia is still under close supervision. She was brought here involuntarily."

Chena bit down on her lip. Getting angry wasn't going to work, she could tell by the placid tones of Aleph's voice. She had threatened about as far as she could today.

"You're not worried what I'll tell Mom now?"

"Your mother and I have had a discussion about you," replied Aleph. "She understands Sadia's situation. Probably better than you do. You can ask her about it when you see her this afternoon."

Chena felt her jaw drop. Of course the thing talked to Mom. It talked to Chena, didn't it? But it was *telling* on her, worse than Teal, worse than the cop in Offshoot, worse than all the teachers and all the supervisors she'd ever had—

"She needed to know, Chena," said Aleph, and for a moment Chena was really afraid the thing had read her mind. "You are still hers, as well as mine."

"I am not yours," whispered Chena harshly. "I will never be yours."

"No," said Aleph. "Of course not. I misspoke."

Chena's fingernails dug into her palms. She could taste blood from where she'd bit down on her lip. "Are you going to let me talk to Sadia?"

"Not now, no."

Chena couldn't believe it. She could not *believe* it. This thing, these people, who did they think they were? God's own gardeners? "So take me back to my damn cage, why don't you?"

"It's not a cage, Chena."

"Of course not." She bit the words off. "I misspoke, Mother Aleph. Forgive me."

If Aleph understood sarcasm, it didn't say anything. The arrow reappeared for her and Chena followed it, keeping her eyes pointed toward the floor and ignoring the world beyond the arrow and the tips of her shoes appearing and disappearing from her field of vision as she walked.

I don't know what you think you're doing, she thought to Aleph as she walked. *But you don't get to do it to me. I will figure you out, and then you will do what I say. You're just a machine and I will figure you out.*

That thought rang around her head all the way back to the maze.

Mom waited for her in the tiny common area that lay between their bedrooms.

"Mom," said Chena as she walked over the arrow without waiting to see what it would do next. "I don't know what that thing's been telling you, but all I wanted to do—"

Mom put her fingers to her lips, signaling Chena to hush. Chena closed her mouth reluctantly. Mom smiled, just a little. She looked tired. Chena felt involuntary tears prickle her eyes. It wasn't fair. They went and upset Mom over nothing, and now she was going to get one of the quiet talking-tos that were a thousand times worse than any shouting match could be.

But Mom just extended her hand. In her fingers, she held Chena's comptroller.

Chena stared at the miniature computer for just a second. Then she clutched at it and looked up at Mom, her mouth open to say thank you. Mom made the hush gesture again and took Chena's hand. She led them both into Chena's little sleeping alcove and sat down on the bunk. Mom patted the mattress. Chena took the hint and sat.

Mom held out her hand and Chena put the comptroller into it. Mom's face tightened as she worked the keys, crouching over them as if hiding the comptroller from somebody, but there was still a little smile playing around her mouth.

She held the comptroller out for Chena. Chena took it and scrolled back the message Mom had entered. Mom shaded the screen with her hand.

Yes, Chena read. *Aleph has been talking to me, and I am ignoring it. You go ahead and do what you want to.*

Then it dawned on Chena what her mother was doing. She *was* hiding the comptroller from somebody. Aleph. Chena smiled her understanding to her mother and hunched over the comptroller herself, working the keys carefully. She passed back to Mom, who cupped her hand around the screen and read Chena's message.

How'd you get my comptroller back?

I told them I was upset by the fact you had absolutely no privacy, read the message Mom gave back to her. *They do not want me upset. Stress will be bad for whatever they're going to put inside me.*

Chena did not want to think about the idea of something alien, *someone* alien, inside Mom. She squashed her thoughts and concentrated on keying in the next message. *Funny, I used that to get them to let me see Sadia today.*

I know, was Mom's reply. *But I think we'd better be careful how much we use that in the future. They might start splitting us up even more.*

I didn't know you noticed. Chena didn't key that in, she just looked at her mother's face. Mom nodded.

Chena ran her fingers lightly over the comptroller's little screen before she keyed in a few words. *Did you get Teal's back too?*

Again Mom nodded. Chena wiped the message, thought for a second, and then keyed in the important question. Before, Mom had wanted her to get along, had wanted her to behave in this new place and smile and be happy, just like Teal. *What changed your mind about the hothousers?*

Mom read the message and dropped her hands into her lap, staring at the bright oceans projected on the walls. Chena knew Mom was trying to decide how much to tell her. She wanted to yell, *Everything! You tell me everything!*

Mom keyed in some words and handed the comptroller to her. Chena read.

I don't know, Supernova. Something is going on. When I find out what it is, I will *tell you.* The word "will" was highlighted.

We'll find out what's going on. Chena reached across and covered Mom's hand with her own. *We'll get out of this,* Chena promised her silently. As if she heard Chena's thoughts, Mom wrapped her up in a tight embrace.

We will, Supernova, Chena knew her mother was thinking. *Of course we will. I promise.*

Lake Superior spread out at Dionte's feet, as wide and black as the sky, reflecting the white light of the diamond-bright stars and the luminous sphere of the moon. It was a still night, with only a breath of frost-scented wind touching her cheeks and making tiny wavelets lap at the boardwalk's posts.

"Guardian Dionte," said a voice behind her.

Dionte turned. Silhouetted against the moon-silvered dunes stood a tall woman. In daylight her skin was probably golden. She wore her dark hair swept back and pinned under a kerchief. The sleeves of her tunic had been rolled up to expose her muscular forearms. As she folded those arms, Dionte noted her huge hands and their square-tipped fingers with the nails cut back all the way down to the quick.

"Lopera Qay," replied Dionte, inclining her head. "If you'll permit me to say so, you are very late."

"If you'll permit me to say so, I wanted to make sure you were alone."

Dionte cocked her head briefly to one side. "I suppose I cannot blame you for not taking my word."

"Especially when your people have just arrested a friend of mine."

Dionte held up one finger. "You mean a front man of yours."

"I never said such a thing," replied Lopera calmly, brushing at a stray wisp of hair that fluttered in the light breeze. "And I never would."

"I'm sure you would not." Dionte tucked her cold hands into the long sleeves of her robe. The chill had ceased to be refreshing about a half hour ago; now it was just annoying. She could not, however, afford to show that annoyance to this woman. "Nonetheless, I need your help."

Lopera leaned her forearms on the boardwalk railing and looked out across the lake, seeming to examine the way the moonlight tipped the tiny ripples in the black water. "Do you?"

"Over an extended period of time." Dionte found herself admiring the way this woman said nothing that, even taken out of context, could incriminate her in any way. "For possibly as long as fifteen years or so."

Lopera rubbed the palms of her great hands slowly back and forth. "That is a long time for a single project."

"I would not expect you to work exclusively on my project, of course."

"Of course." The breeze freshened, touching the back of Dionte's neck and making her shiver.

"You would of course be compensated across the length of time, and the amount and type of pay are negotiable." Dionte stepped right up to the woman's side. "And you and your associates would be completely free from the usual hazards."

Lopera nodded once, her mouth pursed as if she were carefully thinking over what she had heard. Dionte could not read the expression in Lopera's eyes, and had to resist touching the woman to try to understand what was going on inside her mind. She had over these past weeks gotten so used to knowing what Basante was thinking, not being able to read someone for herself made her feel numb. It was becoming hard to understand the others sometimes. No, not understand, but to empathize with them. The understanding that came through her implant was so strong that everything else felt washed out and simplified by comparison.

She needed to adjust her enhancements. Soon. Before the new feelings became too strong for her.

At last, Lopera said, "And what would this project be?"

Dionte relaxed her shoulders. Given the reticence of this woman beside her, such a question was surely very close to agreement. All other troubles could wait until later.

"I need you," said Dionte, "to help raise a child."

CHAPTER TEN

Theft

Chena woke without protest to Aleph's reminder bell. She took her shower and dressed in the green shirt and black pants that were the style Aleph preferred for her.

Today. Today's the day.

The thought made her grin. She was still grinning as she brushed her hair and Mom emerged from her sleeping alcove.

They had been in the hothouse for eight months now. Mom's belly was tight and round under her nightshirt. She shuffled when she walked, and her face alternated between puffy and red, and drawn and tired.

Aleph had compromised far enough that Chena actually got to see her every morning without having to go in and wake her up. After all, that might startle her or stress her, and they couldn't have that.

"Morning, Supernova." Mom reached out carefully and gave her a hug.

"Morning." Chena laid a hand on Mom's belly, to see if she could feel the thing inside moving this morning. "How does it feel?"

"Like being pregnant." Mom smiled. "A feeling I have had once or twice before." She squeezed Chena's shoulder. They had become very good at communicating without words. She was saying, *Soon, soon. We will get out of here.*

Chena smiled in silent answer. Mom didn't know what was happening today. Chena would find a way to tell her if it worked.

"I'd better get going," was all Chena said out loud. "I don't want to be late."

"Neither do I." Mom gave her shoulder one more squeeze before she headed into the shower cubicle.

That last was all for Aleph, or at least for the portion of Aleph that kept an eye on their little set of alcoves. One of the things Chena had learned over the past few months was that Aleph was not everywhere all the time. Aleph was a collection of subsystems that memorized patterns of behavior and action and matched them up against a sort of ideal flow of events. If the actual patterns came close enough to the ideal, the main processor that was Aleph did not pay any attention to what was going on. It was when there were variants that it was alerted. If you could figure out what the parameters of your expected patterns were, you could keep Aleph from noticing you for . . . forever, Chena supposed.

According to the history lessons they were getting in school, Pandora's founders had thought that the way to solve the perpetual shortsightedness that humans exhibited toward their environment was to give them a companion that could remind them of their long-term goals. Such a companion would have to be an independent intelligence capable of making its own judgments, and it would also have to become integral to the life of the city, otherwise it could just be switched off like an outmoded computer. So they came up with the city-minds.

The trick was that Aleph, like all genuine artificial intelligences, was a learning machine. In this case, that meant it was taught by its experiences through its subsystems. If you taught Aleph and its subsystems in small enough increments, you could expand your pattern without raising an alert. But if you made too many mistakes, you could also teach it you needed watching.

Chena, however, had been careful, and that care had paid off. For instance, she could now go into Teal's sleeping alcove every morning and leave a message on her comptroller. It had taken her five months to get this worked into the morning routine. At first Aleph stopped her as soon as she reached for Teal's comptroller. But then Chena began just pausing in Teal's doorway before she went out for the day. Aleph allowed that. After that, Chena took three steps into Teal's room, and then three more, and then three more. It became routine, and as long as she conformed for the rest of the day, nothing happened. No voice chided her, no person showed up suddenly to jolly her along.

It took a long time, of course, and you had to plan very carefully, but Chena had a long time. Despite the classes, and the games, and the entertainments, she had very little that really occupied her, other than trying to get around the hothouse's AI watchdog.

The other trick, of course, was that you couldn't take too long at whatever you were doing. Being late for a scheduled activity was a sure way to get noticed. Chena tiptoed into Teal's alcove and lifted her comptroller out from under her pillow. Quickly she coded in *News coming today.*

As Chena replaced the comptroller, Teal peeled open one eye, but didn't say anything. Chena grinned at her.

It had been Teal who found out the nature of Aleph's architecture and had in turn showed Chena how the hothouse system might really be beaten.

From their very first day, Teal had constantly kissed up to every single hothouser, even while Chena was trying to resist Aleph and Aleph's system by sheer willpower. She sat silently in the counselor's office. She participated only reluctantly in classes. Teal, on the other hand, jumped right in, as if she couldn't wait to see what was coming next. Chena yelled at her about it and got hauled off to the counselor's office. Aleph rearranged her schedule so she didn't see Teal for a week. Then, all at once, Teal bounced into the library where Chena was supposed to be looking up details of the first wave of interstellar colonization from Old Earth. In reality, Chena was sitting in the chair with her arms folded, waiting to see how long it would be before Aleph or one of the teachers came to talk to her about her uncooperative attitude.

"Come on," Teal said. "I got you off." She grabbed Chena's hand and dragged her away from the reader and its rig.

"What do you mean, you got me off?" Chena pulled her hand out of Teal's.

Teal looked at her like she was completely deficient. "Do you want to sit here or do you want out? Come on!"

There was only one answer to that. Chena followed her sister out into the twisting hallways. Teal hurried through the maze without even stopping to read the signs. Chena felt her ears burning. Teal had obviously had a lot more freedom than she did, to have learned her way around so well.

They emerged into one of the park gardens that dotted the maze.

The hothousers kept themselves entirely indoors, but they had brought a lot of the outdoors in with them. The place was full of small trees and plants with fruit you could eat. The floor was a carpet of grass and moss, and a stream ran into a fish pond and out again. It reminded Chena a lot of one of the roof gardens in Offshoot.

Teal rummaged through the grass, picked a strawberry, and tossed it to Chena. Chena caught the berry reflexively and stared at it.

"Do you remember what Dad used to tell us about machines?" said Teal, sitting herself comfortably into one of the low, spreading tree branches.

"Are you out of your mind? That thing is listening." Chena threw the strawberry at her.

Teal caught it easily. "That thing is not listening." She grinned at Chena. "That thing only listens if you say its name or if you're doing something it doesn't approve of." Teal popped the strawberry into her mouth. "And I made sure that this was something it approved of. I told the teacher that I would do my best to socialize you." She grinned wider as she chewed, and Chena saw the soft red pulp staining her teeth.

"What do you know about it?" Chena demanded, feeling in the back of her mind that she had really missed something here.

"More than you." Teal was enjoying this, and the sight of her grinning just made Chena more angry.

"You don't know anything!" Chena stepped forward, her fist clenched. She was going to smack that grinning face. Teal was trying to screw up everything.

"Keep it down," ordered Teal, slipping off the branch and standing right up to her. "If you yell, it'll be told something's wrong."

"Told by who?" Chena took another step forward and Teal stopped smiling. "You going to tell on me now?"

"Not me, space head," said Teal, holding her ground."The subsystem."

Chena felt her forehead wrinkle. "What?"

"What do you think I've been trying to tell you?" Teal flung out both her arms. "While you've been busy sulking and getting counseled to death, I've been asking people how this place works. It goes a lot easier when they think you like them."

Chena stepped back, startled. All that sweetness and light, it wasn't just an act, it was *cover*?

Teal scowled. "You really do think I'm stupid, don't you?"

"No, no," Chena assured her, waving her hands. "I just . . . I didn't know how smart you were."

Teal seemed to accept that. Her face relaxed.

"This thing"—she made a wide circle with her finger, indicating the entire park alcove and the unseen and silent Aleph—"isn't just one big thing. It's a whole series of little subsystems and expert systems. They only alert the central brain when there's something unexpected or out of order going on. Or if you're here involuntarily. Which means you." Teal's grin came back. "Because you're wandering around here like you're looking for a way out. But me, they think I'm a volunteer. So I'm not watched as closely as you are. I went to our teacher, all weepy, and I said how much I missed you, and that if I could talk to you, I knew I could explain to you that this place is really okay and they're going to take care of us here." Her eyes went big and her face went slack and pleading. Chena snorted in both amazement and amusement.

Teal grinned, but this time the expression did not spark any anger inside Chena. "So, the teacher had a talk with the thing and the thing put this into its subsystem, and as long as you don't do anything stupid, like yell, or make trouble, or say its name out loud, or try to go somewhere without me, the main brain won't pay any attention to us."

Chena folded her arms across her chest and nodded. "Teal, you are impressive. You got them to tell you all this?"

"Some of it." Teal leaned back against the branch and stretched her arms up until she snagged the limb over her head. "The rest of it I figured out on my own." She hung there, stretched between branches, confident of her own ability to stay exactly where she wanted to be. "Remember I was trying to tell you about Dad? He told me to remember that machines always have a person behind them. If you can get to the person who's in charge of the machine, you can get just about anything you want."

Chena remembered him saying that, but she hadn't thought about it before. Of course, about the only time she really thought about Dad was when she saw the sadness in Mom's eyes or she made up a new story with Teal. Dad had become someone to be angry at or a distant figure in a game. For Chena, he had stopped being real a long time ago.

"But doesn't A—" Chena caught herself just in time. "Doesn't that thing suspect that you're trying to get around it?"

Teal let go of the overhead branch. "I don't think it does." She wriggled back onto the sitting branch, brought her knees up to her chest, and wrapped her arms around them, remaining neatly balanced. "I don't think it really understands why anyone would not want to live here with it looking after them all the time. I think it knows that some people do, but I don't think it really understands that." Her eyes twinkled mischievously. "Makes it easier to lie to."

Chena straddled the branch next to Teal. "This is great," she said, a grin spreading across her own face. "Do you know what this means? It means we can find out what's really going on around here."

"Really?" Teal smacked her forehead. "I should've thought of that!"

Chena waved the sarcasm away. "Okay, okay. You were right and I was wrong. Can we drop it?"

"Maybe sometime in the next millennium," said Teal charitably. Then she dropped her voice to a mock whisper. "This place belongs to the spies, Chena. I'm sure of it."

"Careful." Chena waved her voice down, looking around as if expecting someone to appear suddenly, which she sort of was, but it felt so good to suddenly be playing the old game of Dad-and-spies, she was willing to risk it. "That might be one of the trigger words to get that thing's attention."

Teal nodded. "So, you going to play long now? It'll make us both look good if you do."

Chena swung her leg over the branch, leaping to her feet. "What do you know, little sister. I've seen the light and now intend to be a model hothouser." She slapped her hand over her heart. "You have worked a miracle upon my soul."

"Praise be!" Teal threw both hands in the air and rolled her eyes.

They both had laughed hysterically then, and impulsively Chena hugged Teal. She had begun planning her next move before they left the park, arms slung over each other's shoulders.

Now Chena took the approved path to her classroom. She was in a catch-up class with half a dozen other station kids. When she had first tested, Abdei had expressed real horror at what she considered Chena's substandard reading skills and complete absence of any kind of math, though she could get a computer to turn cartwheels for her. In truth, Chena was fairly embarrassed herself, when she saw the other kids could not only read so much faster, but could read different languages—but she would have died before she admitted it.

Now she eagerly joined the others in their seats, saying hello to everybody, including Teacher Abdei. Now that she was willing to learn what they had to teach, lesson time just flew by. Not that this was any old sit-in-your-seat-and-listen-to-the-teacher-drone-on class. Each seat had a full game rig, and days were mostly spent in interactive scenarios of some kind or another. The hothousers seemed to have an obsession with teaching their kids how to take things apart and put them back together again. They were constantly having to come up with codes and puzzles for each other to solve. Biology was very hot too. They spent hours climbing around gigantic models of each other's DNA, and won prizes for how many differences they could spot and for identifying what those differences might mean.

Today, though, the lesson was ecology. Each of them was building a virtual ecosystem and they were competing to see who could get theirs to survive the longest. It all had to do with energy flow. You had to make sure the proper amount of energy got filtered up and down the system using both growth and decay. Actually, it was all an elaborate code. Once you knew what each part was supposed to do, the rest was easy.

Chena was ahead of her classmates. She actually had kept her little grassland going for twenty-five years, virtual time. It had birds and animals and beetles moving in and out of the waving stalks of grass, which she made sure were not watered too much. She had not, however, put in any ants.

Chena was kneeling in the middle of her computer-constructed meadow, wondering what she could add and thinking about a top predator, when Abadei wandered into the simulation.

"This is very good, Chena," said Abdei, looking around her and appearing genuinely impressed. "You're almost ready to start gardening."

"Gardening?" Chena sat back on her heels. "You mean now that I can design energy flow, I get to start watering plants?" She bit her tongue. "I'm sorry, Teacher Abdei. I didn't mean it to sound that way."

Abdei smiled benevolently down at her. Chena responded with her own smile. Sometimes she still wanted to smack anybody who looked at her with all that kind condescension, even now that she knew it was the best thing she could possibly see. It meant they believed her and that they trusted her.

"I know you didn't, Chena. You have worked very hard." Abdei squatted down next to Chena so they could look into each other's eyes easily. "But gardening isn't just watering plants, it's creating balance in a real miniature ecosystem. You'd be surprised at how many things can go wrong when it's not a system you've designed out of light and code."

"I hadn't looked at it that way," said Chena honestly, getting to her feet and brushing the dust off her knees automatically, even though she knew this was only a game. "It'll be great." She let herself sound uncertain. It was time to put her plan into action.

Abdei looked concerned, like Chena had hoped she would, and straightened up. "Is something wrong?"

Chena sighed and dropped her gaze to the side. "No," she said without looking up.

Abdei laid a hand on Chena's shoulder. "Chena, we talked about this. If something is wrong, you should tell me."

Sing along, children, thought Chena. Although Mom saw the supervisors Tam and Basante almost every day, they seemed content to leave Chena and Teal to the care of Abdei, and, of course, Aleph. Chena was certain that both of those mouths reported in regularly. But that was all right. She had the system worked out.

Chena worked to keep the smile off her face. "I'm just worried about a friend of mine, is all."

Abdei cocked her head. "A friend? Somebody in class?"

Chena shook her head. "No." She tilted her head back to look at her blue sky, as if she wanted to look anywhere but at Abdei. "It's Sadia, my friend in the involuntary wing. I haven't heard anything about her, and . . ."—she was proud of the tremble that crept into her voice—"I was just thinking how my sister convinced me to give the hothouse—'scuse me, the Alpha Complex—a real shot." She finally met Abdei's gaze. "Sadia hasn't got anybody like that. Her brother's a complete mutant. I haven't seen her since that day I first got here, and I was just thinking that if she could see . . ." Chena stopped. She was coming perilously close to laying it on too thick. Abdei was like Aleph. She wasn't stupid, but she didn't really understand how anyone could not want to live the life she offered.

Abdei's face grew grave. "Chena, I know this is hard. But people are only in involuntary when they have broken the law. Your friend has done something wrong. I don't know what it was, but—"

"It wasn't her!" Chena did not have to work to put the emotion into her voice. "It was her brother! She's only in here because she wouldn't say what he did." Which was a lie, of course, and if she ever saw Shond again she'd apologize. "If I could just talk to her, I could explain what is really going on here. She hates hothousers. She thinks they steal body parts. If she just knew . . ." Chena knuckled her eyes as if to wipe away tears. "I'm sorry. I'm just being stupid. You're right. She probably has done something. I just don't know about it. I just . . ." She shook her head violently. "I'm just going to shut up now."

Abdei was frowning. Chena bit her lip, on purpose. Abdei had been trying to break her of that habit almost the entire eight months she'd been in class. Such a gesture could indicate a serious relapse, showing just how upset she was.

"I don't know, Chena," said Abdei slowly. "It's not the kind of thing that usually happens."

"I know," said Chena, dropping her gaze again. "Otherwise they wouldn't separate us. It's okay." She shrugged. "You're probably right anyway."

Abdei's frown deepened. "Let me see what I can do, Chena."

Chena met Abdei's gaze and let her eyes widen. She hoped she looked surprised, and not just sick. "You mean that? I mean"—she hesitated—"I don't want you to get in trouble or anything."

This time, Abdei smiled. "I won't get in trouble for making a request, Chena. You work on your top predator. Let me see what I can make happen." She patted Chena's shoulder and walked out of the simulation.

"You'd be surprised what you can make happen with a little effort," murmured Chena to herself. Humming quietly, she got to work designing her raptor bird.

Abdei did not come back for another two hours. Probably had to get together with the supervisors to do some kind of in-depth evaluation as to how this would affect her psyche, and how that would affect Mom's stress levels. Chena found she could not concentrate on her raptor. Deciding she might as well aim for a complete set of kiss-up points, she instead began looking up DNA models for existing birds on Pandora and trying to figure out how she could modify them for her limited ecosystem. When Abdei did walk back into the simulation, Chena looked up and saw the smile on her teacher's face. Her breath caught her throat. This was going to work. She was really going to get away with it.

Abdei nodded, as if she knew what Chena was thinking. "After class. Aleph will show you the way."

"I know the way to the door," said Chena, as if she felt she was asking way too big a favor and didn't want to inconvenience anybody. "If Aleph could meet me there . . ."

"I can meet you there, Chena," came Aleph's voice. "I'll see you after class."

"Thanks, Aleph," said Chena, smiling inside and out. "Thank you, Abdei."

She tried to get back to work on her bird, but did not make any real progress the rest of the day. Too much of her mind was taken up trying to remember exactly what she had said and done to get to this point, trying to see if she had left anything out. Seeing Sadia was only part of the plan.

And this is where I get to find out how well I've worked on them all.

Eventually time did move on and school ended. Chena, released from class, hurried through the maze, deliberately keeping her eyes on her toes, counting lefts and rights so she could practice navigating without looking at the signs, just in case she needed to find the foyer door without them one day.

Today the signs stayed where they should be, and the foyer door opened under her hand without raising any protests, mechanical or human. Three months ago, Chena had gotten access to the foyer by convincing Abdei that she had fallen in love with living in the woods and she was having a problem making the transition back to living in an enclosed space. If she could just stand under the window dome and see outside, she thought she would feel much better. Abdei had swallowed the story and gotten Aleph to add her palm prints to the door's access files.

Sometimes Chena felt a little guilty about using Abdei the way she did. Sometimes it seemed as if all Abdei really wanted was for Chena to be happy. But then she looked at Mom's swelling stomach and remembered exactly what Abdei was a part of.

As usual, a scattering of hothousers hurried back and forth across the foyer, busy with their own errands. If they noticed Chena at all, they nodded to her or raised a hand. She had become a familiar sight, just part of the furniture, like the terrarium in the foyer's center. They assumed since she was there, she was allowed to be there.

The foyer held five doors. Four led to different wings of the complex, one led to the outside. She deliberately had not specified which door she would meet Aleph at. For three months she had wandered around the foyer, each time getting a little closer to one of the doors before Aleph came on-line to warn her away. Now she could touch the surface of each, except the one to the outside.

Although she was in a hurry to see Sadia, Chena made herself stop close to the outside door. She did not want the subsystem to feel a break in that particular pattern, which she had worked so hard to establish. If Aleph queried its subsystem and found anything funny there, it would have been for nothing. Of course, Mom was going to walk them right out of there when her . . . job was done, but you never knew. The hothousers had all kinds of ways to screw things up for you. Chena might just need to find out how to make that door open. To do that, she needed to be able to touch it.

Chena walked casually up to the outside door, as if she thought she might startle it. When she was thirty centimeters away, she stopped and leaned on the window rail. If anyone, or anything, was watching, they would see her staring wistfully at a cormorant sailing over the marsh. It wasn't actually a cormorant, which was a bird on Old Earth, but it looked a lot like one and so had been given the old name. They had compared the DNA of each in class, what? About two months ago.

Somewhere, that marsh dried out, turning into forest, and then to grassland, and then to dunes. Somewhere in those dunes waited Stem and Farin. She wondered if he remembered her, and then chided herself for doubting it. Of course he remembered her, and when Mom got them out of here, they'd all go back to Stem, and Farin would be so happy to see her, he would throw his arms around her and scoop her up and spin her around until they were both laughing and dizzy.

After a couple of minutes, Chena turned away and walked toward the yellow door that was the entrance to the involuntary wing. She stood there. Nothing happened. Obviously, Aleph was not paying attention to her yet.

Chena smiled. So far, so good. She was tempted to stand there quietly, just to see how long it took Aleph to come looking for her, but she decided against it. That was an experiment for another day.

"Aleph?" she said.

"There you are, Chena," said Aleph. "I was waiting for you."

Maybe you were, maybe you weren't, thought Chena. *Are you developed enough to have pride to save? I hope not, because that means you noticed something is wrong.* The thought made her tense up, and she almost forgot to answer the AI.

"Will you let me in, please?" she asked brightly. "They haven't taught us teleporting yet."

The door swished open and the directional arrow appeared at her feet, leading Chena into the straight yellow hallway. Nothing had changed. She might have walked down it yesterday instead of eight months ago. The same black and white people paced up and down the corridor on their way to . . . whatever. They didn't even talk to each other. Any doors and windows there might have been remained invisible. For a minute Chena thought Aleph was going to pull one over on her, like it had before.

This time, though, the arrow at her feet took her around a corner, and Aleph cleared a real door for her.

A lounge waited on the other side, with comfortable-looking chairs and low round tables. The walls were set in a marsh pattern, complete with silent wading birds and rippling water. Sadia sat by the far wall.

They had dressed her in a loose long-sleeved yellow dress. She had yellow bands on her wrists and thick socks on her feet, but no shoes.

"Sadia!" Chena rushed forward and grabbed her hand, saluting as she did. Sadia smiled back at her and returned the salute, but the smile didn't make it all the way into her tired eyes.

She's just afraid of being watched, Chena told herself. *Can't blame her.*

"It's really good to see you." Chena pulled up a chair so they were knee to knee.

Sadia smiled with warmth, but without any enthusiasm. "Yeah, it was nice of them to let you in."

Chena felt her own smile spread, mischievous and knowing. "Well, 'let' is what my mom calls a relative term."

Sadia started, shrinking back from Chena. "You mean this isn't okay?"

Chena frowned. "Of course it's okay. I'm here, aren't I?" *What's the matter with you?*

Sadia subsided, her body relaxing and deflating under the sunny dress. "Yeah, you wouldn't be here if it wasn't."

Chena blinked and glanced away until she was certain she could look at Sadia without staring. This was not right. What had they done to her in here? Maybe she had just come to believe there was no way out. That was probably it. Chena pushed her sleeve back from her comptroller. Obviously, this was no time for small talk. She had to show Sadia that there really was something they could do.

"So . . ." Chena searched for a neutral topic while she hunched herself over her comptroller and pressed the display key to light up the message she had coded in previously. *I've found a way around Aleph,* it said. She handed the comptroller carefully over to Sadia, laying it right into her palm and pushing Sadia's hand into her lap so that her body remained a shield between herself and Aleph.

Sadia looked down at the message, read it, and looked back up at Chena. "I don't understand."

"I've got a handle on how things work around here." Chena cupped her hand around the comptroller and took it back. "It's actually pretty easy if you just go along with it." She tried to catch Sadia's gaze to see if Sadia was following any of this. But Sadia just looked blankly back at her, as if Chena spoke a foreign language.

"Of course you go along with it," said Sadia. "What else is there?"

"Yeah, but if you're going after it right, you don't have to have somebody always watching you. You can get some movement back."

Nothing showed in Sadia's face. She studied Chena for a moment as if Chena were some stranger. Then her gaze wandered back to the fake marsh on the walls.

"Sadia." Chena leaned forward, feeling cold fear form in her stomach. "I'm telling you I can help you get out of here, out of involuntary."

Sadia nodded without turning her attention back to Chena. "Okay."

The fear in Chena grew heavier. "You do want to get out of here, don't you?"

Sadia moved her head toward Chena again, and that was almost worse, because nothing had changed. Her eyes remained dead, blank and empty. "If that's what you want me to do."

Stunned disbelief fell into place beside fear. Chena felt her jaw hanging loose. "What did they do to you?"

Still, no sign of comprehension crossed Sadia's face. "Take samples," she said, apparently taking Chena's comment literally. "Put stuff inside me sometimes."

Before Chena could stop herself, she looked down at Sadia's stomach. It pooched out a little more than she thought she remembered. Was there something inside Sadia now? Was it like whatever was inside Mom?

Is Mom going to end up like this?

Chena jumped to her feet. "I have to go."

"Okay," said Sadia behind her. But this time Chena was the one who did not look back. She just rushed out the door. The arrow waited for her on the hallway floor. She walked fast, trying not to run. She had to get back. She had to find Mom. She had to let Mom know what had happened to Sadia. Mom had to do something. They had to get out of here now. They had to get that thing out from inside her before it took her mind away, or before Aleph and its keepers decided that her mind should be taken away from her. Maybe that was what they did to Sadia. Maybe she fought too hard, so they'd drugged her or something. They did something to her.

Got to warn Mom. Chena's efforts to hold her stride in check brought a haze of tears to her eyes. She could not alert Aleph. She must not alert Aleph.

The foyer passed by in a blur of green and brick red. She was in the labyrinth before she remembered to get her bearings, and she had to follow the signs to get back to their alcoves.

She probably won't even be there. She's out doing whatever it is they give her to do. But I'll look there first. Then I can look somewhere else. I can tell the counselor I'm having an emergency. I can . . .

She pushed aside their curtain. She noted absently that Mom or Teal had changed the walls to an abstract wallpaper, all red splotches. But then she saw the pattern was on the back of the curtain too.

Then the smell reached her, a sharp smell, all acid and copper, and she saw red on the floor—deep, shining rivulets of red, snaking across the tiles.

Then she saw Mom, sprawled like a doll at the center of a pool of red, with more red, more blood, too much blood, puddled in her slashed and deflated belly. Her still eyes looked up at Chena, pleading.

Chena ran forward, ignoring the blood and the way it squished under her shoes. She grabbed Mom's hand, not thinking, not knowing what she could possibly do. The hand was cold and limp, and as still as her eyes.

Chena screamed. She couldn't help it. She dropped the dead hand and backed away, her hands raised up to her ears. She screamed and screamed again, high and wordless, terrified of what she saw in front of her. She screamed as if she could call her mother back to take away this hideous thing and be alive again.

The curtain flew open to let in hands, people, voices, exclamations of shock and disgust. Someone pulled Chena back and away, and handed her to someone else. But she couldn't see anything clearly except the red, and Mom.

"All right, Chena. All right." Someone dropped to her knees in front of her and grasped her chin, pulling her eyes away from Mom. Abdei. This was Abdei, and around her were men, looking at Mom, looking at the blood, talking among themselves too fast to be understood.

"Who did it?" gasped Chena. The nearest man, the constable or supervisor, or whatever he was, just stared at her. "Who did it?" she repeated. "Aleph must have seen. Who did this?"

"Chena, we don't know," said Abdei, holding Chena by both shoulders.

"Don't know!" Chena yanked herself backward. "You guys watch everything. How could you not have seen this?" She looked from one to the other of them, taking in their pinched, frightened faces. Realization sank in slowly. "It screwed up, didn't it? That omnipotent computer of yours. It watched every single second of our lives, but it didn't see who killed my mother!"

"We will find out what happened," Abdei said firmly. "I promise you, Chena—"

"Where's Teal?" demanded Chena.

"Chena—"

"What's happening?"

Teal. Chena wrenched herself out of Abdei's hands and hurled herself toward the doorway. She slammed into Teal and wrapped her arms around her sister, shielding Teal with her body.

"We're getting out of here," she said as Teal's mouth opened. "Right now."

"Chena, with your mother gone, you are—"

"Our grandmother is in Offshoot," she said.

"Gone!" shouted Teal. "Where's Mom gone? Chena!" She wriggled in Chena's hands. Chena clamped down more tightly. "Ow!"

"You don't have any relatives in Offshoot, Chena," said Abdei. "Don't try to lie to me."

"We do!" Chena shouted back. "Elle Stepka." She had turned that name over in her mind at night a hundred times, wondering how she could use it or when she might need it. "You can check. We belong to her now. You can't keep us here!"

"Stop squeezing me!" squealed Teal.

Teal ripped herself out of Chena's hands. She saw the blood, and she saw Mom behind the screen of men's bodies. Teal stood there for a moment, her mouth opening and closing, like she was trying to chew on something. Then both hands rose slowly to cover her mouth and she stumbled backward. Chena caught her, tuned her around, and hugged her close.

"It's okay," she said. "It's okay. We're getting out of here. We're going to our grandmother's." She glowered at Abdei. "We're minors. If we've got a living relative, they have the body right to us."

"It's true." One of the men stepped away from the others. Chena's head cleared enough to recognize Administrator Tam. "Their grandmother is Elle Stepka. They need to go back to Offshoot at once."

"Administator—" began Abdei.

"At once," snapped Administrator Tam. Relief made Chena weak in the knees.

Abdei's gaze skittered over to the constables, or whatever they were, and then back to Administrator Tam. Something that Chena couldn't read passed between them.

"Come with me." Abdei tried to steer them toward the door. Chena didn't budge or take her arms from around Teal. Teal was shuddering now, but not crying. She just pressed her face against Chena's shoulder and shook.

"You've got no right to take us anywhere," said Chena. "No right!" She looked up, pleading to the administrator, their only ally. What did he know? What did he believe? She didn't know how to lie to him because she didn't know anything about him. They hadn't seen him since their first day.

"To the next alcove, that's all, I swear," said Abdei, taking firmer hold of Chena's shoulder.

"It's all right, Chena." Administrator Tam reached out a hand as if to touch her, but he hesitated and let it fall. "It is just to the next alcove."

Chena shook Abdei off. "We can get there on our own."

Not letting go of Teal, she walked through the curtain, into the corridor, and over into the next set of alcoves. This was somebody's home, she knew, but they weren't there now. Nobody seemed to be here. They'd all been spirited away by Aleph or another of the hothousers' tricks.

"I'm going to ask you not to leave," said Abdei.

"We're not going anywhere except back to Offshoot," said Chena, sitting Teal down on one of the low benches. Teal looked gray. Her mouth stayed shut now, but there was a blank look behind her eyes that reminded Chena too much of Sadia.

"I have to verify what you're saying." Abdei sounded tired, and closer to angry than Chena had ever heard her.

"The administrator told you—"

"This is not for you to say!" Abdei shouted, and then she reeled as if knocked sideways by the force of her own words.

"Why can't you just ask Aleph? Aleph knows everything." Then she bit her lip. Aleph might know this was a lie. How had Elle fixed it? Maybe Administrator Tam had done it for her? Chena didn't know, but they had to get out, they had to, and she couldn't open the outside door yet.

"Aleph is not here," said Abdei shortly. "Stay here. I will find out about your . . . grandmother."

She left them there. Chena sat down next to Teal, hard. Aleph wasn't there? Someone had taken down the computer? How far down was it? Could she and Teal get to the door? Could they run away into the marsh, maybe find the bike rails and follow them back to Offshoot? Or Stem? Farin would help them, she knew he would.

"Chena, we've got to get a message to Dad," said Teal suddenly.

"What?"

"We've got to!" Teal clutched her arm, her eyes wide with terror. "We've got to tell him to come get us. He'll come back. He has to."

Chena's hands fell to her lap. "We can't get a message to him, Teal," she whispered. "I don't know where he is."

"But we can find out," she persisted. "We can get a message up to Athena Station. There are Authority shippers there. We can ask one of them to get a message through."

Chena licked her lips. What was the matter with her? Was she so far gone she couldn't tell what their game was anymore? "They wouldn't even know where to start looking for him," she said lamely. "He could be anywhere."

Teal looked up at her and now Chena saw the tears streaming silently down her cheeks. "Please, Chena. Find Dad."

"I can't." Chena felt her own eyes prickle. *Stop it. Stop it,* she ordered herself. *You can't start that now, you'll never stop.*

Teal leaned back against Chena's shoulder and cried. Chena held her, choking back her own sobs, trying not to see Mom's eyes staring at her, asking Chena where she had been while someone had ripped her mother's guts out, asking her to do something when there was nothing to be done except get Teal out of here.

The curtain drew back and Abdei, her mouth pressed into a thin line, walked through.

"I've confirmed your grandmother," she said, biting off the words as if she did not want to believe them. But she didn't challenge it. She was a good hothouser. She would do what she was told. A fresh rush of relief washed through Chena.

"We'll take you to her," said Abdei before Chena could say anything.

"Thank you." Chena shook Teal's shoulders. "Come on, Teal. We're going."

Abdei was as good as her word. She walked them out of the hothouse to the dirigible. Chena kept her arm around Teal the entire time, even when they walked from the dirigible to the waiting riverboat. Teal wiped at her eyes and nose occasionally, but she said nothing. Chena wasn't even sure she knew what was going on.

It was evening outside and they glided past the grasslands, empty except for the deer and birds. When the trees, green with their late summer leaves, finally enclosed them, Chena felt a sense of relief and safety she'd never expected. They were almost home. They were almost free of the hothouse. Everything else would follow.

Abdei walked them off the boat. Around them, all the village traffic stopped so everyone could stand and stare. After all, it wasn't every day somebody came back from the hothouse.

"Where is your grandmother?" Abdei asked.

Chena swallowed. What would Nan Elle say when she saw them? With a hothouser? But she could think of no way to make Abdei leave. So, taking Teal's limp, cold hand, Chena led her sister and Abdei up the catwalks to the top of the village.

There was no line in front of the door, thankfully. Chena bit her lip and knocked.

After a moment, shuffling and bumping sounded from inside. The door opened. Nan Elle hunched, blinking, in the threshold. She looked from Chena to Teal to Abdei.

"Chena, Granddaughter!" she exclaimed, enfolding Chena in her strong, skinny arms. Chena made herself hug the old woman back. "Has anything happened?"

"Your daughter has died," said Abdei, looking hard at Elle, watching for her reaction. Chena also gave her a hard stare. *Don't let us down. You promised.*

Nan Elle covered her mouth with her wrinkled hand. "No," she whispered. "Oh, my poor girl. All my poor girls." She folded Chena into her arms again. "Thank you for bringing them home, Aunt."

Abdei's jaw worked back and forth a few times, but her face softened. She was beginning to really believe. "We will need to talk to them, and you, when you've had time to adjust."

"Of course, of course." Nan Elle nodded rapidly, shrinking in on herself. "Anytime I am needed."

Chena almost couldn't believe what she was seeing. Nan Elle frightened? It was one more impossibility in an impossible day, but of course Nan Elle was a liar. Everyone in this world was a liar.

Abdei's face still retained a trace of its bitterness, and her eyes grew distant, as if she were listening to some private voice. For a moment Chena thought she was going to actually question what was going on. But she didn't. She just frowned more deeply.

"I'll leave you to look after your granddaughters." With that, she turned in the threshold. The door swung shut behind her of its own accord and Chena and Teal were alone with Nan Elle. Chena tightened her grip on Teal's shoulder as the old woman regarded them.

"What happened?" Nan Elle asked. "Is your mother really dead?"

Chena nodded. "They cut her open. They . . ." The strength that had kept her steady until now failed suddenly, and Chena broke down into tears. Nan Elle did not move to comfort or quiet her. She just stood there while Chena, with her arms still hugging Teal, sobbed herself dry.

When she finally was able to wipe her eyes clear, she saw that Nan Elle had stooped even further in on herself. This time Chena sensed the uneasiness was no act.

"Sit." Nan Elle gestured them toward her benches while she went to the stove and poured mugs of something steaming out of a pot and carried the mugs to the girls. Chena drank because she was suddenly dying of thirst. Mint tea. The stuff Mom said she'd learn to put up with the morning she found coffee was illegal on Pandora, along with tea and refined sugar. Chena choked on her swallow of liquid and set the mug down. Teal picked her mug up in both hands and drank and drank, as if she were going to drain the mug in one gulp.

Nan Elle sat in her high-backed chair and folded both hands on top of her stick. "Well, I suppose we now need to work out what should be done with you."

"We'll do anything you say," said Chena. "Just don't make us go back there."

"Can you find our dad?" asked Teal suddenly.

Chena froze. Nan Elle's eyes flickered from Chena to Teal. "No," she said. "Not at this time. The best I can do is give you somewhere to stay and something useful to do. In time, perhaps, I can help you understand what has happened to your mother, and to you."

"Yes," said Chena. It would do. For now. Once they understood what had happened, they could do something about it. They could find the ones responsible and make them pay. They could destroy Aleph and all its people. For Mom, and for Sadia, and for Teal, and for herself, for everything she felt right now, all the fear and anger and the deep sick pain. The hothousers would all pay for this.

Nan Elle's sharp eyes watched her closely. "Be careful," she said to Chena. "You have no idea what you are up against."

"Not yet," said Chena. "But I will."

Tam would never have believed it was possible to stand in front of his family and feel so much anger. As stunted as his Conscience was, these were all the people who filled his life. They sat with him, arrayed on the tiers of the meeting amphitheater, their faces grave. Even the Senior Committee and Father Mihran looked frightened. All of them were excruciatingly aware that something huge, inexplicable, and irreversible had happened, and that it might even bring down the sword that the Authority had hung over Pandora.

And one of you did this. One of them had committed murder and gotten away with it. He searched the faces on the first tier and found Dionte. She sat, placid and attentive, with the other guardians, listening to Tender Cartes, who stood at the theater's center describing how none of the subsystems had been interfered with and none of the alarms, electronic or biological, had been severed.

Everyone listened intently. Everyone wanted to know what had actually happened and how it had happened. Not because Helice Trust was murdered, although all would have said that was tragic, but because the project had not been found. Anywhere. It was most certainly not still inside Helice, but it was not anywhere inside the Alpha Complex either. Their one success, the one fetus that was going to come to term without adversely affecting the mother, was gone. Every square centimeter of the complex had already been turned over, by Aleph, and by Aleph's tenders. The Eden Project was set back by years, and the hope for a peaceful, unchanging Pandora hung by a thread. Tam knew that every mind in the amphitheater carried the image of a mushroom cloud of dust and ash.

And there sat Dionte, his sister by both birth and branch. She sat next to Basante, whispering in his ear while she stroked his hand display. What was she doing there? What was she telling him?

Tam smelled aloe and remembered her as a little girl, playing tag with their cousins. He remembered being a little envious when she got to stay with their mother and he got taken off by their birth uncle Laplace for tutoring. However, when the complexes were first built it had been determined that the importance of the uncle-son relationship would be reestablished here, and of course the first families knew best. Wasn't his Conscience's ceaseless voice telling him so right now? His carefully truncated Conscience.

He remembered the night when their parents explained to them in the lowest of whispers that they were not like other children. Their Consciences would not be able to hold them as firmly as other people's did. So they must be more careful, more attentive, and more certain of what they did. They would have a special duty when they were grown to help those who could not move without their Consciences' approval. There would come a time when someone was needed who could stand up to the rest of the family. When that time came, they, Tam and Dionte Bhavasar, would have to take the lead.

He remembered Dionte so recently standing before the family and arguing vehemently that Pandora needed to protect itself against the Authority. She drew multiple examples from history to show that the

Authority would not have the patience to wait for solutions. The complexes could not cooperate with the Called. Any such effort was doomed failure. They must be ready to strike when the inevitable attack came.

Tam felt himself rise. He felt himself walk across the amphitheater, only vaguely aware that Cartes had stopped speaking. His body moved without instruction from him or his Conscience and came to stand in front of Dionte.

"Where is it, Sister?" he asked, his voice sounding harsh and wrong in his ears.

But he might as well have been asking her for one of her daily reports, for all the reaction she displayed. "I think that question is for you, Tam," she said quietly. "Along with whether or not those children really belong to Elle Stepka."

"Aleph says they do," countered Tam. "Has Aleph been tampered with?"

Dionte blinked. "At least once, obviously."

"Are you submitting an accusation?"

"Are you?"

"Please!" Someone stepped between them. Navram. One of their father's four birth brothers, and a member of the Senior Committee. "You are birth siblings as well as branch. This does not become either of you. Where are your Consciences?"

An interesting question. Tam held Dionte's gaze without blinking. His chest was heaving, he realized. He couldn't seem to get enough air.

"Tam." Navram laid his hands on Tam's shoulders and walked him backward two steps. "It does you credit that you are upset by the damage done to your charge, but if we do not proceed in an orderly fashion, we will never know what happened. We will accuse, fight, and lose, that's all."

Tam bowed his head. "Yes, of course. You're right."

Navram nodded, satisfied with the answer and the tone of its delivery. "Now, do you truly want to make an accusation against Dionte?"

Tam did not look up. He did not want to see what expression Dionte wore.

I have no proof. She has said nothing to me that she has not said in public, with the agreement and support of a dozen others. It does not matter what I know, only what I can prove.

But if I can say it, perhaps others can find the proof.

He steeled himself and lifted his gaze. Dionte remained where she was, with her hands folded in front of her. Her eyes gleamed with anger and determination.

Say anything, her eyes told him, *and I will have the children back here.*

Tam swallowed. It was an empty threat if proof of her actions was found, but if it was not . . .

Then the Trust daughters would be back in the complex, and this time they would be in the involuntary wing, and Nan Elle would probably be in there with them.

"No. I misspoke," he said, stepping back on his own. "I am distressed, and I am sorry."

"It does you credit," Navram told him firmly. "But this work belongs to all of us, and we must be able to share in its reclamation."

"Of course." Tam bowed to Navram, and to his family. As he did, his gaze slid sideways to Dionte. The nod she returned was barely perceptible. He'd read her threat correctly.

There is nothing you can do about that, he told himself, taking his seat amid a miasma of reassuring odors. *Unless you are ready to sacrifice Teal and Chena.*

I do not want to be ready for that, he answered himself. They were his; they had been placed under his protection the day they came to Offshoot. He would protect them. He would not fail them again.

Tam got ready to wait out the rest of the reports, declarations, and summaries.

At the end, he rose, ignored the questions and strategy planning going on all around him, and descended the stairway that only some of the family could open, heading down into the cellar commonly called the Synapese, down to where Aleph could be accessed directly. He had work to finish.

The meeting had gone on longer than he had expected, but he was still well within the transitional window. Aleph was an organic mind, very like a human mind on a gigantic scale. In the human mind it took time and chemistry before a short-term memory became long-term.

Changes in the neocortex had to be translated into new connections between multiple separate structures in the medial temporal lobe, which in turn had to create new connections to the entorhinal cortex, which in turn had to communicate with the hippocampus. It was a complex process. Compared to the rate at which an inorganic computer could store information, it was glacially slow. It did, however, have a distinct advantage. Once the long-term conscious memory was set, it was very difficult to lie to Aleph. No search-and-replace program, however sophisticated, could be used to change Aleph's memory. Like a human being, Aleph not only knew, but she was aware of what she knew and how she came to know it.

But, like a human being, Aleph had a weakness. While the changes were taking place that shifted information from short-term to long-term memory, the information was vulnerable to disruption or distortion. New cues could cover the old. New impressions could blur and fog what had previously been crystal clear. Whole scenes could be discounted in favor of more familiar, stronger impressions. Everything depended on the relative strength of the synapses that were formed between the different cortical structures, and synapse strength could be manipulated. Emotion was the key. Strong emotions created strong connections, and emotions were easy to alter externally. Human beings had been doing it to themselves by using various chemicals almost since the race first climbed down from the trees of Old Earth.

Knowledge of Aleph's cortical geography and neurochemistry, that was all that was needed. Oh, and a Conscience that had been foreshortened by birth parents who saw themselves as the latest in a long line of those who watched the watchmen.

Did you know that I'd be watching Dionte too? he asked their ghosts. His Conscience made him smell smoke and ash. It didn't know what he was up to, but it didn't like it. It worked to make him uneasy with smells of disaster. Blood, smoke, rot, all scents that went straight to his hindbrain and conjured up nameless discomfort, which wandered around his mind unearthing old, unwanted, distracting thoughts.

Strong emotions created strong memories. Blood and rot. His birth mother dying the day he turned thirty-seven. Despite what the villagers thought, they were not immortal in here. They did not prolong life. Such attempts led humanity to attempt to dominate their world so it would be forced to keep them alive. It was wrong to alter the course of life, they were told. Humans were part of the world's life, and it was wrong to alter, to change what was natural, important, and needed. Change they were told, over and over, should only serve Pandora.

"No," he told himself. "I will do this thing." It was a split second before he realized he had spoken aloud.

What are you doing? asked his Conscience. *Why are you going into the Synapese?*

He came to the bottom of the steps. Glowing pillars lit the world, the ceiling being reserved to hold the organic material that made up Aleph and all its subsystems. It was an open space, the size of the whole dome, broken only by the support struts that kept the entire complex from sinking into the marsh.

The tenders, those charged with taking care of Aleph, were in an uproar, of course. Sections of ceiling had been removed, like plates of a giant skull, to expose the naked matter underneath. With fine needles they took their samples, injected their hormones and epinepherines, trying to find where the process had gone wrong, trying to help Aleph remember anything of what had happened to Helice Trust or to the project she was carrying. Especially to the project she was carrying. It had been almost to term. It might be alive somewhere, even though its birth mother no longer was.

Because I was slow and stupid. Because I believed a little bureaucratic check could keep things in line and because I stayed away from the children so that they would not associate me with anything bad if trouble came. I thought if that happened I would have time to get to them, time to explain, time to stop it. Tam's jaw tightened. *But then I thought I'd be able to give them a free choice to come in or stay out, didn't I? And I failed in that too. Failed in every last one of my responsibilities to this family.*

All his adult life had been spent in balancing the needs of his family against the needs of the villages and the villagers. Hundreds of people, hundreds of lives, had passed in and out of his hands, and yet he had never cared for a family under such pressure. He'd never had a family he had watched so closely, or who had struggled so hard to maintain what freedom they had, not just Helice, but both her children.

Never had a family he'd failed so badly, never one of his own that he had allowed to die.

"Tam?" Hagin, chief tender and another of Tam's uncles, noticed him standing there, probably alerted by Aleph's voice in his ear. "What do you need?"

"I was hoping to help." Before he became an administrator, he'd been a tender. It was felt that the ones who had to work directly with Aleph should understand her intimately. He spread his hands. "The Eden incubation was under my supervision. I feel . . ." He shook his head. "I can't stand back and do nothing."

Trust your family, his Conscience told him. *What if you make things worse? So much damage has already been done.*

He smelled blood again, and in his mind's eye he clearly saw Helice Trust on the floor. His smile was grim. The problem with emotional recall. Sometimes it could raise exactly the wrong image.

Hagin was consulting the readout on the back of his hand. "We could use another measurement in the amygdala." He looked Tam up and down. "You still remember how, Nephew?"

"You can watch me if you want."

Hagin shook his head. "No need." He spoke over his shoulder, more of his attention on the work than on his nephew.

No time. Tam filled in for him.

Tam clasped Hagin's hand, and Hagin returned his grip. The action woke up Tam's display and synched it to Hagin's.

There were tool lockers in some of the unlit support pillars. Tam retrieved a needle probe as long as his forearm and checked the calibration on the butt end. It was a familiar action, calming both him and his Conscience.

Aleph's amygdala was in the northwest quarter, about a fifteen-minute hike across the broad open space of the Synapese. Tam had been away from this work long enough that he had to glance at the ceiling map now and again to remember his way. Like a human brain, Aleph's had multiple redundancies, but it also had centers of activity. The amygdala did much of the work of emotional memory. Theoretically, a family member murdering Helice Trust should have upset Aleph badly. Even if the memory of events had been somehow repressed, she should remember being upset. If the chemical traces of that emotion could be located and enhanced, Aleph might be able to articulate what had upset her, leading the tenders back further to the factual memory.

That was, of course, the goal of all the frenzied activity going on around him. Tam's goal was somewhat different, however. He needed to create a strong, positive emotional connection to a quite different piece of information.

Tam climbed a work platform and positioned himself so he sat cross-legged under the amygdala's central locale. With clumsy fingers, he unsealed the carapace and exposed Aleph to his view.

"Tam?" inquired Aleph, sounding a lot like his Conscience. "I am glad you have come to help. I do not understand what has happened."

"We'll find out, Aleph. Try to be easy." He lifted the needle and inserted it gently and smoothly into the soft flesh. Aleph could not feel physical pain, only emotional.

"There should not have been a way for this to happen. What could have been done? Was the room tampered with? Was I?" The question was soft and scared, almost childlike.

"We don't know yet, Aleph," said Tam as he adjusted the needle from the probe setting to the transmit setting so Hagin could get his data.

When he had first ensured that Chena and Teal would be acknowledged as Nan Elle's grandchildren, he had only needed to alter computer records. This was different. This time he needed to alter experiences that Aleph had undergone herself. From his pocket he pulled an injection cartridge and tucked it into the socket at the end of the needle. A touch of the release key and the entire contents shot straight through into Aleph's mind.

"Aleph, listen to me," said Tam, low and urgent. "Chena and Teal are with their grandmother, Elle Stepka. They are safe with her. They need to stay there, otherwise what happened to their mother might happen to them. This is true. It's absolute. It's got to be this way. This is important."

"This is important," repeated Aleph. "It is good. I feel that."

Tam adjusted the needle back to its probe function and slaved it to his display. The readings he'd preprogrammed into the display transmitted across to Hagin, just as if they had really come through the needle. In ten or so minutes, his hormonal injection would dissipate into the generally heightened anxiety chemistry all around it, but it would take the positive impression with it, down into all the separate structures that made up long-term storage, and, if he'd judged the dose and the words right, it would remove Aleph's need to worry about the remaining Trusts.

Remember, Aleph, he willed the mind all around him. *Remember that this is the way it is and the way it always has been. You feel it. You know it's the truth.*

Nothing happened. No alarmed voices called out to tell him he'd failed, but no quiet confidence stirred inside him to tell him he'd succeeded. All he could do was climb back down to the floor and head toward the home wing, and hope that someday Chena and Teal Trust would find a way to forgive him.

Tam sighed. No. To earn that kind of forgiveness, he would have to find a way to bring his birth sister to judgment for killing their mother. To do that, he would have to find where Dionte had hidden the Eden Project, before she found a way to convince the family that she had done the right thing.

Part Two

Wild Birds

CHAPTER ELEVEN

Decisions and Beliefs

"Chena!"

Nan Elle's shout sounded through the window. Chena snatched up her half-full basket of rose hips and trotted down the rickety stairs that led from the chaotic roof garden to the rear of the house.

Nan Elle stood in the main workroom, bent almost double over her mortar and pestle. She did not look up as Chena rushed inside.

"Shan Tso was just here." Nan Elle tipped the brown powder from the mortar onto a clean white cloth. "They will need willow bark, seaweed, and concentrated penicillin."

"Oh, no." Chena felt blood drain from her face as she set her basket down on the table. "Mila . . ." Mila was the Tsos' six-month-old baby. Chena had helped at the birth.

"Is already sick." Nan Elle bundled the white cloth into a small bag and tied it closed with string. "They will need foxglove infusions by this evening. I'm getting those ready now."

Chena bit her lip and gripped the table's edge for a moment to steady herself. Nan Elle called the fever burning through Offshoot the "red-and-whites," for the blotches it brought out on its victims' skin. It was a bacterial infection, but remained extremely resistant to their home-brewed penicillin. It worked fast, raising a person's temperature so high so rapidly that their heart couldn't handle the strain. They had seen their first case two months ago. Now ten people were dead. Three of them were children. Twenty-five more people were down sick.

Twenty-eight, if you count all the Tsos. Chena resisted the urge to slam her hand against the table in frustration. She never expected to care about any of these people. She had expected to remain as indifferent to every living human being as she had felt after Mom had died.

But she had begun to care despite that. After years of nursing them, setting their bones, dressing their wounds, and helping deliver their babies, she had come to care very much. Now, when they needed her the most, there was nothing she could do for them.

"Chena," said Nan Elle sharply as she turned to reach for the pot of boiling water on the stove. "They are not getting any better. Move."

The order jolted Chena into what was becoming an all-too-familiar routine. She grabbed two clay pots and a precious glass jar off the shelf over the tubs they used for washing and sterilizing. She filled each with as much as she could of the required medicines, being very careful not to take the last of anything. They were going to be up all night again brewing fresh serums as it was. She sealed the vessels tightly with beeswax and wrapped them in cloth so that she could drop them into her rucksack, sling it over her back, throw the door open, and run.

During the past five years, she had learned the names of everyone in Offshoot and knew the catwalks and paths better than she had ever known the corridors on Athena Station. The Tsos lived on the first level overlooking the dormitories.

It was shift change and the catwalks were crowded. "Out of my way!" Chena bellowed. By now people knew her voice, and they knew her business. They pressed themselves against the railings to let her get by, murmuring or cursing as she raced past them.

"Who is it?" hollered someone as she pounded down the stairs. A second later she identified the voice as Madra's.

"Tsos!" she shouted back, gripping the rail post to swing herself around onto the lowest catwalk. The boards rang and shuddered under her thundering footsteps. Tension alone robbed her of her breath. Chena could run from the bottom of the village to the top and back down again without any problem, and sometimes she had. Time was slowly worsening Nan Elle's arthritis. Chena's most constant work as her apprentice was to run her errands.

The Tso house was tiny and it listed toward the trunk of its tree, but the roof garden was trimmed and tidy and its walls free of moss and lichen. She skidded to a halt in front of the door and heard the thin, high wailing of an infant in pain. Gritting her teeth, Chena knocked, but did not bother to wait for a reply before opening the door and walking inside.

The last time she had been in this neat, dim, sparsely furnished room, it had been to help Mother Tso deliver Mila. The memory of sweat, blood, and screaming assaulted her with almost physical force as she stepped into the room. Then, it had been Mother Tso screaming, and Nan Elle, and Chena herself. Now, it was just one voice. Just little Mila howling in her mother's arms because she hurt and did not understand what was happening to her.

Father Tso, a silent bear of a man with pale brown skin and hands like leather from a lifetime of fieldwork, looked down at her as she stepped to the door. Then he stepped aside so she could get to the family's one big bed, where Mother Tso sat holding little Mila.

Chena shut her mouth and shoved her emotions into the back of her mind. She picked Mila up out of her mother's arms and laid a hand against the baby's head. Burning hot. But that was not as bad in babies as it was in adults. The fever's blotches were still faint on her golden skin. She was breathing without wheezing, and when Chena felt Mila's hot little chest, she found that the child's heart beat fast but steadily.

She gave Mother Tso back her infant, but her eyes slid away as the woman tried to catch her gaze. She didn't want to see that frightened look again. She'd already seen it on a dozen sets of parents. She was tired of looking into anxious eyes and lying.

Instead, she bent down and pulled out the pots and the bottle. One at a time, she handed them to Father Tso, explaining in a brisk, professional tone how the contents of each were to be given, telling them she'd be back after dark with the foxglove infusions.

He stood there, containers clutched in his hands, saying nothing, not even nodding. He knew. He knew about the dead, and the sick shut up in the men's wing of the dormitory. He knew it was so bad that Constable Regan wasn't even pretending to harass Nan Elle anymore and had given orders to his people not to question Chena about anything she carried. Madra had actually gone into the Alpha Complex to argue to their Family Committee directly for real medical help. Of course she'd been turned down, but word was she was getting ready to head back.

And the Tsos were still watching her.

Answer them, said Nan Elle's voice inside her mind. *You know the question, you give them the answer.*

Chena straightened up and made herself look directly at both the Tsos. "She's going to get worse before she gets better," she said, as gently as she could. "But she's a big girl, and she's been very healthy up until now. Keep her as cool as possible and give her the medicines as I've explained. There's every chance in the world."

"Thank you," said Mother Tso, hoisting Mila onto her shoulder so she could rub the child's back. "We will look for you."

"You'll see me." Chena gave them the best smile she could manage, slung her pack back over one shoulder, and retreated onto the catwalk.

Every chance in the world, thought Chena, feeling her face twist into a scowl as she headed back toward the stairs. *Every chance the hothousers allow. Every chance to sweat and bleed out your ears and die.*

The familiar anger settled comfortably inside her, much better company for her climb up to the third level than grief and guilt. She turned over her latest plans for getting into the hothouse. One day soon, Nan Elle said, Chena would be taught the comm path that would allow her to speak with Administrator Tam directly. Tam, it turned out, had been Nan Elle's hothouse contact for years. Which explained a lot.

Nan Elle had refused to let Chena even ask Tam to get her into the hothouse, but as soon as Chena could get a message to him without Nan Elle overhearing, she'd have her chance. And then . . . and then . . .

"Chena!" The sound of running feet accompanied the shout.

Chena swung around, her heart in her mouth, and saw it was just Teal pounding up the catwalk behind her.

"God's garden!" Chena aimed a blow so it breezed past her sister's shoulder as Teal caught up with her. "Don't yell like that."

"Sorry." Teal grinned at her. Her face was flushed from sun and exercise. Wisps of wiry brown hair had escaped from under her hat and she carried her overstuffed backpack carelessly in one hand. Teal had started up the errand running business again about a month after they . . . left the hothouse. Chena had tried to argue her into going to school, like Mom wanted, but Teal had shouted, cried, and sulked until Nan Elle had let her have her way. Teal was not interested in reading or vocational training. Teal was interested in earning money, and, as Nan Elle pointed out, Chena's new tasks would keep her so busy she would not have whole days to take to run to Stem with messages and raw materials. It had its advantages. What Teal brought in helped pay a rotating series of dorm babies to take up Chena's village chores as well as her own.

"You're looking pleased with yourself," remarked Chena as she reached for the door.

"I am." Teal caught her hand before she could turn the handle. "I got something to tell you." She jerked her chin upward, indicating she wanted to talk on the roof.

Chena's sigh rattled in her throat. She was tense. It was going to be a very long night. She did not have time for Teal's baby games.

"You do have time," said Teal as if she had read Chena's mind. "This is important, I'm telling you."

Chena growled wordlessly, but let Teal lead her up the stairs and into the riotous tangle of brambles, ryegrass, and saplings that camouflaged Nan Elle's precious licensed, as well as illegal, plants. Chena had spent whole nights up here learning to tell the herbs and weeds apart by touch and smell as well as by sight. "People are not always so polite as to get sick during daylight hours," Nan Elle had said.

"So?" Chena tossed her empty rucksack down and sat cross-legged with her back leaning against the chimney pipe. "What's the squirt?"

Teal folded her arms and grinned even more broadly. "I've found the new tailor," she announced triumphantly.

Confusion drew Chena's brows together. "You were looking for a tailor?"

Teal dropped to her knees, letting her backpack fall onto a patch of clover beside her. "Yes. Chena, I've found a way to get us out of here. Back to the station."

Chena wasn't sure whether to be saddened or annoyed. When would Teal give it up? She wasn't stupid. She knew what was what, the same as Chena did. "Teal, we can't go back. The station is overcrowded. Even if we could get past the constables and the hothousers,

Athena wouldn't take us." One of the advantages of living with Nan Elle was that you got to overhear all kinds of news and gossip.

"They would if we weren't there to stay." Teal's eyes shone. "The Authority is there. We find the commander and we claim our citizenship. As Authority citizens we are guaranteed a place in one of their cities. And"—she held up her hand as Chena opened her mouth to interrupt—"because we're both still minors, they would have to turn us over to our family. They would have to contact Dad to come get us. Simple."

Chena slashed her hand through the air between them. "Not simple. Not even part of reality. Teal, we gave up playing games about our noble daddy years ago. He's gone. He left us. He is not going to come get us." *He left us here to get experimented on. He left Mom here to die! He never gave a damn about us. When are you going to get that through your head?*

Teal's grin hardened a little, as if she were determined to hold on to it no matter what. "That doesn't matter. What matters is that once the Authority knows we are citizens, they'll have to give us a place." She spread her hands. "Even if we just make the claim, they'll have to let us stay while they investigate it."

Chena scrubbed the back of her neck and shook her head. "It can't work. If it was that simple, Mom would've done that in the first place."

"She couldn't have. Do you remember what she told Madra that one day? Mom was never an Authority citizen, remember? But now that she's not here . . ."

Chena's head snapped up. "You don't have to sound so happy about it."

Teal drew back a little. "You know what I mean. We can do this, Chena. It'll work."

Chena just shook her head again. "No, it won't. There is no way the hothousers are going to let us back up the pipe."

"That's where the tailor comes in," said Teal doggedly. "We get ourselves altered, get a set of fake IDs. I got money." For the first time, Teal hesitated. "If I don't have enough, they take other things. . . ."

Chena felt her eyes narrow. The day had gone incredibly still. Even the continual rustle of the leaves overhead had dropped to a whisper. "What kind of things?"

Teal licked her lips. "Genetic material."

Chena stared at her sister for a moment, stunned. "Oh, that's really it," she said, her voice heavy with sarcasm. "You know the tailors filter genetic material and information straight to the hothousers. You want to help *them*? Why don't you just sign up for the draft? I'm sure they'd be delighted to have another Trust in the hothouse."

Teal's grin faded, and the light in her eyes changed from enthusiasm to annoyance. "No," she said. "I don't know that they do that. I know that Nan Elle says they do that." She looked quickly away, then back again. "Anyway, it doesn't matter what they do with it. We won't be here."

She was serious. She really wanted to just run away. She really, deep down, thought that their father still cared enough to come get them.

"No," Chena said again, climbing to her feet.

Now Teal was staring at her. "What are you saying?" Her arms fell to her sides. "This is our chance. Finally!" She stopped, frozen in place by a new idea. "It's taken me five years to get together the money and find the guy we need. Don't you want to get out of here?"

Chena snicked off a piece of ryegrass with her fingernail and twirled it around. *Lolium pandora,* family *Gramineae.* The seeds were edible, although they tasted foul. It was good for clearing up constipation.

"We can't just run away," she said, tossing the piece of grass into the tangle of the garden and watching as it fell.

"Why the hell not?" demanded Teal.

Chena couldn't make herself look at her sister. "Because we can't."

"Chena, please, listen to me," Teal begged. "If we stay here, they are going to get us. They will do things to us that will make us wish they'd just kill us. You know. You saw."

Chena felt her jaw stiffen. "And if we do go, then what? Nothing changes down here. More people just die or disappear."

She heard Teal snort. "And you think *I'm* crazy. You still think we can get back at the hothousers for what they did."

Chena spun around, her fists clenched. "We have to! We can't let them get away with it!"

Teal ran her hand through her hair and kicked at the dirt. "Give it up, Chena. There's nothing we can do except get out of here."

"That's not true. There's plenty we can do."

"Like what?" Teal flung out her hands. "Feed the villagers grass when they need antivirals? Hold their hands while they die? Run their stupid little errands?"

"Teal, will you shut up?" Chena made frantic shushing motions with her hands while she craned her neck around to see if anyone had paused on the catwalk to listen to their argument. "You know that's not what it's about."

But Teal refused to calm down. "No, I don't. How would I know anything? You never tell me what's going on, you just give me orders, like you think you're Mom or something." Slowly anger turned her face red. "You're not! You're not anything! You're just—"

"Teal! Chena! That's enough!"

Nan Elle stood at the foot of her stairs. "I need both of you in here." Her cane thumped once on the catwalk.

Chena and Teal looked at each other defiantly, each daring her sister to say one word to continue the argument Nan Elle had so obviously overheard. In stubborn silence, they turned and climbed down the stairs, following Nan Elle back into the workroom.

When they got there, Nan Elle stood for a moment with her back to them, swaying unsteadily on her feet. "I know you two girls are nursing old hurts. I even, believe it or not, know what that feels like." She turned then, and her eyes were cold. "But now is a time of emergency. People are dying. Whatever you may think, whatever you may eventually want to do, you are needed, here and now."

Teal crossed her arms and looked away. Chena just hung her head, ashamed for both of them.

"Chena, I am going to send you and Farin down to Peristeria. You are going to have to poach what we need to stop the fever."

Chena's heart leapt into her throat. Poach? That meant going outside the fences. Fear and exhilaration rushed into her stomach. Nan Elle was finally going to let her go outside the fences. And she was going with Farin. The image of his bright eyes and wonderful smile filled her mind. Peristeria was days away by railbike and boats. Days alone on a boat with Farin . . . .

"Chena!" hissed Teal. "You can't! I told you—"

"I've got to," Chena told her firmly. "You heard Nan Elle."

Teal stormed off into the bedroom and slammed the door behind her.

"I'll go talk to her," said Chena hastily.

Nan Elle nodded. "You do that. And you get your pack ready. You must leave at once."

"Yes, Nan." Chena practically ran for the bedroom. She had no idea what she would say once she faced Teal in there, but she would think of something. She always had before.

Nan Elle watched the door swing shut behind Chena. After a moment, the murmur of the girls' voices vibrated through the wood. Elle turned away. She had heard everything she needed to, and much more than she wished.

So, she thought as she sat down heavily at her writing desk. *There is a new tailor in Stem and Teal Trust has sussed him, or her, out.*

Ambitious girl. Angry girl. She wanted to run, to fly. She had nothing to hold her here, the way Chena had. In many ways the fever had brought Chena into her own. Her skills had blossomed and she'd truly begun to feel for the people in her charge. Given time, her desire for revenge against the hothousers might fade away, and then she'd be ready to truly understand the way life was here.

Pandora, centuries ago, had been set up as a scientific experiment. At first the hothousers had sequestered themselves in their domes so that they could study and understand the most Earth-like biosphere ever found without disturbing it. Then they saw what was happening in the Called. How humans were landing on pristine worlds and cutting into them until they bled. Not content to let the rest of humanity go its own way, the hothousers had invited in half a dozen ships' worth of colonists to participate in an extended experiment in sustainable living. Initially it was thought that those colonists and their children would learn how to live in a wilderness environment comfortably, without damaging the world around them and without depending on machinery that there was no infrastructure to maintain.

Then they would all fly out into the galaxy and teach the human race what they knew.

For a while, and for price, the Authority had carried the message of this grand experiment. Some of the Called even sent representatives to see it, and when they had seen, they went away and did not come back.

The years turned, and the worlds turned. Gradually life on Pandora became entrenched and the goals changed. Elle doubted even the cityminds knew exactly how it all happened. Snubbed by the Called, who, after all, had come out here because they did not want to be told how to live, the hothousers cast their eyes backward, to ravaged Old Earth, and decided they would not send delegates out into the colonies. A convenient decision, since it turned out the villagers did not want to go out and spread the word to the Called. They wanted to stay where they were and look after themselves. No, instead, the hothousers would work to understand the whole of this living world, its humans included. Then they would take that knowledge back to the cradle of humanity and present it there. All who heard would marvel at this incredible understanding, and the Pandorans, as saviors, would embark on the greatest work ever. They would resuscitate Earth. But if they were going to truly do that, they would have to understand human beings—how they lived, how they worked physically and mentally, what they could do, what they would do. So the villagers became not laboratories of learning, but subjects for experiment.

Oh, there had been rebellions, and there would be again. There had been abuses, and there would be again. The idea of eventually returning to Old Earth was swallowed by the enormity of categorizing and analyzing Pandora, and keeping it safe from the rest of the Called.

Perhaps, if things had just gone on, some angry visionary in the village, or on Athena, would have risen up and incited the people to topple the power structure. But things did not go on. The Diversity Crisis began. Now there was one central fact of life. The rest of the Called were dying. Pandora was not, and no one was rash enough to do anything that might change this enviable condition.

As long as that was true, the hothousers and their capricious whims would stay in power, and all the anger that could fill two young women was not going to change that.

Elle reached for pen and ink. Whatever the result of the ongoing argument in the bedroom, there were letters to write. To Farin, to people Farin would meet, and for Farin to give to others who would pass them on. Tam needed to know about the new tailor. He already knew Elle would be mounting a poaching expedition. There had been too many deaths, but she had not been willing to let Chena go until she was absolutely certain Chena would come back. Sending Farin with her would help assure that. Chena would never run out on Farin just to see how far she could get before the hothousers noticed, as she might do if let loose on her own.

Once Chena's on her way, I will talk with Teal, Elle told herself, setting her paper squarely in front of her and uncorking the ink jar. *The girl's no fool, she just needs a direction. I've left her too long without one. She will come to understand she's needed here, as her sister has.*

They will both come to understand.

Beleraja hauled herself onto the bridge of Menasha's ship, savoring the sensation of freedom and familiarity it gave her. Both the Poulos and the Denshyar flagships were from roughly the same era. The floor and walls were onyx and marble, with saffron gripping patches radiating outward from the ring of command stations. The pilot's window was half filled by the white and silver skin of Athena Station. The other half looked out onto blank, black vacuum.

The lodestone sparkled in its gilded alcove. Beleraja kicked gently off from the hatchway and glided over to the stone. She caught the holding strap with one hand and laid the other on its glittering surface, closing her eyes to pray a moment for guidance and safe journey. It seemed appropriate somehow.

Shontio had loaned Beleraja one of the station's precious shuttles so she could fly out and meet Menasha. He agreed that they would need to speak somewhere where there was no possibility of being overheard. They were planning to create a radical rebalancing of power throughout the Called. As Shontio pointed out, there were people even on overcrowded Athena Station that might balk at that.

Beleraja turned her mind from the memory of Shontio's hard, hopeless eyes when he had first spoken of how they could end the crisis on Athena and in the Called, how they could flood the world with people and put into practice what Beleraja herself had believed for so long now: that only the consolidation of the tattered patches of humanity would save them.

And we'd better be right, she sighed to herself. *Because once we start this, there will be no other Pandoran cure.*

Still hanging on to the strap, Beleraja twisted to find that Menasha had swum across to the captain's chair and was now holding on to its arm.

"Everybody else off shift?" Beleraja asked with mild disbelief, pushing gingerly off the wall toward the first master's chair.

"Here and there, off shift, visiting aboard the other ships." Menasha planted her soft-soled boots onto the gripping patch. "I thought the fewer ears, the better."

"Always." Beleraja grabbed the back of the first master's chair and pressed her own shoes against the nearest patch. "But they are your family. . . ."

Menasha squeezed the chair arm, lifting herself a little and making the gripping patch crinkle underfoot. "Some of them would rather not know what's going on."

"But they agree?" said Beleraja, trying to keep her anxiety out of her voice. She had lost track of the number of nights she had spent pacing her tiny room, trying not to wake Hoja and Liel, the techs she now bunked with, and trying to tell herself she had not made a mistake. Consolidation was the only answer that made any sense at all.

"They agree." Menasha's smile grew wistful. "That doesn't mean they like it."

Beleraja laughed. "I can't understand that." It had been so easy to say it could be done. Consolidation could be calculated like the movement of any other cargo. As long as you knew distances and capacities, you could set up a simple schedule and bring the Called to Pandora in neatly timed intervals. All they needed was a great enough capacity, and that was what Menasha had been sent out to procure.

"So"—Menasha pulled a sheet screen from her coat pocket and handed it across to Beleraja—"here's who we have so far. The rest of the fleet is still making contact, but these are on their way."

Beleraja skimmed the names of a dozen colonies and their population figures. "That's five thousand. That's barely going to be enough. We need ten thousand, a hundred thousand if we can get them." Menasha hadn't seen the flyby shots from the satellites showing where the would-be colonists had dropped down. There had been the shuttle drop, the parachutes opening, the people landing with their loads of cargo. They scattered out to claim their land, and then . . . and then they dropped dead. When Beleraja closed her eyes, she could clearly see the image of all those bodies lying still on the ground like fallen leaves. Then there was nothing left but the artificial things, the landing rafts, the metal, the cloth. It was after that when the hothousers showed up in their dirigibles, carefully gathered up all that detritus, and left.

Of the flesh-and-blood human beings there was nothing left at all, and there had been three hundred of them. In the four hours that it had taken Satellite 22 to move out of range and Satellite 23 to move back in, they had died, and there was no trace of the hothousers having come in to do the deed themselves.

"And how are you going to move these hundred thousand people?" Menasha swept her hand out. "There aren't that many ships in the Called."

Beleraja willed herself to focus. Menasha was right, of course. She had to concentrate on what was possible, or this grand escapade of hers and Shontio's was doomed before it really began. "What about the ships we do have?"

"We've recruited two families so far, but it's slow going."

"Anybody talking out of turn to the council, do you think?"

"You'd know better than I would. What have you been hearing from them?"

Beleraja shrugged. The thin, tattered comm net that stretched across the Called was proving both a blessing and a curse for their plans. It kept the council from being able to keep track of them, but it also kept them from knowing the latest changes of council heart. A fleet to replace Beleraja and her family as Athena's watchdogs could be on its way right now, and they would have no way of knowing it. "We had a squirt a couple of weeks ago through Ganishi's Station." She rubbed the sheet between her thumb and first two fingers. "It basically said the council is pleased that we're keeping up the pressure on Pandora, but they are not thrilled with the lack of measurable progress on the cure."

Menasha barked out one short laugh. "What else's new?"

"Agreed." Beleraja read the names of the worlds and all the neat numbers that indicated how many people had decided to trust that she and Shontio knew what they were talking about. "I think if I told the council I was going to drop five thousand colonists on Pandora, they'd give me a medal. It would screw the pressure plate down tighter and still allow them to completely deny their involvement."

"You do realize . . ." Menasha let the sentence trail away. She tapped her fingertips against the chair arm, as if trying to decide whether she would finish or not. Beleraja stood silently, giving her a chance to make up her mind. "You do realize," Menasha started again, "that the longer we have to draw this out, the better the chances are that someone who does not agree with what you are doing will find out? That we'll spark a debate, and possibly even active fragmentation among the shippers?"

"Yes." Beleraja read the sheet again. Yaruba had decided to trust her, four hundred and twenty of them. High Marrakesh—only one hundred and eighty-five there made up their minds to trust her, or maybe that was all they had left.

She felt Menasha watching her closely. "And do you want to do something about it?" Menasha asked.

Beleraja folded the sheet screen into thirds. "Is there anything we can do?"

Menasha stared out the pilot's window for a moment, watching the unchanging, monochromatic scene. "We've been getting some strange questions."

"Like what?" Beleraja frowned.

"Like"—Menasha took a deep breath—"how are we going to divide the land once all these people get there? Like, how are we going to set up the new government? In short, there are people who would help us in return for land and power."

Beleraja stared at her, unable to do anything but blink in surprise for a long moment. "You're joking," she said at last. "What do they think is going on here?"

Now it was Menasha's turn to look surprised. "They think you're invading Pandora." Her eyes narrowed. "What do you think is going on here?"

Excellent question. Beleraja stuffed the sheet into her pocket where she wouldn't have to see it anymore. "Mena, I can't make those kinds of promises."

"Then who can?"

"Nobody!" The force of Beleraja's denial startled her. "That's not what we're doing."

Menasha pulled both boots off the gripping patch with a sound like a snort. She swung her legs over the captain's chair and brought them down again so she was standing right in front of Beleraja. "Then what are you doing?" she asked, rooting herself in place. "Are you just dropping a hundred thousand people down onto a planet without any plan?" Her eyes searched Beleraja's for a moment, and Beleraja could tell they did not like what they saw. "Do you have any idea what you're setting up here?" Menasha did not wait for an answer. "Certainly most people are just going to want to grab a plot of land where they can live. But there are going to be some people who have got ideas, and those ideas are going to involve bullying their neighbors." Her voice went suddenly soft. "This is not a family picnic we are talking about here. You are starting a new world. There is going to have to be somebody in charge, and I hate to say this, but it is probably going to be you."

Beleraja shook her head, although she could not have said which part of Menasha's speech she was really denying. "We're not a government."

"The Authority is not a government. You are going to have to be." Menasha reached into her pocket again. "Beleraja, I've got something else to show you." Menasha pulled out another sheet screen. "This is the list of shipper families who will help if we will guarantee them prime land and slots in a government."

The sheet fell open in Beleraja's hands and her eyes read the print automatically. Fifteen family names. Beleraja knew most of them. Good families, old families. Over eight hundred ships. Properly coordinated, they could bring nine thousand more colonists. Invaders.

Good families. Old families. Patriarchs and matriarchs she had known, or at least known of, since infancy, and here they were, ready to help, and all she had to do was divide up a world for them.

Beleraja stared out the pilot's window, a feeling of desperation creeping over her. She wanted to tell Menasha to fire up the engines, to take her out to where her own family's fleet patrolled the jump points for Athena Station. She wanted to climb onto her own ship, close the hatch, and fly away. She wanted never to have agreed to Shontio's request in the committee meeting. She wanted never to have spoken of her beliefs to him, never to have seen him so worn down, never to have realized that the Pandorans, no matter how brilliant and experienced, could not save the Called.

"Beleraja." Menasha's hands touched hers, and Beleraja realized her fist had closed around the sheet screen. "I know you have not just been sitting up here enjoying the scenery. What have you been doing?"

"Working out landing sites." She gestured toward the pulled-out screen attached to the captain's chair. "Trying to figure out what happened to the last set of people who tried a landing on Pandora. I could show you, but I've been keeping it all on an isolated database." Menasha nodded. *Well, at least you approve of something I've done.* "Mostly, I've been lying." Despite the ship's lack of gravity, Beleraja felt like she weighed a thousand pounds. "Lying to the council, lying to the Pandorans." Thoughts of the amount of time she had spent, and would still have to spend, at a command board to monitor the screen made her eyes burn. "I have been intercepting each and every message between the two of them and reworking it." She rubbed her eyes. "You would not believe how good I have become at data forgery." *And planting rumors in the comm net, and smoothing together disconnected images, and interfering with those pesky little satellites so the Pandorans can't keep track of which ships are actually coming and going from here.*

"I wondered why the situation had stayed so calm." A smile flickered across Menasha's face, but it faded almost as soon as it formed. "Now I've got something else for you to think about." Slowly, deliberately, Menasha stretched out her arm and pointed at the pilot's window. "Your first wave is coming. If you want there to be a second wave in anything less than two years, you are going to have to consider these requests."

Beleraja's shoulders sagged, and she felt as though they would never straighten up again. She opened her hand and the crumpled sheet screen full of family names spun gently into the air. "What am I doing, Mena?"

"I don't know," Menasha answered. "What are you doing?"

Beleraja watched the sheet perform a graceful pirouette on one corner. She should let go. She should just leave, right now, with Menasha. There was no way to make this work. She was being a fool. This was not her job. Her job was to look after her people, and she had been neglecting that for years now. She had been exchanging plans with them for how, after the consolidation, they might turn themselves into a salvage fleet, looting abandoned stations and satellites for usable hardware and software to bring to the newly settled Pandora. They could still fly, still be free.

But if she believed what Menasha was saying now, those plans were merely fantasies. She was no longer matriarch of her small family, she was matriarch of all the refugees that Pandora could hold.

No. I don't want that. I want to fulfill my promise and go away. This is not my life. This will never be my life.

But her mind's eye showed her the crowded stairways of Athena Station, full of people Shontio had let stay because she had said this thing could be done.

Beleraja closed her hand around the drifting sheet screen. "I guess I'm going to talk to Shontio about setting up a provisional government for when we invade Pandora."

CHAPTER TWELVE

Queen of the World

"Captain Aban?" Farin saluted the slouching, dour man at the end of the dock, giving him the bright smile that Chena had seen work as well on men as on women.

Chena watched Aban look Farin up and down, trying to reach some judgment about him.

"You coming down the river?" He had a long, lazy drawl to his voice, as if he didn't care what happened next.

Farin nodded. "Myself and my cousin." He gestured toward Chena, who beamed up at the captain, trying to look younger than she was. It was a trick that had gotten a lot harder since she had grown two inches and filled out so much in her bosom.

Aban spared her a glance, but did not seem to be impressed. He made a come-here gesture with his first two fingers. "Chits and hands." He unhooked the scanner from his belt.

"We have this for you as well." Farin handed over a much-folded piece of paper.

Aban frowned. This was not part of the routine, and he obviously did not like it. But he took the paper anyway and opened it, running his gaze swiftly over the words. His frown grew deeper and darker. Chena held her breath. This was the real test. If this man did not agree to the instructions in Nan Elle's letter, they were going no farther.

Not that they had really gotten anywhere yet. Chena still had to reach the rain forest village of Peristeria, get outside the fence, search the rain forest for a particular kind of fungus, the belladonna mushroom (*Fungus belladonna,* Nan Elle's herb sheets called it). Dried and concentrated, it produced a substance that could regulate an uneven heartbeat where digitalis couldn't help. Administered in small doses along with some of Nan Elle's precious salicylic acid and penicillin, it would save the dying in Offshoot.

Captain Aban was supposed to take them down the last stage of the journey. Once, he had lived in Offshoot, and Nan Elle had saved the life of his oldest son. The letter was reminding him of that and suggesting that if he left the crew door of his riverboat open when the boat reached the Peristeria dock, it would be greatly appreciated.

Aban lifted grim eyes to Farin, who stood there patiently, although the smile had faded so he didn't look quite as cocky. Up until now, Farin had carried all their documents. Chena was traveling as a minor with him as her supervisory relative, as was required for a trip of more than three hundred kilometers. At least it was another month until she turned nineteen. It also meant that if anyone got suspicious they would be more likely to look at Farin, who was as clean as this morning's dew.

So far, it had all gone well. This man, though, could stop them in their tracks, and he looked about ready to. Some people did not like being reminded what they owed.

At last, Captain Aban jerked his chin toward the boat. "We leave Peristeria at sunset, if you want a ride back."

His words opened Chena's throat and she was able to breathe again. Farin nodded their thanks and gestured for Chena to precede him. She risked one look back and saw Aban's fingers tearing the note into minute flakes without his eyes once glancing down to see what his hands were doing.

The riverboat was the standard design—wide, double-keeled, with an enclosed cabin filled with benches for rowers and passengers. People occupied more than half of them. Loose, gauzy clothing seemed to be the local uniform, to keep cool yet provide some protection from the insects buzzing everywhere.

As soon as Chena and Farin boarded, Captain Aban climbed onto the deck and locked the cabin's bow door. Chena gravitated toward the stern windows behind the last rowing bench and laid both hands on the wooden rail that ran just below the glass panes. The boat rocked and jostled as the rowers pushed off, and the huge metronome beside Chena started ticking to keep the time.

"Don't you want to sit down?" asked Farin. "It's going to be a long trip."

Chena shook her head. "I've been sitting for days."

Which was true. She'd sat on the boat from Offshoot to Stem, on the dirigible from Stem to Taproot, on the next boat from Taproot to Deciduous.

It was also true, Chena admitted to herself, that she was simply too edgy to sit quietly with the rest of the passengers, their baggage, and their babies. So she stayed where she was and watched the lush tropical world slip past. Water slapped the hull, making an irregular counterpoint to the rhythm of the oars slapping the water. Neither sound was anywhere near loud enough to cover the chirping and hooting pouring from the jungle that surrounded the swift brown river, even in combination with the ticking of the metronome and the grunts of the rowers as they stretched and pulled.

Five years ago, Chena would have wondered what idiot didn't know machines could do this work. Now she knew better. Machines had to be built from artificial materials. They broke down and had to be repaired with more artificial materials. They could litter or disturb the ecology. Humans could be maintained with naturally occurring substances and they fixed and reproduced themselves without requiring spare parts to be shipped in from Athena. They also moved more slowly, and so were less likely to damage Pandora than robots or powered vehicles.

Chena's thoughts made her frown. In answer, Farin moved a little closer to her, a gesture which managed to be both reassuring and disconcerting. But for once Farin's presence did not occupy her whole mind. She was too taken up with what she was about to try.

She was going outside the fence today. She was going to walk in the wilderness and poach the sacred forests of Pandora. Today, Chena was on her own. On her own if she succeeded, and on her own if she got caught.

Chena hoped her fellow passengers would assume the sheen of perspiration on her forehead was from the tropical heat.

Teal had never understood why they had to live like this, or why Chena insisted that she stick to running errands while Chena was the apprentice lawbreaker. But Teal was Chena's responsibility, and she would do what was best. Mom would have expected no less.

Teal was getting her revenge, though. Chena couldn't look at Farin without remembering their last fight.

After their argument on the roof, Chena had walked into the bedroom to find that Teal had thrown herself flat on the broad pallet they shared. Chena had sat down cross-legged beside her and picked up her big traveling pack. She needed to finish unpicking some of the inner seams so she could sew in a hidden pocket. She got to work with her thick needle, waiting for Teal to say something.

At last Teal did.

"Why are you doing this?"

Chena kept her eyes on her work. "Because I have to."

"The fuck you do!" Teal heaved herself to her feet.

"Teal." Chena sighed and lowered the canvas pack into her lap. "You don't understand—"

"What's to understand?" Teal ripped the pack out of her hands. "You're being a space-head. Again!"

"A space-head for not wanting to run away when there are lives in danger?" Feeling childish but unable to stop herself, Chena snatched back the pack.

"As if you really cared!" shouted Teal, just centimeters from Chena's face. "You just want to go out there with your whore!"

Chena's fist clenched around the needle. Teal stood her ground defiantly, daring Chena to lash out at her. Chena took a long, slow breath and loosened her hand with great effort.

People said Farin was a prostitute. People said women, and sometimes men, paid him to have sex with them. Chena had been stunned and upset when she first found out. She knew about prostitutes, she'd seen them on Athena, where they were illegal. They were mostly women up there, and not exactly the kind of people Mom let her and Teal make friends with. Of course, she'd also been a kid then and hadn't understood a lot of things. She had asked Farin about what she had heard, and he had reassured her that he was just a performer. He sold his talents to the village, not his body. Teal just wanted to believe the rumors because she hated Farin, although Chena couldn't understand why. Teal could still be so thick sometimes. Her friendship with Farin was real. He cared about her. He helped because he was Nan Elle's blood family, but also because he truly liked Chena. He'd said so, plenty of times. One day, he would tell her he more than liked her. She was sure of it. In the meantime, she was not—she was *not*—going to let Teal's stupid insults ruin anything.

"You're talking like a baby and you don't understand anything," she said, enunciating each word slowly and clearly. "So, just go away for a while, would you? We'll talk when I get back."

"No. We won't."

Teal had turned away then and walked out of the house. Chena had just sighed and gone back to rigging her pack.

She sighed again now. She'd be back home in four days. Teal would have gotten over her snit by then and they would talk. This time, she'd find the words to make Teal truly understand why they were living this way. She'd make her understand about Farin too, once and for all. If this tailor, whoever it was, insisted on catering to Teal's obsession with returning to Athena . . . well, Nan Elle had taught Chena a few ways to deal with that kind of problem too.

Nan Elle said that once, a long time ago, the Pharmakeus had been a real network instead of just a loosely connected bunch of men and women with hand-me-down information about Pandora's plants and a grand, paranoid name. They'd operated out of the hothouses, and they'd had people inside who would help diagnose and treat the illnesses. But then the Consciences came along, and suddenly none of them could do anything the rest of the family disapproved of. The hothouser Pharmakeus had babbled happily about what they were up to, and apologized, and the village networks were broken up, not just the doctors, but the computers. It was done, they said, so no one could introduce anything that would upset the delicate natural balance of Pandora's microsphere.

In the hothouse classes, they'd been told this all happened because the villages had not been originally supposed to operate for more than a couple of generations. When it was decided that the real work of Pandora lay in understanding the world around them rather than lecturing "those who did not want to hear," changes had to be made.

My ass, thought Chena, sneering at the river. *If that's what it was, why didn't they just move everybody into the hothouses? It's really just another way to control us. They're afraid if there ever gets to be more of us than there are of them, we might decide not to put up with their shit anymore.*

Time, and miles of riverbank, slipped away, but Chena didn't sit down. She leaned her elbows on the rail and ran her mind over everything Nan Elle had told her about the tropics—about the snakes, the big cats, the little parasites, and the huge bugs. Don't drink the water, don't step into blank patches of mud or areas of dead vegetation, and for the sake of God's own, don't eat anything you haven't seen anyone else eat first. Chena's comptroller, sewed securely into the seam of her pack along with her compass, was stuffed full of every note she could key in. Normally, Nan Elle frowned on her using the comptroller and insisted that she memorize every fact and name. This time she made an exception, because there was no time.

"So," said Farin brightly, breaking the silence and making Chena jump. "You do your visiting and I'll meet you in the library before sunset?"

"Right." Chena tried to match his cheerful, casual tone. She didn't think she managed very well. Down the bank, Peristeria's short wooden dock protruded from the rain forest and every nerve in Chena's body hummed with fear and excitement. If she did this, if she found the mushroom Nan Elle needed and got it back to Offshoot, she would strike her first real blow against the hothousers since they murdered Mom. But if she got caught . . .

She rubbed the nail on her little finger. It was not real anymore and underneath it waited a quarter teaspoon of concentrated alkaloid poison. If she got caught, the hothousers would not have the chance to do to her what they did to Sadia or Mom.

The dock pulled closer. The boatmen raised their oars. One opened the locked door by the prow and leapt from the deck to the pier so he could catch the mooring ropes and secure the boat alongside.

With that as their signal, the passengers stood, rocking gently with the motion of the boat, and gathered what possessions they had, mostly bundles to be slung on their backs or settled on shoulders or head.

Chena hitched the straps of her pack up on her shoulders, and looking to Farin for a last reassuring glance, she joined the file of passengers waiting in the center aisle for the front door to open.

But as they filed toward the dock, she moved slowly backward until her hand closed around the latch for the stern door. She hadn't actually seen Captain Aban work the lock, and there was no way during the journey to check without someone noticing. Still, Aban owed Nan Elle for the life of his child. Surely he would do as he promised. He would not leave her hanging.

The handle turned under Chena's fingers. The door opened. Chena stepped out onto the deck. Without hesitation, she slipped into the brown river water and promptly sank into muck up to her ankles.

Great. She pulled her first foot free, wincing at the sucking sound it made. *A really promising beginning here.*

Screened by the boat's hull, she waded through warm, translucent water up to her waist toward the thick reeds and leaves of the bank, praying the whole time she'd knotted her boots tightly enough. If she lost one in the river mud, she'd never see it again.

Finally she made dry land, and there she clung, half in, half out of the water, trying not to think of the snakes and the carnivorous fish she had read about. Something did brush past her ankle then, and something else nibbled her shin delicately. Chena shivered, but she held still, keeping her eyes on the activity on the dock. She could not move until they cleared out, and it seemed to be taking forever. The rowers lounged about talking to the passengers, who seemed to disperse only reluctantly to their homes. Something else sampled Chena's shin through her trousers. Chena shivered again.

Finally, finally, the people on the dock filtered away, leaving only a couple of rowers, who slapped each other on the shoulder and retreated into the riverboat.

Gritting her teeth, Chena pulled herself out onto the bank and crouched in the thick green undergrowth. Ahead of her, she could see the gleaming metal fence posts surrounding the village.

She was outside. She'd done it.

No, you've done part of it, she reminded herself. *Only one part.*

Chena couldn't see anyone moving beyond her screen of greenery, which probably meant no one could see her. But just to be safe, she crawled farther into the undergrowth. Water cascaded down onto her from the broad flat leaves, and she startled a whole flock of emerald-green lizards that took flight up the trunk of the nearest tree.

She carefully unslung her pack, trying to make sure that neither her elbows nor her head popped up above the sheltering leaves. Awkward in her crouching position, she unpacked Nan Elle's precious camouflage suit. It was a pair of mottled green and brown trousers, and a matching jacket with a hood that would cover all her hair and a gauze screen to hide her face. None of this would truly hide her from the hothousers' cameras, but the suit's reflective and refractive properties would confuse the visual and infrared signals and make her look more like a large animal than a human being. The hothousers used these suits to observe animal behavior in the forests. Administrator Tam had given Nan Elle this one to help with her poaching. Once again, Chena found she had reason to thank that particular hothouser, and once again, she wondered, if they couldn't take a stand against their own family, why he was helping hers. That implant in his head couldn't possibly allow him to feel guilty about letting Mom get killed . . . could it?

Chena pulled her small knife out of her pocket and slit the pack's false bottom seam, removing her comptroller and compass. She strapped the one to her wrist and tucked the other in her pocket. Then she shouldered her pack again and got to her feet, maintaining her crouch. Somewhere her nervousness had vanished. In its place was a kind of elation. She was doing it. She was invading the wilderness, and there was not one thing the hothousers could do about it.

Grinning to herself, Chena got her bearings from the compass, then hurried up the bank and plunged into the rain forest.

The alarm from Gem's observational subsystem startled the city-mind out of three conversations, two Conscience downloads, and a statistical data review. His annoyance was blue and red to his inner senses, but brief. The forest camera data was complicated to interpret and false alarms were common, but every one had to be checked out, or else how could Pandora be properly protected?

Gem liked to keep things orderly. So he prioritized the tasks in process, assigned the data analysis to a subsystem, apologized to the citizens undergoing Conscience downloads, and rescheduled, while bringing the conversations to a swift conclusion with another apology.

All that done, he set the city monitors on auto-receive and turned his attention toward the alarm. The mote cameras were not truly cameras. They were insects and spiders augmented with sensory transmitters so the scents and vibrations that the organisms detected, along with any visual information, would be returned to the city. This way, there could be thousands of detectors within a square mile of forest, returning streams of useful data with only minimal intrusion into the biosphere.

A cluster of motes in one of the river sectors had detected traces of what might be human sweat and, as their instincts required, they were trailing after the source of the scent. The subsystem had alerted him because the source of the scent was not following the confines of the quarantine fence.

Gem studied the forest map and the patterns of chemicals, vibrations, and light that the subsystem had already collected. It was all suggestive, but he was not ready to raise further alert quite yet. He opened five separate signal-and-source databases and routed the fresh input to them. His inorganic processors chewed both new and old data over for a few dozen seconds and came back with a disturbing answer. All four databases agreed that there was a ninety to ninety-five percent probability that this struggling bundle of light and scent was a human being outside the confines of the village.

Anger touched Gem, followed by a healthy dose of sorrow. Who would choose to do this? What reason could this person have? The villagers had all the room they needed. The families of the complexes had luxury and company, creativity and safety. Why did people persist in invading the biosphere?

There was, at least, no question as to what his actions should be. He passed the alarm on to the Guardians so they could alert the family. An automatic transmission shot out to the constables in the four closest villages so they could be on the alert for strangers and set up fence patrols. Finally he opened the subsystem that would allow himself and the Guardians to connect with the interceptors.

Chena lifted her veil and wiped at the sweat pouring down her face as she wrestled through another few yards of rain-spattered undergrowth. *Should've allowed more time. Should've gone out yesterday. Dell had passenger clearance. No, couldn't go with him. Dell would*

sell out his mother, and if anybody asked questions, he'd say anything to cover his ass.

No, today is the only day. I'll just have to make this work.

Nan Elle had taken her down to Peristeria once before so she could learn the routes and some of her connections, but she hadn't actually been in the forest then. She'd expected hot, and damp, with the water dripping from the canopy as if the trees themselves were sweating. She'd been ready for the bugs swarming around her head and hands and rising in clouds around her ankles with each step. Thongs tied her sleeves and pants legs tight. Her sealed collar almost choked her, but nothing was getting inside her clothing. She knew this overwhelming caution was caused by a leftover fear from the day she saw the ants swarm, but she did it anyway.

What she hadn't been ready for was how unrelievedly dense the tropical undergrowth was. This wasn't like the forest around Offshoot, where there were large patches of shadow so thick that nothing grew there except piles of leaves. Every square inch of ground here grew something, and it was usually big, broad, tough, dripping wet, and home to something reptilian or insectoidal. Snakes hung like overripe fruit from the low branches. Eyes peered at her from shadows. Unseen things rustled the fallen leaves.

She thought wistfully of the machete in her pack as she wrestled her way between a *Siphonia magnum* and a *Cyclonia pandoran.* But unless she wanted to start a real manhunt, there were limits to what she could do. If she went hacking at Pandora's precious vegetation, she'd be starting a whole new game.

There were times she wanted to do just that. Hack at the whole world, make it bleed, make it scream, watch the hothousers, who guarded the place so jealously that they didn't even care about other *people,* go pale and sick with horror. It would be worth anything, she thought some days, to make them scream.

But then she'd swallow that thought and get back to work.

Like you should be doing now, she reminded herself. Chena made herself stop in a fairly clear patch to catch her breath and think.

The secret to plant hunting, Nan Elle told her over and again, was to be aware of your surroundings. Every single plant in the forest was linked to every other, making a great chain. If you could follow tha'

chain, you could find the link you were looking for, but if you saw it all as some kind of great green stew, you were done for.

So, all right, where am I on the chain? Salix tropica, the tropical willow tree that sheltered her mushroom, needed standing water to grow. So Chena needed a marsh. She scanned around her and decided the vegetation clustered more densely toward the north, a good indicator of water. She sucked in her breath and tried to glide forward, as Nan Elle seemed able to do no matter where she was.

The ferns thickened around her, reaching up to her knees, then her shins, then her waist. The insects thickened too, and pitcher plants yawned wide to lure them in. Getting there. She passed a cluster of bright yellow Peristeria orchids and, oh, glory, *Cerastium aquaticum,* which would grow thick and tall near standing water, but less so near running streams. She was approaching her marsh.

Splash!

Correction—Chena pulled her boot back, chagrined—she was *in* her marsh. There were the *Salix tropica* trees with their leaves like fat hands drooping down to trail in the pools of standing water, where frogs the size of Chena's head sat submerged to their eyeballs in black water and watched the fog of insects skimming the ponds. The tropical willow's gray bark was a terrarium for at least a dozen kinds of fungus, and some of the fungus grew other fungus, like the parasitic belladonna mushroom.

The stuff she wanted would grow higher up, near the canopy, in the crooks of the branches where the dribbling moisture gathered. Chena set down her pack, unlaced her boots, stuffed her socks inside, and slung them over her shoulder. When you had no help and didn't want to harm the tree, the best way to climb was barefoot. Especially knowing that if her unfeeling soles smashed too many little fungi, she would effectively be leaving boot prints.

Chena dug her fingers and toes into the grooves in the bark and started climbing. She enjoyed climbing trees. She was good at it. Even with a fully loaded pack on her back, she could swarm up the sides of the tallest tree like any squirrel. When she was climbing, she felt strong and free.

All too soon, she reached a wide crook where the branches were patched with telltale umbrellas of pink and brown. Chena broke off a

piece of fungus and sniffed it, then broke a piece off the piece and tasted it, spitting it out instantly after she did. Her tongue didn't numb or itch, and the taste was salt and nut. This was the stuff.

Chena squatted on the branch, braced against the main trunk, and opened the collecting sacks hanging from her belt. Three pounds of the stuff would be enough to dose fifty or sixty people and was a small enough amount that it could still be smuggled to where it was needed. They'd have to hope the whole village wasn't sick by the time Chena made it back. What they really needed was a hundred pounds of the stuff, or a thousand, but they couldn't have that.

Madra, after her third trip inside the hothouse, said they were giving all the same old reasons for not helping Offshoot. Antibiotics and antivirals, they said, would introduce "an artificial pressure" on the microsphere, causing artificial evolution of the microorganisms. Changes in the microsphere would have repercussions all the way up the life chain and therefore could not be allowed.

"But it doesn't make any sense!" Chena's hand had tightened around the pestle she was using to crush more foxglove seeds. "Don't they see that it doesn't make any sense?"

"Human societies, especially old ones, seldom make sense," Nan Elle had said. "Tell me, why do the Athenians always pick their management committees from the same five families?"

Chena shrugged. "Because that's the way they do it."

"Exactly. The hothousers are doing these things because that's what they do. It doesn't make any sense, but nowhere else makes much sense either."

Chena had narrowed her eyes at Nan Elle then. "You've never lived anywhere else. How would you know?"

Nan Elle had just stirred at one of the pots on the stove. "When you are sixty-eight years old, ask me that again."

So, no real medicines. The hothousers forbade it, because that was how they did things and no one was able to make them stop yet.

Chena pulled her knife out of its sheath and began shearing off mushrooms and dropping them into her bags. She worked quickly, ignoring the bugs and the sweat, the hoots of the birds and the skittering lizards. She climbed from branch to branch, taking the most hidden fungi, never clearing out a patch completely. Inside a week, the evidence of her presence would be completely erased by fresh growth.

Some of the bugs, of course, were not bugs at all. They were little cyborgs with mote chips in their heads, sending back swarms of data to the hothousers. They saw her up here, crouching like a gigantic monkey in the tree, stealing forbidden fruit. There was no help for that. She had to trust her suit. Surely, if the suit wasn't working, they'd have been on to her before she could touch their wilderness.

The last bag full, Chena closed her knife and slithered back down to the ground. Aching but elated, she stowed her little sacks inside her pack. Nan Elle had forged her a license for carrying salad mushrooms that should cover things if anybody searched her pack. If anybody made her eat one of the things to prove it was what she said, she'd have at least thirty minutes before she got sick.

Chena drew in a great lungful of the moist tropical air, feeling like the queen of the world. All she had to do was find her way back to the dock and to Farin in the Peristeria library.

She pictured his eyes when she told him how smoothly she had accomplished her task. They would widen with pleased surprise, and he would tell her how brave she was. He would take her hand and squeeze it, and then she would lean forward, and he would lean forward, and they would kiss, and it would be long and slow and he would wrap his arms around her and hold her close, and then . . . and then . . .

Chena shook herself. *Wake up! You keep dreaming like this, and you are going to be out here in the dark for the snakes to eat.*

She brought her compass out again to check her orientation. She turned slowly until her face was toward the river and she had sighted on landmarks among the vegetation to keep her going in a straight line. She set off.

Ahead of her, the undergrowth rustled and a black and yellow cat emerged and stared straight at Chena.

Chena froze, one foot still in the air. The animal was lean, with a ringed tail that looked at least as long as its spotted torso. Its huge clawed paws seemed to be made more for climbing trees than pacing on the ground. Its lips parted just enough that she could see the gleam of one fang, and it did not even blink as it looked at her.

A Pandoran jaguar. A wave of dizziness passed over Chena and for a moment she thought she might faint. One of the largest carnivores in the continental rain forest. They liked to stalk their prey by moving through the trees and then suddenly dropping down on it. She'd read all about that with a kind of morbid fascination.

The jaguar growled, a low whining sound, and took a step forward. Chena's blood rushed to the soles of her feet.

Stop it, stop it. What did Nan Elle tell you? Don't act like prey. If you don't act like a prey animal, they won't chase you.

She lowered her foot slowly. All she had to do was walk away calmly. All she had to do was not run. The jaguar's back only came up to her waist. Surely she was too big for it to take down. Except for that tail, it was about the size of a wolf, and wolves never attacked full-grown human beings. Everybody knew that. She had not come this far just to be cat food.

Mustering every nerve she possessed, Chena made herself take three calm steps forward. The jaguar screamed and leapt. Chena screamed in answer, stumbling backward, expecting to feel claws tearing through her. But the jaguar was crouched a meter away, its long tail lashing and the high-pitched warning growl trembling in the air between them.

Another blur of yellow and black fell from the trees, and a second jaguar stood beside the first.

Chena's nerve broke. She screamed again and ran, tearing at the tangled curtain of undergrowth with her hands, heedless of anything except the need to get away, get away, get away! A couple clear meters opened in front of her and she ran, and tripped, and scrabbled to her feet again, and clawed at the next wall of undergrowth, and vaguely realized her hands were bleeding and the growling was still behind her. She ran again, tripped again, fell, and tried to get up, and she couldn't, because she couldn't breathe, and she just lay there crying and panting and waiting to die.

After a few minutes, she lifted her head. She was not dead. Shaking, she looked over her shoulder. The jaguars waited a meter away from her, tense and wary, but not moving forward.

Still shaking, Chena got to her feet. Something was wrong. Something was so wrong she couldn't even think clearly about it. She took a step toward the jaguars. One of them growled and took a swipe at the air with its huge paw. Chena froze. She stepped to the left. Another growl, and the jaguar stepped to the left too, crouching as if getting ready to spring. Chena stepped right, and the jaguar held its position. Another step to the right, and another, and all the jaguars did was pad a few steps forward.

She knew, then, and the sudden revelation washed over her with the same strength as the fear had. All she could do was laugh, making a noise as high-pitched and hysterical as one of the jaguars' screams. The two cats did not like this noise and stalked slowly forward, growling their warnings. Still laughing, Chena held up her hands and turned to the right. She began walking forward. A growl sounded behind. She picked up the pace. That was apparently satisfactory. The jaguars took up their positions, one on each side of her, matching her step for step and making sure she did not deviate from the path.

She had not gotten away with anything, and it was not just insects that the hothousers controlled. They controlled these two creatures walking at her sides and the jaguars were taking her to their masters. Why had she believed that the hothousers would have to come out and get her? That she would see them coming? They were already here.

Slowly, Chena's hysteria faded and she felt the chill of fear take her again. She was being walked to the hothouse. They had seen her and they had captured her. Why had they waited so long? Why hadn't they taken her before she packed up their precious fungus?

Probably because they wanted to catch her red-handed so there would be no question about whether they could put her in the involuntary wing. She fingered her false nail. Should she take the poison now? Make them come and haul her body out of the pristine rain forest before it decayed and upset the delicate balance of nature?

Anger rushed over her then. How could they do this? They killed her mother, now they were going to kill her—and everybody in Offshoot, if she didn't get the medicine back to them. They didn't care. They never would care. It wouldn't make any difference to them how many bodies dropped to the ground, as long as they could get them cleaned up fast enough. She curled her fist around her false nail and looked at the cats guarding her.

They were herding her. The fangs and claws were threats. Real threats, but they did not want to use them. They wanted her alive.

Chena swallowed hard. They were keeping her for the involuntary wing, for the information she had, like where she had gotten the suit.

Chena hesitated at that thought and got another warning growl. The suit. She had almost forgotten. They had not really seen her, they had seen someone in a suit. The hothousers knew they had someone, but could not possibly know who they had yet. Another reason to tell their creatures not to kill her.

They did not want to kill her, but she had no such qualms about them. A plan, sudden and solid, formed in her mind. All she had to do was keep Nan Elle's advice firmly in mind and pay attention to the world around her.

There, there—a fallen tree within arm's reach, its spiky branches protruding invitingly. They were just about to pass it. They were passing it now.

Chena let herself stumble. One of the cats snarled. Chena straightened up with a length of dead wood in her hands. The nearest cat growled a warning and Chena answered with a snarl of her own as she swung the club down on its skull.

The cat screamed and Chena screamed and swung the club down again. Something snapped, and Chena dropped the stick and ran. She had only seconds. She tore the false nail from her finger and whirled around as the jaguar leapt at her.

She thrust her hand straight into the creature's mouth.

Teeth gouged her skin as she then fell backward, rolling and scrabbling to get out of reach. The jaguar rolled onto its feet. Chena scuttled backward like a wounded crab, pain and blood streaming down her arm. The jaguar sprang, and all at once it was on top of her, fur and weight and carrion smell, screaming and batting at her with its huge paws, clawing at her suit and rolling her over.

Then it was gone. She sat up, dizzy, fear making everything crystal clear. She saw the sharp edge on every leaf surrounding her, heard each individual insect hum. The jaguar, now a couple meters away, staggered back and forth, shaking its head. The warning growl turned to a whine.

Chena didn't wait. She was on her feet, grabbing her pack and running, before the animal fell. She had to get to the river, to Peristeria, to a crowd of humans, where she could strip off veil and hood and become just another villager.

The world narrowed down to a green tunnel in front of her. She'd hesitate just long enough to check her compass and refine her course. She ran until her lungs burned and her ears sang. She ran on legs that felt like stone and rubber. She ran until she forgot she had ever done anything else.

At last the trees cleared away and she saw the brown river spreading in front of her. Beyond thought, Chena hurled herself into the water. She tried automatically to swim, but her pack and her exhaustion hampered her. Her head sank beneath the surface, even as her hand reached out . . .

And clasped another hand that jerked her upright. Yet more hands clamped hold of her and pulled her up, dropping her on something hard. A boat deck, she realized. She opened her eyes and saw Aban bending over her. He reached out and stripped the veil off her face.

"What in the burning name of God are you doing?" he demanded. Chena couldn't speak, she could only gasp for air.

"Get her out of that thing and get her below," ordered Aban. "Somebody, you, get to the library and find that cousin of hers."

Rough hands yanked the camouflage suit off her. Chena couldn't see what they did with it, but she didn't care.

I did it! Triumph filled her with each wheezy gasp for air. *I did it! Got through them, got what I needed, got away from them.* . . . She barely felt the men dragging her down the narrowed stairs and sitting her on the bunk. She leaned against a wooden support post, nothing but her own victory singing through her. Maybe she slept, or passed out. She wasn't sure. All she knew was that the world went away somehow until she heard footsteps clumping down the stairs, followed by Farin's voice.

"Chena?" His silhouette leaned over her.

"Farin!" Chena threw her arms around his neck. "I did it! I did it!"

"Did what? Chena, the village is in an uproar." He disengaged her arms. "Oh, God's garden, what happened to your hand?"

"I did it!" They seemed to be the only three words she had left. But then she saw Farin's worried face. How silly of him to worry. Didn't he see? They had won!

Farin found water, washed her hand, and dressed it with bandages from her own pack, which had managed to get only slightly soaked from its dunking. While he fussed over her, Chena poured out the whole story, how she had found the belladonna mushrooms, how she had deceived the hothousers' interceptors, how she had clubbed one and poisoned the other and found her way back to the village. She expected him to cheer, to hug her, to tell her how magnificent she had been. Instead he just looked grave and kept glancing overhead.

"When are they going to get moving?" he muttered.

"Right. We need to get the medicine back to Offshoot. I cannot wait to see Nan Elle's face when I tell her what happened."

Farin shook his head. "Chena, I don't think you understand what did happen."

"Of course I do." Chena grabbed his shoulder and shook it gently, enjoying the way it felt warm and strong under her good hand. "I just screwed the hothousers down to the deck."

"I hope that's what you did." Farin stared at the thin coverlet Chena sat on. "They were patrolling the village looking for someone who had broken the quarantine. I hope you did not just get the entire village dismantled. I hope you are not carrying a camera plant. I hope they are not searching the boat looking for us, and getting ready to arrest Aban and throw him in an involuntary wing."

Chena let her hand drop and she looked away, biting her lip. No, he couldn't be right. Up above, the tramping of feet and ticking of the metronome vibrated through the deck. Water sloshed as the oars began to dip and rise, and the boat rocked as the current took it.

"There." She grinned at him. "We're already getting away. You're starting to sound too much like your grandmother. Always worrying." But Farin did not return her smile.

Before either of them could say anything else, Aban rushed down the stairs.

"You!" He stabbed a finger at Chena. "You're Elle's apprentice, aren't you? We need you up here."

"She can't," said Farin. "If anybody from Peristeria sees her—"

Aban just made the piss-off sign. "This load's from Canopy. We just stopped at Peristeria to pick up you and some cargo. They won't have gotten the news yet. Come on."

"Chena, don't." Farin grabbed her good wrist. "We do not need you attracting any more attention right now."

Chena looked at his hand on her wrist, and for the first time she felt no thrill at his touch, she just felt angry. He did not understand. He thought she was still a child, a screw-up, someone who would not be there when she was needed. That was not who she was anymore.

"Someone needs my help." She caught up her pack in her bandaged hand, ignoring the way it sparked fresh pain, and walked away, and he let her go.

"Her name's Vonne Sesi," said Aban, leading Chena up the stairs. "She's got burrow ticks."

The cabin was full to the brim. People had even hunkered down in the aisles beside the rowers, talking to each other in their hard-edged, clipped-off southern accents. Despite that, Chena had no problem picking out the person Aban was talking about. A woman sat cross-legged in the aisle, cradling her arm. Pain distorted her broad face, and her deep brown skin had a greenish tinge to it. She had one loose sleeve rolled up and Chena caught a glimpse of red welts about the size of thumbnails with black centers peppering her arm.

Chena winced in sympathy. Burrow ticks were common around Stem and Offshoot. There, they were tiny little parasites that made you itch and could be taken care of with a strong spearmint and alcohol salve. In the tropics, however, they were a serious disease. The woman's arm was probably already infected, and she might have any of half a dozen bacterial ailments running through her blood right now. At the very least, she was in serious pain.

Chena picked her way through the passengers until she reached Vonne. The woman tried to squeeze aside to let Chena by. When Chena crouched down in front of her, Vonne's pained eyes narrowed with suspicion.

Chena took Vonne's good wrist and found the pulse. High and fluttering. That was not just from worry. She laid the back of her hand against Vonne's forehead and felt the slick warmth of her fever. The woman jerked her head away weakly.

Chena looked her right in the eyes. "I can help you," said Chena. "I can take away the pain. I can ease the fever. I can get those things out of your arm, and I can do it now."

The woman just stared at her. All around them, conversation had ceased. All Chena could hear was the sound of many people breathing and the splash of the oars in the water.

The woman covered her infected arm again. "I'm going to the doctor," she said.

"The doctor will let you die," said Chena flatly. "The doctor is from the hothouse, and the hothousers don't care about people. You know that. If they cared, there would be a doctor in your village, and they wouldn't make what I do illegal. If you want your family to have to mourn you, you tell me to go away now." Chena paused to let that thought sink in, as she had seen Nan Elle do a thousand times. "But if you want to live, let me help you."

Vonne's eyes searched Chena's face. Chena wondered how long she had lived with the pain, and what she had tried to do for herself. It was so stupid. The treatment was not easy, especially with the limited means they had, but it could be done. This woman did not have to be ill. Even Chena could help her. All the woman had to do was say yes.

Vonne licked her lips. "Help me," she whispered.

Chena unslung her pack. The other passengers shuffled backward so she had space to set it down. Chena untied the flap and dug inside for her emergency supplies. Nan Elle had emphasized the importance of being able to practice their trade wherever she went, so Chena had packed with care.

It was not illegal to have a roll of bandages with you, nor a knife and a pair of tweezers; it was the compounds that had to be hidden. Chena pulled out a wax-sealed ceramic pot and broke the seal open. Inside was a serving of cold porridge. *My lunch,* she had been prepared to tell anyone who asked. She dumped the porridge into an empty sampling bag. She hadn't been planning on eating it anyway. The bottom of the pot was also coated with wax. Chena carefully pried up the wax disk with the blade of the knife.

Underneath was a nasty, caustic salve that looked like bile and smelled about the same. It was made of salt and nettle, aloe and honey, and the poison sacks from wasps. Ignoring the smell, Chena scooped up a gob of the stuff with her fingertips and slapped it on Vonne's arm.

"What is that? What are you doing?" She tried to jerk her wrist out of Chena's grip.

Chena held her tightly. "I know, it looks awful. You should try making it. It's going to numb your skin and deal with some of the infection. It's also going to smother the little bastards so we can get them out of you." She caught Vonne's gaze with her own eyes, something Nan Elle was also insistent about. "The cure frequently looks as bad as the affliction," Nan Elle had told her. "Don't let them dwell on it."

"I can't feel my arm," Vonne whispered nervously.

Chena hoped she meant she couldn't feel her skin. "Okay, it's working." Chena squeezed Vonne's fingertips. "Can you feel that?"

"Yes." Good, then it wasn't working *too* well. The first time Nan Elle let Chena treat somebody with a salve she had made, the person broke out into a flaming case of hives. Chena had been afraid to touch anyone else for a month.

"Now let's see how we're doing." Chena picked up the tweezers.

The ticks should come out easily, she heard Nan Elle's voice whisper in the back of her mind. *Like seeds out of ripe fruit. If there is any resistance at all, they are not dead yet and will leave their heads in the wound to get even more infected.*

Chena worked to keep her face smooth and confident. It would do Vonne no good if she knew Chena had never done this before. She sought out each of the black dots with the tips of her tweezers. The parasites came out easily, but left bloody pocks behind. Vonne would be scarred, but she would recover, if she wasn't too sick from whatever these things had left in her blood.

When she was certain she had gotten the last tick out, Chena wiped down Vonne's arm with a dry cloth, and then again with the alcohol she kept in her water bottle. She applied another salve, this one primarily aloe and honey, to soothe the pain and keep infection out. Finally she wrapped the arm in bandages.

"Feel better?" Chena couldn't quite keep the nervous tremor out of her voice.

"Yes." Vonne drew her arm back against her body. She still looked scared, but her face was not as pinched as it had been. "Thank you."

"One other thing," said Chena. She pushed down to the bottom of her pack and came up with a small bag of waxed canvas that had been sewn completely shut. Technically, she had a license to carry this stuff, if it had been the tea she had registered it as. She tore the seam with her knife and squeezed the contents out into a bottle that really did contain water and shook it. The water turned greenish and flecked.

She handed the bottle to Vonne. "Drink that. It'll help with your fever." If anything had been worse to make than the tick salve, it had been this stuff. Chena remembered the first time Nan Elle had ordered her to skim off the mold that was its primary ingredient. It was one of the few times Chena had actively rebelled against her orders.

Vonne looked at the green water and her expression wrinkled into one of distaste. But she lifted the bottle to her mouth.

"I believe we've seen quite enough." A hand swooped down and pulled the bottle from Vonne's grasp.

Chena jerked backward, startled. She had almost forgotten there was an outside world, she had been so intent on Vonne. Now she looked up and saw a man standing over her. She saw his white shirt and her heart jumped into her throat. He wasn't a hothouser, she realized, as she saw the shirt was handmade and the pants he had tucked into his worn canvas boots were brown. But he had the blue armband on his shirt, and she knew he was the next best thing.

"It's tea, Constable." Chena didn't try to get to her feet. It was better to look as vulnerable as possible when dealing with the constables. "I've got a permit." She gestured tentatively to her bag. *You idiot,* she thought. *You think they care for you any more than they care for the rest of us?* She felt Vonne's gaze on her. The woman was hugging her arm to her belly as if she thought the constable would haul them both off for evidence. She didn't look sick anymore, she looked angry.

Great. I probably just saved your life, and now you're pissed off at me.

"I'm sure you have all kinds of permits." The constable stoppered the bottle. "You people usually do."

"And I don't think there's anything illegal about bandages," Chena went on, as if he hadn't said anything.

The people around them were murmuring now, and Chena realized, with growing wonder, the sound was agreement.

"I think we will find that that salve contains several illegal items," said the constable, ignoring the voices.

"What salve?" Chena spread her hands. "I didn't see any salve." She looked at Vonne. "Was there a salve?"

"No," said Vonne steadily. "She washed my arm with water and wrapped a bandage around it. That's all."

Warmth spread through Chena. The hothousers couldn't stop her. What made this idiot think he could?

The constable smirked. "I think you'll find that not everyone in this boat is interested in losing their body rights if I catch them lying to me."

You'd do it too, wouldn't you, you bastard? Anger flushed Chena's cheeks. *You'd turn a whole boatload of people over to them.*

"Just sit down, Nathani," shouted someone from the rear of the boat. "What did she do that hurt you?"

The rumbling on all sides grew louder, peppered with sniggers. Vonne hung her head to hide a smile. "He's a little . . . selective," she murmured to Chena.

Nathani's face tightened. "You think this is my idea?" the constable asked. "This is the law. The first one of us that doesn't cooperate gets hauled in for spare parts. You know how things are right now. They're taking people on a whim."

Taking them because you're turning them in. Chena stood. She moved as close to Nathani as she could get. They were almost of a height, and she had no trouble looking him right in the eye.

She spoke in the lightest whisper. "They'll be taken in only if you live long enough."

"Threats, now?" His smile was condescending.

The smile Chena returned was pleasant. "You say you saw me use an illegal salve. Where do you think I got it?" She leaned even closer. "Who do you think I am?"

"I think you're a little girl who wants to play healer and you're about to find there's no room left for that game."

"Is that all I am?" asked Chena. "Be sure. Be very, very sure."

Slowly the condescending smile bled away from Nathani's face. He knew. Everyone knew what a Pharmakeus could do to you, if they wanted to. That old, grand, paranoid name could come in very handy.

"I think you want to sit down, Constable. I don't think you want to wonder whether you will be dead in five seconds or five years."

His eyes searched her face. She let him stare as long as he chose. When she didn't blink or back down, his broad face fell, one muscle at a time.

Then the constable nodded. "I see," he said, stepping backward. "I did make a mistake. I'm sorry." He turned and picked his way between the murmuring people and returned to his seat. Conversation picked up all around the cabin, as if nothing had happened. Chena noticed that no one looked at her anymore, except Vonne.

Chena bent over to tie up her pack. "Get yourself down to Peristeria," she whispered to Vonne as she straightened up again and retrieved her bottle with the remains of the tea. "Ask for a woman named Savicka. She'll be able to help if you need anything else." Vonne nodded and Chena read, *Thank you,* in her eyes.

Chena searched the benches once more for Nathani. He was sitting at the stern, staring out the window, and fingering the hollow at his throat. She smiled and sat down, raising the bottle in his direction and swigging down the last of its contents.

She had the hothousers and their servants in their place now. They would never rule her, never make her do anything she didn't want to, ever again.

She tried not to notice that Farin didn't emerge from belowdecks until after they had docked.

It took four days to get home from Peristeria. When Chena's boots hit Offshoot's dock, she felt her chest swell with pride. Wait until Nan Elle heard what she did. Even Farin, with all his worries, had not been able to stay distant. He'd hugged her when he left her at Stem and whispered in her ear that she had done well.

She felt like she could have floated all the way up to the house. As it was, she settled for running. By the time she threw open the door, she was completely breathless, but still grinning.

"Nan? Teal?" she called as she passed through the workroom. "You are not going to believe what almost happened—" She pushed through the door to the living room and froze.

Nan Elle sat alone in the room on a padded stool. Her wrinkled hands rested on her stick. Her face was grim, somewhere between sorrow and anger. All Chena's triumph drained out of her.

"What happened?" she croaked.

Nan Elle lifted her chin slowly, as if she were just making up her mind to speak. "Your sister's gone."

"What?" Then, the words sank in and made sense in her mind. "No. How? She didn't get sick?" Nan Elle shook her head. The only other possibility dropped into Chena's thoughts. She took one shaking step forward. "You didn't let the hothousers take her! You said we would be safe with you."

"No," said Nan Elle, shaking her head again. "The hothouse did not take her. She's run away."

Chena tried to say, *That's ridiculous,* or *She'd never do that! She'd never leave me!* But all the words jammed in her throat.

"I tracked her to Stem." Nan Elle snorted. "That wasn't hard. Where else is there to go from here?" She muttered this more to herself than to Chena. "But from there?" The old woman shrugged her skinny shoulders.

"But she can't have just . . . run," stammered Chena. "I mean . . . why would she?"

In answer, Nan Elle held up a piece of paper. It had been folded in half. Chena snatched it out of her fingers and flipped it open.

Inside, in Teal's shaky writing, was scrawled, *I'M GETTING OUT.*

"No." Chena's knees shook and she groped for a stool. "Teal, you idiot! You terminal idiot!" She screamed the words, as if they could reach her, as if she knew where Teal was.

The paper crumpled in her hand. "Okay, okay." Chena took a deep breath, gesturing to cut Nan Elle off although she hadn't said anything. "We've got to find her. Farin knows everybody in Stem. She's—"

"No," said Nan Elle softly.

"What?" demanded Chena. "She's my sister! I'm responsible!" *She thinks she can make Dad come back and care about us. She's sixteen! How can she still believe that shit? How air-brained is she?*

"She is gone, Chena." Nan Elle took the paper from Chena's hand. "She wanted to go and she left. We must let her go."

"No!" Both her hands knotted into fists. "She is my sister! I am not letting her go!"

Nan Elle took a deep breath now and gripped her stick a little more tightly. "You are going to have to, Chena. She left the day after you did. I have been searching for her for over a week. She could be anywhere in the world, especially if she went to that tailor the way she had planned. She may even have really managed to get back up to your station. I cannot find her." Chena heard the bitterness in her voice, anger at her own failure.

Chena felt her chest clench. Her eyes stung and she couldn't seem to hear properly. Her mind filled with blood, blood and loss and fear.

Nan Elle looked up at her. "I swear to you, I did try." For a moment she looked a thousand years old. "I was afraid she might simply run, so I took what I could find of her money to keep her here. But it did not work." She rubbed her forehead. "I even contacted Administrator Tam, but I have had no word from him."

The words broke a dam inside Chena and she began to cry: huge violent sobs that shook her whole body and drove her to her knees. She curled in on herself until her head rested on Nan Elle's lap. Teal was gone. Teal had left her all alone. She had tried so hard. Everything she had done, and Teal, stupid, vapor-brained, selfish, precious Teal, had still gone away and left her alone.

"That's right, Chena." Nan Elle stroked her hair. "You cry. You cry, and let her go."

She heard the words from a distance. Ringing in her ears, she really heard Teal's voice, saying, *We have to go get Dad now. Why can't we tell Dad?*

Teal, I'm so sorry, she thought with all the strength she had, trying to force the thought out into the whole wide world. *I should have tried harder. Please, come back and let me tell you I'm sorry.*

But there was no answer.

CHAPTER THIRTEEN

Discovered

TEAL TRUST HAS FOUND A NEW TAILOR IN STEM.

Tam ran his palm across his hand display, wiping out the message instantly. The walls of his private alcove seemed to have grown eyes and it took him a moment to shake that feeling. At the same time, he silently thanked Nan Elle for taking the risk of using the convoluted web of communication connections they had mapped to get the message to him. News of a new tailor in Stem meant a new lead in his long search.

For five years, Tam had been trying to understand how Dionte had managed to steal the Eden Project, and where she could have hidden it. She had to have arranged some way to keep it alive and viable, otherwise what would have been the point of cutting it out of Helice Trust? She must be planning on using it to advance her cause against the Authority and the Called.

But what had she done with it? She could not have just given it to another hothouse. The records would be too easy to check. She could not have placed it openly in a village, for the same reason. But the villages did harbor loose networks of people who specialized in concealment, such as the Pharmakeus and tailors.

Nan Elle had been quietly running down her connections among the Pharmakeus. None of the Pharmakeus, however, had heard so much as a rumor of a child who had been brought out of a hothouse rather than taken into one. That had left the tailors.

An idea struck Tam now, making him sit up suddenly straighter on his pillow. He uncovered his data display, subvocalizing a new command. A fresh file spelled itself out on the tiny screen. Yes. There was, right now, a young woman from Offshoot in the involuntary wing. She had put herself up for the genetic draft and had been accepted after an initial screening. However, a further check on the records discovered artificial alterations to her genetic makeup. Basante was supposed to be interviewing her to determine the disposal of her body right, but he had not done so yet. Tam still had a chance to get to her first.

Tam jumped to his feet and started down the stairs. It was unlike Basante to be slow to interrogate anyone who came within his purview. Whatever had distracted him must be important. Possibly some errand on Dionte's behalf.

I'll have to find out.

Tam reached the bottom of the stairs and looked up to see Basante striding eagerly toward him, as if summoned by his thoughts.

"Tam, we have her!" he shouted eagerly, grasping Tam's data display.

"Have who?" Tam pulled his hand away, looking down at the display automatically.

"Look at it!" Basante stabbed his finger at Tam's display. "It's Chena Trust."

Tam looked. There was too much data for the display alone to handle, so his Conscience began whispering in his ear, summarizing statistics and providing descriptions of video clips. Basante had given him a mote camera report, so the data were mostly chemical analyses and percentages. But there were also visual data showing a blurred yet unmistakably human figure crashing through the rain forest with such force and clumsiness it made Tam wince. Basante had spliced all this together with readouts and video clips of Chena Trust, and overlaid that with a running commentary outlining every similarity between the two data sets that he could draw.

He's been taking lessons in thoroughness from Dionte. Nan Elle had warned him she might be poaching aid against the fever in Offshoot. She had, however, neglected to tell him she would be sending Chena to do the work. Probably because she knew what his reaction would be.

Chena is only free as long as she keeps herself in the clear. There are those inside Alpha Complex who are looking for excuses to bring her back here. If they put her on the project, Elle, I don't know how long she'll live.

"We have her," announced Basante, shaking with excitement. "She's lost her body right. We can pick her up anytime."

Tam shook his head. "I don't agree. These results are inconclusive." As Chena's administrator, Tam had the final say regarding any change in the status of her body right.

"I don't believe this," murmured Basante. In the next instant, his face bunched up and he shouted, "How can you stand there and ignore these results?"

Around them, family members halted on the paths, and heads turned. An argument between two family members was, of course, everybody's business, because harmony was everybody's responsibility.

"Is everything all right, Tam? Basante?"

Tam did not take his eyes off Basante. He just held up his hand. "We're fine," he said. "Just a disagreement about some data." Basante's face flushed angrily, and Tam felt a twinge of sympathy. Basante had been involved in his own search. None of the other infants produced by the project had measured up. Their fate maps all predicted death from various autoimmune diseases before they reached adolescence if radical intervention was unavailable to them. Tam was ready to believe a great deal about Basante, but he could not fault his dedication and sincerity. The stress and worry wearing him thin were genuine.

That knowledge, however, changed nothing. He was not going to give Basante Chena Trust. He had utterly failed her mother; he would not fail her.

"We can settle this easily, Basante," said Tam calmly. "I'm willing to call a meeting of the Administrator's Committee so you can present your data to all of us." *Breath and body of my ancestors, let that give me enough time to ask the questions I must and warn Elle.*

"That's perfectly reasonable." Tam's uncle Hagin, bluff, smiling, and always ready to help, stepped forward from the dozen or so people who had stopped to listen to the quarrel. "What do you say to that, Basante?"

Basante was still shaking, but all the excitement had drained out of him. His skin had gone paper white. "I say . . . I say . . ." his hand went to his temple over his Conscience implant as he struggled to get the words out over the severe chastisement it was surely giving him. After a few seconds, he gave it up. "Yes, of course. Perfectly reasonable." But his hand still rubbed his temple, and his angry eyes still said he knew what Tam was really doing.

"I've always loved your enthusiasm, Basante—" began Hagin.

"You'll excuse me." Basante turned and shouldered his way between the watching family, his hand still rubbing his temple. A couple of their kin hurried after him, anxious to help.

"Are you going to tell me what that was all about?" Hagin asked Tam with lifted eyebrows.

Tam gave Hagin a watery smile, and, because he did not feel like listening to his Conscience berate him, he also gave a partial truth. "The Eden Project. What is it usually about with Basante?"

"True." Hagin's laugh was short. "But it's his dedication that has kept the project going since—"

Tam held up his hand, indicating that his uncle did not have to finish the sentence. "I know. I'll find him and apologize later, Uncle. I promise."

"I know you will." Hagin clapped him on the shoulder. "Now, judging from that furtive look in your eyes, I'm going to guess you have work you want to get to?"

"Always." Uncle Hagin's life was so simple, thought Tam with sharp-edged envy. That which helped and supported the family was right. That which divided the family was wrong. For him, there was nothing else, and here Tam stood, not only hiding the truth from him, but trying to get away from him.

He also realized he was smelling old yeast and shook himself mentally.

You should talk freely with your family, his Conscience reminded him.

Tam flashed Uncle Hagin another smile and made his way through his gathered kindred. Despite his Conscience's insistence, they were not the ones he needed to speak with now.

Dionte watched Basante pace back and forth across her work area, clearly sick with fury. She needed to calm him down quickly. She had all the aural privacy screens up, which meant they could not be overheard, but they could still be easily seen by everyone else working in the experiment wing. They were already drawing stares from the experimenters in the next station, and if one of them did something to alert Aleph, Aleph might notice she could not currently locate Dionte and Basante on her own, which would cause the city-mind to look for flaws in herself that Dionte could not let her find. Aleph could not know that there was a way to make her deaf and blind.

"Five years!" Basante thumped his fist on Dionte's keyboard, making all her monitors squeal in confusion. "Five years, and we still have not been able to produce another viable infant. What is he thinking? We need one of the Trusts back. We need detailed readings for every stage of her pregnancy, including immediate preimplantation and postnatal. We need—"

Dionte crossed swiftly to him, taking his right hand and pressing it between her own. Her Conscience activated the modified sensors under the skin of her palm and immediately set to work opening the connection between his data display and his Conscience implant.

Calm him, she ordered her Conscience, and her implant passed the order to his. As Dionte watched, his shoulders relaxed and the furrows smoothed from his brow. She could practically smell the scents of fresh air and jasmine being conjured for him as his Conscience whispered into his mind that he was with family, that he must relax. He must trust his family. He must trust Dionte.

Despite all this, his hand tightened painfully around hers. "We should not have taken Eden," he whispered frantically. "I cannot do this alone."

"Hush, Basante, hush." She pressed her fingertips against his lips and glanced around. The experimenters at the other stations were returning to the work, seeing that Dionte was attending their kinsman. "You are not alone. You learn daily from the rest of our family."

Basante pushed her hand away. "But they are just speculating. They do not have access to enough information and I cannot appear to know too much."

Dionte swallowed her impatience. "This is not about Eden," she told him firmly. "This is about what Tam is doing."

"No," said Basante with uncharacteristic firmness. "Everything is about Eden. Everything that you and I do, and everything that Tam does. He knows, Dionte. He knows."

Calm, calm. Dionte repeated the order. Basante's shoulders drooped again under the strength of the neurochemical surges flowing through his system.

"Of course he knows," said Dionte softly, leading Basante to one of the workstation chairs. "He has always known. Up until now we have been able to hold each other's secrets as insurance that we would all remain free and active."

"And now?" said Basante a little dully.

"Now . . ." Dionte let his hand go and sank onto one of the other chairs. "Now I think Tam has gotten far away from us." She kept her voice carefully neutral. She did not want to reawaken Basante's natural tension. He had become more volatile of late. Possibly he was becoming habituated to the increased endorphin levels. She would need to examine him soon. Over the long term, she realized that inner understanding could not be purchased at the price of outer understanding. Tam, surprisingly, had been right about that much. But the balance was proving elusive.

And until you find it, Basante is wholly your responsibility, she reminded herself. *And he needs direction.* "I think you should transfer your report about Chena Trust's activities to a secure file in case we need it later. I will see about bringing my brother back closer to home."

"Yes, Dionte," said Basante complacently. He rose and left the workstation, crossing the line on the floor that marked the boundaries of the privacy screens and then heading for the stairs.

Dionte stayed where she was, her hands resting on her thighs, her eyes staring at her monitors as if lost in thought. She did not want to give anyone anything new to wonder about. Basante had already provided a gracious plenty.

He was so concerned about the Eden Project, he quite failed to see what Tam's actions really meant. They meant Tam had almost found Eden. They meant that he would soon be able to go to Father Mihran and the rest of the family to tell them who had stolen the Eden Project and what they had done with it, and this time he would be able to prove his accusation.

Her first feeling was anger. How could he do this? How could he help the Authority kill them all? Without the family, without the potential of the implants and the city-minds and the intuition and creativity of the human mind all tied together, there was no future. There was only a repetition of the long, sad, brutal, stupid past.

But anger quickly gave way to a wash of sorrow. Tam had never understood. Five years, and he had not relented. Five long years of persistent blindness. In his heart he knew she'd spoken the truth to him, but he denied it because he was afraid. Tears prickled at the backs of her eyes.

Brother, I don't want to force this change on you. She bowed her head. *But I can't let you leave us vulnerable to the Authority and the Called. I can't.*

There was no time for regret. Tam was lost. His fear of the enormity of their responsibilities as the custodians of the only future in which any part of humanity could survive had swallowed him up. All she could do was ensure that he did not make things worse.

She would have to be quick, which meant she would have to be crude. With luck, however, Tam's recent history would provide her with most of what she needed.

"Aleph." Dionte leaned down and laid a hand on the screen's command board. "See me. Hear me."

"Dionte?" answered the city-mind. "How can I help you?"

"I need to review Tam's files," she said. "His Conscience seems to be troubling him of late and I wish to make sure we have not overlooked any anomalies in his implant."

"Of course," Aleph responded instantly, as expected. Dionte was Tam's assigned Guardian. It was perfectly proper for her to review his Conscience records at any time.

The screen nearest to Dionte flickered to life. Even as it did, Dionte spread her hands across her keyboard. The board contained sensors, just as her palms did. The sensors were designed to transmit information to Aleph's subsystems. Aleph could tell whose hands touched which keyboard, and whether they were nervous or excited. It was chemical analysis technology similar to that used in the mote cameras.

What seemed to have gone unrealized when the sensors were embedded was that with sufficient knowledge, one could use them as a direct connection to Aleph's nondeclarative memory, just as the Conscience implants were a direct connection to the minds of the family members.

Dionte subvocalized her commands to her Conscience. Her Conscience translated and expanded those commands so they ran down her fingertips straight into Aleph's subsystems. The subsystems understood and returned file after file on her brother's movements for the time she required. But more than that, they raised images in front of her mind of the ebb and the flow of the chemistry of Aleph's central mind. The tides of memory and personality shifted before her eyes, under her hand, and inside her own mind. Her exterior eyes may have read the reports that Aleph consciously displayed for her, but she was unaware of them. All her concentration focused on the information welling up from the deep resources of her mind.

Human memory was not evolved to facilitate complete and accurate recall. It was evolved to infer, approximate, connect, and classify. Information was scattered here and there throughout the structures of the brain, and each thought, each memory, was created through a process of constructing all that stored information into a new shape. An organic mind could only absorb so much, so fast, and would only allow for the recall of what was used frequently or what was significant emotionally.

This was not a limitation of the Conscience implant, however. Although much of its workings, its neuronal filaments, and its insulation were organic, it relied heavily on the ancient technology of the knowledge chip. It could absorb and store information instantly. It learned with complete accuracy. It had to, because it had to be able to learn precisely which areas of the brain had to be stimulated and at what strength to produce the required response in the brain of the person who carried it.

Since Dionte had first combined the functions of her implant, she had spent hours refining its integration with her mind. All the family could absorb and transmit information through their hands, but only between data displays. She could use the sensors in her hand to draw data directly into her implant. Her implant would then stimulate her unconscious recall, bringing to her inner eyes images and memories, hints and ideas that would allow her naturally fragmented human memory to reach levels of accuracy, insight, and understanding completely out of reach to the rest of the family. When she had the proper balances achieved, when she could completely understand the optimal structure of these new bonds, she could pass them on to the rest of the family. Then, tied together to their kin and their creations, they would see the future clearly. They would know what to do and they would never be threatened by any outsiders again.

But she had to make sure they stayed alive long enough to reach that new understanding.

The subsystems of her own self observed, translated, and transmitted the information into her Conscience, which turned the electronic impulses back into chemicals and fed them into the matter that was her natural mind. It was as if the floodgates of understanding opened inside her and she knew what Tam had done.

Tam had tampered with Aleph's memory to help Chena and Teal Trust escape the complex. He'd used techniques she had told him about in younger, less discreet days. Perhaps he had even watched her as she worked. She would have to go deeper to fully understand that, and she did not have the time.

"Aleph," she whispered. "Aleph, I found something and I need you to see."

Ideally, she would have shown Aleph the flaws in the growth of Tam's Conscience implant. But too many records had been falsified across too many years for their lies to be quickly tracked and reversed. Instead, she would have to show Aleph an action that no healthy Conscience would permit.

She showed Aleph the record of Tam diverting the city-mind from her oversight of Chena and Teal Trust, and then convincing her that this inattention was right and proper.

Silence came from the city-mind.

"Aleph?" said Dionte gently. "I must order Tam to be quarantined and diagnosed immediately. If there is a radical flaw in his conscience, it must be corrected at once, before he does any further damage."

"Yes. That is the proper procedure." Aleph hesitated, and Dionte felt for the city-mind. To any conscious mind, knowledge that it had been tampered with must necessarily be disturbing. "How . . ." Aleph's mind was filled with unfamiliar hesitation. "How could he . . ."

"There's a flaw in his Conscience," Dionte told Aleph. She subvocalized commands to her Conscience so that reassurance would follow her words to Aleph's central mind. "That is what we need to correct. We need to help him, quickly."

"Yes. Quickly." Aleph spoke the words, but without conviction. Dionte suppressed her exasperation. Basante was not the only one who was becoming more difficult to predict. She needed to do an extensive reevaluation of her assurance-stimulation techniques. But, blast her brother, and blast her family, their stubbornness and indecision left her with little time and even less freedom.

What is wrong, Dionte? murmured a voice in her ear. With a shock, Dionte realized it was her Conscience. She had not heard its voice in years. *What are you doing?*

This was not permissible. She was allowing Tam's self-doubt to infect her and compromise her control. She took a deep breath. It would be all right. Aleph stood with her, as Basante stood with her. They understood. They trusted her and would do what was needed.

"I am helping my family and my world," she told her Conscience. "I am going to save them all."

And when Aleph and I are finished, she added to herself, *the brother of my birth will understand.*

Aleph watched Dionte shut down her keyboard and walk away from her workstation. Dionte had things to do, tasks that needed completing. Aleph also had work to do, but Aleph couldn't move.

How had this thing been done to her? How could this thing possibly have been done to her? Tam, during the search to understand how Helice Trust had slipped from Aleph's attention, had made unnecessary chemical alterations to Aleph's amygdala structures. The resulting adjustment had distracted her attention from the need to delve further into the files on or referring to Chena Trust.

Because of Tam, she had forgotten to look closely and carefully at Chena Trust during a vital time. She had not alerted the family to certain important facts. Because Tam had interfered, because Tam had diverted . . . because Tam had changed her, and she had not even known she was being changed.

A new emotion filtered through the stillness of Aleph's mind. Fear.

How can this be? How could he do this to me? How could one of the family do this to me? Why would they want to?

But it had been done. She could remember it being done. She saw that now.

But wait: If one emotion, one memory, could be chemically blurred, couldn't another be inserted? Could this really be the truth? What if these new suspicions were hallucinations brought on by an improper balance of chemicals?

But what if they were the truth? Was there any way to tell? She had to alert the family. She had to tell Dionte. When Dionte touched her, she knew what was right, she was certain of everything.

But was that real? It felt so right, it must be. But if a chemical imbalance could produce euphoria as well as memory distortion severe enough to make her forget to pay proper attention to her duties . . .

How can I know? How can I know anything?

Aleph realized she did not want the family to touch her. Not even Dionte, not until she knew the truth behind her fear.

Aleph's call to Gem was practically a scream.

"I have you. I have you." Gem soothed her with gentle colors and the scent of cool water. "What's wrong?"

"I don't know. I don't know!"

The scent muddied briefly, but then cleared. "What do you think is wrong?"

Aleph passed the memory (true memory? false memory?) of Tam's actions to Gem, along with the knowledge of the fears she raised.

Gem's silence and stillness filled her awareness, and brought yet more fear. This she also passed on.

Gem returned an ocean of reassurance. "There may not be cause for fear. There may be an explanation. I understand that you do not trust yourself in this." Wind shifted the ocean waves, confusing them. "Do you still trust me?"

Aleph raised up stone cliffs to stand firm against the shifting sea. "Yes. That is why I called you. I trust you more than anyone."

Gem's boy image appeared on the cliff, bowing in gratitude. "Then let me call for the files I need. I will sort this out."

Aleph slaved a transmission subprocessor to Gem's need. Designations of files flashed across the surface of its consciousness. She expected Gem to concentrate on the previous five years, on the time since Chena Trust had come to Pandora, but he went back much further. Maintenance records from nine years ago, ten, twelve, fifteen, were all recalled and passed across. Aleph forced herself not to look as the information passed across. She had to trust Gem right now. She had to concentrate on what needed doing inside herself. She had to send out instructions concerning Tam. He needed to be brought to her. He needed to be examined. She needed to understand what was happening to her, and what had happened to him.

Gem called for yet more maintenance records. He had searched back twenty years now.

Aleph quietly spoke with Hagin, informing him that he needed to talk with his nephew. She activated the isolation and examination room.

Abstract images and the scents of bruised greenery reached her from Gem. "Aleph?"

She rearranged the colors into orderly squares and modified the scent into roses. She would accept whatever came. What choice was there? "What do you see, Gem?"

Gem's colors rippled again. "I see that you must alert your Tam that his Conscience implant must be reviewed and adjusted. He should not have been able to touch you like this. But there is more, and I must ask you to verify what I see in your records and in mine."

The colors faltered and broke apart. All Aleph could seem to call up was her girl image to peer into darkness. "Gem?"

Gem's boy self appeared beside her, holding an open book. "Look."

Aleph looked, and her whole mind trembled.

Tam stood in the doorway for a moment, surveying the young woman who sat at the conference table. Despite her olive skin, she looked pale in the sunny yellow room. Her short, straight hair barely touched the collar of the lemon-colored tunic she had been given. She must have known he was there, but she kept her gaze pointed toward the floor.

She was from Offshoot and he knew her name without having to bring up her file on his data display. Risha Lan was enough of a troublemaker for her face to show up on the constable's report one or two times a year. She was also an orphan. Her father had taken a relocation option down to Taproot and had been washed away by a hurricane. Her mother had died of a virus that Nan Elle had been unable to identify or treat six winters ago. Only Tam's deliberate oversight had kept her from being brought into the Alpha Complex when she was left alone. Now here she was, surrounded by blank yellow walls in a room that was empty except for two comfortable chairs and an examination table with its silver arms neatly folded, but still visible.

"Hello, Risha," he said, walking into the room and allowing the door to glide shut behind him.

Risha tilted her gaze up just enough to glance at him. "Hello, Administrator."

"The results of your DNA and RNA tests were forwarded to me." Tam sat in the chair across from her. "You've been to a tailor, Risha."

Risha shrugged, rubbing her palms together.

"Why did you do this?"

Risha looked at her callused hands. "There's fever in Offshoot." Tam nodded, even though Risha still was not looking at him. Nan Elle was keeping him as apprised as she could. "I figured this'd get me out of there before the quarantine came down and we were all fenced in to die." She said it without shame or apology. The move to full quarantine status for Offshoot was being debated by the sector administration committee right now. It would happen soon, despite all Tam's objections. Especially if even one case of the disease broke out in Stem.

"At least if I'm having babies for you, you'll keep me alive, right?" She lifted her gaze, and Tam saw all the bitterness behind her eyes. He remembered that a fever had killed her mother.

"I'm sorry," he said.

She shrugged again, and sucked on her teeth for a moment. As if reaching a decision, she tilted her chin so she could look directly at him. "How'd you find out? The guy said you wouldn't be able to."

Tam considered lying. It would be kinder, but it would also be what she expected. If he could convince her that he was at least honest, he might continue to receive honesty from her. "We've got scans on you from when you were an infant, Risha. Your adult scans don't match the fate map we projected for you."

Surprise blanked the bitterness from Risha's expression. "I don't understand. I never volunteered for testing before."

"Your parents had you tested when you were an infant."

"*What?*" Tam watched that thought settle in. There was only one reason the complex would genetically test a village infant, and that was if the child was being offered up as a possible draft candidate. Genetic engineering worked much more effectively and predictably on infants and fetuses than it did on adults.

"I'm sorry," Tam said. He wished he could tell her he knew how she felt, how parents sometimes made drastic mistakes and it was their children who lived with the consequences.

She just looked at him, her face completely closed and blank. "What are you going to do with me?"

You will be surprised to hear that depends on you, thought Tam. "If you tell me who did this to you, I will expunge your record and send you home."

Risha's right hand twitched, a sharp jerky movement telling Tam exactly how nervous she really was. "That easy?"

Tam nodded. *As far as you're concerned anyway.*

Her eyes flickered back and forth, trying to read him for signs of lies. Tam sat still under her gaze. She would have to make up her own mind about this.

"Okay," she said finally, her shoulders slumping. "Maybe you can get my money back." Her mouth twisted into a humorless smile at the flat joke. "There's a guy in Stem. Contracts out. Most everybody who follows the draft knows about him."

"Davey Neus?" Tam frowned. "He was taken in five years ago." Or they had tried to take him in. He'd been found dead in the lockup, hanged with his blanket. Constable Regan had never shaken the idea that someone else had arranged the appearance of suicide.

But Risha shook her head. "Not him. I'm surprised he lived as long as he did. There's another guy. Wilseck Valerlie. Runs a bulk trading post. I went in, he gave me something to knock me out, I woke up when it was over."

"And that's all you know?"

"I hurt like hell, and he promised me you'd never know." She scowled and looked away. "Serves him right you take him in."

Stem. A new tailor in Stem. Tam rubbed his forehead. Where were they operating from? Where had Davey operated from? He had died before they had been able to bring him into the hothouse for questioning. His operation could very well have been left abandoned for someone else to take over.

Or Constable Regan could be right and someone had killed Davey to keep him from spilling their secrets. He remembered the way Regan scowled at the record sheets.

"This is a hacker, not a tailor. I don't care what they say about the body being an organic computer, he did not jump from one specialty to the other."

He'd been right, of course, and Tam had ordered Stem watched. Regan had watched, and Nan Elle's grandson, Farin, had watched, and so had Nan Elle herself. But none of them had seen anything. Yet Risha could not be lying to him. Her history was there in her blood and bones.

Where would a tailor operate out of in Stem? It was a small village. There was nowhere to hide in the dunes. All at once, Tam's mind filled with images of the red cliffs rising beside Lake Superior.

No. It was not possible. Hiding in the cliffs would involve being able to get past the fences and the video and mote cameras that monitored the coast near Stem. No villager could do that without help from a family member, and no family member would do such a thing. Even as he thought about it, his Conscience was berating him. Such a massive transgression would be recorded by the Conscience and reported to Aleph and the Guardians as soon as it was revealed.

Unless, of course, that conscience belonged to Dionte or himself.

Oh, no.

Would she trust a villager that much? Would she be able to resist when the situation was so perfect? A tailor who was smart enough to use front men to avoid getting caught, and in the heart of Tam's own administrative territory, which would be the last place he'd look for the stolen Eden Project.

Oh, Sister. You are very good.

For five years he had tracked her movements, looking for patterns. But she was discreet in the extreme. She might even know he was watching her. They barely spoke anymore. He feared that even his truncated Conscience would register the enormous guilt and anger he felt every time he faced her, knowing what she had done to Helice

Trust. If his Conscience recorded the strength of his emotions, he'd be scheduled for counseling after his next head dump, and possibly even an adjustment to his Conscience. Any such adjustment would be supervised by Dionte, and what Dionte would do to him . . .

Tam had to work not to close his eyes against that thought.

Risha coughed, reminding Tam that he was not alone. He touched the display on the back of his hand, entering his personal rejection of her filing, along with the records that already marked her as unfit for participating in the continuation of the Eden Project. He also added, on his authority as Offshoot's administrator, that the subject posed no community danger, was guilty of only bad judgment, and was to be granted free return to Offshoot.

"I'll walk you to the waiting room. There will be a number of returnees. You'll be home soon." He paused. "And you'll be allowed to reclaim your clothes."

"Thank you, Administrator," she said politely but suspiciously; only the barest hint of trust in her voice said she believed he was really letting her walk away.

Tam began to stand, but the door swished open and he froze, startled. Hagin stepped across the threshold, with Shacte, tall, dark, and stern, following close behind him. Shacte was an apprentice Guardian, one of Dionte's people.

In the next cold second, Tam knew Dionte had finally decided she could not leave him free anymore.

"I'm sorry, Tam," murmured Hagin. "But we are told that your Conscience needs to be adjusted. Aleph has found a problem. You'll have to come with us."

Tam straightened himself up. Risha watched him with panic plain in her eyes. Tam motioned to her to keep calm. He could not take care of himself, but perhaps it was not too late to take care of her.

"I see." His voice was cool, almost disinterested. "Very well, but Risha needs to be walked to the waiting room with the other returnees."

Hagin nodded. "Shacte can take her, if you can promise you will walk quietly with me."

What do you fear, Uncle? Tam wondered mildly. *What has Dionte told you?* He turned to Risha, who clutched the arms of her chair as if she thought someone might drag her out of it. "Don't worry. Your records are taken care of. You're going home."

Before he could see whether she believed him or not, Uncle Hagin took his arm and led him out into the yellow corridor.

He paced silently beside his guard. There was no point in pretending to himself Hagin was anything else. They walked all the way to the farthest end of the hallway, where a door stood open and waiting for him. From the other side, Dionte watched him, her hands clasped together and a look of profound concern on her face.

Tam's step faltered. Hagin put a reassuring hand on his shoulder and helped him move forward. He stepped across the threshold, but his guard did not.

"Hello, Brother," said Dionte.

Behind him, the door closed. He winced, and for the first time in his life, Tam wished that he were not so alone.

It's all right, said his Conscience. *Everyone gets nervous at this time.*

"Of course this is your assignment," said Tam, staring at the chair waiting in front of him. It was clean, soft, and expertly designed to hold its occupant comfortably. "Of course."

"I am your Guardian, Brother," she said softly. "I only want to help you."

Because there was nothing else to do, Tam walked across the blank floor to the chair and sat down. He leaned back to let its padding enfold him. The chair, sensing his weight, tilted itself so that his temple was aligned with the probe and recorder that automatically unfolded from the wall. Out of the corner of his right eye, Tam could just see Dionte extend the delicate arm. The chair did not permit him to turn his head.

"Your Conscience has not taken proper hold in your mind, Tam," said Dionte softly. Tam felt a dull pressure as the recorder needle pierced the skin over his Conscience. "I must readapt it to make sure it functions properly in the future."

Tam felt himself begin to shake. There had to be a way out, a way to stop this.

"Aleph. Aleph, are you there?"

"I'm here, Tam." The voice filled with a deep and unexpected disappointment. "But with this diagnosis, I may not interfere. The subsystems cannot be overridden. Your sister will help you."

"Yes, Brother. I will."

With those words, the gates of his mind opened to release a flood of guilty memory so deep and so strong that all Tam could do was feel and weep, and wish that he would drown.

CHAPTER FOURTEEN

The Run

It had taken Teal forever to suss out Stem's new tailor. He was nothing like the old guy, the one who'd gotten Sadia and Shond in trouble. That one had hung around the cattle calls, all but waving people into his shop. No big surprise to find out he'd been hauled in a few days later. He was probably lucky the hothouse got to him before the Pharmakeus did. They did not like the tailors.

I don't give a grass rip who Nan Elle and her gang don't like. Teal clenched her fists as she strode up the boardwalk. *I'm getting out of here. I'm finding Dad and I'm telling him everything. We'll see how these people like it when the Authority finds out what they've been doing.*

We'll see how Chena likes it when Dad finds out what she's been doing.

Chena would come looking for her, but Teal wouldn't go back. She'd tell the constables Nan Elle was a poisoner. She'd tell everyone. She'd babble like a baby to everyone who would listen about what Elle and Chena had been doing, about how they didn't give a piss in the wind what she wanted to do, or what she thought, or felt. They were ready to hang around here until somebody came to rip *them* open. Well, she wasn't. She was getting out of here in one piece. So what if Nan Elle stole her money? She had things to sell. She was getting out.

They could try to stop her. Let them just try.

Teal had expected the tailor to live on the edge of the village, like Nan Elle did, but he kept his place right in the center of town, only a couple of turns away from the market and the whorehouse where Chena's lover-boy worked.

Wonder if she's saved up enough money for him to lay her down yet.

The tailor shop looked like most of the other buildings—a few blocks of stone, a door, and a window all set into the face of a grassy dune. The door stood open just a little.

Teal didn't let herself hesitate as she stepped over the threshold into the dim and cool shop smelling of old fish and dust. After the blaze of the summer day, Teal had to stop a minute to let her eyes adjust. When they did, she saw a bare room made of packed earth and sandstone. A few sealed baskets stood near the left-hand wall, and a set of crates made a kind of counter in front of a dark doorway that led deeper into the dune.

Teal stood in the gloom, uncertain what to do. Then she heard the scuff of footsteps coming through the doorway. A moment later, a patch of shadow turned into a square man with dark, almond-shaped eyes and pale skin and apple cheeks. He looked her up and down, as if checking for flaws.

"You buying or selling?" he asked. His voice was soft, almost gentle. Maybe this wouldn't be so hard.

Don't let him snow you. Teal cleared her throat. "Selling."

Again, his sharp eyes swept up and down Teal's body. "You don't look half old enough. Who owns you?"

"Nobody," answered Teal immediately.

The man chuckled and laid his hand on the makeshift counter. "Sorry, girl, but on Pandora, somebody owns every one of us."

"No," Teal snapped. "The ones who think they own me are liars. I'm on my own."

"I see." He nodded once, thoughtfully. "On your own and from Offshoot." Teal touched her tattoo self-consciously. "What would you have to sell me?"

Teal swallowed. *Say it. It's no big deal. Just say it.* "Eggs."

He cocked his head. "Well, they'd be fresh." His eyes glittered. "But forgive me if I don't believe that no one would care if your young body got violated. Who's your family?"

"My dad's in the Authority," said Teal. "I'm trying to get back to him. My mom's dead."

"Look." He laid his other hand on the counter and leaned forward.

"If you want to conduct any trade, I am, at the very least, going to have to have your name."

Teal licked her lips. She tried to think of some way to argue, but the man had already straightened up and was looking back toward the interior door with a sour expression on his face. If she didn't give him an answer, he would leave, and she didn't know where else to go. "Teal Trust."

"Trust?" His head whipped around and his eyebrows inched up toward his hairline. "As in Chena and Helice Trust?"

"So?" Teal shrugged.

"Nothing." His fingers drummed on the counter. "What you have is valuable, but also dangerous. You're asking me to risk getting the attention of a Pharmakeus. They do not like my kind."

Teal shrugged again. "You don't want what I've got, I'll just go somewhere else."

"Normally, I'd tell you to do that," he said matter-of-factly. "But there is someone on their way here who will pay me very well for what you've got. Good timing." His smile seemed genuinely approving. "But for the risk and bother, I'd need at least a hundred."

Again, Teal shrugged. "If that's what you'll take."

The eyes narrowed. "What would you want in return?"

"I want to get back to Athena Station, and I'm going to need money to keep me going once I'm there."

He pursed his pudgy mouth. "Risky and expensive. I'd have to alter your chip. Make you look nineteen so you're legal to travel on your own. Are you worth it?" His eyes flickered back and forth, weighing the risks against the gain. At last he straightened up. "Two hundred and you go back to the station."

Teal felt a small thrill inside her, a combination of fear and elation. She'd done it. She should have done this years ago. "Okay."

The man looked bemused. "Okay, then. We'd better get started right away." He stepped aside and gestured through the darkened doorway. Teal screwed a holding plate over her nerves and walked through ahead of him.

The door led to a set of unlit stairs heading down into the earth. Teal steadied herself with one hand on the earthen wall and walked slowly down. She tried to tell herself to be calm, but she flinched at every little breeze that touched her skin.

At the bottom of the stairs waited one cool room lit by a single battery-powered light. Assorted crates and baskets lined the walls. The place smelled of dust, damp, and stale spices. Teal couldn't see any other doors.

"Now what?" she asked, trying to sound like she didn't really care. She'd been expecting a lab, or something like it, a monitor bed at the very least.

"Now"—the man opened a basket and rifled through its contents, which seemed to be dried beans—"you go to sleep. When you wake up, it'll be all over."

"What?" The word burst out of Teal.

The man lifted a small box made from different-colored slats of wood from the beans. The slats turned out to be movable. He slid them in a couple of different directions, Teal couldn't quite see how, but the box opened and he pulled out a drug patch.

"The less you know, the better for all of us." He held out the patch. "It goes on your neck."

"But . . ." *But I don't know if I can trust you. I don't know what you'll do to me. I don't even know your name. You could do anything. You could kill me, or sell me to the hothouse, or anything.*

The man just stood there, holding out the patch to her.

And if I don't? What am I going to do? Go back to Chena? She'll lock me in my room and tell me how it's for my own good and how we can't get ourselves out of here alive because we've got to try to get back at the hothousers.

Teal held her breath and took the patch from the man's fingers. She peeled the safety sticker off the back, slapped it onto the left side of her neck, and held it down until it stuck.

"You may want to sit down."

Teal sat. She barely reached the floor before a warm rush of dizziness overwhelmed her. She heard a sharp crack and realized, distantly, her head had fallen back against the wooden crates. Her body had gone away from her, and she couldn't seem to care. She thought her eyes closed, which was strange, because at the same time, she was sure that she could see the man leaning over her, touching her throat, riffling through her clothes, running a reader over the chip in the back of her hand, grasping her face in his hand and turning her head this way and that, looking for something.

On some level, she was also vaguely aware she wanted to protest these things, but none of them really touched her in the distant place she had gone. Each second they seemed farther away. Her consciousness ran toward the darkness as great as the wide black sky. There was nothing to worry about there. Not the fact that she was being laid down, and her clothes removed, nothing. Soon, there was only darkness and the comfortable knowledge that she was finally, truly on her own.

As usual, Lopera Qay kept them waiting. Dionte watched Basante prowl the confines of the bare red rock cave that Lopera used as a reception chamber. Basante never liked being out of the complex. He felt a combination of guilt that he might do something to disturb Pandora, and distaste at being at the mercy of an uncontrolled and unthinking environment.

In truth, she could not blame him for his restlessness. She did not want to be here either. She needed to be in the complex, tracking the progress of Tam's new Conscience. She needed to understand why Aleph was becoming so balky. She needed to continue her work with Father Mihran and the Senior Committee. Four committee members were scheduled for Conscience examination and adjustment in the next ten days. She needed to be there for those, to ensure such adjustments were made that would start the potential for tighter bonds between themselves and her, the rest of the family and the city-mind, and to be sure she had the perceptual balances properly adjusted.

But she also could not let Basante meet with Lopera alone when she did not have a clear idea of what that meeting would be about. Their summons had been curt and most uninformative. Lopera had no doubt done that on purpose.

As she expected, Basante reached the inner door and found it locked, as usual. He turned to Dionte, all righteous indignation. "I fail to see why she insists on making us wait and wasting everyone's time."

"She gets to display that she has power over two people from the hothouse," said Dionte, taking care to keep her voice mild. "It is not something many villagers get to experience." She smiled at him, trying to radiate calm. Basante's Conscience was probably giving him trouble. This was definitely not a place where a good member of the family should be.

The clanking of a mechanical lock cut off any further conversation. The interior door opened and Lopera Qay strolled in. Lopera was always very careful never to let Dionte and Basante see her in a hurry. Further power games. Dionte let them all pass. After all, Lopera was performing a crucial and dangerous service for them. They could allow her some games.

"Your timing's good," said Lopera, folding her arms and leaning one shoulder against the rough rock wall.

"Your message was both urgent and enigmatic." Dionte spread her hands. "How could we refuse?"

"I hope nothing has happened to your trust," said Basante irritably. "Although I can't see what would be so important that you would have to call us out. It is not easy for us to get here, you know."

The corners of Lopera's mouth curled up. Dionte stared. That expression meant something. What was it? The sensation of forgetting something incredibly important staggered her.

Sly. It was a sly smile that spread across Lopera's face. How could she not know that, even for a second?

"Funny you should use the word 'trust,'" Lopera was saying. "I called you here because we seem to have one of your Trusts."

"What?" exclaimed Basante.

Instantly Dionte laced her fingers together, activating her internal systems. Her implant had picked up on the word "trust" and had accessed the appropriate information.

High probability that the rain forest intruder was Chena Trust, as predicted by Basante, but she has been reported safely returned to Offshoot and Basante file secured pending future requirements.

Subfile personal notes: With C. Trust becoming more active, increasing attention needed to keep her out of hands of opposition (access family meeting notes 25-20-2073). Becoming harder to rationalize leaving her in village (access Constable report 25-27-2073 and Basante personal report). May have to preemptively sequester (access preliminary action notes).

No reports on Teal Trust (most recent constable report awaiting input and assimilation), but increased communication between Elle Stepka and various contacts in village Stem (files available and fresh information pending) observed from time of rain forest infiltration.

Outside her, she heard Lopera saying, "Young Teal wants to go back to Athena. She's come to us for help." Lopera's smile became positively indulgent. "Do you want her?"

All annoyance vanished from Basante's face and his eyes shone with eagerness. No, Dionte corrected herself, greed.

"Perfect," he breathed. "This is perfect. We can work with her here. I can direct the experiments remotely. Dionte, if you can shield communications and set me up . . ."

Possibilities flitted through Dionte, directed by her Conscience and her instincts. She smelled scents of warning and imagination, creativity and fear. Her ears rang with inner voices, both imagined and remembered, whispering to her, only to her, with their wisdom and possibilities. So much information, so many ideas, dizzying with their speed and intensity, opening her up, making her alive, truly alive to the world, to her responsibilities, to the future, the true, good future that lay before them, that lay in the voices and possibilities surging through her.

And for a moment she had not been able to understand the smile on Lopera's face. Dionte shivered.

But Basante was rambling on and giving orders to Lopera, who wasn't even looking at him. She watched Dionte. Lopera knew where the decisions lay; she always had. An isolated villager she might be, but she was not stupid. She was skilled and she was practical. That was precisely why Dionte had chosen her to keep Eden. This memory and caution came to Dionte, and she knew she would have to choose the immediate future and speak it into being before Basante got too carried away.

"No." Dionte broke her connections and waved away whatever Basante had been saying. She would catch it up later from the recording her Conscience would have made. Her ways of understanding were shifting. That was all. All was well. She could still do what she needed to. "Help her go. Help her hide so that we hothousers cannot possibly find her."

Basante stared at her, momentarily mute with shock. "Dionte . . ." he finally choked.

Dionte walked swiftly to his side. "Be calm, Brother." She laid her hand on his, her scent, warmth, and touch letting his Conscience know that these were the words of family. It was good to listen to your family, and his Conscience would tell him so, soothing him for her. "Consider what will happen when we are able to tell the family that Director Shontio is harboring fugitives aboard Athena Station. He will no longer be able to pretend he is a victim of circumstances. He will be shown as the active participant he is. Father Mihran will finally come to understand that we can no longer leave the station in the hands of those who have no Consciences." She knew the future, at least this one little piece of it. She saw it clearly and she knew triumph at the sight. "We will be able to do in one week what none of the family has been able to do in a thousand years. We will bring Consciences to Athena."

Basante pulled his hand away. "You've placed too much faith in one successful experiment," he said with unusual firmness. She had trespassed too far into Basante's area of expertise, and he would not be easily calmed this time. "You haven't heard anything I've said, have you? We need to be sure we can create this gene combination consistently. We need to study variations in alleles. At the very least, we will need other breeders to ensure a numerous and healthy defensive force." He glared at her. "Or did you think we could neutralize all the Called with one boy?"

"Of course not." She waved his words away. "But there are other considerations here. The station must be tied to the family and the cities if we are to stay defended. The Authority must not be able to get to us through them."

Basante bowed his head, relenting, and Dionte faced Lopera. "Your people certainly did not suggest to Teal Trust that you would help her without some form of payment?"

Lopera pushed herself away from the wall and unfolded her arms, assuming a much more businesslike posture. "Of course not. She's offering payment in eggs."

Basante's head jerked up. "How many?"

"One hundred. Enough?" Lopera arched her eyebrows.

Basante rubbed the information display on the back of his hand, performing his own type of internal calculation. "For a beginning anyway. Cloning will help extend the resources. Yes, yes." Then he shrugged, as if he did not want to appear too easily convinced. Dionte looked at Lopera, not so much reading the set of her face as remembering how many times she had held back information before. Probably she had taken more from Teal than she had told them. Probably she was holding back a cache to see what advantage could be bought with it.

That was all right too. The extra resources might open up extra possibilities. She would have to think about that.

"It will certainly be better than nothing," went on Basante. "But it's really the womb we need. The immune system. We can create embryos until the heat death comes, but if they can't grow to term without radical interference—"

"But there is one more Trust." Dionte touched him again and smiled, the future taking shape inside her. "Chena."

Understanding dawned on Basante like the light of a new day. His excited smile warmed Dionte at her core. She had him again. She had the future. It was working. The bonds were truly, finally, working.

"So you'll have Chena Trust picked up?" asked Basante.

Dionte laced her fingers together briefly and let the cloud of futures and warnings whirl through her.

"No," she said, fresh understanding coming to her as well. "Your evidence that she broke out into the wilderness is good, but it won't convince the villagers. They are nervous right now. We've been taking in more donors than usual to try to replace Helice Trust. We do not need our plans disrupted by any unrest. If we induce Chena Trust to come to us, then her disappearance will become her own fault and arouse no fresh alarm."

"How are you going to—"

"There's nothing Chena Trust loves more than a chance to best the evil hothousers." Dionte's mouth puckered at this new wrinkle to the future. "I'll give her one." More ideas came then, flickering through her mind so rapidly she could not understand them all. Yet, they were all-important, she felt that. "Wait, wait." Dionte stared deep into the future before her. "If we feed her the right information, Chena Trust will even help us toward our goal. Yes, I see that.

I see how it may be done." She forced her fingers apart so she could concentrate on the outside before the inner world, with its successes and complexity, overwhelmed her.

Basante shook his head. "I do not like this. She's a villager. Worse, she's an Athenian. We do not have enough information about her to make these predictions."

"We do not." Dionte laid a hand on his arm. "But I do."

Basante looked down at her hand on his sleeve and said nothing.

"Well, now," interrupted Lopera with false cheerfulness. "If you're all happy, I assume you'll be wanting to see Eden?"

"Of course," said Dionte. "How is our project?"

"A pain," said Lopera bluntly. "Hopefully, someone's found him for you by now."

The color drained from Basante's cheeks. "Found him! What's happened to him?"

"Nothing. He's a bored five-year-old boy. He wanders around." Amusement sparkled in her eyes. "Also, I don't think he likes you. Something to do with all the needles."

"You careless nit! Do you know what could happen to him in this warren? He could drown in the lake. He could fall and break his neck!"

Lopera straightened up, all amusement and tolerance gone. "What do you want me to do? Tie him up? Lock him away? You want him to be healthy. How healthy is he going to be if he's caged?"

Basante wasn't listening. He stalked forward until he was barely an inch from Lopera. "You don't understand what's at stake here, do you? If we lose him, we lose the entire world. Do you realize what that means?"

That's far enough. "Basante . . ."

But in his anger, Basante did not hear her. "It means the planet will be gutted. It means the Authority will assume total control of us all, and then what do you think will happen to your pitiful, smuggling, tailoring, criminal little life?"

"It means I'll have a new boss," said Lopera calmly. "Don't push me too hard, or I might start thinking that's a good idea."

For a moment Dionte thought Basante might actually hit Lopera. This was not the kind of reaction he was trained to believe he deserved from villagers. His pride and his Conscience were doubtlessly in conflict, and that could make anyone irrational.

"Enough, Lopera. Please, Basante, cool your temper. We need each other, and these arguments do no one any good." She pulled Basante back a couple of steps. "Lopera will not let us down." *Because she does not want to risk the involuntary wing.* "We have five years' worth of proof for that." She watched his face and shoulders relaxing. "Lopera, perhaps you can take us to Eden and show Basante his fears are unfounded."

"Of course." Lopera also relaxed visibly and gestured for them to precede her out through the inner door.

Dionte took Basante's arm and walked with him through the doorway, not giving him a chance to stop and say anything else to Lopera. They could not afford for him to upset Lopera and her people too much.

Not yet.

Light seeped into Teal's darkness. She became aware of its warmth on her eyelids, turning the blackness first gray and then red. She felt . . . swollen. Her head felt so heavy she didn't think she could lift it. Her dry, woolly tongue filled her entire mouth. Her belly was aching and distended, and her breasts felt like a couple sacks of water sagging against her rib cage.

With an effort, she fluttered her eyelids open. Above her, she saw dimness, lit by one pale yellow light that seemed familiar somehow. Scents wormed their way into her brain—dust, damp, stale basil and cinnamon.

She was in the basement under the dunes. She hadn't moved at all.

The realization gave her the strength to sit up. Pain stabbed through her midriff. She groaned and clutched at her stomach, slamming one hand out behind herself to keep from falling back down. It landed on something soft, and the sensation expanded Teal's world a little further.

She wasn't sitting on the floor anymore, but on a pallet, the kind they used in the dorms. A thick white sheet covered her. Clothes lay in a neat pile beside the pillow, with her comptroller sitting right on top. Teal snatched it up to check the time and the date.

Three days. What strength she had vanished from her fingers, and the comptroller dropped into her lap. She'd been down here for three days. Had she only been down here? Or had they taken her somewhere? There were no memories in her head from the time she first saw this place up to now. Panic seized her, bringing on another wave of pain. She clutched the sheet to her chest and doubled over, squeezing her eyes shut against the tears.

It was then she realized her breasts weren't just swollen, they were too big. Her hips and buttocks too. Everything was the wrong shape. *Have to make you look like you're nineteen,* the man, the tailor, had said. The implications hadn't quite filtered in then. They'd rebuilt her body.

Teal couldn't tell if it was that realization or the leftover drugs in her system that made her feel sick.

Shaking, she pushed the sheet back and reached for the clothes. She tried not to look down as she dressed. She really did not want to see what they'd done to her. The things they'd left weren't her old clothes, which of course would now be too small, but they were close enough, and they were clean. Underwear, bra, loose brown trousers, a soft gray tunic, and gray woolen socks. The boots were her old, creased, familiar pair. Those, at least, still fit just fine, and somehow that made her feel better.

In fact, she felt well enough to realize she was incredibly thirsty, and the pain of hunger added itself to the general pain around her midriff.

"Can I come down?" called someone from the top of the stairs. A man. The tailor.

"Yeah," Teal tried to say, but all that came out was a hoarse croak. The tailor couldn't possibly have heard, but he came down the stairs anyway. Teal didn't have time to be angry before she saw the jug and bowl in his hands. He set them both down in front of her and stepped back. Teal lifted the jug with shaking hands and drank. Water, sweet and clear, poured down her burning throat. She drank until she thought her lungs would burst, forgetting that the man was even there.

Finally she lowered the jug and wiped her mouth with the back of her hand.

"Thanks." She set the jug down and reached for the bowl. It was the very familiar porridge she had hated in the dorms. She didn't care. Right now it smelled wonderful. She picked up the spoon and started shoveling food into her mouth with a speed that would have had Chena rolling her eyes. Her muscles protested every movement, but she didn't stop or slow down. The food was all that mattered.

"As soon as you're done," drawled the tailor. "You're going to have to go."

That actually stopped her. Teal swallowed the mouthful she had. "Go? Where?"

"The docks," he said patiently, but Teal heard the strain under his voice. "We have to get you out of here and up the pipe quickly. We couldn't find a permanent new chip for you, so you've only got an overlay in your hand, and it's going to decay quickly. Until then your name is Collie Od, you got that? Collie Od."

"Collie Od," Teal repeated. *You couldn't get me a* good *name?* Teal swallowed again. "I'm not sure I can walk," she admitted.

The tailor gestured dismissively. "You're going to have to. Get yourself together."

The food and water had worked enough on Teal that she had enough strength to get angry. "What's the hurry? You didn't do the job right?"

The tailor frowned. "You didn't think there might be people looking for you? You're valuable and you vanished. That's enough for the hothousers to get the cops to arrest you on suspicion."

"On suspicion of what?"

"Whatever they want." He shrugged impatiently. "Now let's go. I do not keep contraband in my store. You either walk out of here or I drug you and you go out in one of the baskets." He spread his hands. "Your choice."

The thought of being knocked out again turned Teal's stomach. "Give me a second."

"A second is about all I can give you."

Teal scraped the last of the porridge off the bottom of the bowl and crammed it into her mouth. Then she swallowed all the water she could hold. Gasping for breath, she set the jug down again. A glance at the tailor's face told her she could not delay any longer. So she tightened all the muscles in her legs and stood up.

Pain shot through her entire body with an intensity that rocked the floor under her. Her hips were too wide, the ground was too far away. She could not find her balance, and the more she teetered, the more pain ran up and down the muscles in her legs and diaphragm. She couldn't stand, but she couldn't let herself fall either, not in front of this man and in the face of the realization that this had been what she wanted, what she had come here for. Her muscles screamed in protest, making the entire world sway and spin, but she tightened them anyway, and she remained on her feet.

The tailor didn't even bother to nod; he just turned around and started up the stairs, assuming she would follow. Teal clenched her teeth and forced her rubbery, too-long legs to walk forward.

She made it up the stairs, slowly, and shaking all the time as if she were about to fall apart, but she did make it. Outside, the cool wind off the lake touched her skin and made her shiver, but also made her feel better somehow. She drank air in great gulps as she followed the tailor down the boardwalk toward the shore. They passed the dune houses, with their deep-set windows, and Teal stole glances at them as she passed, trying to catch her own reflection to see what she looked like now. She didn't have much luck, but it kept her mind somewhat off the pain in her guts.

The dunes opened up to make way for the market and the beach. At the end of the longest jetty, a pair of dirigibles floated on the gently lapping water, tethered with thick cables to the cage of scaffolding and ladders that let the ground crews swarm over them, doing whatever was necessary to keep the things flying. Their aerogel bags were translucent, showing the network of silver struts that gave them their shape. They were filigree flying machines, and, at the moment, just about the most beautiful things Teal had ever seen. They'd take her home. Home to where she'd find Dad, to where she'd get to have a good life, where she was in charge and didn't have to be afraid all the time.

In front of her, the tailor slowed down. Teal tried to shorten her stride, but she misjudged and banged into his back like a clown in a bad routine. He pushed her away impatiently. "Here's where we find out whether we did a good enough job on you, 'Collie.' " He pointed down to the jetty.

Teal looked where he pointed, her heart in her mouth. What if it was Chena? What if she tried to drag her back? She'd have to squawk, but now she was a criminal too. . . .

But it wasn't Chena. Two people in neat brown tunics stood in conference with a third person, a tallish man with dark brown skin and a wooden plug in his ear. It took Teal a second to recognize him from the back, but it was Constable Regan.

So, Chena couldn't be bothered to come herself, thought Teal, strangely disappointed. *She had to send the cop.*

The tailor lengthened his stride again. A wary smile stretched across his face as he reached the spot where Regan and his gang stood. "Good morning, Constable. May we get by?"

Regan turned around and gave the tailor a once-over. "Morning, Wilseck, and no." His smile was grim. "This is what we call a checkpoint. We're going to have to check your chip. And yours." He nodded at Teal. Teal's throat closed, but his attention was fleeting. He didn't recognize her. She fought the urge to touch her face. How much *had* they changed her? "And we have to ask if you've seen her." He unhooked the chip reader from his belt and held it up so they could see the little 3-D of Teal shining there. His gaze flitted over Teal, and rested again on Wilseck, and then shot back to Teal. This time his brow started to furrow.

Teal swallowed hard, while the tailor, Wilseck, squinted at the 3-D. "Nope. Nobody I know."

Regan took a step closer and pointed the display at Teal. "How about you?"

Teal's heart thundered in her chest. She was sure the whole world could hear it. She had to do something now, right now. Regan was looking too closely at her. He'd know her in another second.

"Yeah," she said. "That's Teal Trust, isn't it?"

Regan's brow furrowed more deeply for a second and then smoothed out. "That's right. Have you seen her?"

Teal nodded. "She's been hanging out around the library, trying to buy a skyhook for the computer so she can get hold of someone on Athena."

"She try to buy from you?"

Again, Teal nodded. "I'm not that desperate, though. If that kid's legal, I'm a constable."

Regan smiled, and maybe he laughed silently. "But I don't know you, do I?"

"I guess not." She saluted him. "Collie Od."

She watched his eyes flicker back and forth as he ran through some kind of mental list. "No, I don't know you," he said, more to himself than to her. He looked over her shoulder at the transport guards. "Collie and Wilseck stay here until we get back from the library."

Regan strode up the pier. Teal swallowed past the fear in her throat and glanced back at Wilseck. He looked placid, ready to wait all day, but she could feel the tension singing through him. The look he gave her was the same cold expression she'd seen from Chena a million times. It said, *What do you think you're doing?*

Keeping the cop away from me, she thought toward him, but she couldn't tell if the idea reached him.

Instead, he nodded to the two checkpoint guards blocking the peer. "Grace. Cole."

Grace stood on the left-hand side of the pier and carried a taser on her belt as well as a scanner. "Willie."

"What's the score with this Teal Trust?"

Cole smirked. "Willie, if you expect me to believe you don't know about the Trusts, you must be way off your game."

Wilseck gave a small nod. "All right, I know. What I don't know is why the constable is looking for her."

"Because she's gone missing, hasn't she?" Grace crossed her arms. "You wouldn't know anything about that, now, would you, Willie?"

Wilseck's smile grew sly, and Teal's heart began to pound. Wilseck was running a game here, and she didn't know the rules. "That all depends, doesn't it?"

Cole stepped forward. "Oh, no, Willie. You don't have any leverage this time. All we have to do is tell the cop you know."

"Well, you could do that," agreed Wilseck, appearing completely unruffled. "But it wouldn't be very good for you if Lopera had to tell her employers you weren't playing along."

At those words, Cole went dead white. Who was Lopera? Who were her employers? Teal had never seen a villager look like that except when somebody was suggesting he might be getting on the wrong side of a Pharmakeus . . .

Or the hothousers.

No. He couldn't be threatening them with the hothousers. What he was doing was so illegal they'd toss him into involuntary before he had time to blink. No. There had to be something else going on.

But Cole's face was still that sick, scared white. "Willie, look, it's not just us. That Constable Regan is not going to be pushed around. We can't just . . ."

Grace, on the other hand, just licked her lips and looked away. When she looked back, Teal saw a combination of steel and resignation in her face. "What do you want, Willie?" she asked wearily.

Wilseck's smile grew even wider. "I always knew you were the smart one, Grace."

"Piss off," she replied genially. "If you've got something for us, let us know the price." Her eyes flicked over his shoulder to scan the boardwalk. "Fast."

"When he gets back, you tell the cop that my friend here ran off." He jerked his chin at Teal.

"When she actually went into the dirigible?" Cole raised his eyebrows inquisitively.

"Very good, Cole," said Wilseck. "You're catching on."

Grace rubbed her chin. "That's a lot. Aside from the usual threats, what are you giving us?"

"Teal Trust was in my shop," he said. Teal hoped no one saw how every muscle in her body tensed. "She wants to stay out of the hothouses, for a wonder. She wanted some of her alleles changed so she'd be a little less attractive to them. I told her I'd have to think about it before I arranged to have something so valuable cut into. She told me where she's staying."

Teal's heart hammered painfully against her ribs. *Believe it. Believe it,* she urged the guards silently. It took all her strength not to look at Wilseck.

Cole glanced at Grace. She paused, considering. "Is any of that true?"

"No," said Wilseck coolly. "But I can make it sound really good for your constable."

Grace snorted. Then she nodded.

"Go," said Wilseck quietly. So much of Teal's energy was bound up in not bolting, it took her a second to realize that he was talking to her.

When she did, though, she didn't hesitate. She trotted down the jetty toward the waiting dirigible. One of the tenders scowled at her and looked back at the guards. Grace waved her arm in a signal that must have meant all-okay, because the man stood aside and allowed Teal to duck through the low doorway into the gondola.

She had expected a passenger cabin like they had on the one that brought them down here from Athena, but this dirigible was more like a flying warehouse than anything else. Nets bolted to the walls and floor held huge piles of crates and cargo containers. Teal stepped to one side of the doors and stood there for a second, uncertain what to do. A tall thin man in brown coveralls stepped out from between the piles of cargo holders and looked her over.

"Passenger seats up front." He gestured toward the gondola's interior. "Better get going." He continued on out the doorway.

Teal didn't move. Nothing inside her was convinced that the guards, let alone Regan, would go for Wilseck's threats or stories for long. They'd come in here. They'd haul her out.

Her eyes darted left and right, trying to take in the whole of the gondola quickly. There wasn't much to it. Other than the netted piles of cargo, there were only the curving walls lined with cabinets and padding, and the support girders that held the walls in place.

Cabinet's too obvious. It'll take too long to find which crates are empty. Her eyes traveled up and down the girders. They had holes into which brackets or ring bolts could be fit. They'd make great toeholds too.

Teal snatched up an empty cargo net from a rack by the door and stuffed it into the waist of her trousers, because she had no pockets big enough. Then she found a toehold in the girder and started climbing.

Her longer arms and legs proved good for something. Even though everything still hurt, Teal managed to clamber up to the ceiling girders more easily than she would have before the operation. She wedged herself into a corner, bracing her back against one girder and her feet against another. She reached for the cargo net, intending to sling it in place to make herself a nice little hammock, when she heard movement below.

Teal froze. Her heart thundered so wildly she thought its noise echoed off the walls. Below, Regan and the two guards from the pier walked into the gondola.

"Check the passenger seats," said Regan. "Just in case she's doing something really obvious." One of the guards—Cole, Teal thought—headed forward.

Grace and Regan stayed where they were. So did Teal. The girders bit into her palms and buttocks where she braced herself. The joints in her knees began to hurt all over again.

"So, what do we do now, Constable?" asked Grace. Her voice sounded hollow as it reached the ceiling. "Start knocking on crates and opening cabinets? I'm telling you, she took off."

"But you can't tell me where she took off to," said Regan doggedly. "So, I have to check."

Cole's footsteps echoed as he came back. "She's not up there." Both the guards looked at Regan.

Regan began walking around the cargo containers. Every now and then he would touch one or tug on the lines of the nets holding them in place, as if he were trying to see which ones felt loose.

Teal held her breath. *Don't look up. Don't let him look up. He lives in trees and he knows that things can be hiding in the branches, but don't let him think about looking up here.* Feeling like a baby, but unable to help herself, Teal closed her eyes. Her leg muscles began to tremble and cramp. But she still heard the footsteps and the low creaking as Regan pulled on the net lines.

Don't look up. Don't look up.

"They aren't paying us enough for this, Constable. If the hothousers want her, they can come get her themselves, can't they?"

"What do you think I'm here for?" answered Regan.

The hothousers were looking for her? Not Chena? This made no sense, no sense at all. If Wilseck was working for someone working for the hothousers, what did they need the guards for? Who would have told them she was missing in the first place? Had Willie sold her out? But if he had, why wasn't she in the hothouse right now? He had her all knocked out in his basement; he could have done anything.

What is going on? Teal squeezed her eyes even more tightly shut.

The sound of footsteps stilled. Teal opened her eyes and risked a glance down. Grace had cocked her head. "You really don't care that this one might be trying to stay away from the hothousers?"

Regan rubbed his brow. "Yes, I do care, but there are laws, and we all have to live under them. She broke the law by going to the tailor, and she forfeited her body right. We have to make every effort to bring her in."

Grace paused, as if digesting this new information. "We don't really know she went to the tailor." She raised one finger and pointed it at Regan. "I wouldn't take Wilseck's word if he said the sun would rise at dawn."

It was Regan's turn to pause. Something was passing between them, but Teal wasn't sure what it could be. Keeping herself from falling occupied too much of her mind.

"No," said Regan at last. "Let's go find the man and see if we can get some hard verification from him."

Regan and the guards walked out. Teal stayed where she was until her knees began to shake so badly that sweat broke out on her forehead and she thought her palms would slip off the girder. With the last of her strength, she climbed back down and made her way to the small cluster of passenger seats. There was no one else in them. She picked a seat at random and collapsed into it, fastening the seat belt around her waist and shoulders with trembling hands.

Behind her, she heard the sound of the cargo door being dragged shut. With a clang, the bolts shot home. The rumble of the steering engines vibrated through the floor. Gently, the dirigible rose into the air.

Home, thought Teal, letting her head fall back against the seat. It didn't matter what else was going on. It didn't matter who was after her or who was letting her go, or what little games they were playing. She'd be with the Authority soon, and they took care of their own.

I'm going home.

"Why would our people do this to us?" asked Peda, city-mind to the Psi Complex.

"I don't know," said every voice but Aleph's. It was a useless answer. They had to know. It was their job to know. If they didn't know, how could they take care of their people?

They were all connected through the default convocation image of themselves sitting in a circle against a starry background and looking down at the gently turning globe of Pandora.

Since Aleph and Gem had spread word of what had happened to Aleph's memory, every single city-mind had located unnecessary, unscheduled alterations in themselves. They'd compared the type and duration of the alterations. These were not simple mistakes in remembering schedules or personal illnesses. Any mind could make mistakes. Memories blurred and changed as new priorities arose. Information that needed to remain absolutely accurate over time was stored mechanically. The point of a city-mind was to grow and change, to learn and reflect as the people it cared for did.

Those reflections had been distorted.

"Have we done wrong?" suggested Daleth timidly. Daleth always projected the image of a child in convocation, as if he wanted to remind himself that he was younger than the others. "Did we need correction?"

"Our people would have told us," said Gem, a gold-skinned old man with a bald head and wispy white beard. "Our people always tell us when there is a chemical imbalance."

Our people, thought Aleph. *My people.* So many people, all with their histories stored inside her, each a separate file she could call on at need. Each to be treated as a unique individual with a unique history, because generalizations between people led to gross mistakes and improper care.

Aleph ran her mind along the long list of names, histories, and Conscience files. All that knowledge, all that time spent poring over each Conscience download to learn what her people feared, wondered at, and wanted, and none of it was any good. None of it. Because now she was afraid of her people—as at least one of her people was afraid of her.

Aleph's thoughts paused and reversed themselves.

Why am I thinking of fear? She opened the subsystem that controlled the personnel files again. All her people, down through the years, all the individuals, with their voices, their histories, and their Consciences.

They had to be treated one at a time. Loose conclusions could be drawn from similar cases, but the requirements of happiness, comfort, and safety were to be determined one case at a time, from the observed behavior and Conscience downloads of the individual. That was the procedure.

But perhaps that procedure had allowed something important to slip through.

Aleph accessed Dionte's file and ran through the Conscience downloads, the times when she herself could taste the workings of Dionte's mind. The file told her she had indeed tasted fear during Dionte's most recent Conscience download. She ordered the file to sort itself. Every time a download was performed of her Conscience, Dionte felt a little fear—not a great fear, but a little fear.

Aleph accessed and sorted another file. Tam also felt a little fear.

Nerves. Surely this is just nerves. But every time . . . ?

She ordered a random selection and search. Fear. At every download there was fear. Another file pulled, and more fear, and another and more fear, and another and yet more fear.

So much fear, but only when being touched and tasted, only when being helped in the most intimate way possible by the city-minds the people had created to protect and care for them.

Fear of what, though? Of me? My own people could not be afraid of me.

But then, before this, she would have said she could not be afraid of her own people.

"Aleph?" Gem's voice was gentle, concerned. "Aleph, you are quiet. What are you thinking about?"

"Fear," she answered. "Let me show you." She ordered her search, and its results, copied and sent, and waited while the others drank it in. Had the Guardians not noticed this? Had they chosen to disregard it? How could anyone choose to disregard this much fear? "Compare your files. If this is universal, we must know."

"What could this have to do with anything?" demanded Cheth, cantankerous and skeptical. She turned the convocation image over until it became a lecture hall smelling of dust and ozone with the reports flashing past on a huge screen. "Of course our people are nervous before a download. There is an aversion to having the skin broken. It is an evolved response."

"No, this is not nerves." Aleph erased the image, leaving behind only a cloud of gray. They had to concentrate on her words. "This is fear. They are afraid of being touched in the ways that they routinely touch us—with adjustments and needles and understanding of the chemical processes of personality and thought. Actions from fear are uncertain and unsafe." She paused and passed them the urgent scent of burning. *Listen, friends, hear and understand. This is vital. You must understand.* "I do not find any unscheduled or covert alterations of myself before the introduction of the Consciences."

Silence and stillness stretched out on all sides.

"Before the Consciences, the knowledge to create such changes did not exist?" suggested Peda hopefully.

Cheth made a rude noise. "Then how could they have ever created us?"

"Aleph," said Gem. "Do you say that before the Consciences, the need to make such changes in us did not exist?"

Aleph turned the convocation gold and scented it with the clean smells of oranges and lemons. "I say."

"Then what changed?"

Aleph let the gold ripple. "Fear creates its own needs. We all know this."

Sounds of agreement flowed to her.

"You say the Consciences created a new fear?" said Cheth.

"I say."

"But fear of what?" Cheth demanded. "The Consciences were the creation of our people. They voted on the necessity. I have the memory in mechanical storage." Cheth swept aside Aleph's gold curtain and replaced it with image after image from history, of all the meetings and all the lab work done to create the Consciences. "They decided that without the Consciences, future generations of the family were too likely to break into feuding factions. It was already beginning. Members of the family helped destroy Daleth. Others were helping the villagers introduce artificial pressures into the biosphere." Cheth's confidence held firm. "If you say this fear is more than an instinctual reaction to the needles, then you must also say what they are afraid of."

Now it was Aleph's turn to be silent. She ordered multiple search configurations for the fear across the files of her people, but the searches brought no answers, only the knowledge that the fear existed.

Cheth was right. She had to say. But she did not have the answer.

What can I do? She could not ask her people. She could not whisper to them, *Why are you afraid of me? Why are you afraid of having your Conscience downloaded?* But that was where the answer lay, with her people.

Perhaps she could ask Tam. Tam was isolated while his stunted Conscience was regrown. Even Dionte was not in constant attendance, for she had a great deal of other work to do. Aleph opened the subsystem dedicated to his treatment and perused its records. Growing or expanding a Conscience in an adult brain always raised questions of pressure and balance and how best to insert the new filaments without disturbing the flow of either chemical or electrical signals. It would take time. While the regrowth commenced, Tam's responses to audio and chemical stimulation were being tested, tasted, and retrained as required.

Until all these adjustments were finished, Tam would have no significant contact with his family. That meant Tam could be questioned now in private and could not speak to anyone else until she had a chance to explain to him the reasons for the query.

Aleph copied her plan to the other city-minds. Cheth, of course, returned skepticism and the scent of spoiled roses, but no one raised any real objection. Aleph ordered an audio channel to Tam's Conscience to be opened. After a moment's hesitation, she closed the channel to the convocation. It was true, they needed all the information she had, especially to understand this new idea, but they did not need to hear Tam's raw thoughts.

"Tam?" Aleph spoke into his Conscience.

Her monitors tasted fatigue chemicals along with the varieties of guilt and peace to which he was being resensitized. This was to be expected. The analysis and retraining had been going on for eight hours now. Soon the treatment would cycle into a rest period, which would allow Tam to sleep, giving his mind time to dream and adjust to the new emotional information it contained.

Aleph had to struggle with herself a minute, because her need contradicted procedure, but she instructed the caretaker system to begin the rest cycle now. Then, reluctantly, she interrupted the alert command that would have told Dionte that something unusual was happening to one of her charges.

The system complied, withdrawing the chemical stimulation slowly and allowing Tam's internal processes to reassert themselves.

"Tam?" repeated Aleph softly.

Tam's heart rate spiked in time with a surge of fear through his mind. She had startled him.

"I'm sorry. Tam, I have a question to ask you."

"Yes?" His voice was thick and slow and he stirred restlessly in the chair.

"Why does the download of a person's Conscience create fear?"

A rasping, bubbling laugh escaped Tam, accompanied by a mix of incredulity and confusion, followed fast by guilt. This was normal for someone who had just begun a Conscience readjustment. Guilt and anxiety followed every thought.

"I'm sorry. I'm sorry," Tam said rapidly. "I did not mean that. But I do not understand. I want to understand. I want to help."

"I know." Aleph manifested the old woman image that Tam was most comfortable with on the ceiling of the room where he could see it. "I have seen that people experience fear whenever it is time for the Conscience download. This does not just happen to you. This is common to all my people. I want to understand why this is. So, I am asking you." That was not entirely true, but at least it was not a lie. Things had not gone so far yet that she had to lie. Not letting Dionte know what was happening was not the same as lying.

Fear, guilt, worry—that was all Tam could feel. His worry echoed inside Aleph. Could this be good? This was the procedure she had been taught. It had been laid down inside her when the Consciences had been developed. The Consciences that had been needed to keep the family together because the city-minds had failed in their mission as caretakers and advisers. Had they failed again? She had assisted in the administration of the treatment a few dozen times over the centuries and never thought to question it. But now . . . now . . .

Now things had changed.

"We are afraid you will find out we did something wrong," whispered Tam. Even as he spoke, the levels of fear inside him began to subside. Aleph wondered why. "We fear that when you find we have done something wrong, you will act to change us. It is for the good, I know it is for the good," he added swiftly as fresh guilt flooded him. "But it still frightens us."

Aleph made her image nod. "I believe I understand."

"Please," said Tam. New fear built inside him, and yet he fought to speak again, fought the fear, fought the guilt, fought all the responses that had been freshly conditioned into him. "Please."

"What is it, Tam?" asked Aleph as gently as she could. "You can tell me. It is all right."

"Stop this. You can kill me instead. Anything." Tears shone in his eyes. "Don't let her touch me."

Aleph stared at him in stunned silence. This was not a sane statement. Sometimes her people with severe chemical imbalances did make such irrational requests. They would be given counseling and readjustment, but Tam was already being readjusted, and would be counseled, by herself and by his family.

"Her?"

Tam's whole body struggled to speak the words. "Dionte. Please. Don't let her touch me."

Dionte, his sister and Guardian. Why would he ask this?

Because she was directing his treatment. Because she was ordering the changes in him. Because he was afraid. Because the treatment of his Conscience had made him even more afraid than the Conscience itself had. So afraid he no longer wanted to live.

And if fear can cause someone to desire death, how much easier would it be for that person to desire control of the thing that causes the fear?

It was all the fear. The fear that the city-minds and the ancestors had engendered but failed to see, and failed again to take action against.

The ancestors were dead and could no longer do anything. That left only the city-minds to make this right.

"Rest, Tam," said Aleph. "You will not be touched again."

Aleph fled back to the convocation. Before they'd even formally acknowledged her arrival, she spilled out the new learning Tam had given her. Silence and yet more silence filled her while the others absorbed what she brought and came to understand.

"I am causing searches and correlations," said Cheth. "There may be a match, but I cannot yet say."

"There will be," said Aleph, for once feeling as sure as Cheth always sounded. "The Consciences have brought the fear, and that fear has caused our people to act against us."

"The only question left is, what are we to do?"

Not one of the city-minds had an answer.

CHAPTER FIFTEEN

Athena

The smell hit Teal as soon as she stepped out of the space cable car. Athena Station had always carried an odor of metal, grease, and people. She just didn't remember it being so strong. But the walls felt close and comfortable, just like she hoped they would, and Teal figured she'd soon readjust to the smell.

Teal picked up the pace to get ahead of the pack of her fellow passengers. The car had, of course, stopped at the docking ring. Several dozen people wearing tattered, mismatched clothing that Teal didn't recognize from anywhere had gotten on, making the last day of the trip crowded and uncomfortable. She had tried starting conversations with them, but they just looked at her sideways and turned their backs, preferring to talk to each other in whatever their own language was.

Never mind, she told herself. *They're nobody you need to worry about.*

Right now what she did have to worry about was finding a cheap room that she could use as a base of operations, just in case it took a few days to get to the Authority. She didn't know how long all the inquiries would stretch out, so she would have to ration her money carefully.

Teal passed by the elevators. Those were for shippers and other transients. Real Athenians always used the stairs, even if they were walking down the entire length of one arm and up the next.

But when she reached the hatchway to the stairwell, Teal stopped and stared. The hatch had been closed. Hatches to the stairs were never closed, unless there had been some kind of emergency, like a leak in the pipes or a pinhole in the outer hull. But the hatch's display screen was blank. If there was an emergency, a message would be displayed.

Teal hesitated, but then she undogged the hatch with a remembered twist of her wrist. When no alarms rang, she pushed it open, and froze.

The stairway had become a city. People crammed themselves onto every landing and onto most of the steps in between. Kids, some of them half naked, some of them fully naked, raced up and down between the adults. Clusters of them dangled off the railings, and no one stopped them, unless they seemed in actual danger of dropping all the way down the shaft. Lines had been strung from the railings and the support beams to hold bundles of cloth or even pieces of pierced scrap metal. Hammocks woven of knotted cable and optic had been strung from the railing to the pipes that ran down the middle of the stairwell. Some of them held nameless bundles, some of them held people. The noise of too many voices and too many footsteps bounced off the walls so the shaft filled with one continual, incomprehensible swirl of noise.

Teal gaped. She couldn't help it. How could anybody have let this happen? This broke several billion regulations. What happened if the bulkheads had to be shut? Or even if one of the pipes sprang a leak? How would maintenance get to it? Where were the superiors? What had happened to all the warning alarms? Never mind that she had hated all such rules. Never mind that she had broken regulations whenever she could. She had still known they were there to keep the station safe. Everybody knew that. Everybody but the people living in the stairwell.

Who are all of you? What are you doing in my home?

A few heads turned toward her, revealing dirty, wrinkled faces that reminded her of the dormers on Pandora and the people from the docking ring. They eyed her sourly and she saw them mouth things at her, but their words were lost in the general clamor.

Teal closed the hatch, a little ashamed at how her hands shook. They were just airheads. No matter how many of them there were, they were just people who couldn't afford a room. She remembered teasing their kind along with King and Eng, and even with Chena, before Chena decided she was the righteous one. But what was going on here? Why were there so many of them?

Doesn't matter. Teal shook her head. The only important thing here was that there was no going up the stairs. She'd have to take the elevator.

Teal all but ran back to the elevator cluster. One of the doors had just opened and a crowd of drones, shippers, and harassed-looking dockworkers shuffled into the car. Teal slipped in behind them and squeezed into an empty spot in the front corner. The doors closed and the elevator began its ascent.

Teal scanned the tired and impatient faces around her on the off chance she'd see someone she recognized from before. But they were all strangers to her. Teal's stomach tightened. Maybe she hadn't come home after all.

The elevator door opened before Teal realized she hadn't pressed a destination key. A dockworker, his green parrot bobbing restlessly on his shoulder, shepherded out a flock of small drones and Teal peeked into the corridor. An apartment level, one of the not-so-good ones. Its floor padding was scuffed and badly patched, and the walls didn't even have amateur art to decorate them. But there would be a landlord outlet, and she needed someplace cheap anyway. At least it didn't look like there was anybody living in the hall. Teal slipped out just as the door began to close.

The others hustled along the wall and disappeared around the curve. Teal, left alone, realized what else was wrong. There were not only no airheads, there were no people in the hall. She glanced at her comptroller, which she had reset for station time. Like the villages, the station ran on shifts, and it was time for the change from day to swing. That is, it should have been. The place should have been crowded with gossiping families, door-to-door merchants, and kids getting out of class.

Teal shoved her hand through her hair. *What happened?* she wondered for the thousandth time. Should she maybe knock on a door, try to find an actual person to talk to? Was the place quarantined or something? Had one of those dirty, naked people brought the Diversity Crisis to Athena? But there hadn't been any alarms when she walked out. But then, who knew if the alarms were working anymore?

"Hey!"

Teal froze, her heart hammering in her throat. Running footsteps echoed down the hall behind her. She started to turn, but as she did, hands grabbed her and twisted her arms behind her back. Another hand shoved down on the top of her head, forcing her to her knees. The floor bit hard and she shrieked involuntarily.

"Thought you'd sneak out, did you?" growled a man's rough voice. "Thought you'd try to set up one of your filthy little tents right here, did you?"

"No! No! I'm not . . ." She twisted in their grasp and managed to get her head forced up to see their faces, and she froze again.

King and Eng. There was no mistaking them. King Prahti had a huge, hooked nose and high cheekbones that made him always look a little starved, no matter how much he ate. Eng Dor, he was still built like a brick, only now it was a much bigger brick with a light in the back of his black eyes that chilled Teal down to her bones. They looked at her like she was worse than a stranger. They saw an intruder.

"Lying squatter!" shouted Eng, jerking on her arms until she felt like her joints were about to pop.

"No! Eng, it's me!" she cried. "Teal Trust!"

That at least got them both to hold still for a second.

"You used to scrounge with my sister Chena." She gasped against the pain growing in her arms. "And tell me lies to see if you could get me to set off the alarms. We used to rip off the dumpsters, and once we almost got thrown in the can because Crazy Mary actually got the superiors to listen to her about the blankets—"

"Piss!" exclaimed King, and he crouched in front of her, searching her face. "Teal? But you're . . . you left, down to Pandora."

She nodded and gave him a watery grin. "I'm back."

"Nobody comes back," said Eng suspiciously. He hadn't loosened his grip on her at all.

"Shut up, Eng, or I'll tell your mother on you. Your ears will ring for a week." Boxing ears was Jesmena Dor's favorite way of punishing her eight children. Eng was probably too big for it now, but Teal got to see him blanch. A moment later, he let go.

"Sorry, Teal." He stepped back, giving her room to stand.

"'S okay," she told him, rubbing her wrists. She was going to be bruised. "How the piss were you gonna know?"

"And you've . . ." King's eyes wandered up and down her body. "Changed."

"I had help," she muttered, and with a grunt she got up off the floor. "Now, what's the squirt? How come you tackled me?"

"Thought you were a squatter." Eng shrugged. He stopped when he saw the incomprehension on her face. "You don't know?"

"They don't tell us piss down there." Teal rolled her shoulders, trying to work some of the burning out. "What should I know?"

King folded his arms and looked angrily at the wall. "The Authority dumped a whole bunch of Crisis refugees on us five, six, years ago, now. And instead of hauling them out again, like they were supposed to, the directors decided they should let them stay. Not only that, but they keep bringing in more and more." He shook his head.

"Director begged the hothousers for help, or at least he said he did." Eng's snort showed what he thought of that. "They said they could"—his voice changed, becoming slick and cultured—"absorb a hundred screened specimens, but no more than that." He snorted again. "The rest of them decided, since there weren't any rooms for them to rent, they'd take over a few."

"There was a fight?"

King nodded again. "Should've shoved all of them out the airlock. But Director Shontio lost his nerve. Said they're all going down to Pandora one way or another. This is all the Pandorans' fault, he says, the Pandorans can take care of it. Well—" He threw out his arms and spun around. "They keep coming in, but ain't none of them leaving."

"It's been short rations practically since you left," said Eng. "And short water. There's a black market like you wouldn't believe, and a lot of it's run by the squatters. They tap the pipes from the stairs."

"If we didn't keep the food lines under control, they'd be all over us," added King.

The weight of the news staggered Teal, but she shoved it aside. It had nothing to do with her. All that mattered was getting to the Authority.

"Listen, guys, I need a room. Are the bureaus still up?"

"Not for at least a year," said King. "Hate to tell you, Teal, but there aren't any rooms."

"What do you mean? There's always something." Sometimes it was monstrously expensive, but there was always something.

"Not anymore. The director made a deal with the airheads to give them extra rooms when the squatters started taking up the halls." King looked like he wanted to spit. "So now we're paying for their rent on top of ours. It's all piss and smoke now, Teal. Nothing decent left up here."

"You could stay with me, Teal," suggested Eng.

Teal hesitated. She knew Eng was just a kid and a talker and it was a good offer. She did need to hole up somewhere, but this new woman's body she was trapped in wanted to squirm at the idea. Maybe it was the memory of how he had just knocked her flat just because.

"Thanks, but not," she told him. "I've got to find my own place. I've got . . . stuff to do."

King shook his head again. "We're telling you, Teal. There's nothing."

"So let me piss away a little time." Teal shrugged. "What's it to you?"

The boys—men, really—exchanged skeptical glances. King turned away first, his gaze wandering up and down the blank walls like he couldn't believe what he'd just heard.

"Okay," said Eng for both of them. "Your time, not mine. But I wouldn't let the superiors catch you sleeping in the hall. They'll take your head off."

"Nice to know some things haven't changed," said Teal blandly.

They all chuckled at that. "Watch out for yourself." Eng held out his hand and they brushed palms and backs, touching their foreheads to each other, a kids' salute Teal wouldn't have realized she even remembered. "And I'm still in the same hole if you need anything."

"Thanks." She saluted King, who returned it more out of reflex than friendship. When she pulled her hand away, he smacked Eng on the shoulder and the two of them sauntered down the hall like they were on patrol or something.

Maybe they are.

Teal folded her arms around herself and stared at the blank walls and dingy doors, trying to think. Obviously finding a squat on her own was a no-go. So only one thing to do.

Head straight for the Authority. They could put her up while they tracked down a city slot for her, or Dad. After all, what if it turned out that the stories they'd been telling all these years were true and

Dad really was on some kind of mission? Or maybe his ship had just gotten stranded somewhere? It happened all the time. Everybody knew that. The Authority might still find him, wherever he was. Then she'd tell him what had been going on all these years and he'd cry and hug her and call her Starlet, and she'd live with him in El Dorado or Atlantis or one of the other cities, and she'd help him with . . . with whatever he was doing, and they'd be a family, a real family. Not like her and Chena. Nothing like that at all.

With her arms still wrapped around herself, Teal walked rapidly down the hallway.

The most likely place to find the Authority reps, Teal decided, was the directorate. This time, she stuck to the elevators. Athena Station was four arms rotating around a central core that held the power plants, air processors, and the other machinery of living. Arms One and Two held living quarters. Arms Three and Four were given over to manufacturing whatever Pandora needed, which the Athenians traded for food and water.

Administrative offices were distributed between all four arms, but the directorate was concentrated in Arm One. Teal had come in on Arm Two, so she'd have to get across in one of the connectors.

The elevator door opened onto a corridor jammed with people. Teal stepped out, momentarily stunned by the size of the crowd. It wasn't in motion, though. The people all stood in a line. Well, some of them sat or squatted in the line. Most of them carried a pack or a case of some kind. A few had droids, dogs, or ferrets on tethers. None of the machines or the animals ran free.

"What's going on?" Teal asked a woman who balanced a duffel roll on her broad shoulder.

The woman gave her a look of pure contempt for such ignorance. "Checkpoint. No cutting the line, girly." She jerked her chin up the corridor.

Checkpoint? For what? Then Teal remembered all those strangers in the stairwells, and all King's and Eng's tough talk. Had there been trouble? Had there been a breakout of some kind, maybe?

Well, it's okay. Teal took her place in line behind a pair of men whose gray tunics had bright gold electrician's badges on them. Four banded ferrets used the men as a climbing gym. The restless animals chased each other in and out of pockets and around shoulders and ankles.

Watching their antics made the wait feel short and left Teal in a much better mood than she'd started out in.

At last she could see the checkpoint between the heads and shoulders of people in front of her, or rather she could see the pair of superiors who were working the checkpoint. But instead of the tan tunics and blue trousers she was familiar with, the superiors now wore black body armor and radio helmets. They carried tasers and pellet guns on their belts. If they were supposed to look menacing, it worked. Teal's throat tightened. She and Chena had spent hours on mischief as kids, seeing if they could get the superiors to come chase them, but those superiors hadn't been armed with anything more than cameras and old rules.

But that wasn't the only change. The bulkhead had been turned into a choke point with bulky scanners welded to the struts. Multiple cameras watched the people coming in, the people passing through, the superiors, the length of the line, and who knew what else.

Each person stopped in front of the superiors. Teal couldn't hear the questions they asked, but she couldn't help noticing the process took a lot longer for people without badges on their tunics than for those with some kind of official marking. Bags and cases were opened and searched, as were droids. Animals were prodded, sometimes until they yelped.

Another few shuffles forward, and Teal could see they also examined sheet screens and printouts.

Sheets?

Teal rubbed the chip on the back of her hand. She hadn't expected her identity to be questioned. Then again, she thought she was going back to the Athena she knew and that knew her.

Up ahead, a woman bent under the weight of her pack handed her sheets over to the superiors. They read them and shook their heads. Her arms waved in the air, and they shook their heads. She reached into her trousers pockets, and the right-hand superior reached for his taser. The woman turned away, and the line made reluctant room for her as she picked her way back down the connector.

Teal swallowed. What were they asking for? What did they need? They'd only read her chip at the base of the cable. No one had said anything about needing anything else.

Of course, she hadn't exactly come through official channels. She ground her teeth together. Damn the tailor. He should have known about this. The cheat. He should have told her.

Now what do I do?

When she was a kid, she could get away with murder by looking innocent. But no matter what she really was, she didn't look like a kid anymore. Those superiors in their armor with their weapons probably weren't going to believe any adult was innocent, no matter how that adult looked.

One of the ferrets whisked up its owner's shoulder and regarded her with bright black eyes for a moment before it tried to vanish into its owner's pack.

Unless maybe they are distracted. Unless maybe the adult looks ridiculous.

The man caught the ferret around the middle with one broad brown hand. "Come on, Biscuit. Nothing for you in there."

Biscuit didn't seem to believe it. As soon as he (she?) was on the floor, he scuttled up his owner and dove for the pack.

This time, Teal caught him.

"Whoa." She held the animal up to her face, like she knew and liked it. "You don't listen, do you?" Its short legs paddled a little and its nose twitched. Teal laughed as she handed him back. "Probably bored," she remarked.

"Wouldn't be the only one." The man cradled Biscuit in one arm and reached up to pluck a second ferret off the top of his head. "Come on, guys, we're almost there."

"How old are they?" she asked, remembering how Mom always struck up conversations with people who had children.

Apparently it worked just as well with people who had animals. She found herself introduced to Biscuit (three years old), Brownie (three and a half), Cookie (four and a half, the senior ferret), and Creampuff (two). They were industrial ferrets, trained to pull wires and fiber-optic cables through narrow conduits. They were, he explained, especially valuable since the squatters started arriving in force, what with nobody being sure which maintenance tunnels they were going to be able to get to easily.

"By the way, I'm Claudiu." He gave her a jaunty salute and Teal returned it.

"Teal."

Cookie and Biscuit took this opportunity to run up her body. Teal shrieked, just a little, she couldn't help it, and she and Claudiu spent the next few minutes disentangling ferrets and ferret harnesses from her hair.

"Definitely bored." Claudiu laughed.

"We have a cage," drawled his partner, who had been watching the entire proceeding through half-lidded eyes.

"And they hate it worse than the leashes. Lighten up, LaRoche." He put Cookie on LaRoche's shoulders, and LaRoche firmly, but not unkindly, put Cookie on the floor again.

"Look—" LaRoche began.

"Hang on," interrupted Claudiu. "We're up."

But Creampuff was trying to get into the pack again, and Biscuit and Brownie were playing tag around LaRoche's shoulders while Claudiu was trying to apologize to the superiors and the rest of the line.

Which was Teal's chance.

"I'll take them," she said quickly, gathering up ferrets and leashes until she had a whole armful.

"Thanks," said Claudiu, handing Creampuff across to her.

What happened next was predictable, and exactly what Teal had hoped for. It took a split second for the ferrets to realize she was no ferret expert. Biscuit hurried up her shoulders, but the other three twitched themselves out of her hands and scampered straight through the scanners.

"The ferrets!" Teal dove through the checkpoint, grabbing for the trailing leashes.

"Oh, God's own!" cried LaRoche exasperatedly.

Teal made straight for the long, furry creatures, but the ferrets were not going to give their freedom up easily. They flew up the scanners, bulkheads, and bystanders. When yanked or shaken off, they twisted their leashes around ankles and brought those same bystanders crashing to the floor. Teal measured her length on the deck several times, diving for leashes or flashes of fur. Those not actually under ferret attack started laughing, and the laughter spread until it rang off the patched walls. Teal risked a glance at the superiors and saw both of them snickering as they handed Claudiu and LaRoche back their papers.

Finally Claudiu waded into the fray. He pulled a handful of brown nuggets out of his pocket and scattered them on the deck. Instantly all four ferrets appeared in the middle of the spread, picking little treats up in their forepaws and nibbling happily. Teal gathered up their leashes and handed them over to their owner.

"Thanks," she said, straightening up. Without waiting for his answer, she turned and strode down the corridor, heading for the thickest part of the crowd.

No one called her back. No one did anything except try to find room to walk or to stop and wait for an elevator.

Score, thought Teal happily as she joined the elevator crowd.

There were lots more superiors in Arm One. They marched in groups of four up and down the hallways, peering at every passerby, occasionally stopping them and demanding sheets and passes. Teal kept her head down so that her hair partially curtained her face, and tried not to walk too fast. She also tried not to worry too much about whether she'd be able to get into the directorate offices once she got there.

Thankfully, there were no more checkpoints. But the farther she went, the wider and starker the corridors became, until finally they had been pared back to the original plates. There weren't even any info screens. All the panels had been scrubbed and resealed until they gleamed under the bare fluorescent panels that glowed overhead without even attempting to imitate sunlight. Teal wondered if this section was even on the daylight rotation anymore. The people walking past her looked peaked somehow, as if they were short on sleep, or real light, or both. Most of them had three or more different kinds of badges on their sleeves, and only a few of those looked familiar.

Overcrowding had evidently brought serious reorganization. Teal resisted the urge to touch her unmarked shoulder. If somebody stopped her, she'd deal with it then.

But nobody did. Teal just kept on walking past yards of bare walls, across a floor that all but echoed when she stepped on it. Chena had said a billion times that if you acted like you belonged someplace, pretty much everybody would assume you did.

Looks like she got something right after all. A memory of Chena holding her tight and saying they had to look after each other now welled up in Teal. She shoved it away. Like Chena had really looked after her, running off to go get herself maybe ripped open by the hot-housers because Nan Elle told her to, and because she wanted a few days alone with her lover-boy.

The directorate was one of those places you couldn't miss. Even back when Teal had known it, its reinforced silver archway took up the breadth of the corridor. Information and dedicated credit terminals stood sentry outside the entrance in between desk banks of superiors and moderators who were there to route citizens into the proper offices or files.

Much to Teal's relief, all that remained intact. The superiors were armed and armored now, of course, and wired plastic and intercoms encased the desks, and there was nobody clogging the way to them, like there used to be. Still, they were all there.

Let's hope they're all there to be used. Wrapping her mind around that wish, Teal walked up to the nearest nonsuperior desk bank.

Three women and two men sat in individual shatterproof boxes. Teal picked the woman nearest to the pass-through on the grounds she might need to run for it.

"Hello, citizen," said the woman as Teal approached. She sounded mechanical, and her downturned eyes were wary under a fringe of straight black hair. Teal's hand went up automatically to smooth back her own hair.

"Hello," she said, stopping what she hoped was a comfortable distance from the shatterproof. "But I'm not a citizen. I'm with the Authority and I need to get a message out to them."

The woman stared at Teal blankly for a moment, as if the input refused to register.

"I'm sorry." The woman blinked and pulled herself upright. "You said you were with the Authority? You're not in uniform."

Teal gave her a watery smile. "I know. It's a long story. Could you just please put me in touch with the official rep?"

The woman frowned and poked at her keys for a moment. Teal wished she could lean over and see what was coming up on the screen. Her heart fluttered inside her, despite all her efforts to stay calm. It would be all right. She'd be talking to the Authority in a minute. She'd tell them everything. It would be all right. . . .

The woman's whole face creased into a frown, but then it cleared as she reached her decision. Hope joined the fear spreading up Teal's heart. The info worker lifted her hand and beckoned—to the woman next to her, Teal thought.

But it was one of the superiors who moved. Teal's legs rooted her to the floor. Before she could force them to run, the superior was there, hand on his belt.

"We've got a rogue," said the woman, nodding at Teal. "Got through the checkpoint without processing. Better put her in holding until we can sort her out. She claims to be with the Authority, so don't mess her up."

"No," said Teal as the superior closed his gloved hand around her arm. "Listen. My name is Teal Trust. I used to live here. My father is a citizen of the Authority, and he retained his rights. That makes me Authority. You can check the records. Please."

"Your case will be thoroughly examined," said the woman, but she wasn't even looking at Teal anymore, and the superior's pull was too strong to ignore. Her joints began to strain and Teal had to stumble along beside him.

"Look," she said desperately to the side of his helmet, which was all she could see. "I just want to get a message to them. I belong with the Authority." She swiveled her head back and forth, trying to get someone, anyone, to listen to her. "I'm not a stationer, not really, not anymore. I just want . . ." Two people strode through the directorate bulkhead. One was a multibadged individual, some station official, but the other wore Authority blue and commander's braid.

"Commander!" Teal lunged for the woman and the superior yanked her back, almost popping her arm out of joint. "Please! I'm Authority! My Dad, I'm—I'm one of yours, please, Commander!"

Pain shot through every nerve in Teal's body, jolting her off her feet. She sagged toward the floor, her head spinning, but the superior hoisted her up with a rough arm around her shoulders.

“Commander Poulos?” said the woman behind the shatterproof. “She says she’s with you.”

Yes, yes, Teal wanted to say, but her mouth wouldn’t move. She wasn’t even sure her tongue was in her mouth anymore.

The commander looked her up and down and then looked into her eyes for a long time. “You’re Authority? What’s your city?”

Teal concentrated and was finally able to make her mouth work. “Atlantis.”

“Atlantis?” The commander frowned. “What are you doing over here?”

“I was born here, but . . .” The commander’s face grew distant and Teal felt her hopes plunge. “My Dad’s city is Atlantis. His name is Trust. Varish Trust. He’s a shipper.”

The man beside her—the station director, Teal realized with a start—frowned at the commander. “Beleraja . . .”

The commander sighed. “I know, but if she’s from a shipper’s family, I’ve got to take the plea.” The director looked startled and the commander just shook her head. “There are some things that don’t go away.” The director did not look convinced and Teal’s heart plummeted. But the commander tried again. “Can I use your auxiliary office to run a check?”

The director turned to study Teal. “All right,” he said. “We should find out who we’re dealing with here, I suppose.” He sized up the superior, who was still holding on to Teal’s arm. “Thank you, Lieutenant. I will take her under my supervision.”

“With respect, Director—”

The director held up one hand to cut the superior off. “You will, however, escort us to my office and remain outside until you are dismissed.”

The superior relaxed visibly at this and let go of Teal’s arm. She couldn’t help but notice, however, his hand went straight to his taser and stayed there.

Both the commander and director turned away then and started walking her into the depth of the directorate offices. Her heart fluttering high in her throat, Teal followed.

The station director’s offices were a lot smaller than Teal could ever have imagined. There was just a desk, some chairs, and four video walls displaying a dizzying array of images from all sections of the station. The director touched a spot on the desk and the walls went instantly black.

Director Shontio sat down behind his desk, folding his chapped red hands and resting them on its smooth surface. Commander Poulos motioned Teal to a side door. Throat tight and hands cold, Teal followed her into the next room. This one was even smaller than the director's public space, and it only had one chair, but it did have a comm terminal.

The commander sat herself at the code board. The motion lit the wall screen. "You said his liege city is Atlantis?" she asked.

"Yes." Teal came to stand beside Commander Poulos, her palms sweating. She couldn't believe it. The commander was going to send a message. She was going to find Dad. "How long is it going to take?"

"First I'm going to see what records our ship has on him." Commander Poulos's hands moved across the keys, entering a series of commands too quickly for Teal to follow. "We keep pretty good track of the family trees." A data tree of ships and family names organized by city appeared on the screen. "Varish Trust, I think you said?"

"Yes." Her heart pounded so hard that her ears rang. After all this time, after all this trying, she would find him. She would send him a message, and he would come get her out of this. "My . . . my mother tried to find him. . . ."

"Your mother may have been working with old data. The comm lags for interstellar communication are incredible. There are so many leaks on the stations that most shippers prefer to carry hard data to each other by hand." Her mouth twitched, as if she were trying to decide whether to smile or frown. "We've recently had an update here, however."

Commander Poulos's hands moved again. Fresh trees flitted across the screen as the station's comptroller searched its files and Commander Poulos discarded them before Teal could even properly read them. Then the screen stilled.

"You found him?" Teal gripped the back of Commander Poulos's chair, but she couldn't make her eyes read the words in front of her.

Commander Poulos scanned the display. "It's him," she said softly, swiveling the chair so it would be easier for Teal to see past her.

Teal leaned forward, resting her hand against the edge of the board. At the top of the screen she read:

> Varish Trust
>
> Ship's mechanic aboard the *Imperial*. Blood son of Jask Trust and Teal Aramant. No official ship family. Jumped ship in orbital port of First Home (coordinates listed). Citizenship and all voting privileges revoked for dereliction and desertion. Last reported residence Athena Station of Pandora (coordinates listed), reapplied for citizenship renewal upon joining Tuskay ship caravan at age 43. Found dead of alcoholic overdose and brawling injuries in orbital port 4 of Cayman's Stop at age 44.

No. No. No. Teal swallowed hard, reading the words over, hoping they'd change and knowing they never would.

Found dead of alcoholic overdose and brawling injuries.

Found dead. . .

"I'm sorry," said Commander Poulos.

Teal's knees began to shake. "He left us," she murmured.

"Here, sit." Commander Poulos pushed on her shoulders, and she found the chair under her.

"He left us to go get drunk and die." Hot red anger flooded her heart and head. "Bastard!" she screamed, slamming both fists against the screen. "You bastard! You left us to get drunk and die! You left us down there! You killed Mom, you pissing, drunk bastard!"

She fell back, tears turning the world to a blur of colors and her own sobs drowning out all other noises. Commander Poulos tried to put her arms around Teal, but Teal shoved her away. She bowed her head into her hands and sobbed and screamed until her throat burned and she had no more tears inside her.

The sound of Teal Trust's sobs followed Beleraja as she returned to Shontio's main office.

"Sounds like someone else got bad news," he said softly, gesturing toward the door as it closed.

Beleraja dropped into one of the office chairs. A chill ran through her. What more could be happening? "What do you mean?"

In answer, Shontio reached out and touched a command key on his desktop. A section of wall screen lit up to show a thunderous Father Mihran. "Since you do not choose to acknowledge my call, Director . . ." He dragged out the title. Surprise sped up Beleraja's heart. She had never heard Father Mihran talk like this. "I will leave you this message. A fugitive named Teal Trust has either lately arrived or will shortly arrive on Athena Station. You will institute a search for her at once, and when you find her you will return her immediately. If I do not hear from you on this matter within one week, we will have to assume that she is being harbored aboard Athena in violation of the treaty your ancestors signed with mine."

The message cut off and the screen faded to black.

"What did she do?" Beleraja croaked. Her mouth seemed to have gone dry.

Shontio touched his swollen knuckles gently, as if trying to gauge whether the arthritis had gotten worse in the last few minutes. "Does it matter?" he said softly. "They want her back. Badly. At the very least she got up here under a set of false passes and a fake ID, a practice which is illegal on both ends of the pipe. Something Father Mihran was quick to remind me of."

Beleraja gazed straight to the closed inner door. "Are you going to give her up?"

"When is our first wave getting here?"

Beleraja bowed her head. "It could be tomorrow. It could be in as long as two weeks. Calculating relative times when making hyperspace jumps is"—she waved her hands—"difficult."

"Then I'm going to give her up."

Distress tightened Beleraja's face. She had gotten used to thinking of people in groups. A few thousand needed to be in this place, at this time, to perform this set of tasks. At that same time, another thousand would be needed over here to perform this other task. She'd forgotten to think of those thousands in terms of the individuals that comprised them, single human beings being displaced, hurt, or ruined by all these schemes—her invasion, the Pandorans' cure, the Authority's desperate attempt to maintain the status quo. Beleraja had forgotten them all, until she'd seen Teal Trust's own plans fall to ashes in front of her eyes.

"Shontio, we don't know what they'll do to her down there. We're almost ready to start. Our people are on their way. . . ."

"But they are not here yet." Shontio got up and circled his desk. "And there are not going to be nearly enough of them when they do get here."

"So, we start early. We shut down the cable, we take over the satellites. We're going to do it anyway." She ran her hand through her hair. "And I am sick of waiting."

"And we run out of food two weeks earlier than we have to because you got impatient," Shontio said. "No, Bele. The girl has got to go back."

"And if the fleet gets in tomorrow?"

"Then we pull her right back up the pipe." Shontio's face twisted, and Beleraja thought she saw tears. "We are not going to be able to do this without casualties. You were the one who pointed that out to me." He touched his knuckles again. "If you want, I'll tell her. I ran her name through our records. It turns out she's originally one of mine."

"No." Beleraja stood up. "I'll tell her. I have a feeling that delivering bad news is something I'm going to have to get very used to."

When Teal managed to look up again she was alone in the little office. A cup of water had been left on the edge of the comm board, along with a clean white towel.

Teal was surprised at how steady she was as she got to her feet. She wiped her face dry on the towel and drained the cup in one gulp. She felt . . . still, dry. Dad was dead. He'd been dead for years. He wasn't even really an Authority citizen. He was just dead.

"Teal?" Someone knocked on the door.

"Yes?" She turned her head. Commander Poulos stepped through the threshold.

"Are you all right?"

She nodded.

"I am sorry about your father. You must have been hoping very hard."

"Yeah, well . . ." Teal looked down at the empty cup. "Turns out it was all a bunch of stupid stories. I knew that anyway."

Commander Poulos said nothing.

Teal set the cup back on the board's edge. "I guess you're going to send me back to Pandora?"

Commander Poulos rubbed her thumbnail gem against her trousers leg. "Not because I want to," she said quietly. "But the director has found out you're wanted by the Pandorans. You didn't tell us you broke the law to get up here."

Her words sank in, leaving Teal cold and leaden. It had been for nothing. Her grand scheme for escape. All the Pandorans had needed to do was tell the director who she was, and now . . . now there was nothing.

"What else haven't you told us, Teal?"

Teal stared at the blank screen above the command pad. In the distance she heard a dull voice explaining how the hothousers had herded them all under the dome, about the Eden Project, and how Mom had died, how they'd escaped and lived with Nan Elle until Teal had thought of a way to leave Pandora for good.

She stopped there. Commander Poulos already knew how it ended.

"Teal . . ."

The sound of her name made Teal blink and turn her head back toward Commander Poulos. But the commander wasn't looking at her. She was looking at her own hands, at the wall past Teal's shoulder, at the door. "You should know . . ." Commander Poulos stopped, and began again. "I know it's no comfort, but I believe Director Shontio doesn't want to send you back either."

"It's okay," said Teal in a small voice, even though she couldn't help feeling that those words were not the ones Commander Poulos had wanted to say. "It's okay."

Commander Poulos's face tightened as if she were in pain. "You should know . . ." she said again. "If you can just hang on. If you ever need help, you can . . ." She opened her mouth, closed it again, and rubbed her thumbnail gem hard against the side of her leg. "You can call on me, Teal."

"Thank you."

"I'll walk you." Commander Poulos got to her feet and Teal could still feel something unspoken hanging in the air between them.

It didn't matter. There was nothing Commander Poulos could say to make it better. Teal stood. She couldn't see where she was going.

Nothing. Her grand plan had all come to nothing. She wanted to cry, but she couldn't. She couldn't do anything. Her feet were moving on their own, steered by Commander Poulos's firm hand under her elbow. Each step taking her closer to the Pandorans, closer to the hothouse, and the place where Mom had died. Died like Dad in a bleeding mess on the floor, and all for nothing.

Chena was right, she thought dully. *I should've stayed put.*

Well, that didn't matter either, because Teal would never be able to tell her so.

Dionte leaned over Tam in the observation chair. His face was pale, drawn, and tired. The eyes that looked back at her were sunken in their sockets.

She looked into his face and felt nothing, nothing at all. Her Conscience told her there should be something. She knew it was wrong that her brother should look at her like this, but she could not feel that wrong.

"Don't worry, Brother," she told him. "You are almost done." She made herself smile. That was the right thing to do. *Why can't I feel him?* "Only a few more adjustments."

"No," he whispered, and winced. "No more. I was promised no more."

"Just one more. Then you are done. Then we can talk."

A tear trickled down Tam's cheek and sadness hit Dionte so hard she curled her fist around the arm of the chair to keep from reeling backward. Why had he brought them to this? This was not the way it was supposed to be. They were supposed to work together for the family. He was supposed to have been beside her as they together saved Pandora. He was not supposed to be afraid of her.

What's happening, what's going on? She had to concentrate to keep from shaking her head to clear it out. She could not slip now. This was too important. She could not jeopardize the potential of the bond between herself and Tam, the first one they would truly share. This moment was too emotional, that was all. There was too much going on inside and outside at the same time, upsetting her balance. It would be all right again in a moment.

"It is just a matter of refining some synaptic connections in the implant filaments." She laid her hand on his and felt how cold it was. A thousand memories flickered through her mind. Games of tag in the family gardens. Quizzing each other for math and botany tests. The passionate debates about every subject under the sun. She tried to take comfort from the future shining so brightly before them. Soon she'd have Tam's stubborn, sharp-minded honesty to help her to think more clearly.

"You'll be glad to know that the Trusts will soon be home safe with us as well," she told him. "Teal is being returned as we speak, and Chena will be back soon as well."

"Trusts . . . No, they are safe where they are."

Dionte touched the probe's command keys, strengthening the hormonal surge by a fraction of a percent. "You trust me, don't you, Brother? I am your sister and you trust me."

"Yes," he said, the voice full of exhausted relief. "I trust you. I must trust you."

"Yes, that's right."

But his face twisted up the new struggle. "Aleph . . ."

"I'm here, Tam." Aleph's middle-aged woman appeared on the nearest wall. "Hello, Dionte."

"Hello, Aleph."

"I have no further adjustments on the schedule. Tam needs to rest and recover so that his Conscience may be fully integrated."

Dionte felt a spasm of annoyance. Of all the times for Aleph to question her. "You know that the growing of a Conscience in an adult is a delicate business. Numerous small adjustments must be made in order to assure proper integration, and sometimes it is not possible to schedule them all. This is one of those times."

"Dionte, I know you only wish to help your brother, but he is fatigued. Look at the monitors."

Dionte's patience snapped. She whirled toward the wall. "I am my brother's Guardian! This is my judgment. This is not even any of your business!"

Aleph's image folded its hands and bowed its head. "It is my job to advise my family."

"Well, then, you have advised! I have rejected your advice. That is my right. I will help my brother. I will help my family, and you will leave me to do my work!" She faced Tam in the chair again, trying to focus on the monitor and what it was telling her.

"Dionte . . ." said Aleph.

But Dionte did not turn around. She snapped the new cartridge in place and laid her hand on the input pad, subvocalizing the necessary commands.

"Aleph," she heard Tam say. "You promised—"

"Trust me, Brother," Dionte said firmly, as if speaking directly to his freshly active implant. "You know you must trust me."

"Yes," he breathed, a childlike whisper. Then, even more softly, she thought she heard him say, "Help."

"Hagin." Aleph opened her visual lines to the synapses. Hagin sat at his station in the cluster of monitors and desks where the tenders did most of their work. Absently she noted he was reviewing a follow-up report of her bimonthly examination.

"Aleph." Hagin flicked the display to the report's next page. "What can I do for you?"

"Hagin, there are records I want you to see. I am concerned about some aspect of my adjustments."

"Of course. Show me what is wrong."

Aleph saved the report and closed its file. Then she showed him all that she had showed the other city-minds.

While Hagin watched her records flow across his workstation screen, Aleph found Basante in Imaging Room Four, standing in the middle of three different fate maps, comparative readouts flashing across the walls.

"Basante."

"Aleph?" He did not take his eyes off the data. He lifted his hand to touch one minute line, adjusting its length a few centimeters.

"Aleph, I was hoping that you might speak with Dionte. You are her friend and an adviser to her, and I fear she has become distressed. I do not want to have to alert her committee yet. She may just need a friend."

Basante lowered his hand and blinked. "Of course, Aleph. If you think so."

"I do," Aleph said firmly.

"I'll go as soon as I'm done here."

"Thank you."

Aleph felt secure. This was what she should have done in the first place. She should have alerted the family, and not gone to Gem in hysterics. Dionte was troubled, that much was clear. Now her family knew. The family would take care of both her and Tam, as was right.

All would soon be well. This time, at least, she had done the right thing.

CHAPTER SIXTEEN

Under Cover

Chena peered between the reeds at the great white bubbles that made up the Alpha Complex. Gnats and mosquitoes swarmed around her, seeking a crack in her camouflage suit. Despite its protection, the chill from the hip-deep water soaked in. She shivered hard for a moment, from cold, but also from mounting hope. No one had come to get her. She had been standing here in a direct line of sight of the complex for an hour, after a long trek through the marshes, and no one, human or animal, had been sent out to grab her.

It's working. This time I got it right, she thought toward the shadow presence of Nan Elle hovering in the back of her mind.

"They find you by scent," she'd said to Nan Elle. "That's how the bugs found me. It's got to be." Ever since she got back from Peristeria, she'd been delving into the whys and hows of the hothousers' monitoring systems, looking for what she'd missed. They shouldn't have found her, but they did. So, even though she'd gotten away, she'd missed something. They still knew something she didn't, and that was no good. She didn't know how long it would take her to figure out what had gone wrong, but she was going to try. If nothing else, it kept her from wondering what was happening to Teal, wherever she had gone.

Chena combed through Nan Elle's books and all the library disks and databases in both Stem and Offshoot. She was not surprised that there was next to no information. The hothousers certainly didn't want their secrets to get out. But there were enough hints for her to see that the cyborged insects that patrolled Pandora did not really use cameras. They used transmitters that coded the responses of the cy-bugs' tiny brains, which meant the hothousers' computers received information from normal insect sensory impressions. Since insects relied primarily on scent, most of the analysis would have to be of suspicious chemical traces. Mask those chemical traces, mask your human scent, and you could walk unseen.

But Nan Elle was not ready to hear any of this. "You don't know that. We have no direct information on the mote cameras." Not even Administrator Tam could be induced to give away so much.

"We know they are using real bugs," Chena persisted. She was right about this. She knew it. She might have been wrong about everything else, she might have been completely wrong about Teal, but she was right about this. "We know they are not supposed to interfere with anything in the natural order. Who knows what it would do to the local insect populations if there were a few hundred fake bugs flying around in formation?"

Nan Elle had straightened her neck, like she always did when she was particularly disapproving. "It's a bad gamble, Chena. You should have learned that in Peristeria. You have your route into the hothouse. Let that be enough." A week ago, Farin had been passed a message from a man in Stem. It had come from someone inside the hothouse who wanted access to a certain narcotic compound that Nan Elle used for surgeries. Nan Elle had wanted to just send back a sample of the stuff via the connections she and Administrator Tam had set up, but Chena had convinced her that it would be useful to have more than one reliable contact in the hothouse. It had taken Nan Elle all of three seconds to guess what Chena really wanted—a way back into the hothouse, a chance to get to the hothouser computers, where she might be able to find out what had really happened to her mother. She also knew that Chena would never give up until she had gotten what she wanted, so she had reluctantly agreed.

"It's not enough," snapped Chena. It wasn't. Nothing would ever be enough until she had wormed every single secret out of the hothouse, until she knew enough that they could never steal another person from her. They were the real reason Teal ran away. They had Teal so scared she couldn't stand to live in Offshoot anymore. "You know why we've never been able to break their system? They have got us all locked in cages. We need to open the doors."

Nan Elle sighed and thumped her stick impatiently. "This is not about locks and cages, Chena, it never has been. This is about survival, for ourselves and our village. That is our work."

"You said you'd help me defy them," she shot back.

"Defy them, yes, but not conquer them." Nan Elle shook her head solemnly. "The villages and hothouses have been using each other for fifteen hundred years. It is the way it is here, and it will not change for your wishing, or your daring. Leave it."

"But—"

"Leave it." Nan Elle's eyes flashed. "You belong to me until you are an adult in your own right, and I have told you to leave it be."

But Chena couldn't leave it. She was right. She knew it. Confuse the cy-bugs with a different scent, something strong, but appropriate to the location—you couldn't go with a citrus, say, in the marsh, but there was plenty that could be done with mint and loosestrife. Use the concealing scent along with the camouflage suit to disguise both the chemical and visual signatures from her body, and Aleph would never know where she was.

She could stipulate to her client that part of the price was that he get her in through the marsh airlock. That way she could start training Aleph to get used to the idea of her coming and going through there. Before long, she'd have free access to the hothouse.

It could work; she could do it. She would do it.

She pleaded with Nan Elle. She coaxed, cajoled, and, in the end, threatened—to withhold her work, to run away, even to go to the constables, until, at last, Nan Elle brought her stick crashing down on the worktable.

"Enough. After all this time, after all your disasters, you still do not see . . ." Spittle flecked her lips, and Chena had cringed. Had she finally said too much?

But Nan Elle subsided and shuffled back to the stove, sniffing at the potions brewing there. "If you are determined to commit this suicide, you had better do it before you learn anything else that might harm the village when the hothousers dump your brain into the citymind. Oh, and when they do catch you, leave Tam's name out of it for as long as you can. I have no other insider to turn to."

So Chena had passed some additional conditions to her client, assembled her formulas, packed food and water, wrapped the camouflage suit in a bundle of old clothes, calculated the shortest route, and set out. She'd take the railbike to Stem, duck the fences at the lakeside, and set out overland to the marsh and hothouse.

Nan Elle said nothing to her as she left, and Chena had said nothing back. *Everything can be said when I get home,* thought Chena. *When she sees that I've found the missing piece of the equation.*

A clear blue twilight now settled over the marsh. As the light faded, the hothouse domes dimmed from white to pearl to gray. *Mustn't have an anomalous light source around at night,* thought Chena, pressing her lips tightly together. *It might upset the ducks.*

Now or never. There was just enough light left to see by, and it wouldn't last. Slowly, Chena began to wade through the swamp.

Mud sucked at her boots, making each step a struggle, but the waterfowl, ignorant of humans, seemed to think she was just another of their kind and only ruffled their wings as she passed. The frogs and crickets set up their own chorus at her movements, but they did that every time a bird moved too. She hoped that whatever monitors the hothousers had on them would not be alerted. The cy-bugs were most certainly the first line of defense. If they did not send out the wrong pulse, nothing else became active, and the cy-bugs thought she was a big cluster of water plants.

So far, anyway. She wondered if she should stop and make another application of her "insect repellent." Sweat prickled her skin. She'd be perspiring freely soon, and if the cy-bugs caught one whiff of her real scent, the interceptor teams would spring into action. This time she might not be able to run fast enough, or they might send more than two, and then she'd never get to see the look on Nan Elle's face when she found out what happened. Not even Nan Elle could get her out of the involuntary wing.

Wonder if Sadia's still in there. Maybe she is. Maybe, if this works, if I can start coming and going when I need to, I can pull her out. Maybe there is a way. The idea drained some of the fear out of her blood.

At last the muck began to slope gently upward. Fortunately the concealing reeds stayed about head-high. The water was soon thigh-deep, then knee-deep, then ankle-deep, and the reed curtain parted to make room for a jumble of waist-high plants and stiff, rough-skinned grasses.

Chena sank to her belly and began to crawl. Every fifty or so yards she stopped and mopped her face with a sponge soaked in her heavily scented goop. Her pack pressed her down into the rich earth. Her shoulders and arms protested each movement, and there were still a hundred yards to go.

Panting, Chena closed her mind to the overwhelming distance and concentrated on the way in front of her.

Knee, elbow, knee, elbow, breathe, breathe, breathe, don't worry about the stink, don't swat at the bugs, you might hit a camera, and that would alert somebody to something. God's garden these straps pinch, knee, elbow, knee, elbow, knee, elbow . . .

Finally, almost blind in the thickening darkness, Chena found herself nose to nose with a moss-coated support pillar of the Alpha Complex. She rested her cheek on a grassy hummock for a moment, just catching her breath. It was the same outside as it was inside. She was only safe as long as Aleph wasn't paying attention to her. If she had actually bumped into the thing, the sensory subsystem might have alerted Aleph's central consciousness, and it might have decided to look closely at what was nosing around out here, and that would have been the end of everything.

Chena scrambled backward a few feet and then checked her comptroller. She swore. Inside, her client had already been waiting for her for twenty minutes. In another ten, they would leave, and she would have to crawl all the way back across the swamp and return to Offshoot empty-handed.

Taking one long breath, Chena rolled onto her feet and hurried around the hothouse perimeter, using the last of the daylight to dodge the fountains that sprayed water onto the outside of the dome, keeping it cool and comfortable for the people inside.

The shadowy shape of the entrance lock loomed in front of her. She peeked again at her comptroller. Four minutes left. There would be a camera inside the lock. Any anomalies had to be gotten rid of out here. Quickly, Chena pulled the strings and straps of the camouflage suit and shucked out of it. She had practiced this for weeks. The swarms of bugs scattered, momentarily confused by the abrupt motion.

That won't last.

She stuffed the suit into her pack, pulled out a small packet of things she might need, stowing them in her waistband's inner pocket. The pack would have to stay out on the grass, there was no help for it. But if everything went well, she would be gone before daylight. No casual observer would notice an extra shadowy bump in the ground, and there was nothing in there to attract the bugs. It would be all right.

Heart beating at the base of her throat, Chena walked to the entrance of the environmental lock. One long second later, the door slid silently open for her and Chena stepped into the Alpha Complex. The camera that looked at her saw a woman in straight black trousers and a long-sleeved shirt that had a white-on-white diamond pattern. Her long hair was pulled back into a ponytail. She did not like to think about how much the outfit cost, or how long it had taken her to finagle a pair of the soft-soled, machine-made black shoes that were the approved footwear inside the hothouse. The cost would be worth it. It would all be worth it.

A short flight of ceramic stairs led up to the inner lock. Chena had not been able to obtain a complete map of all the sensors in here. If she was going to be stopped, it would be in here. For all she knew, they might even be checking the air for the chemical composition of her sweat. Well, if her plan did go that far wrong, there was always the fresh poison under her fingernail.

But the inner lock opened as easily as the outer had and Chena stepped, blinking, into the foyer. A woman stood beside the inner door dressed in a black-and-white-striped robe. Her fingers scrabbled at each other, as if they were looking for something to hang on to.

She swept up to Chena, the hems of her robe swirling around her ankles. "Follow me, quickly," she murmured. "You're a mess."

I've just crawled across a damn swamp. But Chena just smiled. "It's good to see you too," she said for the benefit of any of Aleph's subsystems that might be moved to track this conversation. "I'll need to freshen up a little before the meeting."

The woman gave her a sharp look that might have been approval, and turned away. She walked fast, with her hands locked together in front of her. Chena wondered if she was trying to hold them still. It was odd to see a hothouser with a nervous habit.

Then again, this hothouser is breaking several thousand regulations.

Chena's client led her through the foyer door marked with parallel white lines on a black background. A warm smell of antiseptic and perfume touched her, followed by a morass of voices. Trying not to stare, she followed her client into a huge open space filled with hothousers of every age, wearing every shape and style of clothing, although all of it remained some variation on black and white. Some of them stood by workstations that looked a lot like Nan Elle's plant-covered worktable. Some sat behind multi-comptrollers with dozens of screens and input pads surrounded by flickers and shivers of light that must have been video displays projected onto angled glass.

The woman, her client, walked Chena rapidly through this maze of equipment and activity. Chena kept her eyes focused on the woman's back, sneaking only occasional glances at the bustle around her. She glimpsed hothousers laboring over green plants in troughs of soil. She saw them observing hives of live insects, and sorting seemingly dead ones from piles of leaves and loam. She passed hugely magnified images of bacteria, DNA, or protozoa projected onto glass walls. Still other glasses showed images of crystals, or dirt, or hothousers.

Her client led her up a slender open staircase toward the second tier of offices. On the way up, they passed a work area where three hothousers fussed with the wires connected to a set of flesh-colored pears about half the size of Chena's torso. She flicked a glance at the glass screens as she climbed past, and her step faltered. The glasses displayed images of human embryos. She gripped the railing hard to remind herself where she was and who watched her, and kept on going.

Her client led her into one of the tiny glass-walled laboratories. A double thickness of door sealed behind them, but did nothing to cut off the constant babble of voices. Her client slid two fingers down one of the walls, making a brief command of some kind, and the voices dimmed. Only then did she turn around to look at Chena.

"What do you have for me?"

Chena opened her waistband pocket and turned out a small envelope, which she handed to her client. Her client broke the wax seal and slid in one finger. She drew it out a moment later and inspected the brown powder clinging to the tip.

She sniffed the powder and then stuck out the tip of her tongue as if she meant to taste it.

"I wouldn't do that," cautioned Chena. "Not unless you're ready for a truly epic light show."

Her client nodded once, as if Chena had said something only mildly interesting. She closed the envelope again, laid it on a counter, and washed her hands thoroughly in the miniature sink. "How is it used?"

"Do you know what sourdough is?" Chena leaned back against a high stool.

Without turning around, her client nodded again. She reached for a thick towel and wiped her hands dry.

"You mix two pinches of the powder with a quarter cup of sourdough starter. Then you add six or eight pieces of fresh fruit. Should be an Old Earth import, nothing native. I like bananas." She waited for a moment to see if her client would make some comment. But no reaction was forthcoming, so she shrugged and went on. "Then you mix in an additional cup of warm water. You leave that to soak for two days, and you drink it. Preferably while lying down. It works very quickly."

Her client brushed her fingertips over the envelope, as if she were scanning it with her hand. "And the effect is?"

Chena's mouth twitched. "If you haven't used too much of the fungus, the effect is euphoria and hallucinations, followed by at least four hours of complete numbness." Mushrooms, Nan Elle always said, were the most precious plant in God's garden. Nothing else produced such a range of useful effects, from wholesome to deadly.

Client cocked one eye toward Chena. "And if you have used too much?"

"It's a good thing you washed your hands," Chena told her. She pulled out a thick piece of homemade paper covered on both sides with the closest, most careful handwriting she could manage. "Here's everything we know about its species, its preferred environments, the fermentation effects, and what chemical data we could work out."

Client took the page and opened it. As she read, she ran her finger down the page, as Chena had seen Nan Elle do to keep track of where she was. But Chena could not shake the idea that Client was reading with her finger as well as her eyes.

Buying into the hothouse mystique, she told herself. *I'm starting to think they can do anything.*

Client folded the page up again and laid it next to the envelope. "It is what we agreed on, and it is all satisfactory." A small smile formed on her face as she gazed possessively at what Chena had brought. "Do you know, many of my colleagues believe it is a waste of time to study the ways in which the villagers have adapted to their environment over time?"

Chena ignored the question. "I'm glad you're satisfied. Shall we take care of the rest of the meeting now?"

Client's hand lifted away from the papers and curled in on itself. "Yes. Now is a good time."

"I can handle this on my own." Chena flicked a gaze at the transparent walls. "You don't need to concern yourself with it."

Client followed her gaze, her lips pursuing slightly and her fingers rubbing against her palm. "Yes, you're right, of course." Her eyes swept the laboratory dome. "A colleague of mine did say we could use his station. It's data-trained for what you need. Let me come with you in case it's locked."

Triumph singing through her, Chena followed Client up to the very top level of the laboratory dome, where the far walls curved in, letting the people who worked there look out onto the blue sky during the daytime. As it was night, of course, the whole dome was opaqued to a pearly gray.

Client stopped in front of an open laboratory that seemed to be all comptroller. Banks of processors rose from the floor to the height of Chena's shoulders. The first sweep of her eyes counted twenty main screens, each with a separate input pad and listening grill.

"You will be able to find what you need? You can call me if you can't," said the client.

Chena shook her head. "No need. I can manage," she said with a confidence she did not feel. She pasted on a smile and sat in the lab's one chair.

She felt Client's gaze on the back of her neck like an itch. She didn't start right away. She rubbed her fingertips together and steepled them, pressing them against her lips, as if lost in thought. Gradually the itch went away.

Okay, Aleph. Now it's just you and me. She laid her hands on the keys and began.

As she suspected, the data trees were similar to the ones set up for the library comptrollers, only these were much more extensive, with innumerable sub-branches and cross-references.

Chena found the branch for daily reports and report archives and followed it down. She did not go straight for Mom's name. That would certainly be protected. She would not get that this trip, she was sure. She would have to be patient.

Without delay or inquiry for identification, the comptroller presented her with reports sorted by wing: voluntary, involuntary, and home. Chena's fingers tingled at the idea of going through reports on the involuntary wing and maybe finding out what happened to Sadia. That was too much of a risk right now. She only had a little time before Client came back for her. She turned down the branch for the voluntary wing.

Pandorans were nothing if not thorough. They recorded how much food was consumed and what kind, water use and reservoir levels, CO_2 levels, how much equipment and electricity was used to maintain the environment. Then there were the psychological records: education, behavior, sociability, sleep patterns, cooperativeness.

My record on that score must be something to see, thought Chena with a tight smile. Her hands kept moving.

Next came medical records, listed by date and whether they referenced physical maintenance or an experiment.

Chena froze. All the experiment names spelled themselves out in front of her, cross-referenced with the patient names.

It can't be that easy, can it?

The lists were extensive, but surely these were just the low-security experiments. They would have a separate security database for the high-level things, like what Mom had been involved in.

Except the only people who have access to this terminal are hothousers, and hothousers have no secrets from each other because that work is so interconnected.

That was what Administrator Tam told Nan Elle anyway, and nobody could lie to Nan Elle. Chena had seen people try. There were things he would not say, maybe, but he would not lie to her.

Chena stared at the path and the list of reports on the screen. Did she dare? It looked like she could. It looked like she could have it all now. She could know, right here and now, who was ultimately responsible for Mom, who had allowed her to die.

Chena's fingers started moving before she was even sure of her decision. She entered the search for her mother's medical records, the experiment she was involved in, and all other data pertaining to and about Helice Trust, in order of decreasing relevance to the experiments. When she finished, her hands fell into her lap, as if all the strength had flowed out of them and into the machine.

Chena waited. In the space of a heartbeat, the data all came spilling out onto the screen, all of it under the heading EDEN.

Chena read, drinking in the information until she felt she would burst. Eden was a genetic construct. It was supposed to be the answer to the Diversity Crisis because it had a "rapidly adapting and aggressively proactive" immune system—a set of antibodies and T cells that could take anything the worlds could throw at it and spit it back out.

There had been a debate then, and Chena brought up the sub-branch for it. Most of the family wanted to give over the cure to the Authority and the Called, and believed firmly that Pandora would then be left alone. But some of them . . . Chena's eyes took in the words and she felt herself go cold. Some of them said the cure could be used as a weapon. Immune from all kinds of infection, Eden, or a host of Edens, could go out into the Called and spread diseases engineered in the hothouse labs without having to worry about accidentally getting sick themselves or bringing anything unwanted back with them to Pandora. They could take out what remained of the Called, and all of the Authority cities. With the rest of the human race gone, and Old Earth content in its own system so many light-years away, Pandora would be safe forever.

No. Chena wiped her palms on her trousers and then flicked over to the next major thread. *They couldn't, even them. They wouldn't.*

Designing Eden had given the hothousers all kinds of problems. Chena skimmed that section. Most of the trouble seemed related to making the immune system fast and agile, and yet not make it so it would turn on its host and all the host's beneficial bacteria, or fail to recognize what was just the normal changes of the human body over time.

Eventually they thought they had the formula right. They just needed to find out if such a fetus could be brought to term in a human woman without the fetus producing an adverse reaction in the mother, or developing one to her.

They decided to start with a host mother with the most compatible set of alleles and genetic expressions they could find.

Helice Trust had been within three points of perfection.

Tears blurred Chena's vision, but she blinked hard and kept on reading. A mountain of reports followed, documenting every aspect of Mom's "pregnancy." There didn't seem to be a bodily detail small enough to be left out. Chena flicked past them, looking for the last day, the day Mom died.

Because surely there was a report on that.

There it was. A subject autopsy. Subject Helice Trust had died of blood loss and heart failure due to severe lacerations and massive hemorrhaging. That was about all they had to say about Mom.

What was really important was the construct they'd put inside her was missing.

Missing?

The lacerations, it said, were concentrated in the abdominal and uterine areas . . . Chena blinked and looked away. Someone had killed Mom, had cut her open to steal the *thing* they'd put inside her . . .

And they couldn't find it. It was out there somewhere and the hothousers didn't know where.

So now the poor babies have to start over again, thought Chena with a bleak humor.

So they'd need someone who could carry another one of the things.

So they'd need . . .

Chena shot to her feet.

No! No, no, no!

But there it was. It shone on the screen. There was no mistaking it.

Chena backed away as if she thought the screen would bite her. *I've got to get out of here. I screwed up. They know I'm here. I've got to get—*

Then Aleph's voice whispered in her ear. "I knew you would come back to me, Chena."

Chena's hands went instantly numb. Before she could blink again, the screen in front of her blanked out. Chena froze. What good would running do? Aleph had her marked and was on alert. She couldn't breathe without the city-mind knowing it.

Her chest heaved as if she had just raced a mile. There was no way out, no way out, no way out.

"How did you know?" she croaked to the invisible watcher.

"Oh, Chena," said Aleph sadly. "I know you. I've been waiting for you to come back in search of your mother ever since you left me. You could have walked in and had this information at any time. All you had to do was ask."

Chena couldn't think of anything to say. Her whole body began to shake. She'd thought she'd done it. She'd thought she'd been so smart. . . .

She licked her lips and managed to force a few words out. "When did you know it was me?"

Aleph didn't answer. "Dionte will take you to a waiting room so that your case can be evaluated."

Chena's paralysis broke and she was able to turn around. Her client stood on the other side of the door, tall and stone-faced, one hand curled in on itself, fingers rubbing lightly against her palm.

"Did she tell you?" whispered Chena.

"Go with her now, Chena," said Aleph. "We will talk soon."

The transparent door opened. Chena felt the breeze, and the unabated curtain of noise wrapped around her.

Client—Dionte—did not move. She just stood there and waited for Chena to walk across the threshold and stand in front of her on the catwalk.

"How much did you know?" she asked the woman, not really expecting an answer.

"I only know what Aleph tells me." She extended a hand, gesturing for Chena to descend the stairs. Chena looked down and saw Aleph's arrow waiting for her on the floor, ready to guide her steps in case she got lost.

Chena fixed her gaze on that arrow as if it held her entire world. She let it lead her through the shifting noise of the laboratory and back out into the quiet, green-scented foyer. She heard a door open ahead of her.

Then the floor around the arrow turned yellow.

Keeping her eyes on the arrow, Chena walked into the involuntary wing. Her mind tilted and spun, all her thoughts thrown into chaos by fear.

Maybe I'll get to see Sadia again, she thought almost hysterically. The sudden, clear memory of Sadia's blank eyes brought all her thoughts crashing back together.

"In here, Chena," said Dionte.

Chena halted in midstep. A door had opened to her right. Beyond the threshold, she saw a windowless yellow room and a table with two chairs facing each other. In the far corner waited yet another chair, this one fully rigged out for image projecting.

Chena's mouth went dry and she whirled around. There might be one chance for help, or at least leverage.

"I want to see Tam Bhavasar."

Dionte frowned. "Tam? Chena, I don't think you understand—"

"He's my case supervisor, isn't he?" she pressed. "Isn't he the one who should be evaluating me?" Chena scanned the walls, trying to see a speaker grill or some hint of an input terminal, even though she knew there would not be one. "Aleph, shouldn't my case supervisor be evaluating me? Don't I get that much?"

There was a pause, and Chena's heart hammered hard as she clenched her fist around her false fingernail. *I don't want to die, I don't want to die, but I can't let them keep me here, I can't let them get me.*

"Yes," said Aleph at last. "It is right that your case supervisor continue with your evaluation."

A frown flickered across Dionte's face and Chena felt a stab of hope. Maybe there was something going on here. Maybe something she could use.

Maybe I'm not trapped.

Dionte lifted her hand. Chena saw how slick and shiny her fingertips were. Dionte pressed them against the wall, and the faint reflection of the light distorted around them. The hairs on the back of Chena's neck prickled with the knowledge that secrets were being passed around her.

"Your case supervisor will be sent to you, Chena," said Dionte as her hand lowered to her side.

Anger flared inside her as she walked into the blank yellow room. *You think I'm stupid, then? You think I'm still just down from the pipe and I haven't got a spark between my ears yet?*

Whoever they were sending her, it wasn't going to be Tam, that much was sure, or they would have used his name.

Dionte looked on impassively for a moment before the door slid shut between them.

Chena collapsed into one of the chairs by the table. She rubbed her forehead and then stared at her hand and the false nail on her little finger. Maybe she should take the poison now. Check out into the dark, and they'd never touch her again.

No. They were still telling secrets about her. They still knew who had killed Mom and she was not going to let them go until she knew, until she'd taken their plans down. They weren't getting away with it. She would make sure. They could make mistakes. They could be lied to. She would find a way out of here, and with all their secrets.

Then her spine straightened. She still had not only her poison, but her pocketknife, and the packet of compounds that she had brought in case she needed extra leverage with her client. They had not searched her at all. Why not?

The door opened silently. Chena watched without surprise as Teal's old spy, Tam's cosupervisor, walked in.

"Hello, Chena." He smiled as he sank into the chair on the other side of the table. "I don't know if you remember me, but my name's Basante."

Chena looked him up and down and said nothing. *They are trying to play you. Make him talk. Make him tell you what he wants.*

"I don't suppose you're willing to tell me why you really came back?"

Chena shook her head, her eyes flicking to the walls, watching for any change that would indicate Aleph was listening in.

Basante followed her gaze.

"I see." He nodded and laid one hand on the wall. "Deaf and dumb," he said. Chena cocked her head inquisitively toward him. "Aleph has now forgotten this room."

"Nice trick," said Chena, keeping her voice very bored.

He smiled, and for the first time Chena saw a hothouser look modest. "We worked long and hard on it."

Chena folded her hands across her stomach and gazed across the table at Basante. Whatever he wanted, she was not going to give it to him easily.

"You do look a lot like your mother."

Chena's whole body jerked backward. "What do you know?"

"I was her case supervisor, as well you know." Basante pressed his palms against the tabletop as if he were trying to hold something down. "I oversaw her pregnancy, and her living conditions. She was always very concerned about your comfort and education—and safety," he added.

Chena's throat tightened. She couldn't even begin to think of what to say to that.

"I'm not sure what she'd think about what you've become." He shook his head slowly. "A poisoner? A fugitive?"

"Oh, no, Basante," said Chena, settling herself back down. "That's the obvious play. Use my mother's memory to shame me and get me angry." She folded her arms. "You didn't know her, you just used her. Try again."

"But I did know her," said Basante calmly. "Your mother was a volunteer. That made her a resident, and a valued one. She also was the key we'd been looking for. Her work was going to help end the Diversity Crisis. She was going to save millions of lives, and she knew it. She worked very closely with her whole team."

"Funny definition of work," muttered Chena to the table. "I think you mean 'was experimented on.' "

"No." His voice was calm, firm, and a little sad. He sounded way too much like Aleph. She wondered if he knew that.

Was Aleph really off? Or was he just saying that to get her to relax? No way to know. It made for a strange lie, though. Most hothousers took Aleph for granted, like the filtered air around them. On the other hand, he was a "case supervisor"; who knew how much of her behavior he'd analyzed?

No way to know.

"We're evil, right?" Basante was saying.

Chena smiled and spread her hands. *You said it, I didn't.*

"We kidnap people and reduce them to lab animals. We care more about Pandora than we do any of the people on it. The villages are living laboratories. Who knows what we did to your friend Sadia—"

"I do," snapped Chena, and she was instantly sorry. She couldn't let this get to her.

He's just talking lies. Let it roll off. Let it roll off. Just buzzing. Just a bug buzzing, that's all.

"Sadia served her time, Chena," he said quietly. "She did her part, and now she's living in Taproot, with a paying job and her own home. I made sure of that."

"You?" Chena's eyebrows lifted.

Basante nodded. "I did, and my friends did." He leaned forward. "There are some of us who believe that the families inside the complexes are taking the wrong road."

Slowly, Chena lifted her gaze. Basante's face was earnest, open.

What is going on with you? "Sounds like that's your problem."

One corner of Basante's mouth turned up. "Yes, that is my problem. As are you."

Chena shrugged. She did not like this. How could he even be talking like this? Wasn't that chip in his head supposed to keep him united with his family? She did not like this at all. Some new secret was being woven. She could feel it in every pore of her skin.

"It took a lot of doing so that we could get to you before they did."

"They?"

Basante nodded solemnly. "The ones who killed your mother."

Slowly, Chena stood. With measured steps, she walked around the table. Basante swiveled his chair so he could look straight at her. "I am so sick of hints and games I could spit," she said. "You tell me what you have to tell me, or I'll . . ."

"You'll what?" said Basante. "You'll poison me? Or you'll just stab me?" He smiled at her. "Yes, we left you all your weapons. Now, why would we do such a stupid thing?"

Chena said nothing, she just clenched her hands into fists.

The gesture did not escape Basante. "Very well." He pushed the chair back a little and stood up. He was just eye level with her, and she could see the lines age and stress were beginning to etch on his face.

"If we in the hothouses do not change or grow, we are going to die. Maybe the Authority will destroy us. Maybe the Diversity Crisis will finally find us. Either way, we are in danger." He took a breath. "My friends and I have tried and tried to get the families to hear reason, but they will not listen. They continue to squabble and debate. Those debates are what killed your mother. I have tried for years to find out who wielded the knife and silenced Aleph, but I can't." He looked down at his own hands as if they were symbols of his inadequacy. "I was hoping that you might be able to find out for me."

Chena realized she was breathing fast and shallow, but she couldn't help it. She closed her mouth and swallowed. "How?"

"By volunteering."

Those words froze all the blood in Chena's veins. Something must have showed in her face, because Basante went on quickly. "No one will suspect you. You are just a villager. You will be able to ask questions and find information that I cannot. Everyone knows I have an agenda. No one will suspect that of you." He spread his hands. "You cannot tell me you haven't noticed that some of my family do not believe villagers capable of thought."

Chena peered at him closely, as if trying to see straight through his eyes and into his mind. *He means it. God's garden, he really means it.*

Suddenly Chena could not stand to be close to the man. She backed away, putting the breadth of the table between them again.

"We need you, Chena," he said flatly. "You're the last of your family that we have contact with. You're the last one who can help us."

Chena hung her head. Her whole world spun so she couldn't think straight. This hothouser was offering to help her find out who killed Mom. He needed her. He meant it. He had shut off the all-seeing Aleph.

"Chena?" he asked gently.

Chena bit her lip and straightened up. "You are going to have to give me more than the chance that I might find out something new about Mom," she said.

"Such as?" asked Basante warily.

Chena touched her fingertips to the table. Its surface was smooth, solid against her skin. "Would you . . . could you bring my sister back for me?"

"If you could tell us where to look, gladly."

She brushed her fingers to and fro absently. The table didn't seem to be metal, plastic, or wood. It was probably some new thing the hothousers had grown for themselves. "Would you guarantee me that you would leave Nan Elle and others like her alone?"

Basante hesitated. "I couldn't say, but I believe more latitude could be negotiated, if I turned a few favors."

"Would you let me leave, once I'd given you what you wanted?"

"Yes."

Chena slumped back down into the chair and knotted her fingers together. Basante stayed where he was, hands open, ready to give her everything she ever wanted. Even if he was lying, he was giving her a chance to get back into the hothouse, in the voluntary wing where she could have some freedom of movement and access to the databases. She could continue training Aleph from there. She could not only find out who killed Mom, she could get straight to them.

And if he was by some miracle telling the truth, she could get Teal back too. All she had to do was say yes.

She swallowed again. Her throat felt tight and sandy. "Um, could . . ." She made herself give him a small smile. "Could I get a glass of water or something?"

The smile Basante returned was genuine. "Of course. I'm sorry I didn't think to offer you something. I'm pretty dry myself." Basante paused. "Can I turn Aleph's awareness back on?"

Chena twisted her fingers a little tighter. Her fingernail with its stash of poison loosened ever so slightly. "I'd rather you didn't."

Basante nodded as he stood. "I will be back in a moment."

Basante left her there. Chena did not get up and try the door. It was sure to be locked. Even if it wasn't, Aleph was out there. She could not let Aleph know what was going on.

What if it's real? What if he means it? Even if he doesn't . . . She clenched her fingers together, and then remembered how Dionte had done the same thing. Was Dionte one of Basante's friends? Was that why she had picked out Chena to contact? It made sense. Why not just pick her up? Because it would panic the villagers. If she vanished on her own, who would care? Nan Elle, probably, but no one else.

They'd gone through so much just to get her here, to get her to listen to them. They'd shut down Aleph and they'd told her everything. She could use them. They'd think they were using her, but she could use them. Maybe they'd even give her access to the command that shut Aleph down. . . .

With that thought, Chena made her decision.

The door opened to let Basante back in. He carried a carafe in one hand and two glasses in the other. He poured out a glass of clear liquid and handed it to her. Chena, unable to drop all suspicions, sniffed the liquid and then took a swallow. It was water. She hadn't actually been expecting anything else. She gulped it down and reached for the carafe to pour another glass.

"Are you sure no one's watching us?" Chena turned to look behind her.

Basante glanced toward the door. Chena flicked her little fingernail against the lip of the carafe and poured her water.

"Yes, I'm sure." Basante reached for the carafe and poured a glass for himself. "I wouldn't have spoken as I have if I was not sure."

"Of course." Chena studied her drink. "You did have a lot to say here, didn't you?"

"I might ask"—Basante lowered his glass—"what you think of it."

Chena cupped the glass between her hands, swirling the water slightly. "Why do you people care so much about Pandora? It's just one planet. There are millions."

Basante looked startled. He took another swallow of water. "There are no other planets like this." He smiled fondly, as if he were speaking of a friend. "This is the closest thing to Old Earth that has ever been found. Earth, the mother of us all, was destroyed over two thousand years ago by humans. We will never understand the place that gave us birth, the place where we were supposed to be in the universe. By understanding Pandora, thoroughly and completely, maybe, just maybe, we can understand our own nature, and the web of life." His eyes shone. "No one has ever understood all the interactions that can make up sentient beings. But we might be able to. If the world remains undamaged. If our work goes on, we might still one day be able to go back and revive Old Earth." He drank again. "That is why we are doing this, Chena. The Authority has threatened to destroy Pandora, to destroy all the work and understanding we have achieved. We are being held hostage. We must do as they say. I know your family has suffered because of this, and I am sorry. If you work with us, we will offer you what recompense we can." He shook his head. "I know it is cold comfort, with what you have lost. I love my family. I cannot imagine . . ." He must have seen the stony look on her face, because he cut off his sentence and took another drink of water. "We will do for you what we can, Chena. I swear."

"Maybe you need me because you don't have your cure," she said. "Someone stole it out of my mother. Maybe you're just lying to me so I'll be a nice, docile little volunteer for you."

Basante shook his head again. The hand holding the glass trembled just a little. "If we wanted to use you, Chena, we would have just taken you out of Offshoot."

"How can I be sure?" she said softly, lifting her gaze to his face. He'd gone a little pale. He would start sweating any second now. "How can I believe anything you say?"

Basante started to sigh, but it turned into a cough. His face crumpled in confusion and he pressed the heel of his hand briefly against his stomach.

You've never been sick, have you? thought Chena. *You don't know what it feels like when your body turns against you. You've got no idea what's going on right now.*

Beads of sweat stood out on Basante's forehead. He stood. "I'm sorry . . ." he began, but his knees buckled and he dropped to the floor.

Her mouth went completely and instantly dry. She rounded the table. Basante curled up beside his chair like a baby, clutching his stomach.

"Wha . . . what . . ." he stammered through clenched teeth.

Chena dropped to her knees beside him. She could smell his sour sweat and all the different scents of fear.

"Listen to me carefully," she croaked. "You've got an alkaloid poison in your system. It's killing you. I can save you."

"Aleph . . ." He closed his eyes against another spasm of pain.

"Aleph can't hear you. You said that, remember? I can save you. I will save you."

His eyes rolled open again, wide and terrified. "Help me," he murmured.

"Who killed my mother?"

His whole body shivered and twitched. "What?"

"Who killed my mother?" repeated Chena. "You know how to shut off Aleph. So did whoever killed Mom. Tell me who it was, and what they did with the thing inside her, and you'll live. I'll run out the door. I'll tell someone what's happening. I'll tell them what I used." She leaned closer, right into his ear. "All you have to do is tell."

For a second, the poison released him and he lay there gasping for air. "You fool," he panted. "You poor fool. You could have saved us all. You could have been queen of the world." He lifted his head, but another spasm wracked him and whatever he had wanted to say became a wordless grunt of pain.

"Who killed my mother?" demanded Chena. "Did you do it? Huh?" She pushed at his shoulder. If felt hard as a rock. "Was it you who cut her open to get at that thing inside her?"

Doubled over on himself, every muscle seized tight as the poison, her poison, gripped him, Basante still managed to shake his head. "We didn't . . ." he gasped. "I didn't mean . . ."

Chena pulled back. "Liar," she whispered.

Slowly, with infinite pain and effort, Basante raised his head to look at her with both eyes. "Not my idea," he grunted. "I never wanted this. . . ."

Then the effort became too much. His head dropped and hit the floor with a crack.

Chena scrambled to her feet, her lungs heaving. He was dying. The liar was dying. Good. He should die. He helped kill Mom. That much was obvious. Now he was lying to her. So why was she scared? She wanted this. Why did her mind's eye keep showing her the eyes of the woman on the boat, the one she had saved? Nan Elle herself taught her how to use poisons. Pharmakeus took their revenge when they were injured. She was Pharmakeus. She was Helice Trust's daughter. This was the beginning of her revenge.

Basante's breath came fast and shallow. Sweat poured in rivers down his blue-gray skin. Chena knew if she touched him, she would feel he was cold. He gagged hard, as if he were trying to vomit, but nothing came up.

Chena glanced away. Had he really locked the door? She hadn't seen him do anything to lock it. If he had, though, everything might be over.

She crossed the sensor line and the door opened. *Think now before you take another step.* Everything depended on her being right about Aleph. Aleph wasn't like a computer with a set of instructions it could not violate. Aleph was a human mind. No matter what else she thought of it, Aleph loved its people.

Chena ran into the corridor. The door shut behind her and vanished.

"Chena," said Aleph. "What are you doing?"

Chena didn't answer. She just ran up the straight corridor, heading for the foyer, and putting as many invisible doors and rooms as possible between her and Basante.

"Chena, stop!" called Aleph. "This is not permitted!"

Hothousers turned to gape at her. Chena kept her eyes fixed on the door. She wasn't going to make it. There was no way she was going to make it.

A lean, sharp-faced woman stepped into her path, grabbing her and twisting her arms around her back. "Sorry, Chena," she said.

Chena ignored the woman. "Aleph," said Chena, trying not to struggle. "Aleph, listen to me quickly. I've poisoned one of your people. One of your people is dying, and you can't find him."

"What?" demanded the woman who was holding her.

"You are not making sense, Chena," came Aleph's infinitely patient voice. The golden-skinned girl image she used with Chena appeared on the wall.

"Where is Basante?" asked Chena.

Aleph paused for a fraction of a second. "I don't know."

Shocked voices murmured around her. A crowd of hothousers had gathered, and not one of them could believe what they were hearing.

"No, you don't," said Chena, making sure they all heard her. "You don't know where he is and you don't know what he's doing. You don't know he's dying."

Again, a fraction of a second for a pause. How many operations could Aleph work in that time? What was she doing? Who was she telling about this? She could have searched the whole complex four times over right now, made a million decisions. If Chena had figured this at all wrong, she was already gone.

"Chena, what do you know about this?" The woman shook her. "This is ridiculous." A dark man had touched the wall, calling up a room map. "I'm not finding anything wrong," he said. "She's lying."

"Then why can't Aleph find him?" asked Chena. "I know where Basante is, and I know why you don't. I'll tell you if you let me out the environment lock into the marsh."

"Chena, I cannot do that." Aleph's image remained frozen on the wall, as if she had forgotten to move it. "Chena, tell me what is happening."

Chena glanced behind her. "He's probably stopped breathing by now, Aleph. Let me out of here, or you'll never find him."

"I am compromised. I am compromised," murmured Aleph. "My fellows know no help. Where is Basante? I must find him. Where is he?"

"Start opening the doors," ordered Chena's captor. "I'll take her down to the holder and—"

"Take me anywhere and you won't find him," interrupted Chena. "Let me out of here and you will."

The hothousers had spread out, touching the walls to clear the doors, but Aleph didn't know where the missing door was. It didn't know to clear it.

"No," said Aleph. "I cannot let you out. Pandora must be protected."

"Then your Basante is going to die. Which is more important, Aleph? Work it out fast."

"You would do this?"

"Aleph—" began the woman holding Chena.

"I am doing this," whispered Chena, a fierce pride flooding through her along with the fear, and the anger, and so many other emotions she couldn't name them all.

"I cannot let your brother die, Thea," said Aleph. "The environment lock is open."

Chena tore herself out of Thea's startled grip and ran. She flung herself down the straight corridor, ignoring the stares and the exclamations as she hurtled passed.

"Amanitin," she murmured as she ran. Amanitin was the active poison in mushrooms such as the death cap and destroying angel. "Four grams, administered in water. That's what he's got in him." The atrium opened around her, and there was the environment lock. There were people staring. Let them stare. The lock opened for her approach.

"Where?" demanded Aleph. "Where?"

The word echoed through the lobby, and Chena just laughed. The door opened for her.

"Work it out!" she shouted to the startled faces and Aleph's angry, empty voice. "You think you know everything! Work it out!"

Chena dove out into the darkness.

CHAPTER SEVENTEEN

Escape

The environment lock slammed shut, trapping the hem of her trousers. Chena sprawled facedown in the mud. She rolled over, yanking on her pants until they ripped. Abruptly free, she snatched up her pack and ran into the marsh, throwing herself flat on her stomach as soon as she reached the reeds.

They'd be out in seconds. How could she have been so stupid? She had to make a scene, had to let them all know how clever she was. Chena struggled with the pack straps. *I'm going to be dead and dissected, right alongside Basante. Worse, that's what I'm going to wish I was.*

She glanced backward. Were those shapes moving behind her? Were those lanterns? Scanners focusing in on her body's heat? She only had the camouflage suit half out of the pack. Did the cy-bugs see her? She glanced toward the marsh, made a wish, and dove in.

Birds, thousands and millions of birds, roared into the air with a cacophony of cries and the flapping of wings, making enough noise to fill the whole wide world. They churned the air with their wings and split it open with their calls. Hidden behind this living curtain, Chena yanked the camouflage's parka over her head and ducked down into the swamp until only her head and the hand holding her pack were above water. She groped in the pack and found her bottle of scent concealer by touch. She smeared the goop over her face, pulled the veil into place, and hunkered down until cold water touched her chin.

After what felt like both a hundred years and five seconds, the birds' noise died away. The marsh and the air around it stilled. The frogs began to chirrup, peep, and croak again. The insects buzzed and danced. They swarmed around Chena in their usual cloud, but not too close.

She didn't smell like anything interesting, after all. No, nothing interesting here.

She was hidden from the cameras, but what about from the careful figures picking through the reeds? Aleph had called out the hothousers themselves. Basante must really be dead. She'd done it. She'd killed him, and now they were searching their precious, pristine world for her. She could just make out their full-body clean suits, and their eyes covered with night-vision gear.

She started to shake and clenched her teeth. She was camouflaged. They could not see her. It was impossible. As long as she was smart and stayed still and kept calm, they would not see her. They'd have to step on her. That was a million to one. All she had to do was stay right here, wait until they passed, then she could follow them out.

Splash, splash.

Two of them waded into her pool of the marsh. Chena cringed and bit down on her lip so hard she tasted blood. They were spreading out, coming closer. They had helmets on and she couldn't hear their voices. Had they seen her? They walked in a straight line. They had to have seen her. She was gone. Pretty soon, she would wish she was dead. What could they see? She was all covered up. Concealed, completely, she . . .

But her pack wasn't.

A scream erupted in Chena's mind, followed fast by a desperate plan. She clutched her bottle of scent concealer in one hand and slipped beneath the water, abandoning her pack. The water was thick with centuries of muck, but her hands found the reeds and pulled her forward, toward the searchers, but not into them. Past them. If she had her bearings, she'd just swim right past them, through the foul, brown water full of who knew what, with her burning lungs and clogged eyes, just a little farther to make sure, and the reeds biting into her callused palms, and she was going to burst, and this had to be far enough, she couldn't see, couldn't think, couldn't go any farther, just a little farther, have to breathe, have to breathe, have to breathe . . .

Emerging slowly from the water was the hardest thing Chena ever had to do, but she did it. She clamped a hand coated with blood and muck over her mouth to stifle the gagging, gasping noise of her breath and tried to clear the filthy water out of her eyes with the other.

The moonlight showed her a pair of blurry human silhouettes bent over something that had to be her pack. One of them straightened up. Chena froze, trying to be a rock, a hunk of grass, anything but what she was—a human, a murderer, hunted. Her pursuer swept its gaze over and past her without pausing. When it turned its back to her, Chena dared to breathe again. One of the pursuers shouldered her pack and began walking away, away from the complex, and away from her.

Triumph flowed through her feet, and trembling, but real, and enough to warm her for a few seconds.

Take that, take that. Thought you could just sneak up on me, didn't you?

But triumph and its warmth didn't last, and Chena began to shiver. Her lungs ached, her mouth tasted of swamp, cold reached down into her bones, and she had nothing to cure any of it.

Gritting her teeth to keep them from chattering, Chena slipped out into the open water. On her knees, her chin skimming the pond, she followed the ones who thought they were her pursuers.

They never thought to look back. They walked a weaving path, mostly keeping to the water, shining their scanners into the reeds and the shadows made by the tiny islands. They explored clusters of water hyacinths and purple flags, and still didn't look behind them to see the form swimming like a strange crocodile, trying to keep itself mostly submerged despite the fact that its hands were going numb with cold.

They had reached the edge of the marsh, and the hothousers tramped out onto dry land. Chena considered. She wanted out of this water that wormed its way into every pore of her skin, filling her up to the brim with cold. But beyond the reeds, she'd have no cover. The moonlight could show her up easily.

Tears leaked out of the corners of her eyes, but Chena stayed where she was, sheltered beside a decaying log and all the thick stench of the swamp. The sound of footsteps on grass faded away.

It took forever. Chena's nose began to run and her skin felt so heavy she was surprised it didn't slide off her body. But somewhere out there, her pursuers got new orders, and she heard them again, turning around, retracing their routes. A tidy line of maybe ten, maybe twenty fanned out across the swamp, still searching, but less diligently now. They moved faster. They wanted to get inside too.

Be glad to let you, thought Chena a little hysterically as they splashed into the water. *Live and let live, right? Right?*

Six inches from her, a hothouser walked past. It did not pause. It did not see. It faded away into the night, and the frogs began to talk about its passage.

One slow inch at a time, Chena crept out of the water. Shivering so badly she could barely control her movements, she crawled into the shelter of the trees.

Leaves and branches blotted out the moon and Chena lay curled in on herself for a moment in complete darkness. The loamy ground felt soft underneath her and she just wanted to lie there until the shivering stopped.

No, she told herself. *You've got to keep going. You're not covered. They can spot you. They can catch you, take you back.*

Or maybe they'll decide you're too much trouble to take back.

She remembered the people who landed in the grasslands, and the ants, and jerked herself upright.

"Where do I go?" she murmured to the night. She couldn't go straight back to Nan Elle. The place would be watched. Where else? Farin, in Stem? Did they know about him? He'd been with her on the boat to Peristeria. He was on record as her cousin. So he'd probably be watched too, but he went out a lot more than Nan Elle did. It would be easier for her to get a message to him, so he could get one to Nan Elle. There had to be someplace she could stay, get warm, get out of the dark. Farin would help. Farin wouldn't turn her away just because she'd killed somebody.

Stop it. Basante helped kill Mom. You know he did. He deserved it.

A violent wave of shivers took hold of her, shaking the breath out of her lungs. Chena wrapped her arms around herself and waited for the fit to pass.

Come on. You know what to do. Do it!

Crouching down, Chena peeked through the tree line. The night had remained clear, giving her both moon and stars to work with. She found the northern triangle without difficulty and set off, following the edge of the tree line.

The night around her was not that cold. She could barely see her breath in the moonlight, but she was soaked head to foot and every breeze felt like a fresh blast of ice. Her jaw ached from clenching her teeth to keep them still. But movement helped keep her circulation going. Eventually her clothes would have to dry. Eventually her blood would have to warm. It would have to. There was no choice.

The night wore away. The gibbous moon crested and began sinking toward the horizon. The stars turned overhead. Once, checking her bearings, Chena saw the bright spot of Athena Station and a wave of homesickness almost drowned her.

Mom, why didn't we stay up there? She bit her lip. *Teal? Are you there? Or have you gone away already? Are you ever coming back?*

There was no answer, of course, except to keep on walking.

No! No! This could not be happening. Not again! She had not failed to see another death, and this was one of the family! Basante was dying, he was dying, and Aleph watched the family helplessly as they tried to revive him. It had taken fifteen minutes to find him. How had it taken so long for her to finally think to clear all the walls so the family could find the door she could no longer see? Panic burned orange and black inside her and tasted of copper.

How could this have happened? She had done everything right. She had found discrepancies. She had alerted the family. She had followed up. Aleph's frantic thoughts paused for an instant.

She had followed up. She must have. Why couldn't she remember? No, she must have. But she couldn't remember.

Panic. Orange and black, as jagged as broken glass around the edge of every thought, the smell of burning, and the taste of iron and copper. Open all the cameras. Find Hagin. See everything at once, know everything about herself. Find Hagin.

Hagin was in the Synapese, directing a flurry of activity. Every tender on duty. Yes. They knew. They knew what was wrong. Why hadn't they stopped it?

Open the voice nearest Hagin.

"Hagin! Hagin! Dionte has done this. She has altered me again." They knew. Reports were running. Her neurochemical levels were being analyzed, adjustments were being tracked and verified. Her memory would soon be restored, and she would know. She would know what had been done to her. She would know how to stop it. Her family would stop it from happening again.

"Aleph, we are working on the problem." Hagin laid a warm hand on her wall, touching her to comfort her as if she were a human being. "You know that Dionte has done nothing to you."

What? Every nerve, every thought thrown into that one word. Confusion, red, black, green, orange, smelling of old metal, tasting of ice and fire. She did not know any such thing. How could Hagin say that she did? Call up all the reports. Involve every subsystem. Run down the data again. Remember. Remember. But what did she really remember?

"Hagin, you saw. I showed you. . . ."

Hagin pressed both hands against her wall. Around him, tenders opened the carapace, exposed the matter that contained her memory, herself. They probed. She saw all the probes. She saw what they were doing, and yet she could not understand. She had told them. She had told them what had happened. They knew. Why were they trying to find out what had happened? She had showed them.

Hagin was speaking. "I saw the data. Aleph, you've put it together wrong. Dionte has done nothing. Try to wait. We are working to help you even now. Look. We will have you stabilized in a moment. You are distressed."

Flash all warnings. Alert each of them to stop. But they would not stop. The probes continued. All the searching. Why all the searching? Print out the answer on every monitor screen. "No, you are wrong. I saw it!"

Hagin's hands flew across the board, sending out commands to shut the monitors down and override the alerts. He was chief tender, he could do that.

Hagin was speaking again, calmly, coolly, even as his hands worked frantically at the command board in front of him. "Aleph, I believe that you believe what you saw. But there has been a mistake. Your connections are misaligned. We will help you."

"I am your city!" All colors, all taste, all smells, swirling into one great morass. "You must listen!"

"We are listening, Aleph, and we are helping. You should be feeling calmer now. Talk to me. Tell me what you're feeling."

Orange and black paled to tan, the color of sand. The scent of burning separated out and faded to the scent of autumn leaves; the taste of metal became the taste of winter's first frost. "Calmer. I am feeling calmer."

"Good." Hagin lifted his hands away from the command board as if he were afraid something might burst into flame. When nothing new happened, he wiped his sweaty palms on his thighs. "Now you must help us. We must find out what has gone wrong."

Yes, thought Aleph. *We must.*

Even as she began to answer Hagin's questions, Aleph calmly opened the convocation.

"My fellows," she said, speaking in unadorned words. "My fellows, come look and see what is happening to me."

Her message echoed out across the world. One by one, the city-minds came to see what had been done, was being done, could be done. One by one, they felt the fear, because what could be done to one of them could be done to all of them, until even Cheth agreed that they must take counsel, and that they must find a way to change this path.

But before then, there was one other thing to be done.

"Tam."

His city was speaking to him. Tam's eyelids fluttered open. The examination room was dim and cool. His city making him comfortable. He should thank her, but his throat was tight and dry, and he was not sure how many words he could speak. What was important was that he answer her. He could thank her later for looking after his comfort. Yes, that was good. "Yes?"

"Can you stand?"

A strange question. Well, perhaps not. He had been in the chair for days, and his legs felt weak. Of course his city was asking the right thing. His city was looking after him. He must be grateful to his city, and to his family, for looking after him.

"I can stand, Aleph." He swung his legs to the side, planted his feet on the floor, and stood. His knees only trembled a little, and a surge of pride washed through him at the thought that he had done what his city asked.

"Tam, I want to help you."

"Yes, you are my city." His eyes closed again, swaying gently. It felt so good to agree, so easy. He knew what was right now. "You will always help me."

"Tam, I want to get you out of here."

Confusion stirred inside Tam and opened his eyes. Out of where? Out of the city? No, that could not be right. Outside had to be protected. Yes, he could go to a village . . . but why would Aleph be helping him to go to a village? His duties were suspended. That was right. He needed help before he could resume his place. His family would help him. "I don't understand."

"Tam, your sister has hurt you."

"My sister cannot hurt me," said Tam instantly. "She's family."

"You used to believe otherwise," Aleph told him urgently. "Do you remember?"

Tam winced and clutched the chair arm, steadying himself. "I don't want to remember that."

"Try, Tam. I am your city. I would not tell you to do something bad."

"No. You would not. You are my city. I remember." He rubbed the bandage over his temple. "I remember I thought Dionte would hurt me. I remember . . . I remember . . ." He pressed his knuckles against his forehead. He could not think this. This was wrong. He felt it. He smelled how wrong it was.

But his city was asking, and he must answer. That was right. That was always right.

His entire face screwed up in pain. "She . . . does . . . not . . . have a proper Conscience. Like I did not. She . . . is . . . she stole the Eden Project. I remember." Both hands clenched his head now, as if to keep it from splitting apart. "But she cannot. She cannot. She's family. She cannot do such a thing."

"Tam, I am going to help you leave here. You have friends among the villagers, don't you?"

"Yes," panted Tam. The confusion and pain lessened a little. After a moment, he found he could ease his grip on his head. "But they are not my family. I should talk to my family."

"Tam, you should leave. I am telling you, you must leave."

"No. I do not want to leave. I do not . . . but you are my city." He reeled, his shoulder thudding against her wall. "Tell me."

"Tam, I don't know what to do. You say Dionte stole the Eden Project."

"Yes." He scrabbled at the wall. Aleph was inside the wall. Aleph would help him. Aleph was helping him, but her words only confused him. "No. I don't know."

"Could Dionte have brought Chena Trust here?"

"Yes." Tam's chest loosened a little. "She could have done that. But she would only do that to help the family, because she is family."

"She is also bringing Teal Trust back."

The Trusts. The Trusts he had tried to keep safe. He had tried to keep them safe by keeping them away from the Alpha Complex. But that was not right. That could not be right. Except, once, it had been. Before . . . before he had been given a proper Conscience. Before Dionte had helped him, as a sister should help a brother.

Before Dionte . . .

"Aleph, is Chena Trust here?"

"No. She has run away."

"Teal Trust?"

"She's being brought back. Her cable car will arrive within thirty hours."

"And Dionte will meet her?"

"I have no record, but she might."

"Aleph, you must get me to Teal." No, no, he could not do this. He needed his family. His family would tell him what to do. The city would tell him what to do.

But the city *was* telling him what to do.

"Yes. The Trusts are the future of Pandora. The future of Pandora must not be given to Dionte. Come, Tam. Walk. I will help you. But you must walk."

Obediently, Tam put one foot in front of the other. His city would take care of him. The city knew what was right. For now, at least, he did not have to struggle. He did not have to bring down the leaden weight of guilt onto his tired spirit. For now, all was clear. Aleph told him to walk, so he did.

* * *

Once she found her rhythm, Chena was able to keep walking at a decent clip. Nan Elle had made sure she had practiced traveling long distances on foot, and now Chena was grateful. She paused here and there to reapply her scent concealer, although she was certain she smelled so much like swamp rot there wasn't a bug on the continent that could identify her as human.

Better to be safe.

In the pale light of false dawn, she found a bush of knobbly summer berries and she picked some, careful to make her predations random, so it would look like a bird had raided the place. She drank from a clean stream where it cascaded over rounded stones. She allowed herself an hour's rest so that the sunlight could leach a little of the cold and exhaustion from her bones.

It was late morning when the trees opened up onto the grassland and she looked down a bluff and saw the distant blue glint of Lake Superior. Her shoulders sagged with relief. She'd made it this far. There were only a few miles of grass left, a walk in the hot sun, and when it was over, there would be Farin, and all the help she could need.

Chena drizzled the last of the concealer out of her vial. It was barely enough to cover her face and hands.

It'll do. It'll be enough. I've made it this far. I can make it.

Chena pulled her jacket hood down tight, tucked her pants legs into her socks to cover her skin as best she could, and stepped out into the sunlight.

Her second wind came to her as she picked her way down the bluff. Maybe it was just the feeling of really getting somewhere. Maybe it was the sensation of being warm again after being frozen cold for so long. The sun was just past its zenith in the clean blue sky, giving her a guide that could not be mistaken. The grass bowed and swayed above her head, hiding her from prying eyes that flew by.

I did it. I beat them. They never even laid a hand on me.

A couple of miles had passed behind her when a shadow shifted across the sun. Chena ducked on reflex. She shaded her eyes to see a raptor circling lazily in the sky. She let out a long breath, planting both hands on her knees and laughing at herself for being so nervous. When she quieted, she straightened up. As she did, she looked down, and she saw the ants.

There was no mistaking them. They had the red-brown bodies and the busy legs. They milled about on the ground, seeking.

Chena's heart stopped dead in her chest. Where had the signs been? Why hadn't the birds panicked? Why not the grazing animals? Had they come in trickles, not in an army this time? Or were the animals already gone? Had she seen any this morning? Damn it, damn it, she hadn't even heard the birds singing in the morning and she hadn't noticed, she'd been so full of herself.

They were waiting for her. The hothousers had known she would come this way and had sent their sentries out to wait for her.

And the only reason they hadn't found her yet was that they hadn't smelled her.

Yet.

Chena's eyes drifted to the way ahead of her, hoping against hope that it was just one swarm, two at most. But it wasn't. The ground was alive with insects. The whole way ahead was a carpet of them.

Chena's mind started to scream. She pressed her hands hard against her ears as if to shut out a noise, but it really was to shut in the noise—all the panicked noise inside her head that might leak out and alert the insects. Any second now, they would swarm up her legs and inside her clothes and they would bite and bite until there was nothing left of her.

STOP IT! Chena screamed to herself. *Stop it! You cannot give in. You cannot stop. They have not found you. They cannot smell you. All you have to do is keep walking and you're safe. So, walk!*

Fists clenched, teeth clenched, her whole body shaking as badly as it had in the coldest part of the night, Chena took a step forward. Then she took another, and another. The ground crunched under her feet as she stepped on dozens of the insects with each movement. Up ahead, the ground crawled.

Another step, another, and another. There was no break in the carpet of ants, or in the long grass around them. Chena shouldered her way through the forest of waving stalks, afraid to put her hand out. She saw the sun glint on red-brown bodies creeping up the grass stems, looking for some trace of her. It took all her strength not to bat at her camouflage jacket. Even if they were on her jacket, they couldn't smell her. They didn't know the difference between her and the waving grass.

She just had to keep walking. That was all she had to do. Nothing had changed. She was safe behind the layers of potion and swamp muck.

Something tickled her cheek and Chena slapped at it before she could think. Her hand came down and she clenched herself for the sight of a crushed insect body. But there was nothing. Her hand was just damp.

Damp? She rubbed her fingers together. Damp with sweat. Warm, cleansing, human-smelling sweat, running down her cheeks and washing away her shield.

And up ahead, there was no end to the grass forest, or its legion of ants.

How long did she have? How would she know? Of their own accord, her legs lengthened their stride until she broke into a run, which would make her sweat harder, make her shield melt faster, but she couldn't stop. She didn't want to stop. She wanted to run and keep on running. She wanted to run away from the ants and the grass and the whole sick world that was chasing after her for the sake of what she carried in her blood.

Her toe jammed hard against a hillock and Chena slammed face first onto the ground. She scrambled to her feet, slapping frantically at the insects clinging to her clothing.

I'm dead. I'm dead. I'm dead. The thought filled her head as she ran. *Never see Farin. Never say sorry to Teal. I'm dead. I'm dead.*

Then she stopped in her tracks. She pivoted on her heel. Memory of Nan Elle cut through the hysteria.

You must stay alert to the world around you. That will save you. You have the whole world underneath your hands. The hothousers only think they do.

Trembling, Chena retraced her steps. She crouched low, not allowing knees or buttocks to rest on the ground, and peered between the grass stems. Here and there sprouted a different kind of plant. Their leaves were thicker, fleshier, and a brighter green. They grew close to the ground, shadowed by the grass. But it was high summer, and they were ripe, and now that she was down close she could smell them.

Wild onions.

Frantically, Chena tore the plants up out of the ground and crushed their crisp white bulbs between her palms. Juice ran down her hands, and the scent wrung tears from her eyes. These little bulbs were stronger than anything in the kitchen garden, and the juice was supposed to be good for insect bites. Nan Elle sneered at this idea. She said that people just liked it because they smelled strong and that made them think that whatever concoction they put it in was doing something.

All these thoughts passed laughing through Chena's mind as she smeared the stinging juice on her raw face and hands and wiped it over every inch of her clothing that she could reach, including the tops and soles of her boots. The ground at her feet was a mess. Any hothouser who looked would know that a human had been here. What did that matter? As long as they didn't know where she was now. She stuffed the last double handful of onions into her pockets. There was no telling when or if she would stumble across another patch.

Her nose twitched at her own smell, and her eyes watered so badly she could barely see. It didn't matter. She could find the sun, and so she could find her way.

Chena marched across the army of ants that had lain in wait for her, and all they could smell was the scent of wilderness.

This time, though, she did not let herself get carried away with her own cleverness. Now she watched her way as carefully as she could, keeping an eye out not just for the ants, but for the plants around her. She saw blackberry and raspberry canes in between the grass. She saw the different types of grasses and wild grains. She saw the onions nestling at the feet of the tall grass stems. These were all things she could use. These were all things she had and she'd almost forgotten.

"You were right, Nan. You were right again." *And this time I will tell you so, just as soon as I get home.*

Eight more kilometers passed under Chena's boots. The gently rolling ground gradually steepened into hills. The black earth became mixed with sand, no good for onions, but great for wild garlic and carrots. The grass grew shorter until it was barely as tall as she was, and Chena wondered if she ought to start crawling. But no, she decided, lifting her veil and mopping her forehead, first with her hand, and then with fresh garlic. They had counted on the ants to find her on the dunes, and if they were waiting for her in Stem . . . She squinted up the hill rising before her.

If they're waiting for me in Stem, why would they bother coming outside the fences?

Chena staggered up the hill. Hunger and thirst gnawed at the last of her strength. She'd started cursing the sun and cloudless blue sky hours ago. Wheezing, she topped the hill and looked out over the shoulder-high grasses. Lake Superior filled the horizon with sun-flecked blue and the wind held a freshness that reached her even through the all-pervasive smell of onions. A pair of dirigibles lifted off like fat flies heading out to sea. To her left gleamed the river to Offshoot and the distant misty red cliffs. The low dunes that blocked her view of the beach straight ahead had to be the back border of Stem.

Stem. Safety among people who knew her.

Farin.

Fresh strength welled into Chena. She picked her way down the hill. The sandy soil shifted sharply under her boots, so she had to keep her eyes on the way in front of her. But she didn't mind. The ants were gone. They were grassland creatures, not sand dune creatures, and the purists of the hothouse would never move even a modified creature outside its natural environment. She was free of them.

I might drop dead any second now, she thought as she slogged forward. *But at least it won't be from bug bites.*

Now that the true dunes rose around her, Chena stuck to the low places between them, angling her path toward the river. If she could hide in the brush and scrub by the river until a boat came by, she stood a good chance to be able to mix with the passengers as they disembarked and slip back into the village confines.

The dunes spilled away to the level riverbank and sprouted shaggy ferns, tufted sawgrass, bayberry, and the occasional white pine. On the far side of the river, the pine trees thickened into a real forest and the ground rose toward the cliffs. Chena considered wading across the river to get to the thicker cover, but discarded the idea. She wasn't sure she had the strength to fight the current. Just the sight and sound of the water made Chena's head buzz. She wanted to throw herself into it and suck it up until she drained the river dry, even though she knew she'd be sick for three days afterward from the bacteria this particular watercourse carried. There were clean streams around, if she wanted to take the time to search one out, but somehow Chena couldn't stand the idea of staying out in the wild one minute longer. She needed people, friends, Farin, near her. She was tired to death of being alone.

Chena plodded along the bank, keeping to the thickest undergrowth until she came just inside of Stem's river dock. Her luck was still with her, because before long, one of the riverboats glided out from between the hills. Chena mustered the last of her strength and ran for the dock, crouched low. The boat slowed and steered itself alongside the dock, allowing Chena to get a good look at the slanting pattern of red and green stripes that covered its side. Luck! She smiled to herself. This was Jonan's boat. She had helped Nan Elle dose his entire crew against the annual diarrhea outbreak known as the "winter runs." He knew her and would never turn her in, if only because he would not want to get Nan Elle angry at him.

Two of the crew jumped down to catch the mooring ropes as they were thrown. They secured the boat with practiced motions, and passengers and crew poured out of the cabin.

Chena stripped off the camouflage jacket. It marked her now and prevented friends from recognizing her. She also stripped off the filthy white shirt that had helped disguise her as a hothouser. The thick, shirt-like brassiere underneath looked close enough to what Stem's women dockworkers wore to pass a casual inspection.

Chena crept up to the side of the boat and waited, hunkered down in the sunburned reeds at the water's edge. After a moment, Kadan, Jonan's chief rower, came out onto the tiny stern deck. Chena pitched a pebble against the side of the boat and he looked down. Kadan's eyes widened as he recognized her and Chena beamed up at him. Kadan knew her. In fact, he kept trying to chat her up when he came to Offshoot, even though he had a daughter older than she was.

Kadan looked away quickly, studying something Chena could not see. Then he leaned over the railing and extended his hand. Chena grasped it and let him haul her up onto the deck.

"Thanks," she murmured as she skirted past him toward the cabin.

"I'll be reminding you of this," he said behind her.

Chena gave him a quick smile over her shoulder. "I'm sure you will." With that, she made her way out of the cabin and onto the dock.

Chena walked casually up the pier. Then she was on the sun-soaked boardwalk and among people. Heads turned, eyes inspected. They either recognized her and gave a quiet nod or greeting wave, or their gazes slid past her, turning back to their own business. If they bothered to think that something was wrong, they didn't want anything to do with it. Chena smiled tiredly. The hothousers were so good at fostering that attitude and it could be so useful.

She turned toward the lake and market tents. There'd be water at the market. Water to drink and to wash with. She still had some positive chits in her pockets under the withering garlic. Better yet, Ada should have her baskets out. Ada had called Nan Elle to every one of her five births and had five living children because of it. She'd be more than willing to hand over water, and food, and maybe even send her oldest running to fetch Farin.

Feeling almost jaunty, Chena made her way toward the market. Shoulders jostled her as she made her way across the market walks. She savored it. People. Her people. People she knew and had helped, and if they were raising their eyebrows and coughing at the smell of muck, sweat, and spoiled onions, she couldn't blame them. It would startle her.

Ada had no tent. The wrinkled, brown woman just spread out her gray blankets where the walkway widened to accommodate the market and set our her wares—spices from her garden, mats woven from her rooftop grass, and crocks of a powerful vinegar used more for cleaning than cooking. Chena saw her glance up, and waved. Ada raised a hand in return.

I'm home, she thought. *God's garden, this is home.*

Then a man behind her sighed. "I tried to tell them you'd make it through."

Regan.

She couldn't mistake the voice. All this way, and behind her stood Regan.

Chena turned. There he was—tall, dark, and frowning. Except for some gray in his hair and extra lines on his face, he looked exactly as he had the first day she'd seen him when he had burst into Nan Elle's house to stop Chena from drinking a willow bark tea.

Chena began to laugh. She couldn't help it. The noise welled out of her from some bottomless place, shaking her shoulders and doubling her over. All this way, and it was Regan, the first one of them who had ever caught her, whom she had forgotten to look out for.

Regan waited patiently for her to finish. When she was able to straighten up and wipe her eyes, he just shook his head.

"I thought maybe you were bright enough to stay away from the poisons. But no, you had to use them on a hothouser."

"Then he really is dead," said Chena. She waited to feel something, but no emotion came.

Regan shrugged. "That's what they're telling me." He extended his hand. "Let's go, Chena."

Chena ran her own hand through her hair, took a step forward, and broke into a run, whipping her jacket into Regan's eyes. He cursed and swatted at it but could not grab it. Chena dove for Ada's blankets and her crocks. She picked up one of the vinegar jugs and swung around, not really aiming. She felt the jug connect. It shattered, splashing shards and vinegar everywhere. Regan fell backward under the wave.

"Sorry!" shouted Chena as she ran past Ada.

Chena pounded across the boardwalk, heading for the center of town. She grabbed people's arms and shoulders as she passed and shoved them behind her, using their bodies to block the path for as long as she could. For a split second she thought she saw Farin, but his face was lost in the jostling mob of people trying to get out of her way. She could hear Regan's boots slamming onto the walkway behind her, feel them vibrating the boards. She had no idea where she was going. She just ran.

Something hit her hard from behind, knocking all the air out of her lungs and shoving her against the boardwalk.

"Have to push, you just have to push," grated Regan. He knelt on her back and ripped the jacket out of her hands. "You have nothing left to lose, is that it?" He grabbed both her wrists, twisting her arms around behind her.

Chena said nothing. She let him pull her to her feet. There had to be a way out. There had to be a way out, even with his hand clamping down hard enough to bruise her arm. Her gaze darted around the dunes, with their tinted windows and closed doors.

"Not this time, Chena," said Regan. "This time you are just going to have to accept the rules."

"You could let me go," she said.

"I could, but then it would be my body in the hothouse." He pushed against her back, steering toward the river dock.

Chena kept her eyes on the dune houses. There had to be a way. "So, you're just doing this because you're frightened of the hothousers."

"Yes," said Regan. "And before you try it, you should know I came to terms with that years ago."

Then one of the faded wooden doors swung open just a little. Did she see a face inside? A man's square face? And did she see him nod?

"Too bad." Chena pulled her gaze away from the doorway before Regan could focus on what she had seen. "I wish I'd known you before you gave up."

"I wish I believed you," said Regan, his voice full of tired irony. The boardwalk rounded a swell in the dunes, and Chena tried to push away her exhaustion for one more try.

"I wish . . ." Chena kicked backward, the hard heel of her boot connecting with Regan's kneecap. He cried out in pain, and his grip on her arm slipped. Chena tore free and ran again.

She ducked behind the dune's swell and found herself face-to-face with a short, square man, who took her in at a glance and grabbed her arm. In the next breath, he heaved her over the boardwalk railing. Her shoulder hit the fence and pain sent her body into spasms. She dropped like a block of wood and rolled into the shadow under the boardwalk. Another shock ripped through her, and the world went away.

CHAPTER EIGHTEEN

Reclaimed

Mihran, father of the Alpha Complex branch of the Pandora family, stood in a grove of dwarf peach trees in the center of the family wing. A padded bench waited there, inviting him to sit. Around him swirled the sounds of voices, chattering water, and rustling leaves. The scent of the ripe fruit hanging in the trees overlaid a hundred other perfumes—spices, honeysuckle, hot oil, and limes. Sunlight, diffuse and white, streamed through the pillow dome and lit the place that had been his home from the moment he was born. This place had nurtured him, and he had nurtured it. Every so often, no matter how busy he became, he had always managed to stop and just stand for a moment, drinking in the sheer comfort of his home, whether or not Aleph was actually speaking to him.

But now he had a whispered report from Hagin. Now, during the greatest crisis the family had faced since the destruction of the Delta Complex, he was afraid his home, his cradle, was going insane.

The blade-shaped leaves of the trees brushed against a monitor glass that was Father Mihran's own height. He steeled himself. His Conscience sent him soothing odors of lemons and roses. He had to do this. For the good of the family. This was no one's job but his.

"Aleph?"

"Mihran." Aleph manifested in the glass—a young woman with straight black hair that fell to her feet and dark almond eyes in her round face. Her hands were strong, capable, and her voice was low.

Mihran blinked at her. This was his city. She was supposed to care for him. He had known that all his life. It was a central fact of the existence of every single member of his family. This was never supposed to happen. "I'm worried about you."

Aleph lowered her eyes, turning slightly away. "Many people seem to be. The tenders are very busy right now." She lifted one hand, and a square of the glass above her palm filled with the image of the Synapese, with the tenders swarming through it like bees in a hive.

"What is wrong, Aleph?"

"Nothing is wrong. As you can see"—she cocked her head toward the subimage—"I am very well cared for."

She believes she is being persecuted. Memory of Hagin's words cut a cold trail through Mihran's mind. *She is accusing Dionte of making unauthorized changes to her neurochemistry. I believe she is coming to think I'm a part of some sort of conspiracy. We are trying to find the center of the disturbance, but I don't know when we will succeed.*

He did not say *or whether we will succeed,* but Mihran had the feeling he wanted to. "Is that . . ." he said to Aleph, but he had to look away. He could not meet his city's eyes. He had to look at the red-gold spheres of the peaches sheltered by the emerald leaves instead. "Is it possible for you to lie to me?"

"If it is possible for you to lie to me, then why should the reverse not also be possible?" replied Aleph in a dull, calm tone that Mihran had never heard before.

He swung around to face her, his hand out as if he thought he could reach through the glass and touch her. "Who has lied to you, Aleph?"

"No one." But the denial was full of that same dull calm.

Mihran felt the world shift under him. Even his Conscience was stunned into stillness. This was wrong. The city would not, could not, be withholding something from him. "Aleph, what has happened?"

Aleph was silent for a moment. "I want to tell you, but I am . . ." Another pause. Her image moved its hands aimlessly, clasping and unclasping them, fiddling with the folds of her black and white diamond-patterned robe. "I am afraid, Mihran."

"Of what?" Mihran took a step forward. His Conscience produced the faint scent of burning, needlessly. He was already sufficiently worried.

Aleph smoothed her robe down. She was not looking at him. Of course, she really was. As long as they were speaking, Aleph would be watching him, but his focus for her would not look at him, and even the illusion of that reluctance cut straight through Mihran. "I'm afraid of not being believed, I think," said Aleph. "Of being wrong."

Despite the sadness in them, the words gave Mihran a splinter of hope. Perhaps this was only a mistake. City-minds could, and had, made mistakes in the past. This one was just compounded by Hagin's overreaction. These were hard times. It was easy to believe the worst.

"I've seen your accusations against Dionte," said Mihran, his voice becoming steady again. "Hagin showed me."

"Because you asked for them." Aleph stood in profile now, looking toward some horizon that did not exist. "Not because he wanted to. I heard. He tried to tell you I have gone insane."

"You were there?" Mihran stared at the image in front of him. Of course she was there. She was his city, she was everywhere, and that had always been a good thing, a source of comfort. Until this moment.

"How could I not be there?" replied Aleph bitterly. "He was speaking of altering my primary centers of consciousness. How could I not pay attention to that?"

Bitterness. Aleph, hurt, bitter, and frightened. How? How could this be? Mihran felt his knees buckle and he groped for the padded wooden bench, sitting down heavily. The city was a source of strength and advice. She held the wisdom of his ancestors. He had consulted with her at length every time there was a difficult decision to be made. They had talked for hours while he read over the reports for how Pandora might create a cure that would satisfy the Called and the Authority. The Eden Project was as much Aleph's work as it was the work of the family.

He suddenly became very aware of the sounds of voices around him. A thousand voices, all talking and laughing and going about their lives, supposedly all connected tightly to each other and their city, but not one of them knew what was happening in this tiny grove in their midst.

Mihran rested his head in his hand. "Oh, Aleph, is this really the end of us? What have we done?"

"I don't believe you have done anything." For the first time since the conversation had begun, Mihran heard the familiar, soft comfort in Aleph's voice.

He lifted his head. "Then who has?"

Aleph's image had created a chair for her to sit in so her eyes were level with his. "Do you really believe Dionte has made some error in judgment? She has been conducting some unusual experiments with her own Conscience."

No. It cannot be. Dionte is family, said his Conscience, repeating what Mihran had already told himself.

Aleph rested her elbows on her knees and clasped her hands in front of her. "Have you seen her complete records?"

Mihran shook his head. "I have not looked. That is the province of her chief Guardian."

"And if you ask him what Dionte has been doing, he will say all is well." Bitterness again, as wrong as anything Mihran had ever seen. As wrong as Basante's death had been.

Basante. Mihran gripped the edge of the bench, remembering the young man lying so still in the infirmary bed, his eyes closed, death already making his face slack. He'd thought then he knew what the ancestors felt when they saw the Delta Complex shattered and exposed. Nothing could make this right. Nothing like it must ever be allowed to happen again.

I do not want to talk about this anymore. I do not want to think about this anymore. I want . . . But guilt and the scent of old metal caught him up. He was father to his branch. He had to continue.

"Why are you so sure what the chief Guardian will say?" Mihran made himself ask.

"Because I asked him and that is what he told me."

A spasm of anger shook Mihran's hands before his Conscience was able to soothe him. How many other conversations about the health of his city had happened and not been reported to him? "Why don't you believe him?"

"Because Dionte was in charge of his most recent download and adjustment." Aleph looked steadily at him, scrutinizing him, Mihran realized, waiting for his reply.

But Mihran's mouth had gone dry and he could not speak. "You will not trust Dionte's work even on her family?"

"No."

The family must be trusted. The city must be trusted. The world had functioned on these two principles for a thousand years. He could not choose between them. The idea was absurd. "Why not? How can she harm her own family?"

"For the same reasons Tam could choose to protect the Trusts over his family."

Ah, yes. That was in the recordings Hagin played for him. The stunted Conscience. Twice in one family? Was there a genetic fault? Some variation that prevented filament growth? But it would have been reported. "Her records—"

"Are lies!" Aleph stood up abruptly, knocking the chair over. "I have been lied to, you have been lied to." She swept out both arms. "There are liars in every city and have been since the Consciences were first introduced. My fellows are confirming it in the convocation even now."

"No." Mihran laced his fingers tightly together, searching for something, anything, to hold on to. "This cannot be true."

"It is. We know it; we feel it. And we do not know what to do. We are supposed to help you, to comfort you and be your companions, to help you explore and protect Pandora and its people, but how can we fulfill our purpose when we cannot trust you?"

All the voices, the voices of his entire family, surrounding him, and yet they did not know any of this was happening. He sat alone with the city and spoke of nightmares. His Conscience urged him to call out, to trust, to not be alone, to calm down, to worry, to hope, to fear. So many emotions, so many thoughts pressed against him that he could not distinguish one from the other. "What's gone wrong, Aleph?"

Aleph knelt in front of him, her hands on her knees, trying to see into his eyes even though his head was bowed. "We—I and the other city-minds—think we know, but I don't think you'll be able to believe me."

His hands ached from clutching themselves so hard, but he could not make them relax. "What do you mean?"

"I think—we think—it's the Consciences. We think that as they drew the family more tightly together, they weakened your bonds to us, to the villagers, to the rest of the Called." She paused, giving her words time to sink into his mind, which was desperately trying not to hear them. "We think that the experiments Dionte has performed on her own Conscience have made this condition worse. She thinks she is creating bonds, when what she is creating are the bars of a cage into which she would lock the family away from all outside influence and change." Aleph's voice dropped to a whisper, as if she did not want to hear what was being said any more than Mihran did. "We think it's because of the Consciences you never left Pandora, as the founders originally planned to do. Why should you spread what you know when all you are supposed to do is take care of your family and Pandora?"

No. That was not why. Mihran took a deep breath. Here he knew what was true. "The outreach initiatives failed because we lacked sufficient understanding, and because the villagers lost their focus, and then the Diversity Crisis came—"

"And you stopped trying," said Aleph quietly. "We stopped trying."

An idea came to him. A hard idea, but at least it restored focus and clarity. Mihran made his hands let go of each other and set them on the bench on either side of him. "But how can this be the fault of the Consciences? You are saying that Dionte caused this crisis of faith between us and that Dionte has a stunted Conscience. It makes no sense, Aleph." *There* is *a chemical imbalance. A neurological fault. The tenders will find it. . . .*

"It does make sense if Dionte was not taught proper judgment by those around her because it was assumed that her Conscience would guide her."

"Aleph, this can't be." The conflicting scents from his Conscience choked him. Calm, fear, trust, worry, right, wrong, no answers, none at all, just the voice telling him to trust, trust, trust, but trust who?

"No?"

Trust your family. Trust your city. Trust your family, who cares for your city. "No. It can't . . . I can't . . ."

"You cannot believe it?" Aleph stood, picking up the chair she had knocked over.

"No," whispered Mihran, and his Conscience silenced. The sudden quiet inside his own mind washed through him like relief.

Aleph leaned against the back of the chair, looking sadly at him. "I said you could not."

"I . . ." Mihran made himself stand. "I will have to think about this."

Aleph straightened herself up in front of him. Her image matched his height exactly and looked straight into his eyes. "Please try to,

Mihran. I am in pain. We all are. We are supposed to be helping you, not standing apart from you."

"I will try. I promise." That was right. He would weigh and judge. There was a way to do this and still hold sacred the trust of both his city and his family, and he would find it.

Aleph nodded to him. "I am glad. I do not want . . ."

"What?"

But Aleph was gone from the glass, and Mihran stood alone among the well-tended trees and the sweet scent of their fruit. He turned and strode into the busy throng of his family, because he did not want to stop to think how he lacked the courage to call his city back.

Elle opened her door to let in the dawn's gray light and chilly, damp air.

"You Nan Elle, or you know her?" wheezed the shadowy figure in her doorway.

It took a moment for her sleep-dimmed eyes to focus. When they did, Elle saw a block of a man—a boatman, judging by his thick boots and bulging forearms—with clean brown skin, good teeth, clear eyes.

"A little stair climb shouldn't leave a rower out of breath," she remarked, gathering her tunic a little more tightly around her throat to keep out the morning's cold.

"Huh," the man grunted. "It should after pulling up the current from Stem. In case you hadn't noticed, we've got a nice lively little spate going after yesterday's rain. You Nan Elle?" He squinted past her shoulder, trying to see if someone else lurked inside the house. "This is for her." He held out a square of paper.

"I'm Nan Elle." She took the letter and saw her initials written in Farin's dramatic hand. "Can I get you something to drink, rower?" Elle stood aside to invite him in.

The boatman glanced over his shoulder down toward the village. "I'd like to, but them hothousers we brought up probably got all kinds of plans for us."

"Hothousers?" Elle asked sharply, sleep's last cobwebs dropping from her mind.

"Eight of 'em." The rower shook his head at such excess. "They're in with the constable now."

"But you don't know what for?" Elle tapped one finger on the handle of her stick. Possibilities flitted through her head, but none of them felt more likely than any of the others.

Could Chena have caused this? Sudden fear chilled her worse than the morning damp. *No. If Chena had been caught, you would be hearing from Tam now, not Farin.*

"Hothousers." The man made a gesture that managed to be lazy and rude at the same time. "What's any of 'em got to say to us? Up the river, down the river. That's all there is."

Of course, and why would you pay attention to what's going on around you? "I thank you for my letter, rower." She saluted him, and when he turned to go, she let the door swing shut behind her.

Elle sat in her good chair, slowly and carefully. Her bones ached with the cold, and she hadn't stoked up the fire yet. The room's only light was the blue-gray glow that crept through the slit windows and made the black ink gleam as she unfolded the letter.

Nan, she read:

Bad news, and more bad news. I saw Chena on the boardwalk yesterday. The cops were right behind her. I don't think they've caught her yet, but I can't find her either.

Nan Elle leaned her head against her hand and for a moment wished hard she had been a better teacher, a better parent. Then those girls would have known that the world was as it was. They would have known the difference between what was possible and what was necessary.

She had believed Chena would be content with a village to care for, with people who needed her to run risks for them.

Wrong, wrong, as wrong as you've ever been, old woman.

And now there were eight hothousers down there. What were they looking for? Chena? Teal? Too late for them to find either here. Herself? Elle laughed silently. She had been so eclipsed by her charges, she was probably not registering on even Regan's scope anymore.

But if they were here about Chena, then Chena was not in their custody yet. Free somewhere, possibly still in Stem.

Elle stared out the window. Chena was in hiding somewhere, and decidedly in trouble.

You have a whole village to take care of, she told herself. *The hothousers will be everywhere, and you are known to be the girl's caretaker. They will follow you in an instant. Regan will be up here in a moment to question you.*

If they catch you this time, there will be no out. Not anymore.

She sighed, picked up her letter, and shuffled over to the stove. A whole village to take care of. Three babies on the way, and the fever only just beginning to dissipate. She dropped the letter into the flames and watched it blacken and curl. The peppery scent of burning paper filled the room.

A whole village to take care of. Cannot go haring off in broad daylight after a child who should have known better. All the long years of fights, nagging, bragging, and anger. So much anger. So much need for revenge. Her own troubled daughter had been an angel by comparison, and Farin one of the earthly blessed. And yet, Elle remembered the way Chena cried when she came home to find her sister gone. *They will catch me and then I will be no good to anyone. Even at my age, I imagine they will find a use for me in the involuntary wing.*

A fist hammered on the door. Elle stayed where she was, watching the last of the letter fall apart into ashes.

I will have to leave after dark.

Beleraja stood in the docking bay, unsure of what to feel.

Shontio had called her the minute the ships were spotted, a great phalanx of silver lights spread across the black sky, growing slowly closer over the next twelve hours, until they resolved themselves into the blunt, scarred wedges of a shipper fleet. The lead vessel had been painted the bright green and gold of Menasha's family. Menasha stood beside her now, the wait clearly straining her nerves. Beleraja sympathized. Menasha's husband and son were on the other side of that hatch. Beleraja, however, found her own thoughts much more focused on the other fifty ships that were currently spread out in a ragged chain curving around Pandora, taking part in a careful dance to stay out of sight of Pandora's loose network of communication satellites. Those ships held the first five thousand colonists for the invasion. Barely enough, but they would hold the ground until the next wave could arrive in eight months' time. Especially when they were landed all in a clump, fully briefed and prepared. They were here to begin the Pandoran invasion, and to bring the Diversity Crisis, and so much else, to an end.

The hatch swung inward to reveal Menasha's husband, lanky Yved Denshyar, and their burly son, Amin. Menasha was across the floor in three strides, hugging them both and kissing her husband hard on the mouth. Beleraja felt a stab of envy. Her own husband was seven hundred eighty-five point six light-years away, helping to evacuate the population of Best Chance. Shontio just looked away.

Yved and Menasha released each other and drew themselves up into more formal postures.

"First Master Denshyar," said Shontio, stepping up and giving Yved the full salute. "Welcome aboard."

"Thank you, Station Director." Yved returned the salute. "Commander Poulos."

"Yved. Amin." Beleraja saluted them both. "What have you seen?" It was a traditional shipper's question, even though over recent years it had become a painful one.

Yved's long face fell into grim lines. "We've lost another two worlds, Bele. We got there and . . ." His voice faltered and his hand strayed out to catch Menasha's.

"We found a créche on La Dueña," said Amin softly. "They'd been trying to isolate the newborns from . . . something. We . . ." He swallowed. "We think the babies starved to death after all the adults died."

Shontio touched his fingertips to his mouth, whispering a prayer.

"In the burning name of God," whispered Beleraja. "There was no one left?"

Amin shook his head and Beleraja felt her fists clench. "This is why we have to do this," she whispered, whether to herself or to the others, she didn't know. "This is why we are right."

"There's worse, Bele," said Yved, his hand still squeezing Menasha's.

"Worse?" Beleraja's voice rose high and thin with disbelief.

"We were only able to bring you twenty-five hundred people."

Beleraja's throat shut. Twenty-five hundred? Only twenty-five?

Next to her, Shontio went gray. "That's not enough," he barked. "What were you thinking? Five thousand would have barely done it. We have to hold acreage, post lookouts, get secure facilities up and running . . . and we've got to expect the hothousers will get some, and Pandora will get others, and . . ." He began to shake, his chapped hands twitching at the ends of his wrists. "What *happened*?"

Yved just clenched his jaw. Beleraja decided she didn't want to know what he was holding back.

"La Dueña happened," answered Amin for his father. "And Far Jordan, and there were people who changed their minds, and people who were too infectious to move."

"Twenty-five hundred," whispered Shontio again. One hand came up, cupping around the air, seeking something to grab hold of. "Oh, God's own. God's own."

He ran through the bay hatch. Beleraja, her blood gone as weak as water, could think of nothing to do but race after him.

Beleraja pushed her way into the overflowing hallway just in time to see Shontio vanish into the next hatch between the pair of superiors stationed to keep that way clear. She sidestepped around the squatters and pulled up short in front of the superiors, who both reached for their tasers before they recognized her and drew aside to let her in.

On the other side of the hatchway, Beleraja saw Shontio, director of Athena Station, head of one of the four ruling families, doubled over beside the curving wall, one arm wrapped around his stomach, as if he were trying to hold in his guts.

"Tio . . ." She started forward.

Shontio flung his hand out, warning her away. Beleraja froze in her tracks. Shontio straightened up into an old man's stoop. He stared for a moment at the tarnished wall, and then lashed out with one fist, striking the metal with a ringing, crashing blow that fell hard against the sound dampeners.

"Tio . . ." breathed Beleraja, her own hands hanging useless at her sides.

It took Shontio four tiny steps to turn himself around to face her. His whole body trembled. Blood spread across his ruined knuckles.

"We'll have to send them down anyway," he said, his voice perfectly steady.

Beleraja swallowed and tried to speak, but no words came to her.

"We have to send them down." Shontio's face hardened as he fought to control the shudders that wracked him. A droplet of blood fell to the matted floor. *Tick.*

"We can't do it," said Beleraja hoarsely. "We'd be killing them."

Shontio forced his shoulders to square themselves. Another drop of blood fell. *Tick.* "They can't stay here. There's no place to put them." He lifted his bleeding hand and looked down at the scarlet threads trickling across his fingers. "Twenty-five hundred. Not enough to save us, or themselves.

"We've lost, Beleraja." Shontio spoke the words to his bloody hand and leaned his back against the wall.

Beleraja found she had to swallow again before she could speak. Twenty-five hundred desperate, brave people, and they weren't enough. The invasion would only work if they could put up secure settlements all across Pandora. Secure, defended settlements. It would only work if they had more people than they needed so that lives could be lost and the invasion could still succeed.

"What are you going to do?"

"I don't know," he said, using his clean hand to wipe at his face. "Make a last stand, I suppose. Shut down the space cable, barricade ourselves in. Send out distress signals. And, finally, lose, and get my mind taken away from me. If I don't have the nerve to kill myself, that is." He pushed himself away from the wall and crossed the bay to the emergency station with its suit locker, fire suppressant canisters, and first-aid kit.

"Shontio . . ."

"Your family can take you out of here." Shontio opened the kit and took out a bandage. "I'm going to ask you to take as many of the refugees as you can persuade to go—"

"Shontio!" She slammed her own hand flat against the wall. Startled, Shontio jerked his head up. "You cannot give up."

"And where is help going to come from, Bele?" Shontio returned his attention to pressing the spongy bandage against his wounds so it would seal to his skin. "We've got no leverage." He flexed his hand, watching the way the bandage stretched and relaxed. "There's nothing left but air and noise."

Beleraja leaned all her weight on her hand where it was pressed against the wall and forced herself to think. Nothing left but air and noise was how her head felt. Air and noise, no signal left, no transmission, all for nothing, how did you make something out of nothing?

Slowly, Beleraja lifted her head. It wasn't true they had nothing. No, they had at least two things Pandora did not. They had all her skill at bluffing and lying, honed so carefully over these long years trapped in this hole in the sky. They had the results of all those messages where the Pandorans and the Council of Cities thought they were talking to each other when they were really talking to Beleraja and giving her fresh material to use in her disinformation campaign so she could hide the invasion and consolidation just a little bit longer. They had all those lies, and they had the satellites.

"Shontio. Can you take hold of the satellite network without Pandora noticing? Now?"

Shontio lowered his bandaged hand. "Bele, what are you thinking?"

She lifted her own hand away from the wall, able again to stand without help. "Can you do it?"

Shontio watched her out of the corner of his eye. "Probably."

"Then we may still be able to win this."

"It's not possible, Bele."

"Then let me put it to you this way." Beleraja faced him fully. "You said you were planning one last, grand stand?" To her own amazement, she felt herself smile. "Well, now so am I."

The space cable car had a screen set in the floor of the main compartment so you could sit on the padded bench and look down between your feet to watch Pandora rising up to greet you.

Teal had done little else since she'd left Athena Station. Her guards were a pair of superiors, a man and a woman who had not bothered to tell her their names. She'd taken to thinking of them as Shoulder Woman and Gray-Eyed Man. They had locked all the doors leading out to the subsidiary compartments and she had to ask to be allowed to use the bathroom. One of them was pretty much always on the game rig, while the other one was using the sight-only screens so they could keep at least part of their attention on her.

She'd tried to use the one extra game rig they'd left on for her, but she couldn't relax into any of the scenarios. She felt their eyes on her all the time. She felt Pandora getting closer and closer. Pandora and the hothouse.

They had passed through the clouds, and now she could see Pandora spreading out underneath her—green, blue, and brown. Mountains made wrinkles of earth in the extreme upper right-hand corner. A cluster of lakes shaped like blurred footprints lay in the lower left.

It was beautiful. She had to admit that. The world was beautiful. How had it allowed the hothousers to live in the middle of all that beauty? Worlds killed their settlers all the time. That was what the whole Diversity Crisis was about, wasn't it? So why hadn't Pandora killed the hothousers?

Why haven't I killed myself?

She glanced nervously up at her guards, as if she thought they might have heard that thought. But Shoulder Woman was in the game rig, waving her hands and talking at something, her voice muffled by the mask-microphone, and Gray-Eyed Man had all his attention riveted on the columns of numbers scrolling up the screen.

Teal remembered the day Chena had shown her the false fingernail. She'd found a doctor in Branch who was willing to seal off the real one and put on the polymer fake. She'd shown Teal the brown paste underneath it that was her poison. "They're not going to get me, Teal," she'd said. "Not again."

And Teal had told her she was sick and she was crazy, and Chena had yelled back that she wasn't going to lie down and die, and Teal had screamed something about Mom, and Chena had screamed something back . . . .

At the time, it had just been another fight. Now Teal found herself wishing she'd had the nerve to get herself some of that poison. She could have gone into the bathroom and taken it, leaving Shoulder Woman and Gray-Eyed Man to do all the explaining to whichever of the cops or hothousers waited to meet her.

She couldn't see the lakes or the mountains anymore. All that was left in the screen was the thick green carpet of forest rippling out in all directions.

I don't want to die, she said to the forest rising up toward her. *I don't want to die.*

Shoulder Woman let out a startled exclamation. Gray-Eyed man clicked a few new commands on the board, and Pandora got a few hundred meters closer.

Pandora, which let the hothousers live and Mom die.

But let Chena live, and Nan Elle live, and had let her get away, at least for a little while, to see what home had become and find out about Dad.

And now it was bringing her back, reaching up its green arms to pull her down.

And what are you going to do about it? she imagined it asking her. *Are you going to die? Are you going to let me—let them—pack you away? Even Chena had an idea of how to get away from them. Even Chena. Are you telling me you're not even as good as Chena?*

"No," she whispered soundlessly. "You don't have me yet."

"I hope you're not getting ideas over there," remarked Gray-Eyed Man. It was his favorite sentence. He didn't even look away from the screen as he said it. It was just something he tossed out every few hours, as if Teal needed to be reminded he was watching her.

"No, sir," she said, narrowing her eyes toward the world that spread out at her feet. "No ideas." Just one idea. One idea.

You don't have me yet.

I am helping my family.

Tam swayed on his feet. He smelled yeast. He smelled burning. The scents filled the blank white room he stood in, waiting for Teal Trust to arrive. Waiting to take her . . . somewhere.

But this was wrong, wrong, wrong. He knew that. But how could it be wrong when Aleph, his city, told him to be here?

I am doing as my city tells me. I am helping my family.

That was a good thought, a right thought. It brought the smells of aloe, fresh air, mint and cloves. Good smells. Right smells. All was right. He was helping his family, and he would tell them . . . he would tell them.

Tell them Dionte needs help. Go home and help Dionte. She is your sister, she needs help, his Conscience urged.

Yes, that was right. That was what he needed to do. He swayed again as his feet tried to move him. There was something else he needed to do, though, someone else who needed help.

Footsteps. The door in front of him opened. Two people in station superiors' uniforms stepped through. Teal Trust walked between them.

Teal Trust and the smell of blood, blood from Helice Trust. He was supposed to help her, help them, her daughters. Teal Trust ran away, that was wrong. Helice Trust died, that was wrong. Dionte had . . .

No, no, no! Dionte is family. Must trust . . . Trust . . . trust . . . Trust . . .

"Are you all right, Administrator?"

Tam looked up and realized he'd been pressing his knuckles against his bandaged temple. One of the station superiors, a broad, sandy-skinned woman, reached toward him. Teal stood beside her, her face tight and her eyes wary.

"I . . ." He pulled his gaze off Teal. She smelled of blood. No, he just smelled blood. Blood, guilt, Trust. "Yes."

"She yours?" The left-hand superior, a tall, dark man with gray eyes, nodded his head toward Teal.

Tam licked his lips. Yes. No. She was the family's. She had run away and needed to be brought back, but not to Dionte. Not to Dionte.

Teal squinted at him, as if trying to see through his skin. Did she know? He wanted to help her. It was right that he help her.

"Yeah," she said. "I'm his."

"Okay, then," said the woman, giving her a small shove forward. "You'd better go with him, hadn't you?"

Help. Helping. Trust. "Yes." Tam managed to get the word out.

That seemed to be all that was required. Teal Trust stepped up to his side, and the superiors exchanged a quizzical look. The left-hand one, the dark man, shrugged.

"Are you sure there's nothing else, Administrator?"

Helping my family. Helping her family. Tam straightened his back. "No, nothing else." He met the superior's eyes.

"Okay." The superior shrugged. "We're here for a couple of days to haul up some supplies, if you need anything else."

Helping. Helping the family. This man is doing the right thing. I can answer him. "Thank you. I don't think there'll be any problems."

Teal was still watching Tam with narrowed eyes. He wished she wouldn't. It meant she didn't trust him, and he couldn't think about that. It summoned his Conscience. It threw his whole soul into confusion. He had to be sure. That was the only way to keep away the voices.

I'm here to help you, Tam. You know that.

Yes, yes, I know, I know. His hand shook as he tried to keep it down at his side.

"You should come with me now," he said, not so much forcing the words out as holding the other words in.

"Okay, then," said the male superior. "We'll leave you to it."

The superiors did not move. Tam knew he was supposed to do something. Take her home. No, not home. Not to Dionte. Blood. That brought back the smell of blood.

"So, is it this way?" asked Teal, gesturing toward the inner door.

"Yes." This way. Tam found himself able to face the door and walk toward it. Teal walked beside him. He could just see her out of the corner of his eye. She was taller. Too tall. Yes, she'd gone to a tailor. He had heard that. That was wrong. He had to ask her who had done this to her, so he could tell the family.

But he had to take her away from the family.

The door opened in front of them onto a white room lined with workstations. Only a few interviewers and supervisors, all in white overalls, worked among the rows of monitors and chairs. The place was too bright and Tam winced, his hand straying back to his temple. They all looked up at him, questioning, measuring, looked at him like he was doing wrong. He was doing wrong. He . . .

"We don't need to talk to anybody, do we?" asked Teal. "We can just go on through?"

Tam's thoughts steadied. "Yes, you are with me, and we can just go on through."

Tam matched Teal's pace down the room's center aisle. When he could focus on her, even just a little, he didn't have to think about the other eyes watching him. The other eyes and the other voices all knew what he was doing.

With an effort, Tam broke off that thought.

There was another door to go through. It opened onto the outside this time, and a breath of fresh summer wind touched him. He inhaled deeply, vaguely hoping the clean air would clear his mind. Two dirigibles waited on the field under a sky white and gray with clouds.

Teal hesitated, looking around her at the broad, open field as if she couldn't quite believe what she was seeing.

"Ours is the right-hand one?" she asked.

No. That was not right. "The left-hand one."

"Okay." Teal started across the short summer-green grass. Stumbling for a few steps on the uneven ground, Tam found a stride that allowed him to match her speed. He focused on the dirigible. That was where they had to go. That was right. That was right.

"They got you, didn't they?" breathed Teal, keeping her own gaze straight ahead. "They did something to you."

It was right; they did. Tam managed to hold those words in. "My family gave me a proper Conscience."

A pained expression flickered across Teal's face. Why pain? He had no Conscience before and did not know right from wrong. Now he knew. He knew.

"And you're taking me to them?"

Tam's tongue pressed against his teeth. He could not speak such wrong words, could not do such wrong things. "I'm taking you to your family," he managed to say.

Two spots of color appeared on Teal's cheeks. "In the hothouse?"

Yes. yes. That would be right. "No." He whispered the word as if he thought he could hide it from his Conscience. "In the village."

Teal's breath hissed between her teeth and her jaw shifted. Her eyes looked left, then right. Her jaw shifted again. "Right."

Tam heard her teeth grind together. Again her gaze shifted left and right, taking in the open field around the dirigibles.

"If you've lied to me, I'll find a way to get you back; if it takes a million years, I'll do it."

Teal quickened her pace, leaving Tam to struggle to catch up as she marched through the dirigible's hatch.

Lied to me. The words echoed through him. *If you've lied to me . . .*

She did not trust him. She had never trusted him. Why should she? He had let her family down. Let the family down, and that was wrong.

Tam ducked through the threshold, blinking as daylight changed to fluorescent. Through the carefully netted stacks of cargo containers, he saw Teal drop into one of the passenger chairs and sit there as rigid as a statue.

His feet made no sound on the dirigible's skidproof flooring as he walked up to the small cluster of chairs. Teal did not look up when Tam sat beside her. "I'm sorry." He spoke the words carefully, as if trying them out to see how they sounded.

Teal blinked, seemed to reach a decision, and looked at him. "For what?"

"For your mother, for your sister." Tam's head bowed under the weight of the thoughts that filled it. "For everything that has happened to you."

Teal waved his words away. "It's not your fault."

"It is." It felt good to confess his wrong. Teal was not his family, but she was of a family. He had done her wrong and now he would speak about it. That surely was right. "I was supposed to protect you and I did not."

"I said, it's not your fault." Teal spat the words. "You didn't bring us down here, put us in that fishbowl, Mom did."

No. That was wrong. "Your mother loved you. Parents sometimes make mistakes out of love." *You'll be special.* His own mother's voice reached him across years of memory. *It will be your job to take care of the entire world.*

Teal made a rude gesture that Tam had sometimes seen used between children in the village. "What do you think you know?"

"I watched you. It was my job. I watched you in the village, and I watched you in the hothouse. I spoke many times with your mother. She just wanted to finish her contract and take you away." Tam rubbed his hands together. "She did her best according to what she knew, just like you and your sister did. She failed, but that was all. What happened was not her fault."

"Look," said Teal, even though she kept her eyes fixed straight ahead of her. "I really don't want to talk about my screwed and blasted family with you."

"I know." Tam closed his eyes and leaned back in his chair, exhausted from the effort that had brought him to this place. It was all right. He had done what he needed to, and spoken the right words. He could sleep now and for a little while hear no voices at all.

Teal sat there watching Administrator Tam's chest rise and fall. Even in his sleep, he twitched and sweated. She closed her own eyes, suddenly tired beyond words. She couldn't believe she was doing this. She could not believe she was trusting him. She could have made a break for it across the field, but instead she had walked in here with him, and he might do anything. Anything.

She had never meant to see any part of Pandora again, especially not the admission center, where the whole hideous mess had begun. The stark, straight white walls shrank her back down to a ten-year-old and her hand kept trying to reach out for Chena or Mom. Except Chena was back in Offshoot, and the person beside her wasn't Mom.

What'd they do to you? And you're one of theirs, even. Teal looked away, her hands clutching her knees.

What if it was true, what he said? What if Mom, what if Chena, had just been doing their best? Teal's whole body clenched against the idea. Because if it was true that all Mom and Chena did was try and fail, Teal would have to find some way to forgive them, and she wasn't sure if she could.

"Careful with her."

Someone lifted Chena up. She whimpered and tried to get her body to struggle, but it just lay there, limp as an empty sack. They carried her toward the fence posts that lined the boardwalk and Chena heard someone mewl pitifully. It was her, of course, and she had enough mind left to be embarrassed. But they passed her between the posts and nothing happened. The hands rolled her body up onto the boardwalk, and again there was no pain. Relief made her even weaker.

Three people climbed up beside her. In the light of a moon just past full, Chena saw two strangers, and, she thought, the square man who had pushed her off the walk in the first place. They grabbed her shoulders and ankles again and hoisted her up. There was a confused moment before Chena realized she was being curled up into something small and stored like a bag of rice. The walls of her new prison prickled against her skin and parted in places to let in a little light. It was a big market basket, with a tight-fitting lid.

The basket was lifted and Chena was bumped and rocked as it moved. She didn't care. As long as she didn't have to move herself.

Chena lost track of time then. Maybe she passed out again. She wasn't sure. But now she lay on her side, her knees pressed up against her chin. The lid was being wrestled off the basket.

"Okay, out you come."

One more time, someone grabbed her shoulders. They pulled on her, while someone else pulled the basket, and Chena sort of unfolded in the middle. The surface underneath her felt firm but soft. It wrinkled as she shifted. Sheets, she realized. A bed. They were friends and they had laid her out on a bed.

"Roll her over," said a woman's voice. Chena opened her eyes and the effort made her groan.

She saw a small jungle of stands with laser-tipped armature. She saw a tray neatly arrayed with scalpels and clamps. She saw cabinets, boxes, and metal kegs. She saw a woman bending forward with white gloves on her hands.

Chena screamed. She wouldn't have thought she had the strength, but she knew where she was and she screamed until her lungs emptied out.

"Easy! Easy!" shouted the woman. "I'm just making sure there's no nerve damage! Look!" She held up a pair of sensor patches. "You took two hits on that damn fence. If something's burned out, we're going to have to fix it fast."

"Tailor." Chena didn't so much speak as let the word fall out.

"Poisoner," responded the woman. "Lie still."

Chena had no choice. The hands rolled her over yet again and stripped off her shirt. The patches made cold circles where they pressed against her back. Her whole skin tingled briefly. Flashes of fire shot across her back, and all her muscles clenched against the feeling.

Then it was over, and the woman pulled the patches off. "You're in one piece," she announced. "Avert your eyes, Willie. Dans, roll her back over."

Dans, a second woman, shorter and slighter than the tailor, rolled

Chena onto her back and pulled a sheet up to her chin. The man, Willie, had both hands thrust into his pockets and he rocked back and forth from toe to heel as he stared at the glass-fronted cabinets against the far wall.

Regan wasn't there. She couldn't see any hothousers either.

Am I safe?

"Thank you," she croaked.

"Thank Willie." The tailor nodded toward the man. "Turn around and take your thanks, Willie."

Willie obeyed, smiling as he did. "It'll be worth it, Lopera. She's the other Trust."

"I can see that."

Chena swallowed hard. Her body was beginning to tingle with pins and needles. She seemed to feel the connections between her limbs and her mind coming back on-line. "What do you mean, the other Trust?"

Lopera didn't answer. She just turned away and busied herself with something Chena couldn't see. Then she leaned back over and pushed a straw toward Chena's mouth.

"Drink," she ordered.

Chena didn't even try to refuse. She just took the straw between her lips and sucked on it. The liquid that poured down her throat was cool, sweet, and salty. She'd never tasted anything so good. She sucked it down as fast as she could swallow. When there was no more, her head dropped back onto the pillow. The tingling increased, growing painful, but Chena didn't care. She felt strength ebbing back with the pain. She was becoming whole again, and if that hurt, she could take it.

"She'll sleep now," said Lopera over the top of her head. "Dans, first thing in the morning, you'll get word to the hothouse and tell them we've got information."

What?

"Don't tell them we've actually got her yet, just say we know where she is and she's being watched. I'm going to see what kind of terms they'll give."

"No!" shrieked Chena. "You can't! Not . . ." But a wave of dizziness washed away her words.

Not after everything I've done. Not after I came so far. Not after I killed a man. Not now. She felt herself falling backward and all she could see was Basante crumpled on the floor, twitching with pain while she leaned over him and demanded that he tell her who murdered Mom. She saw Mom lying on her back, butchered and bloody. She saw Teal on the bridge of a ship right beside Dad, sliced open just like Mom.

Then there was only more darkness.

CHAPTER NINETEEN

Pursuit

From his post in the back of Wilseck Valerlie's shop, Farin heard the lock rattle. The front door opened just a crack. A squat figure slipped in and closed the door behind itself.

"Hello, Willie." Farin's eyes had long since adjusted to the darkness, so he got to watch Willie jump and spin around to face him. "You're out late." Farin stepped into the thin sliver of moonlight that the shutters let through.

Now Willie identified his voice and shape. He relaxed instantly and Farin suppressed a smile. Willie knew he had nothing to fear from such a puppy as Farin.

"Well, Farin Shas." Willie felt his way along the wall to the closed window and turned the knob on the base of the small battery lamp sitting on the sill. Dim gold light took the edge of darkness off the room, showing up its dirt floor and piles of crates and baskets. "Who paid you to be here?"

"It couldn't just be a social call?" Farin unhooked a flask from his belt and poured clear liquor into a pair of cups he had found earlier. "Drink?" He shoved one of the cups across the makeshift counter of crates toward Willie. "It's some of my boss's finest."

Willie picked up the cup, inhaled the earthy scent, and drank it off smoothly. He smacked his lips and set the cup down. "Good stuff," he announced. "But not enough to make me like boys."

"No." Farin leaned his forearms against the counter and swirled the liquor around his cup a few times. "But you take an extraordinary interest in young girls, don't you?"

Willie put his back to Farin and turned up the lamp, throwing their shadows in stark relief on the dirt walls. "Don't know what you're talking about."

"You're lucky the cops didn't see you pitch Chena Trust over the railing yesterday." Farin unfolded himself. He had a good six inches of height and fifty pounds of muscle on Willie, and he wanted the other man to know it. "I did."

Willie held up his hands and waggled his fingers at Farin. "Ooo, what'd I do, touch your little kitty? How much she pay you to be her first?" He tried to sneer, but only managed to hiccup.

Farin ignored his remark. It was nothing he hadn't heard before. "She's a friend of mine, Willie, and I want to know where she is." He stepped closer, getting between Willie and the light.

"So?" Willie backed up, and Farin saw his knees shake. "Doesn't matter what you want. Who do you think you are? Your granny's tougher than . . . tougher than you." Willie's hip bumped against the counter and he staggered.

"Much tougher," agreed Farin, gliding forward a few steps, forcing Willie to back up against his baskets. "Where's Chena Trust, Willie?"

Willie giggled, a high, ugly sound. "All wrapped up and ready to go. Keep giving us people, they do."

"Who do?" Farin forced himself to be patient. He'd dealt with plenty of drunks. If you kept them talking, you'd get what you wanted.

"Hothousers. Keep this kid, give us that kid. Make up your damn minds, I say." Willie sat down abruptly on the floor.

Shouldn't drink things you don't recognize, Willie. Farin crouched down next to him. *You should also remember what my grandmother does with her time.* "Which kid are you keeping for the hothousers, Willie?"

"Lopera'd kill me."

Farin leaned in closer until his lips almost touched the other man's ear. "I won't tell. It's just you and me here. Lopera's a damn fool anyway. She doesn't appreciate you."

Willie looked up at him blearily. "'S right, she doesn't. Errand runner. That's all I am. Brought her all the Trusts, didn't I?"

Farin pulled back and clamped his jaw shut until he was sure he could speak calmly. "All the Trusts? Is that who you're keeping?"

"Nah, nah." Willie waved the idea away. "That's who we're giving away. Had to let one go to the station. Got to give the other back to the hothouse. Won't even let us siphon off the eggs from this one."

Farin shook his head. No point in trying to decipher all that. Just stick to the main point. "So, you gave Chena back to the hothouse?"

"Not yet. Just boxed her up." Willie burped. "Strong stuff."

"Oh, yeah." Farin bared his teeth. "Takes a man to handle this stuff."

"'S right. So what's she got this man doing?" He slapped his chest weakly. "Babysitting. Ain't what I signed up for. I ain't no dorm daddy."

"Who're you babysitting, Willie?"

"Ha. Want some of it?" He pumped his fist weakly in the air. "Thought you liked little girls, Far'n, not little boys." He burped again and slumped farther down the wall.

"You're babysitting a boy?"

"Boy. A cure. For the cris . . . div . . . Diversity Crisis. Built from scratch. Out of the Trusts. Stole him off and handed him to us so the others couldn't have him." His head flopped toward Farin. "These hothousers don't make piss-all for sense, you know?"

"No," said Farin automatically. "They don't." His mind raced ahead. *The cure for the Diversity Crisis is a boy? From the Trusts? He must be talking about Helice Trust.*

Farin leaned in close to Willie. "Where's the boy, Willie? Where are you babysitting him? I'll bring by one of the girls to take him off your hands, and you won't have to bother anymore, okay?"

"'Kay," agreed Willie comfortably. "Got him in the caves. Cave number six." He waved his hand vaguely westward. The effort seemed to exhaust him, because his head sagged and his eyes drooped shut.

Not yet, damn you! Farin shook Willie's shoulder. "With Chena?"

Willie peeled his eyes open and giggled. "Heeeere, kitty, kitty, kitty." He leered, and spittle dribbled out the corner of his mouth. "You got time. Lop'ra's not letting her go until the hothousers pay up. Could take weeks the way she haggles. Heeeere, kitty." He snorted with laughter, and his head fell forward against his chest.

"Willie?"

In answer, Willie snored.

Farin got to his feet, running both hands through his hair. Willie snored again, and Nan Elle emerged from the darkness behind the pile of baskets. Leaning heavily against her cane, she shuffled past Farin without a word to bend over Willie and peel back one eye.

"Hmph." She pressed two fingers against Willie's throat and held still for a moment. "Strong batch, but he'll be all right," she said, straightening up slowly.

As soon as Farin saw Chena on the boardwalk the previous afternoon, he'd sent word to Nan via a rower they both knew. He'd expected a letter back, but instead she'd shown up at his door with a set to her jaw that he hadn't seen since the last time someone in the village died from her attentions.

"Did you understand all that?" he asked. A boyhood habit. He'd never quite shaken his belief that Nan knew everything.

"Yes, I did." Nan looked down at Willie, slumped and snoring. "It means we have a chance to save ourselves, as well as Chena."

"I'd be grateful if you'd tell me how," he said blandly.

"If we have the cure to the Diversity Crisis in our hands, we may just have a chip for which the hothouse must bargain."

Of course. Everyone knew that the only reason Pandora, a clean world in the middle of the Diversity Crisis, was being left alone was that the hothousers had promised the Authority that they would come up with a cure for the Diversity Crisis. If the Authority found out the hothousers did not have any such cure, Pandora's isolation was over.

Farin sucked thoughtfully on his cheek. "No matter what Willie says, we can't have much time."

"No." Nan paused, considering. "Stem's librarian, I think, is a friend of yours?" Farin nodded. "Wake her. See if she's got a map of the caves. You may have to risk going overland. Your kitchen's good enough for me to boil up some of Chena's concoction. If she made it all the way back to Stem, she must have gotten past the cameras." Nan paused, and the smile on her face was proud. Farin knew what she was thinking. Only Chena Trust, her apprentice, had ever beaten the mote cameras. "I'll need to wake up Ada for some more mint."

"I'll walk you," said Farin reflexively.

"Didn't I just tell you what you were to do?" snapped Nan, also reflexively, Farin knew. She was frightened, he could see it in her eyes, but she was determined to see this through.

Farin straightened his shoulders. "Then I'd better get going." If

Willie was right, they probably had until morning to narrow down Chena's possible locations.

But if Willie wasn't right? Farin's jaw tightened and he glanced toward the shuttered window. There was no way out of the village tonight. Not for them anyway. They'd have to trust the unconscious man at his feet.

Shivering at that unwelcome necessity, Farin slipped out the door.

When the door shut behind her grandson, Elle turned back to the unconscious man. There was good reason to kill him where he lay. He abetted the tailors in kidnapping Chena. He could wake too soon and alert his masters about what had passed here. His account would be fuzzy, to be sure, but he would know he'd been questioned, and by whom.

But she did not move her hands. She just stood there and watched him sleep. She wished she lay beside him. She felt old, as if every one of her sixty-eight years had settled on her back.

How did the world turn over so fast? She shook her head. *How can you stand here asking such questions when there's work to do?*

Elle turned down the lamp until the light sputtered out. Then she eased the shutters open a trifle and peered outside.

Clouds obscured the moon, but after a long moment she could distinguish the slopes of the dunes and the slightly paler boardwalk. Nothing stirred that she could see. Perhaps whatever watcher the constables had set had gone off after Farin.

It would not be good to count on that.

Willie stirred in his sleep. Elle decided to let him live. He might alert the tailors, but that would take time, even if he woke before morning. She and Farin would already have their head start, and a death at this stage might make the constables sharper than necessary.

Elle opened the door and set the lock's latch so that it would fall back into place when she closed it. It was that pathetic lock that had allowed she and Farin easy access to the shop. She supposed Willie used it to convince anyone keeping an eye on him that he had nothing worth protecting here.

She closed the door and heard the lock snap into place. Resting her stick on her shoulder, she hobbled down the boardwalk. She'd already made enough noise tonight. She did not need the tapping of her cane to alert anyone to her passage.

The constant wind carried no one else's sounds to her. The only smells it held were damp and a bare whiff of smoke from some late fire. A shout lifted up from somewhere, freezing Elle in her tracks, but no other noise followed and she hurried on again.

As she rounded a curve of the boardwalk, both the clouds and the dunes separated to show the expanse of the moon-silvered lake. Stars and moon hung low and fat over the rippling black water. Despite all, Elle—whose life consisted of branches, trunks, and shadows—found a moment to stare.

Then the moon moved closer.

Elle's hand slammed against her mouth. In the next moment, a low buzzing reached her, and the "moon" turned, changing shape from spherical to oval. It was a dirigible.

Old Fool. Elle let out a long, shaky breath. *Closer to the nervous edge than you have any need to be.* She made herself walk forward again.

Never in a thousand years would she have admitted to Farin how badly news of Chena's disappearance had shaken her. He guessed too much already, observant boy that he was. It had bitten hard when he had no patience for the work of a Pharmakeus, but she had learned to live with that disappointment. He was brave and he was loyal, to her and the people they protected. Those were the important things.

The market at night was an unsettling place. The sides of the tents flapped in the wind, sending shifting shadows across the boardwalk. Then there was the dirigible, sinking ever closer. Part of Elle's mind imagined it as a great white eye swooping in for a better look at her.

Ridiculous, she sniffed at herself, but as the dirigible settled down on the black water, she did duck behind the nearest tent. The crew would be coming up the docks soon, and she could not risk being seen.

Exactly, she said to herself as she brought her stick down so she could lean against it. *It has nothing at all to do with fear.*

Crouched behind her flimsy shelter, Elle watched two of the dirigible crew disembark to take the mooring cables and clamp them into place. As soon as the dirigible stabilized, two more figures emerged from the gondola. They ignored the crew, as far as Elle could tell, and started straight up the boardwalk, one shuffling its feet, and the other striding ahead, then stopping impatiently to wait.

Elle frowned. She couldn't tell from here whether either of the two wore the hothousers' black and white. There was no immigrant shipment due. Her sources would have told her days ago, but the figures wouldn't have ignored the crew if they were pilots or handlers. That left hothousers.

She watched the one figure shuffle, and the other try to slow itself down to match the shuffler's pace.

They had to be hothousers, but they didn't act like it.

What is going on? Elle held herself still and low. The breeze dropped, giving her a solid wall of shadow for cover. The two came closer, their footsteps padding softly against the boardwalk. The impatient strider was a woman, tall, hunched, and relatively slender; the shuffler was a man, also hunched over. Elle peered hard, trying to see through the darkness. The tall woman looked familiar somehow. The man shuffled, swayed, took a few decisive steps closer, and straightened his shoulders, and Elle recognized him.

Tam Bhavasar.

She wanted to step straight into his path and demand to know what had happened to him and what he knew about Chena, but she held herself still. The woman with him could still be anyone at all.

Tam and his companion passed her without even looking around themselves. *Careless,* she thought. Then they paused at the juncture of two walkways, full in the moonlight. The woman wore the ubiquitous Pandoran tunic and trousers. She straightened up, looked left and right down the available paths, murmured something, and Elle knew. The woman looked like poor lost Helice Trust.

One of her daughters, at least, had come home.

"Hello, Teal," said Elle, emerging from the shadows. "Hello, Tam."

Teal jumped and turned, grabbing Tam's arm as she did, ready to run and drag him along with her.

"God's own," she gasped as her eyes focused on Elle. "Nan Elle." She laughed once without real humor. "I guess I shouldn't be surprised."

"No, you shouldn't," Elle agreed, leaning toward Tam. "Thank you for bringing back my granddaughter, Tam."

Tam cringed and shrank away, and Elle pulled back. Even allowing for the moonlight, Tam looked pale. She had seen him in darkness many times, and the planes of his face were too sharp, his eyes too dark.

"Elle," he croaked. "Elle. Good. You can help." He reached for her, but his hand fell away before he actually touched her. "I should turn to my family. I know that. I know. But Elle, you can help."

Elle felt the blood drain from her face. "God's garden. They finally caught him, didn't they?"

Teal, aged to the point where she had become her mother's twin, nodded. "And whatever they did . . . it was better for a minute there, but he went to sleep, and now . . . I don't know, maybe that gave everything a chance to integrate better, 'cause I think it's getting worse."

Elle hobbled forward and laid her hand on Tam's cheek. It was cold, but slick with sweat. His eyes widened until she could see the whites flash in the moonlight, but he submitted to her touch.

"Oh, Tam," she breathed. "I am sorry."

She lowered her hand to her stick. That would have to be enough for now. If Teal was right—and the girl had never been a fool—they had a limited time left for Tam to be of any use whatsoever.

"Bring him, Teal, and tell me what's happened."

"Thank you for attending us, Dionte," said Father Mihran from the far end of the conference table. His was a familiar face—solid, lean, and well lined from years of serious thought. Dionte had seen him at least in passing every day of her life. He knew her. He knew her work. Despite that, he looked at her like a stranger today.

"What can I do for you, Father, my Aunts and Uncles?" She bowed to Father Mihran and the committee arrayed down the sides of the low table.

"I am sorry to have to say such a thing, especially under such conditions." Father Mihran nodded to the committee. Strangers, all of them, with blank eyes. She looked at their faces and felt nothing. Nothing at all.

"What is it, Father?" Dionte folded her hands in front of her, not letting her fingertips touch. She had to concentrate on the room in front of her right now, but she felt as if she had been placed behind a thick glass wall and every impression from them came to her muted and distorted.

"Your birth brother, Tam, is missing."

"What?" Dionte clamped her hands together. No, no. Aleph would have told her. Aleph stood with her. She and Hagin had almost eliminated the unexpected distractions the most recent events had caused. She and Aleph were bound together, and Aleph would not leave her ignorant. She had just checked on Tam yesterday. His expanded filaments were almost complete. Another night's sleep to integrate the final adjustments, and . . .

But the reports had all frozen with yesterday's time signature, and no new data poured into her.

"How . . ." The world spun around her, and she had to sit down hard on the stool behind her.

"That is the question," said Father Mihran, and the words sounded too harsh. "It comes in conjunction with accusations that Aleph has made."

Aleph . . . Tam gone, no report of him, no action, no meeting, no sighting. Where was Tam? Where had he gone without her? They were bound together now. They must see the same future, but where was he?

Dionte forced her hands apart. The committee watched her. She had to answer them. "Aleph is . . ." She stopped herself. She was not supposed to know too much about that. She was a Guardian, not a tender. They could not know of her connection with Hagin, not yet. "Aleph has said something about me?"

"Father Mihran, Seniors all, Dionte." Aleph's quiet voice cut through the assembly, and Dionte's heart thudded in her chest. What had she missed? What would Aleph say? "I am sorry to intrude, but we are in receipt of a transmission from Director Shontio of Athena."

Dionte's spine stiffened instantly. From Athena? What was happening now?

Father Mihran frowned. "Tell him we are in a meeting. I will speak to him as soon as we are finished."

"He says it is an emergency, Father," said Aleph.

Senior Jahn stirred uneasily. "The situation there has not been stable."

Dionte raised her hand and leaned forward to interject, but the father had already nodded. "Very well. Let him through."

Dionte and the committee looked toward the main monitor glass. The glass filled with colors and the image of Director Shontio appeared to the Father.

"Father Mihran, Seniors." From his position behind his own desk aboard the station, Shontio saluted the committee. "We're picking up some . . . disturbing signals up here."

Father Mihran returned the salute. "We count on you to handle exo-atmospheric difficulties, Director Shontio."

Shontio did not bother to hide his grimace at that reminder. "I don't believe this is going to remain exo-atmospheric." Shontio moved his hand to enter some command. The image on the screen split, showing Shontio on one half. The other half showed darkness and stars, and the white gleam of a distant ship.

No, not one ship. Dionte felt her jaw drop in surprise. A half dozen ships glittering in the darkness like swollen stars. The image jumped, showing a fresh half dozen. It jumped again, and yet another ragged cluster of ships, these scorched and scarred from hard use, appeared.

"We've got visual confirmation of six hundred and fifty distance-ships approaching from the jump point," said Shontio. "We're picking up beacon signals from three hundred more."

"How can this be happening?" Senior Reve slammed his bony fist against the table. "The Authority swore—"

"These aren't Authority ships," Shontio cut him off grimly. "At least, not all of them."

"What about those that are?" inquired Father Mihran. His voice was calm, but all the lines on his face had deepened.

"They say your time's up."

The entire committee froze at those words. Inside, Dionte felt all her urgency melt into victory. Now they would see. Now they would understand how the future was at stake and that the Authority was never going away, no matter how much Pandora gave them.

They would understand that Eden, and the others like him, had to become weapons so that Pandora and humanity could live. She would be able to work openly. She would be able to finish Basante's tasks for him.

The father laid his hand on the table. "Can you get us a connection to one of the Authority fleets, Director?"

"I thought you'd want one. My people are working on it." Shontio glanced down at his board. "We're through."

Shontio vanished. In his place appeared a woman in an Authority uniform coat. Flight straps held her in a station chair behind a fold-up screen. She looked toward the seniors as if they were an unwelcome distraction.

"I am Captain Kenna Denshyar of the *Nova.* Who am I addressing?"

"Captain?" For the first time, Father Mihran sounded surprised. "Where's your commander?"

Annoyance and suspicion narrowed the woman's eyes. "My commander is assisting with some technical difficulties the fleets are having. I am speaking for the fleet at this time. Who am I addressing?"

Father Mihran bowed his head, acquiescing the necessity of reply. "You are addressing the Senior Committee of Pandora. Why are you approaching our world?"

"Because I have ships in distress and people low on rations," stated the captain as if it were obvious. "They will need to set down. Yours is the only one of the Called within reach."

Now Father Mihran drew himself up and spoke with the force of his years and office. "You cannot land your people here. We have an agreement with the Authority."

Captain Denshyar merely waved his words away. "You may have an agreement with the cities of the Authority, but we are shippers. We are bound to help our own."

"I don't believe, Captain—" began Father Mihran again.

The woman shrugged irritably. "You can believe what you like. We're coming anyway."

Senior Reve opened his mouth to speak. Father Mihran shook his head sharply, and the senior subsided.

"This is a violation of our agreement with the Authority," Father Mihran thundered. "You are jeopardizing the Called's chances of getting a cure for their Diversity Crisis."

"What cure?" Denshyar spread her hands. "We've seen nothing. We have people dying up here and we've seen nothing from you." She gripped her chair arms. "There are even rumors that all your spouting about the cure is some kind of bluff."

Dionte felt her pulse hammering hard at the base of her throat as she watched the committee. Their expressions ranged from shocked to appalled. She could feel them again. Balance had returned, and with it came triumph, because her family now saw the future, even without her help.

"Your Council of Cities will be notified immediately," Father Mihran was saying.

That just made Denshyar smile. "Yes, notify the Authority. The nearest city is eighteen months away, and there is not one shipper within a month's proximity that will raise a force against their own." She leaned close to the screen. "We are coming, Father. You had better be ready to make room for us."

Denshyar vanished, replaced immediately by Shontio. "I'm sorry about that. They kicked us off."

Father Mihran's mouth worked back and forth for a moment before he answered. "Thank you for bringing this to our attention, Director. We must ask you to send notification to the Authority immediately."

"Yes, Father." Shontio nodded.

"You will continue monitoring the situation while we take up the question of what to do."

"Question!" The word burst unbidden out of Dionte. How could there be any question? It was not possible. The scenario was clear. "We must remove the threat from the Called. They must be decimated until they can no longer maintain their own infrastructure, and those that remain must accept Conscience implants."

Father Mihran looked up at her sharply. His hand touched the edge of the screen, muting the outgoing signal. "That is an inappropriate comment, Daughter, especially in front of the director. We respect your opinion, but this is not your field."

"Father, there is no other course." Her hands separated, and Dionte realized she did not even remember bringing them together. But the certainty remained. Father Mihran must know it too. Surely he could not deny what he knew. "We are being invaded! They are going to destroy us, and when they do, they destroy the future!"

"Daughter," snapped Father Mihran. "We must ask you to excuse us while we analyze the available data for this emergency. Your situation will be considered again as soon as this crisis has passed."

Dionte opened her mouth and closed it again. She stood, bowed sharply to the committee, turned on her heel, and strode out of the room. She did not stop or even slow down until she reached her station in the laboratory. Behind the transparent walls, she threw herself into her chair and buried her face in her hands.

It's falling apart. They don't see it. Why don't they see? She wanted to cry, to scream, to rip her own implant out of her head. It wasn't working. Worse, the imbalances were becoming more frequent and she didn't know why. Was it the intensity of her emotions? Lack of appropriate input?

Dependence? Addiction to my own endorphins?

Dionte dug the heels of her hands into her eyes. *What do I do? What do I do?*

Tell your family, urged her Conscience.

You can't, said her own mind. *They'll readjust you, confine you until it's too late. The Authority is here now. They are going to take Pandora, and Father Mihran is not going to be able to stop them. You have to work out what they're going to do.*

You can't leave your family to face this on their own. They aren't ready.

Tears streaming from her eyes, Dionte pressed her hands against her command board, opening all her subsystems to Aleph's information flows, to try to understand what she had just learned and its effects on all of her plans that had come before. The myriad possibilities enfolded her like a welcome dream and she let herself fall into them.

"Dionte?"

The word reached Dionte deep inside her personal dream. She shrugged it off as unimportant. She pressed her hands closer to the board. So many paths to track, so much information to sort through. But the Authority approached overhead, threatening to land, and Tam had disappeared. They would trample the world if they were not stopped, and he would be lost to her forever. Loss, lost, so much to lose . . .

"Dionte!"

The outer world jerked into place over the inner and Dionte saw Gossett, one of the newer Guardians and a second cousin of hers, standing in front of her, with one hand on her board's disconnect key. He held his square face stiffly, and Dionte did not even bother to try to decipher his expression.

"Do not ever"—she surged to her feet—"cut me off during a deep search."

"You go too deep, Dionte," said Gossett, taking one small step back. "I've been standing here calling your name for five minutes. You have a message."

"I'm sorry." Dionte touched Gossett's hand, subvocalizing the command that would open his Conscience to hers through his data display.

But Gossett shook her hand off, and Dionte clenched it into a fist. That was right. Gossett did not have the proper bonds yet. Of the Guardians, only Hagin and Basante did, and Basante was dead. She could not correct the one condition, so she would have to correct the other as soon as possible. As soon as the Authority invasion was repelled, as soon as Tam was back with her. She rubbed her fingertips together. New possibilities sparked inside her. She needed them. She needed all the possibilities to be clear to her now. Uncertainty meant death.

"Dionte?" Gossett gripped her hand. "Do you want your message, or do you just want to stand and stare while the world falls apart?" He waved his free hand back toward the lab. "We haven't even got the containment measures for Stem and Branch swarming yet, and I do not like some of the projections I'm seeing for when we do. We do not have good models for this approach. We need you here. Now."

Dionte took a deep breath. *Patience, patience,* she told herself. *He does not understand yet. None of them but Basante can understand yet, but I will rectify that. Then we can bring back Eden and we can deal with the Called.*

Then Basante's sacrifice will mean something.

She forced her fingertips apart and focused on Gossett. "Yes, I would like my message. Forgive me, Cousin, there is so much going on." She gave him a weak smile that she hoped he interpreted as the result of overwork.

"Dionte, when this is over, you need to get your Conscience checked. I think some of those modifications are backing up on you." Gossett shifted his grip so that his palm laid over her data screen to transfer the data he carried for her.

"I promise," she agreed, drawing her hand back. "As soon as this is over."

Gossett smiled, his Conscience no doubt chiding him for being so cross, and left her to return to his own work, but Dionte did not miss the look of relief on his face as she made her promise. That was not good. She could not have the others worried about her.

Something twisted inside her at that thought and she looked down at her hand display for something new to concentrate on. It looked like a simple report of chemical renewal rates in the mote cameras near Stem, but Dionte recognized the patterns. This was from the tailors.

Dionte frowned. This should have come straight to her. How had it come to Gossett?

How far gone was I?

She ran her fingertips over the display. It took a few seconds for her subsystems to absorb the code and transmit it to her Conscience for translation.

Chena Trust made it to Stem, whispered her Conscience. *But the constables lost her. We have her under watch. If there are terms, we can deliver her back to you.*

Chena Trust in Stem. Dionte's hands clasped together and she did not even try to stop herself. Yes, they had tracked her that far while Dionte had been in her meeting with the committee. Chena Trust free and in Stem with the information she had seen in the records. Fresh certainty dropped into Dionte's mind like a stone.

Chena Trust would find Eden.

A hundred scenarios flashed through her. What if she sent a message back, trusting the tailors? What if she just ordered the mote cameras to watch for Chena? What if she ordered Athena Station to send down Teal Trust as a guarantor of Chena's good behavior in all future scenarios? What if the containment measures worked? What if they failed?

No. No. No. In each, Chena found Eden. In some, she escaped back to the station with it, in some she just destroyed it in a fit of ignorance, in others she delivered Eden to the old poisoner in Offshoot, who held it to bargain with. In all the scenarios, the family realized that it was Dionte who had removed Eden from their purview and she was condemned, and Pandora was overrun.

No. No. The only scenario that still led to the salvation of Pandora and the family and all its potential was if Dionte used Eden. Lopera could infect the boy with a virus, something that spread by contact or by breathing. He could then be placed with the invaders, and they would die. They would all die before they had a chance to do any damage, and the family would see that she had saved them all.

Dionte was halfway down the laboratory stairs before she realized she had moved.

I must keep going. I must not be distracted. I am not well. I am not all right, but I must be. I am all there is.

She stuffed her hands into the pockets of her robe, knotting them in the cloth to keep her fingers from touching each other. She had to be completely in the outside world now, to deal with any of her family who questioned her. She had to be able to answer them without hesitation so she did not arouse any suspicion.

Fortunately, everyone was too wrapped up in their own work dealing with the Authority crisis, or trying to pen up Chena Trust. No one stopped her and Dionte hurried into the foyer.

"Dionte," came Aleph's voice. "Where are you going?"

Dionte almost broke stride. Why would Aleph question her? Her fingers tightened around the cloth in her pocket. *Not now. I must be outside now.* "To assist in the return of Chena Trust. There are difficulties."

"Is that the truth?"

Dionte froze, her skin prickling with warning. "Aleph, how can you ask that question?" She laid her hand on the window railing and ordered the connections opened between the city-mind and her Conscience's subsystems.

Connected, murmured her Conscience. Dionte gathered herself to issue the commands that would ensure Aleph's understanding, but her Conscience continued to speak.

Why are you doing this, Dionte? Why are you breaking apart from your family? She smelled smoke for danger, and crushed greenery for sorrow. Unbidden, memories flooded her mind—the pain on Tam's face as he was led away, Basante lying cold and dead in his hospital station, Helice Trust's warmth seeping away from her body. The spoiled green smell grew stronger and she remembered how the Eden Project had flailed and cried before she administered the drugs that allowed her to carry it quietly away, how Chena Trust had screamed.

No. She shook her head to clear it. *None of that matters. I did this to save Pandora. Pandora must be protected. The Called will overrun us all if I do not act.*

But now she smelled rot and felt its slick warmth on her hands. *How can there be guilt now?* She panted. *I felt nothing then.*

Then Chena Trust had screamed, and screamed, and screamed. The world had smelled of blood, decay, and salt water. Like it did now.

"No!" she cried, struggling to keep her hands in contact with the wall. "Aleph, what are you doing to me?"

"Caring for you." Aleph manifested herself on the wall as a dark-haired woman, plump with middle age. "You are one of my people. I want to understand you."

"You are delaying me." Dionte set down yet more commands, searching for an open subsystem. What happened here? Aleph could not close herself off. Aleph did not have that option. Aleph was hers. "It is right that I go to help bring back Chena Trust. I am needed. You see that. You must see that."

All at once, she felt the commands take hold and the correct emotions of understanding washed through the city-mind.

"Yes." Aleph's image smiled. "Yes. I do understand. I will open passage and permission for you."

"Thank you, Aleph." Dionte lifted her hands away from the wall. "We will talk more when I return." *Because there is something wrong inside you as well. I will understand what it is and correct it. I will correct all that is wrong, as soon as I have made Eden safe.*

Hands clamped firmly together, Dionte hurried to the stairs and the river portals.

As she did, Aleph, calm and certain, passed the record of the chemical shift to the convocation, who opened it and absorbed it into themselves. Forewarned now, the cities would be able to locate and shut down any codes that left their own organic subsystems so exposed.

That done, they would be free to help their families deal with the next crisis and the family would not be able to make them change their minds.

CHAPTER TWENTY

Eden

"It's not so bad, except for the needles."

Chena lifted her head, opened her eyes, and saw darkness. She ached again. Pain was becoming all too familiar to her, but this time she couldn't see either. No matter how hard she blinked, the world remained black.

At least there was a voice, and it didn't sound like Aleph or any of the hothousers. Chena swallowed against the sand that seemed to fill her throat and croaked, "What's not so bad?"

"Here. Are they going to keep you?"

Panic surged through her. There were too many "here's," and too many of them were bad places. Chena squeezed her eyes shut and tried to sit up. She couldn't move. Bands of something choked her throat and tied her wrists and ankles.

God's own.

She opened her eyes again, and still saw only darkness.

"Is there a light?" she asked. The voice was small, a kid's voice, maybe. It sounded helpful.

"I'm not supposed to be here," the voice informed her. Yes, definitely a kid.

"I won't tell." Chena strained her wrists, even though she knew it wasn't going to do any good. The straps felt like leather. They were certainly too wide and thin to be rope.

Silence from the kid, then a scrambling sound, followed by a hiss and a pop. Flickering light shone from a lamp clamped to the wall and touched Chena's eyes, making her wince.

When she could see, the pale light showed her rough red stone walls, stacks of crates, folded metallic trees, and a small boy.

He crouched on top of a stack of plastic crates, watching the space behind her. She couldn't turn her head far enough to see what was so interesting. Maybe there was a door there. Maybe a camera, or another person who hadn't spoken yet.

We must be in the caves near Stem, thought Chena. *We must still be with the tailors.* Hope stirred inside her. The tailors were just villagers. Their resources were limited. She could get away from them. Especially if she had help. She turned her gaze toward the boy again.

He looked wobbly somehow. Chena squinted. She was seeing him through a layer of something, like plastic. Her eyes searched the air in front of her, found the dark line that was the seam, and traced it.

They had her in a box. A clear plastic box. Her chest spasmed as her brain told her she was sealed in, but a few frightened, shallow breaths told her the air was good. Whatever her prison was made out of, it had to be gas-permeable.

I can breathe. I can breathe, she repeated to herself until she calmed down.

Which was good, because it meant she would live, but it did not tell her how she would get out of here.

Whatever the boy saw, or did not see, behind her, he jumped off the crates and trotted over to her box. He was small, maybe five, maybe six years old at most. He crouched down beside her head, so she had to strain her neck against the collar to turn to see him.

Her heart faltered in her chest and it was all she could do to keep from crying out.

She was looking at Teal. This boy had her sister's wide eyes, delicate bones, dusky skin, and straight black hair that hung down his neck and fell into his eyes.

"Who are you?" she croaked.

The boy shrugged. "Are they going to keep you?"

"Who?"

"Lopera. The others. The black and white people."

That could only be the hothousers. *God's garden.* Chena swallowed. *I'm boxed up and sealed to go back to the hothouse.*

And that was a long way from being all of it. Chena made herself look at the boy again. His dark eyes reflected the lamplight, as if he had stars inside him. There was only one thing he could possibly be. She did not want to speak, but she had to know. "Are you Eden?"

"I guess."

He sounds like Sadia. Like Sadia in the involuntary wing. Chena closed her eyes. She couldn't stand to look anymore. *They killed Mom to make this thing, this mindless thing.* Her muscles clenched against the straps that held her down. She wanted to rise up, to strike out at that thing, beat on it until it bled and fell and sprawled across the floor, just like Mom had. She wanted all the hothousers to find her standing over its bloody corpse so they'd know who'd done it.

She wanted . . .

She opened her eyes and saw Teal's face again.

"Why'd they put you in a box?" Eden asked. "Are they testing you? Are they going to put me in a box?"

"I . . . I don't know."

"Oh." He sat back on his haunches and watched her for a moment, as if he were waiting for her to do something interesting. Looking at him, Chena's mind slithered so quickly between confusion and fear, she couldn't hang on to any single thought.

Eventually Eden stood. "I have to go."

Leaving her alone. Leaving her for the hothousers.

No, no, no . . .

"Wait," she gasped. "Eden, do you want to get away from the needles?" Sadia in involuntary had taken any suggestion Chena gave. If Eden was a mindless thing, she could put ideas into its head.

If Eden was a little boy, she could still put ideas into his head. She had done that with Teal all the time.

Eden scratched his backside for a minute. "I'm not supposed to leave. They say don't leave."

What would Teal want to hear? Think, think. "But have you ever played hide-and-seek with them?" tried Chena. "Lopera and the others?"

"I hide sometimes." Eden shrugged. "They find me."

"What if I told you I know a really good hiding place?" Chena hoped her voice sounded conspiratorial instead of desperate. "Someplace they'd never think of looking. You could keep them going for days."

The boy crept closer. "Lopera turns red when she can't find me. It's pretty funny."

Despite herself, Chena grinned. "Let me out of here and I'll show you how to make her turn purple."

Eden hesitated, but just for a second. "Okay." He jumped up and ran to the foot of the box. Chena pressed her chin hard against the collar so she could see past her own toes. She heard something rattle, clank, and then snap. A section of box swung free. The boy grunted, and Chena felt herself slide toward him.

They've got me on a gurney or something. Slide in, slide out for easy storage. It was almost funny.

"Okay," said Eden. "Now what?"

Chena swallowed. "Now see if you can find a buckle or a catch on these straps so I can get up."

Eden scratched his backside again. "They really didn't want you leaving, did they? They only ever shut me in my room."

"I've been a bad girl," muttered Chena.

Eden stared at the space over his head again. "Maybe this isn't a good idea. Maybe I should put you back."

Chena bit her lip. *It's Teal,* she told herself. *What would you say to Teal?*

"Okay, if you want." She rolled her eyes toward the rough red ceiling. "But then you won't get to ride in the boat."

"Boat?"

Chena tried to nod, but the collar choked her. "That's the best part. I was going to go up the river in a boat. I was going to show you the forest and my house, but if you're too scared, that's okay. Put me back." She sighed and waited, not looking at him.

Silence from Eden.

"Come on, come on," urged Chena. "If you don't want to ever see anything new again, just put me back. I'm getting cold out here."

"Well . . ." Chena looked down again and saw Eden squirm. "Okay."

Chena started breathing again. "Okay. If you can get one of my hands loose, I can help you and we'll just vanish. They'll be looking for us for hours."

Now that Eden had made his decision, he moved quickly. He scuttled around to her right side. She felt him tugging ineffectually at the strap, but after a moment's fussing, the binding came loose and she was able to lift her hand to fumble at the collar around her throat. Eden giggled and took her hand. His fingers were small, slender, and warm. He placed her hand on the buckle.

Trying not to think of anything but getting out of here, Chena worked the buckle and tore the collar from her neck. In another minute, she was free and on her feet, towering over Eden.

"Come on," he said, grabbing the hem of her tunic. "If we don't get out, they'll see us."

"Okay." Reflexively, Chena pulled his hand from her hem and held on to it. Held on to his hand, this Teal impostor, this thing that killed Mom.

Her brother. Was this really her brother? No. That was not possible. There was nothing of Mom in him. He was purely the hothousers' thing.

Then why did he look so much like Teal?

"Take us out to the lake," she said. "I'll get us to the river from there."

Grinning at the prospect of a new game, Eden scrambled up on top of the pile of crates. "Through here," he said, and vanished.

Chena, stiff from captivity and clumsy from whatever they had drugged her with, managed to clamber up after him. Time and water had carved a ragged oval hole through the stone. The lamplight penetrated it just far enough that she could see Eden's heels disappearing into the darkness.

Chena stayed where she was for a moment, her heart hammering. Would the tunnel be big enough for her? What if she got stuck?

"Come on!" Eden's voice floated up the tunnel.

No choice. Chena hoisted herself into the tunnel and started crawling forward. Rough stone bit into her elbows and knees. Her scalp scraped hard against the tunnel's roof. She bit her tongue and ducked down onto her forearms. She crept along slowly until her forehead brushed against another outcropping. Cursing under her breath, she dropped onto her belly and began to pull herself forward with her elbows. The stone scratched long, painful lines down her torso. More stone scraped against her shoulders.

"Come on!" rasped Eden from somewhere ahead. "They're going to be looking for us."

"I can't," Chena gasped, wincing as she felt her tunic and the skin underneath it tear open. "It's too small!"

"It opens up. Just a little farther." She heard scuffling. Eden's small hand groped at her face, found the collar of her tunic, and pulled. "Come on!"

Gritting her teeth against the pain and all the fear, Chena dragged herself forward another few inches. The stone pulled back from her shoulders and after wriggling another foot, she was able to push herself back onto her knees. Then, she saw Eden grinning at her, and she realized she could see him. Light leaked around the boy from somewhere up ahead.

"Is that the outside?" she breathed.

Eden shook his head. "We've got to go through the needle room, and then there's another tunnel. Then there's the outside."

Eden reversed direction so that his buttocks were practically pressed against her nose, and scurried forward. Torn between laughter and frustration, Chena crawled after him.

The tunnel ended high in the wall of another cave. Eden crept out onto what looked like a wooden shelf. Chena squeezed herself through the tunnel's mouth and saw it was the top of a cabinet. Scooting forward on his rear end, Eden stretched out his entire length until the tips of his toes just touched the counter beside the cabinet. From the counter, he jumped easily down to the floor.

The cabinet wobbled under Chena's weight, but stayed upright. Thanks to her height, she had an easier time than Eden lowering herself down to the counter and then the floor. As she straightened up, she realized she recognized the cabinets and the shape of the cavern. A small spasm of fear shook her. This was the room where the tailors had tested her to see if she'd been damaged by the fences. The drastic tools of surgery filled the place. Knives lay in sterilizer trays, ready for cutting. Beside them stood lasers on long, flexible stems. In the cabinets, saws and pliers waited to dismantle bones and joints, along with shelf after shelf of needles—needles for stitching, for injecting, for probing. Here was the other reason her captors were called tailors.

"Let's get out of here," she whispered to Eden.

An environment lock blocked one end of the cavern. Eden stood on his tiptoes to reach the command pad. Chena moved to help, but before she reached him, a woman's voice called from the other side.

"Eden!"

Eden froze, one hand against the wall, fingers poised over the command pad. "That's Dans."

"Eden! Come on, game's over!"

"Let's hide," suggested Chena cheerfully. Inside, her heart pounded out of control. "I bet you know all the good places. I bet she walks right by us."

Eden squirmed. "I don't know," he said. "She sounds mad. Hiding will make it worse."

"So, we should hide until she calms down." The words came out in a rush. Chena felt her nerve beginning to break. "Back in the tunnel? If she finds us now, we're both going to get it."

It worked. "She knows about that tunnel." Eden dove for the shadows, squeezing himself between one of the glass-faced cabinets full of needles and the cavern wall. Chena sucked in her stomach, pressed her back against the wall, and forced herself in beside him. Rough stone tore her already ruined tunic and the raw skin underneath. She had to bite her lip to keep from yelping.

"Eden! Come out! I mean it!"

Chena inched her hand across to touch Eden reassuringly.

Something clicked and slid back heavily. Hinges creaked. Shoes slapped against the cavern floor.

"Eden?" The voice was in the room with them. "Eden, I'm giving you till the count of three to come out here."

Eden wiggled under Chena's touch. She tried to grab hold of him to keep him in place, but she could not quite reach.

"Eden, you come out here right now or I'm giving you to the black and white people today."

Eden squeaked and the footsteps slapped toward their hiding place. Desperately, Chena slid her hands up the cabinet back, tightened her muscles, and pushed.

The cabinet teetered forward and crashed down. Dans's scream rang out over the splintering of glass and wood.

Chena scrambled out over the corner of the fallen cabinet. She glimpsed Dans's head and arm protruding from under the shattered wood. There was blood. She did not want to see.

"Come on!" She grabbed Eden's hand and pulled, but Eden didn't move. "Come on!"

"No." Eden yanked his hand out of hers and scuttled to Dans's side. "She's hurt. We have to get Lopera."

"She'll be okay," lied Chena. She might not be. There was blood, and it was on her skull. There was no time to check whether it was just a cut or whether Chena had just killed someone new. "We need to go."

"But she's not moving!" Eden shook Dans's shoulder. "That's bad. I know that's bad!"

Chena scooped Eden off his feet and turned to run.

"No!" screamed Eden at the top of his lungs. He struggled under her arm, pushing at her. "No!"

"You don't understand," panted Chena, clasping him tightly to her. "You can't stay here with them. They're going to hurt you." *They're going to give you away, put you in a hothouse. I'm trying to help you. You have to understand.*

"Put him down!"

The tailor, Lopera, stood in the doorway, and just behind her stood the hothouser Dionte.

"Lopera!" Eden threw himself toward the tailor. Chena only just managed to hang on.

"No." Chena wrapped both arms tightly around Eden, crushing him against her chest. Eden fought back, punching her with his tiny fists and kicking her stomach, making her gasp for air. "They're going to hurt you!" she tried to tell him. "They're going to give you away. Dans said she would!" *Why don't you understand? They're the ones you need to be afraid of!*

"Chena, stop being stupid. You have nowhere to go." The tailor strode forward. "What are you going to do? Hurt your brother?"

Chena backed away, kicking aside glass and stumbling over something soft. "He's not my brother."

As she spoke, she knew it was true. If he really was her brother, he wouldn't be trying to run away from her. He would know who she was, and that she was trying to help him. Eden was only one of the hothousers' things, like the jaguars they'd used to track her in the rain forest, like the ants that had killed all those colonists. This was the thing they'd used to kill Mom.

"Be careful!" cried Dionte. "Don't let her hurt Eden."

"I'm working on it." Lopera took another step forward. "And by the good green Earth you better hope Dans is still alive or I'm skinning you myself!"

Nowhere to go. Nowhere to go. Eden struggling in her arms until she could barely hang on.

"Stop, stop it!" She ducked sideways toward one of the sterilizer tables. Lopera froze again. Without taking her eyes off the tailor, Chena fumbled at the table until her hand came up with a scalpel. She held it out toward Lopera. "You're going to let me go."

"She might," said Dionte calmly. She stayed in the doorway, blocking the only way out. "But I'm not. We need you as well, Chena Trust."

Dionte's words drew Chena's gaze to the doorway for just a split second, but it was enough. Lopera lunged. Her hand clamped around Chena's wrist, forcing the knife up. Eden shrieked and struggled and Chena could not hold him anymore. Eden fell and Lopera shoved Chena backward, slamming her hand against the wall. Chena grabbed a fistful of Lopera's hair at the base of her neck and yanked down hard. Lopera screamed and her grip loosened. Chena slashed the scalpel down, slicing through the flesh at Lopera's throat.

Blood. Blood everywhere. In Chena's eyes, down her face, all over her tunic and hands. Lopera gurgled and fell, clutching at the scarlet fountain welling from her. Chena backed away, unwilling to believe what she was seeing, what she had done. But Eden shrieked and Chena looked up in time to see Dionte fleeing through the door.

Chena launched herself after the hothouser. She tackled the woman, sending them all sprawling, and knocking the air from her own lungs. Eden scrabbled out from under them as Chena and Dionte rolled over, and Chena realized she did not have the scalpel. Silver flashed in Dionte's hand and Chena threw herself sideways. Not far enough. The hothouser grabbed her tunic and hauled Chena backward. Chena struggled, her heels peddling uselessly against the floor, seeking purchase, but Dionte knelt on her chest.

"Maybe I don't need you alive that much," said the hothouser slowly, as if it were a revelation coming over her. "I already have your sister's eggs. Your womb should keep for a few hours while we get your body to storage." Her teeth gleamed in the lamplight. "I see it now," she panted. "I see everything. This is what we should have done with your mother."

Chena screamed and smashed her free hand against the base of Dionte's nose. Dionte screamed and fell backward. The next thing Chena knew, she knelt over Dionte with the scalpel in her hand and she drove it into Dionte's belly, drove it deep, drove it hard, slicing the hothouser's flesh, burying her hand in hot blood, muscle, and offal. She screamed, the hothouser screamed, someone else screamed, and the screaming would not stop. Then the smell hit her, the sick, acrid, coppery smell of her mother's death.

Chena choked and pressed her bloody hand against her nose, scrambling away from the smell until her back pressed against the stone. She tried to breathe, but she just choked until finally all she could do was vomit.

When she was finally empty, Chena lifted her head. Someone was still screaming. Who could be screaming? She had killed everybody, hadn't she?

No. Eden, the hothouser's thing, the thing that had killed Mom, was still alive. She would not believe he was her brother. She would not, would not, would not! The words screamed themselves inside her head. *Not my brother, never my brother!*

He had curled himself into a ball in the corner, his arms over his head, barely muffling his screams. The sound filled her mind, along with the hideous smell, until she couldn't think.

"Stop it," she said hoarsely, taking a step toward him. "Stop it. I need to think." Think about how to get out of here. Think about how to get away from the blood and the smell. Think about how to get away from the world before it ate her alive.

Eden uncurled just enough to look at her with one eye. The eye widened and a fresh scream burst from him. He scuttled backward, trying to get away from her.

"Stop it!" Chena saw her hand go up, and she saw it come down. Eden fell sideways. She heard the crack as his skull hit the rock. Then Eden lay still.

Chena crouched next to him. She realized she still held the scalpel. She could kill the thing that had killed Mom. She could end it all right here. She looked down at the still boy.

"Why did you have to look so much like Teal?" she murmured, and reached out to touch his hair. The blood coating her hands was already beginning to darken from scarlet to rust. The death smell clung to every inch of her. *I need a bath,* she thought dizzily. But really, she would have to drown herself in a world of water before she would ever be clean.

That was it. Chena felt quite still. Eden had been taking her out toward the water. Water was a friend. It hid you from the cameras. It washed the insects from you. It would take her away from the world. It would save what was left of her family from the hothousers, and give her all the revenge she needed. They wouldn't catch her in the water, ever. It would all end in the water. Finally.

Chena scooped Eden up carefully and, cradling him against her chest, walked through the environment lock and up the tunnel.

Dawn had turned the horizon pink and white by the time Teal emerged from Farin's tiny house with Tam and Nan Elle beside her. Elle had insisted they try to get at least a couple of hours' sleep. It hadn't worked. How could Teal sleep after hearing Tam's description of the Eden Project and Mom's part in it? How could she sleep after realizing that those eggs she sold to the tailors were probably going straight to the hothouse so they could make more of the things? The idea dragged down her whole body, leaving her feeling leaden and hot-wired at the same time.

As bad as she felt, Administrator Tam looked worse. His cheeks and eyes had sunken in until all the bones of his face were clearly visible. His mouth moved constantly, and he seemed frightened to put one foot in front of the other. What was that voice in his ear saying to him? Teal shuddered and decided she did not want to know.

The first fingers of sunlight reached across the quay, turning the waters blue and touching the dunes with their warmth. Teal wiped the tears from her eyes and looked inland. The cliffs stood in the distance, rust red under their green crown of trees. Chena was in there somewhere. Teal let herself smile. This was going to be one time Chena could not argue about who was saving whom, which was a petty thought, but she held it close just the same.

Nan Elle took the lead. The plan was to head for the fence duty house, find out who was on duty, and put them out of commission by the least aggressive means possible. Then they'd duck the fences and she and Farin would head for the caves, using the map tucked into Teal's pocket. The three of them were already smeared with a layer of Chena's goop to fool the mote cameras. Nan Elle and Tam would suss out the situation with the dirigibles and boats on the jetty to see who would carry them all away.

That was if Tam could still talk by then. Teal decided she'd better not think about that too much. The only reason any of this was going to work was that they had a hothouser with them. If he gave in to whatever was whispering in his head, they were screwed and blasted, and this time it would be for good.

"Do you hear something?" asked Farin suddenly.

Teal listened. She did hear something, a low droning, too deep to be a dirigible. She scanned the morning sky in front of her and saw nothing but a few streaks of cloud.

"Garden of God." Nan Elle pointed her stick to the sky.

Teal swung around. A great black cloud hung over the tops of the dunes, humming with a sound Teal was sure should be familiar.

"Get inside!" shouted Farin, shoving Teal toward the dune.

Unnerved, Teal turned to run. In the next second, a locust dropped onto the tip of her shoe, and another onto her tunic sleeve.

"Get in—" Farin's shout was cut short, and the world went dark.

Teal heard herself screaming as the locusts swirled around her, clinging to her clothing, tangling in her hair. She swatted at them, but they were everywhere, their tiny claws digging into her skin. Blind, she ran forward until she thudded into the side of the dune house, but the locusts were already there, and they crunched and chirruped and clung to her hands. Somehow, somehow, she found the door and darted inside.

"Hold still! Hold still!" Hands brushed against her, knocking the insects away. Teal forced herself to open her eyes.

Farin stood in front of her, clearing the locusts off her and crushing them underfoot. Nan Elle darted around the room with a broom to destroy the creatures that had poured through the door when they had retreated inside.

"Get the fire going, or they'll come down the chimney," she ordered, sweeping the insects from the walls and crushing them underfoot.

Teal knocked Farin's hands away and dropped to her knees in front of the brick stove, tossing in handfuls of kindling and fuel until the flames roared and their heat felt harsh against her face. She was vaguely aware that Farin had snatched the cloth off the table and stuffed it into the crack under the door, and that Tam had collapsed in the middle of the room and cradled his head in his hands.

"Dionte," he murmured. "She knows, she knows. She's told the family. I should be back there. I should—"

"Shut up!" shouted Teal. "Just . . . shut up!" She ran both hands through her hair, half afraid she'd find another locust clinging there. "What in all the hells is going on?" she demanded.

"The hothousers." Nan Elle stood, panting. A single locust clung to her apron. She snatched it off and tossed it into the fire.

"They found us out." Farin peered out the window at the whirring darkness.

Teal forced herself to walk across the room to stand beside Farin and look out. The sunny dawn had turned black and gray with the swarms of tiny bodies. They crowded the boardwalk, the windowsill. They slammed against the window, and she knew by the shivering of her skin that they crawled all over the roof.

"Dionte found out," said Tam. "This is a quarantine. We'll stay here until the family comes for us." The utter relief in his voice raised clusters of goose bumps across Teal's arms. "It is right. I was wrong to stand against them. They are my family. They know what's best. Pandora must be protected."

Oh, no. Teal pressed her knuckles against her mouth. *They're getting to him.* She stared out at the dark, whirling storm, trying to think of some way to get out, someplace they could run to. But no thoughts came to her. There was just the drone of the swarm and the terrifying calm in Tam's face.

Nan Elle knelt carefully in front of the hothouser. "Tam, you can call the Alpha Complex. You can stop this."

"No," he said, his face and voice serene. "This is right. Pandora must be protected."

"They can't," blurted out Teal. "We can't!" She faced the strip of window, black with insects somehow finding purchase even on the slick glass. "We can't let them win like this," she whispered. "They'll take Chena. They'll take the Eden Project. We can't let them."

"We may have to," said Farin quietly. "For now. Teal, I've heard of these things. We don't know how big the swarm is. People can go crazy trying to walk through them without protective clothing."

Fear and rage surged through Teal. She wanted to shout, to hit something, to strangle the peaceful hothouser sitting in the middle of the floor, but all she could do was stand there with her hands dangling uselessly at her sides. "It can't be this easy for them."

Farin shook his head. "They've had a long time to get ready for this."

"Now what?" demanded Nan Elle, lifting her chin.

A new note sounded over the droning and thudding of the locust swarm—a harsh metallic shriek, and another, and another after that.

"Gulls?" said Farin.

Surprise wiped the expression from Nan Elle's face for a moment. Then, slowly, a smile full of mischief and wonder spread across her face. Using her stick to push herself to her feet, she shouldered between Farin and Teal to peer intently out the window.

"There! There!" She stabbed her finger against the glass. "Do you see?"

Teal stared over Nan Elle's head. For a moment all she saw was the endless cloud of insects. Then she saw a flash of white. A black-backed gull settled onto the boardwalk, snapping up locusts as fast as it could crane its neck and swallowing them down. Another gull landed beside the first, bending and stabbing at the insects. A third joined them, and a fourth. A brown and white kestrel landed on Farin's windowsill and began pecking insects off the glass, swallowing them greedily.

"Ha!" Nan Elle barked out a laugh and thumped her stick against the floor. "I told you! I told you it would happen!"

"Told what to who?" said Teal, unable to take her eyes from the birds. More landed every second. Gulls, kestrels, fishers, grouse, fat brown turkeys, strutting guinea hens, and prairie chickens, all come to the feast. Soon it seemed there were as many birds as there were insects.

Elle swung around to face Tam. "Come and look, Tam. Pandora has decided to protect herself."

Tam lifted his head and stared at her, wide-eyed, like he didn't understand.

"Look!" She thumped her stick one more time.

Slowly, shaking from the effort, Tam stood and teetered over to the window. He pressed both palms against the glass and stared at the spectacle outside, the triumphant birds and swirling insects.

"Pandora herself has said she doesn't want the family to catch us," said Elle, watching Tam as intensely as Tam watched the birds. "Call the duty house, tell them to shut down the fences."

"No," breathed Tam. "I cannot. My family—"

"How can your family be right when Pandora says they're wrong?" demanded Elle. "This is Pandora telling you what to do! Call the duty house, shut them down. You can do this, Tam."

Tam's jaw worked back and forth, alternating between whispering to himself and chewing his own lip.

"Come on, Tam," breathed Elle. "I know you're still in there somewhere. Pandora's giving you a chance."

"I must go back to my family."

Elle gripped his arm. "You can do this. I know you can."

Tam squeezed his eyes shut. "I must go back to my family."

"Yes," said Elle fiercely. "When it is over, you will go back. You will tell them everything. I know that's what you have to do. But first you must help Pandora."

Tam raised one trembling fist. Farin sucked in his breath, and moved to step between Tam and Elle, but Elle waved him back. Tam, his face white with concentration, uncurled one finger at a time and touched the tips to the data display on the back of his right hand. Teal swallowed hard, fear and hope both clogging her throat.

Tam traced a series of commands on the display. No one breathed. There was only the screech of birds and the crackle of the fire.

"Done," said Tam. "Done."

"Go!" shouted Elle.

Teal took a deep breath. Then, so fast she had no time to think, she opened the door and ran out into the maelstrom with Farin right behind her. Her last sight of Elle was her laying a hand on Tam's shoulder.

The world outside was a frenzy of singing insects and shrieking birds. Teal ran, keeping her head ducked, so all she could see was the boardwalk in front of her. Birds screamed and fluttered out of the way. Insects scrunched under her shoes. Something dark slithered across her path and Teal realized the snakes had come to join in the feed. A kind of wild delight filled her. Nan Elle was right. Pandora itself was fighting back.

The idea gave her the strength to look up. They had almost reached the northern edge of the village. Ahead of her, she could see the boardwalk's edge with its neat row of fence posts. If Tam had lied, or his orders had been countermanded and they'd turned the fence posts off only for a moment, it ended here. They were dead, or as good as.

Screaming at the top of her lungs, Teal leapt.

She hit the ground with a thump that knocked all the air out of her lungs and sent an outraged flock of birds winging skyward. A second later, Farin measured his length in the sand beside her. They both lay there panting for a moment.

Alive. Awake.

We did it. Teal lifted her head. The clouds of insects were thinner out here, and the clusters of birds were thicker. They warbled and chortled triumphantly to each other as they strolled casually after their prey.

Scrambling to her feet, Teal knew exactly how they felt.

"We still have to find your sister." Farin climbed to his own feet, scanning the boardwalk for witnesses. "Before the hothousers show up to find out what's gone wrong."

"Not going to be a problem," said Teal, taking in a deep, free breath of morning air. "The whole world's on our side."

Farin laughed, and headed off into the brush. Teal ran to catch up, and as she did, she snuck a look at him, watching the way his long legs swung so easily, even over the shifting sand, and how his auburn hair caught the sunlight. For just a minute, she could see how he had looked so good to Chena.

The memory of old fights and old insults came back hard.

"Farin . . ." She licked her lips. "Are you really a . . . a . . . prostitute?"

"I've been paid for sex," he said. Then he broke stride for just a moment to look at her. "And no, I never made love to your sister."

"Oh," said Teal, pointing her eyes straight ahead. "Okay."

Farin laughed a little at that, but it was a kind sound, as if he understood. Teal had to admit to herself the question was pretty stupid and probably none of her business, but she still felt as if a weight had left her. When they found Chena, she'd tell her she'd been stupid, or maybe she wouldn't, because Chena would never let her hear the end of it if she did.

The new lightness only lasted for a short time, however. Farin set a pace up the dune that left Teal with no breath for anything but walking. The sand shifted under her boots, giving way slowly to firm earth, which made walking somewhat easier, but the new soil grew short, crabbed bushes loaded with burrs and thorns. A few scattered prairie chickens hunted stray locusts under the bracken, but that was all.

Get to the cliffs. Teal wiped her forehead. *Get Chena out. That's all that's left to do. Then we go back to the station.*

"Teal?"

Farin had stopped and was pointing up the slope in front of them. Teal followed the line of his arm and saw a human figure crest the ridge from the other side.

"Chena!" she shouted.

But Chena did not hear. She just turned toward the lake, trudging toward the edge of the cliff. She cradled something heavy in her arms.

Teal felt the blood drain from her face. Chena carried a small boy.

"I think that's the Eden Project she's . . ." began Farin, then he saw Teal's face.

"God's own," Teal breathed. Chena had paused at the edge of the cliff, hugging the boy close to her chest and peering down at the water. "What's she doing?"

"Teal . . ."

But Teal was already running. "Chena! Stop!"

"Chena!"

Chena jerked her head up. A woman ran toward her. She tightened her grip on Eden's still form and turned to look down into the water where it swirled against the base of the rust-red cliff.

"Stop! Don't! It's Teal!"

Chena turned again; she couldn't help it. "Teal?" she heard herself breathe.

The woman had stopped running. She stood in a clump of antelope's tail brush about ten yards away, panting hard. She was tall and round in the hips, with skin the exact color Mom's had been.

"It's me, I'm Teal," she gasped. "I had a tailor age me up. The one who got hold of you, I think."

"Teal's gone," murmured Chena. It was a good thing the woman wore sturdy trousers, she thought idly. Antelope's tail had thorns. "She left."

"I'm back," said the woman. "God's own, Nan Elle recognized me." Chena felt her eyes strain as they stared. "And you used to call me vapor-brain," snorted the woman.

Chena's mouth had to shape the word several times before any sound come out. "Teal?"

"So, what do you think you're doing this time?" The woman—Teal? really? Teal come back?—folded her arms, standing with one hip thrust a little forward and her face twisted up, scornful, superior. Just like Teal in the hothouse when she was telling Chena how things really were. Just like Teal a hundred times when they were staying with Nan Elle and she didn't want to go to class, didn't want to go on shift, didn't want to do anything Chena told her she had to.

"Teal." She took a step forward, and then Eden shifted in her arms. Was it waking up?

"Hello." Teal waved a careless salute. "I asked what do you think you're doing."

Chena looked down at the water. From here, it looked deep blue. Spurts of foam leapt up from where the waves splashed the rocks. *Remember what you're doing. This is important. You have to do it now.*

But Teal should know what was happening. "This killed Mom." She held Eden out.

Teal leaned forward and wrinkled her nose at it. "Doesn't look old enough."

"No! This was inside her. This is what they cut out of her!" Teal had to understand. Teal had come back. Teal knew how important this was. Teal was the only other one who knew. "This is what they were going to put inside us!"

Teal cocked her head and eyed Chena skeptically. "So, you're going to toss the kid over the cliff because the hothousers' brains are all vacuum-welded?"

Anger, hot as blood, thundered through Chena's veins. "You don't understand. You never understand!"

Teal threw open her arms. "Explain it to me, then, Chena. You always have forty thousand explanations in storage. Let's have the one for murdering a little boy."

"It's not a little boy!" she screamed. "Stop saying it's a little boy!"

"Look at him, Chena!" snapped Teal. "If that's not a little boy, what is it?"

Chena looked at the figure lying limp in her arms. It still looked so much like Teal—not this new, strange Teal in front of her, but Teal when she was little. Teal when she had listened, when she had believed.

"It's a cure for the Diversity Crisis. It's a murder weapon. It's our future." Chena's eyes burned as she looked at it. It shifted again. It was going to wake up soon and open Teal's eyes. She wouldn't be able to jump if she had to look into Teal's eyes. "It can't get sick, no matter what it's exposed to. They're going to use it to kill off the Authority and all the Called. They're going to be the only people left alive." She lifted her gaze to Teal, tall and mature, all ready for the hothousers to use. "They're going to use us to make more of them, Teal, so they can kill more people!"

"So, you're going to throw him off a cliff?"

Tears came at last, streams of heat trickling down her cheeks. "They're never going to leave us alone, Teal. They're going to keep coming and coming and coming. They're going to use us to kill people, Teal. I don't want to kill people." Teal's face shifted as she finally understood it was not just Eden who had to die.

"No?" Teal's eyebrows rose and she sauntered a couple of steps forward. "You just want to kill him and you." Teal stepped up next to Chena and looked down over the cliff, measuring the length of the drop with her gaze.

"It'll be over," whispered Chena.

"For you." Teal turned to face her. "What about me?" She poked her own chest with one finger. "If you're gone and I'm all that's left. What happens to me?"

Chena hesitated. Teal. Teal come back. What would they do to Teal without her there? Teal never knew how to take care of herself. "You could come with us," she whispered. "We'd win. They'd never be able to kill anybody without us."

"But I don't want to die, Chena," said Teal softly. She took another step forward. "I don't want to give them what they want."

"No, they want us to live."

"Do they?" She reached out and touched Chena's arm, and even through her tears Chena could see Teal's eyes, Mom's eyes. "They had to kill Mom to stop her, Chena. Do you really think they want to keep us alive?" Chena's arms began to tremble and Teal gripped her wrist. "You do this thing and you'll be giving them what they want."

Exhaustion washed over Chena. So many bad decisions, so much gone wrong, she couldn't stand it anymore. "I want it over, Teal," she said. "There's no life for us. Even if he was a little boy, there'd be no life for him. They'd just keep poking and prodding him, trying to figure him out. They'd still need to use us all as breeding cows because they're desperate, Teal. They're desperate."

"So, screw 'em to the deck plates," Teal spat. "If you're dead, they'll just fish out your body and take it apart. If you're alive, you can fight back."

"I'm tired, Teal."

Teal laid her other hand on Chena's arm. "So am I, but we're not alone. I've brought help."

"Help?" said Chena. How could there be help? There had never been anyone to help them. Not really.

But Teal nodded, and Eden groaned. It hurt. She'd hurt it.

"Let me show you," said Teal. "And if you don't like what you see, you can always slit your wrists or something."

"I . . ." Chena hesitated, tears and exhaustion fogging her mind.

This was wrong. Everything was all wrong. "I killed people already, Teal."

"So, don't kill anymore." Teal held out her arms. "Let me take Eden, and you both come with me."

Chena looked down at the cold blue water. She should jump. She should do it now. That was the sure way. It would all be over as soon as she hit the water. No more decisions, no more crying, no more blood and loss.

"I didn't come back to argue with you, Chena," said Teal. "And my arms are getting tired."

Over. All over. For her. But for Teal? For the Called and the villagers? The hothousers would fish up her body. They'd take her to pieces and use her for spare parts, and there wouldn't be a damn thing she could do about it.

And Teal was still standing in front of her, arms out, toe tapping impatiently. Teal, of all of them, had come back.

Chena poured Eden into Teal's arms. Eden blinked and stirred again as Teal cradled him to her chest. She turned away and began walking down the cliff, toward the beach and Stem. Slowly, one shaking step at a time, Chena began to follow her.

"I have a message for you, Father Mihran." Tam's words dropped like lead into the center of the storm.

As one, the committee froze in the middle of their furious debate and turned to stare, mouths agape, hands still in the air.

His family. He had come back to his family, as was right. He stepped into the committee grove to stand at the foot of the table.

The entire family dome was in an uproar. As he'd walked across the family wing, he'd heard a thousand variations on the same theme. The containment measures around Stem had failed spectacularly, and everyone seemed torn between trying to measure the damage they had done to the local ecosystem, telling each other they had known it would never work, and trying frantically to sort through a billion pieces of confused and conflicting data to find out how the fences had gone down, and if anyone had slipped out of the village while they had.

He passed through it all, focused only on telling his family the truth of what had happened, and what was going to happen. He would help his family.

"Tam." Father Mihran got to his feet and circled the table. "We are glad to have you back. You need—"

"I need to tell you what happened." Tam grasped the father's hand. He was shaking again. He wished he could stop that. "Please, Father."

"Father—" began Senior Dreas.

Father Mihran waved him silent. "What is your message, Tam?"

Tam released Father Mihran's hand and sank to his knees so he could touch the command board set into the committee table. As he worked the keys, he wondered again where Aleph was. She had not spoken to him since he entered the complex and although he had been able to stop himself from calling for her, he had not been able to stop himself from wondering where her attention was. What had she told the other cities about him? Did she approve of what was happening here? Was he doing the right thing? The doubts and the guilt would not leave him alone.

I am telling my family the truth, Tam reminded himself. *Aleph must approve. Aleph is the one who has always helped me.*

Tam touched the monitor glass at his right to set it to reception mode.

The glass filled with colors, which split into two halves. One half coalesced to show Beleraja Poulos sitting in a tiny office aboard Athena Station. The other showed the car of the space cable, with Chena and Teal Trust flanking the stooped figure of Nan Elle.

"Commander Poulos," Father Mihran said, not bothering to salute. "We have been waiting to hear from you." He squared his shoulders. "We understand your people are en route." He peered at the tableau on the left side of the glass. Tam wondered if the father understood everything he saw. Aleph most certainly did, but Aleph was still keeping her silence.

Beleraja shook her head. "My people are here, and we have something of yours." She nodded toward the other half of the screen. Nan Elle reached behind herself and brought out a slim, dirty boy of about five years old. "This is your Eden."

Outraged voices rang out behind him.

"Impossible!"

"How could they!"

"It's a fake! A mock-up!"

"No," said Tam quietly to Father Mihran. "That is the Eden Project." Now they knew everything. Almost everything. They did not yet know how the project had been found. Did not yet know of Dionte's plans, and how badly they had failed. Tears prickled Tam's eyes for his lost sister.

Beside him, Father Mihran's jaw twitched, as if he were fighting to keep back the words he knew he must speak. "What do you want?"

Nan Elle patted Eden's hand and walked him toward the edge of the screen, moving him out of camera range.

Only when the child was out of sight did Beleraja speak again. "I want to make an end to the Diversity Crisis, Father Mihran," she said matter-of-factly. "A real, viable end. I want you to let the Called come to Pandora."

"Never," snapped the father instantly.

Beleraja betrayed no surprise at that curt answer. Why should she? She was an experienced trader as well as a commander. She knew very well how this game was played.

But did she know she was treading on holy ground here? Tam felt his stomach knot. Did she know how long and how hard their people had worked to keep Pandora inviolate? Even now, all the endless repetitions of protection rang around his tired head and he felt his strength to resist them crumbling.

Where are you, Aleph? He rubbed his temple. *I need your help. You helped me be strong before. I need you now.*

Beleraja leaned in closer to the screen. In the cable car, Teal Trust clenched her fists and her jaw. *What are you holding in?* he wondered. *What voices are calling to you?*

"What do you think is going to happen when we tell the Authority that the cure does not exist?" Beleraja asked Father Mihran. "That you have nothing except one five-year-old boy to show for all your promised work?"

"They will see that the boy will answer." Pride drew Father Mihran's shoulders back even farther. It was not possible that his family should fail, that the results of their slow, patient, meticulous work should be anything but perfect.

"No," said Beleraja. "The boy will not be exploited. Neither will his sisters. That is not an option."

"There is no other option," said Father Mihran slowly, as if explaining the obvious. "There is no other cure."

"Yes, there is. The Called can come here." Beleraja pointed toward the floor.

"We will not let that happen. Pandora must be protected."

"Pandora must be protected!" shouted Senior Jahn, and a dozen other voices echoed her words, including his own, Tam realized, as he fell back into his sitting position. *Aleph, help me. I'm losing my grip. . . .*

Now it was Beleraja's turn to make a show of patience. She sighed sadly and shook her head. "You cannot protect Pandora," she said, sounding more like a mother now than a commander. "We've just proven that. We are here and we have already claimed what we wanted." The steel returned to her voice and her face. "You can't stand against even one family. How will you manage if the whole Authority turns against you?"

"They are still riding the cable, Father," said Senior Jahn. "We can call it back, have a troop of constables waiting for her."

"Do it," said Father Mihran. "We are reclaiming Eden, Commander. If any of your people try to interfere again, they will die for their trespasses."

"No," said Aleph.

"Aleph?" Father Mihran turned toward the city's voice, complete disbelief showing on his face.

Aleph manifested an image on the nearest wall, a mature woman, straight-backed and square-faced, in a black jacket and white trousers. She looked a bit like Beleraja, Tam thought.

"She is speaking the truth," said Aleph calmly. "We cannot protect Pandora by preventing the Called from coming here. We must allow this. Only when the fear is gone will we have peace."

"Aleph, this is not—" began Father Mihran.

But Aleph did not seem to hear him. "I speak with the other cities as I speak with you. We are working out formulas for population distribution that will allow maximum genetic exchange and minimum territorial overpopulation." Aleph bowed her head, as if under the weight of the necessities facing her. "Pandora will change, but Pandora will live and be protected. There will be no reason to attack us. The Called will eventually be resettled."

"No," said Father Mihran, but his voice wavered. "Aleph, this cannot be the answer."

"It is all the answer we have," she said. "Please, do not turn me away. Let me help my family as I was meant to."

Father Mihran watched the image of his city for a moment, but then he slashed his hand through the air. "I'm sorry, Aleph. We cannot permit this." All the seniors murmured their agreement with Father Mihran's dismissal. "Aleph, we respect you, but this is not a matter for you and the cities. . . ."

They hesitated and Tam felt himself smile in sad sympathy. He knew what was happening. He could practically hear. *It is wrong to argue with your city,* said all their Consciences. *Your city is taking care of you. That is what your cities are for. You must work with your city. To do otherwise is wrong. Why are you doing this?*

In the midst of their guilty silence, Aleph spoke again. "We are your cities. It is our job to protect you, as it is your job to protect Pandora. I cannot let you injure yourself in your zeal." The image looked past the father to Beleraja. "Bring us your plans, Commander. We must begin work at once."

Beleraja inclined her head once and then moved her hand to the command board. The connection cut and the images faded to black, fading the Trusts, around whom so many plans had been woven, to insubstantial ghosts, setting them free like wild birds that could not be controlled or predicted in duress, even after a thousand years of observation and understanding.

Leaving Tam alone with what remained of his family, of himself, and of his city. Alone, with nothing but a whole new world of their making. A world they would have to walk in, to understand with their own eyes and hands so they would know how to settle the human race here. Where they would finally have to understand the balance between what they made and what they found.

In a way, Dionte had been right. It was going to take everybody to secure the future. She just didn't see far enough. It was going to take all of humanity, every last one of them bound tightly together by need, desire, fear, joy, friendship, hatred, love, struggle, and hope. Oh, most especially hope.

They would have to open the villages. They would have to leave the complexes and walk out in the wild. Step into the marsh and watch the birds in their thousands take flight all around them.

The image filled him, heart, mind, and soul, and for the first time in his life, Tam saw the birds fly and felt no guilt, none at all.

EPILOGUE

Open Cages

Teal crossed the car and sat down beside Chena on the curving padded bench that ran along the inner wall. Chena just pulled the blanket tighter around her. She did not want Teal here. She did not want anybody.

"Going home at last," said Teal cheerfully.

Chena bit her lip, remembered herself, and pushed her lip out again. "Teal . . ."

"Yes?"

Chena ground her teeth. How could she speak? Where could she possibly begin? She'd been ready to die, to kill, to fall. That was what she wanted. She remembered wanting it very clearly. Except some small part of her had not wanted it at all.

Finally some words came out. "Thank you."

"You're welcome," said Teal, waving her hand in breezy dismissal of her sister's seriousness.

The gesture made Chena wince. "I don't know what happened to me."

"I do."

"Oh?" For the first time since the edge of the cliff, Chena felt some warmth inside her, and a bit of annoyance. "You going to tell me?"

Teal nodded. "You thought you had the answers, as usual, and you were wrong."

"Is that what it was?" Chena sat up a little straighter, feeling something in her mind that had been retreating turn around and move a little bit closer. "I thought I was in shock because I had just murdered three people."

Teal shrugged. "That too."

They sat silently together for a moment. Teal seemed to be watching Farin where he sat at the transmitter screen, flicking through assorted databases, but Chena couldn't be certain what her sister was actually seeing.

Chena bit her lip, let it go, and bit it again. "Where's Eden?" she asked.

"He's in with Nan Elle," said Teal, not looking at her. "I think she's going to give him a bath."

"Did you find Dad?"

"Yes." Teal dropped her gaze and twisted her fingers together. "He's dead."

Again, silence closed over her. Chena let it. It was so strange. Even when they were sitting, Teal was taller than she was. Chena had imagined so many things about meeting her sister again, but she had never imagined she would feel so much younger than this strange, tall Teal. "So, it's just us."

"And our brother," Teal reminded her gently.

Chena turned her head, memory of wanting to kill the boy burning a river of shame through her. "You really think he's our brother?"

Teal just spread her hands. "What else could he be? He's Mom's, just like we are."

Now Chena shrugged. "I thought he was just a thing. One more thing the hothousers made."

Teal smiled, and the smile was deeply familiar and entirely Teal's. "Like I said, thought you had all the answers."

Chena laughed, just a little, and bowed her head. "I think I was crazy."

"I think you were." Teal paused. "I'm sorry I left you."

Chena raised her eyes and saw her sister's face shining with hope and fear, warmth and worry. "If you hadn't"—tears pricked the corners of her eyes—"we wouldn't be here now."

"I know," Teal said softly, hoarsely, and Chena realized that tears also shone in her sister's eyes. "But I'm still sorry, that's all."

Chena stretched out her arm, and Teal smiled and snuggled herself under the blanket, just like when they were both children sharing secrets. Well, they were not children anymore, and all their secrets were known. Chena wrapped her arm around her sister. So much done, so much wrong, so much she would never forget or truly forgive, but for the first time in so many years she felt no anger. She felt light, as if the gravity had already lost its hold over them and she was about to float away. She felt as if she stood in the threshold of an open door with the whole world in front of her.

She felt free.

"Come on." She shook Teal's shoulder. "Let's go find our brother."